PRAIS
HARPER FALLS APART

"Shauna Robinson has created a small town brimming with friendships old and new, with a lovable cast of townspeople who care deeply about community and identity against a corporate foe. Hope shines through this satisfying second-chance story."

—Sierra Godfrey, author of *A Very Typical Family* and *The Second Chance Hotel*

"*Lauryn Harper Falls Apart* may be the title of Shauna Robinson's latest gem, but the reality is that Lauryn Harper puts herself back together. This feel-good tale of escaping corporate greed and finding a home in the very last place one imagines is a love letter to lifelong friendships and a reminder that it's never too late to start again. I dare you to not reach out to your childhood best friend after reading this entertaining and witty novel!"

—Sara Goodman Confino, bestselling author of *Don't Forget to Write*

"Funny, heartwarming, and brimming with small-town charm, this book is a delightful reminder that life isn't about the rat race but the people who give you the courage to slow down."

—Anna Johnston, author of *The Borrowed Life of Frederick Fife*

PRAISE FOR
THE TOWNSEND FAMILY RECIPE FOR DISASTER

"I savored this heartwarming and delicious tale filled with family roots, twisty secrets, and mouth-watering food! Shauna Robinson taps into the longing we all share to find our people and our place in the world and gives us a soul-satisfying story that will linger long after the last page."
—Rachel Linden, author of *Recipe for a Charmed Life*

"Hilarious and heartwarming, this book is like a warm drink on a cold winter day. Shauna Robinson stunningly explores our perceptions of family and race and if what divides us is more important than what brings us together. An indispensable read for anyone who has tried to figure out their place in spaces where they never quite fit and a beautiful meditation on accepting yourself and accepting the people you love with your eyes and heart wide open."
—Alex Travis, author of *The Only Black Girl in the Room*

"A heartwarming story about belonging, family secrets, the breaking of generational curses, and forging of new bonds, Shauna Robinson's *The Townsend Family Recipe for Disaster* will have you reaching for the people you love and holding them close."
—Shirlene Obuobi, author of *On Rotation*

"*The Townsend Family Recipe for Disaster* is infused with the warmth and humor that readers have come to expect from Robinson's work. Shauna has always excelled at building worlds that readers want to spend time in and writing characters they want to spend time with, and the Townsends are her best yet. This book is a moving delight, satisfying as a summer barbecue."

—Eva Jurczyk, international bestselling author of *The Department of Rare Books and Special Collections*

"*The Townsend Family Recipe for Disaster* is a heartfelt story of finding identity amidst complicated families and untold secrets. Robinson's writing brought Mae's journey to life, a perfect mix of deeply sad moments and laugh-out-loud inner monologue that kept me turning pages well into the night. True to real life, our histories—familial and racial—hold the best and worst of memories. This story doesn't shy away from hard topics. Rather, it approaches them through a unique, sincere character who wins hearts from the start. More than just a feel-good read, *The Townsend Family Recipe for Disaster* will leave readers cheering for Mae, hoping the best for humanity, and longing for a taste of Southern food! Kudos, Shauna!"

—Michelle Stimpson, author of *Sisters with a Side of Greens*

PRAISE FOR *THE BANNED BOOKSHOP OF MAGGIE BANKS*

"A sparkling bookish story about rules just begging to be broken... I couldn't get enough!"

—Abby Jimenez, *New York Times* bestselling author of *Part of Your World* and *The Friend Zone*

"Shauna writes for the girls without dream jobs, the pandemic babies who moved back in with their parents and are just trying to figure it out, and the extroverts who find purpose in bringing people together. This novel is a booklover's dream, with subtle social commentary to boot."

—Iman Hariri-Kia, author of *A Hundred Other Girls*

"*The Banned Bookshop of Maggie Banks* is a charming rom-com about finding your own path and never being scared to break the rules. It's also an uplifting celebration of the power of books to change people's lives. Visit your favorite bookstore, curl up in a comfy chair, and savor every word!"

—Freya Sampson, author of *The Last Chance Library*

"Delightful and deeply felt, *The Banned Bookshop of Maggie Banks* is one woman's instantly compelling search for herself woven into a celebration of how stories enliven and inspire community. It's the perfect book for booklovers."

—Emily Wibberley and Austin Siegemund-Broka, authors of *The Roughest Draft*

"Consider me an official member of the Maggie army! I found myself rooting for every character in this warm, welcoming tale of a woman coming into her own. If you've ever found comfort in a book—or a bookstore—then you'll enjoy watching Maggie discover how powerful the right story in the right hands can be."

—Lucy Gilmore, author of *The Lonely Hearts Book Club*

PRAISE FOR *MUST LOVE BOOKS*

"*Must Love Books* is a heartfelt and exciting debut. With a relatable protagonist in Nora, frank discussions of the millennial experience, and pitch-perfect sweetness, Shauna Robinson puts forth a wise and honest story of how it feels to be a young woman in search of yourself."

—Taylor Jenkins Reid, *New York Times* bestselling author of *The Seven Husbands of Evelyn Hugo* and *Malibu Rising*

"A book for booklovers that takes a hard look at the predatory approach of the corporate world with a heroine who's easy to love and root for. I enjoyed all of the inside look at the publishing industry from the perspective of a young woman scraping together all of her wits just to get by. It's impossible not to root for Nora!"

—Jesse Q. Sutanto, bestselling author of *Dial A for Aunties*

"Honest, relatable, and real, *Must Love Books* is a tender reflection on finding your person while you're still desperately searching for yourself rolled up in a thoughtful novel about the changing work world."

—KJ Dell'Antonia, *New York Times* bestselling author of *The Chicken Sisters*

"A compelling love story, dishy publishing goss, and a chic urban setting? Yes, yes, yes! But like the works she shepherds through publication, Shauna Robinson's true-to-life story of a struggling editorial assistant is much more than the sum of its parts. Within the pages of *Must Love Books*, the lucky reader will find themselves on a poignant journey of a young booklover with too little support and too many dreams—a place we've all been at one point or another. With emotional honesty and a surprising wit that I found addictive, Robinson's debut is everything a book-about-books fan wants in a novel."

—Kelly Harms, *Washington Post* bestselling
author of *The Overdue Life of Amy Byler*

"Readers will be rooting for Nora from the first page and experiencing her grand highs and heartbreaking lows with their entire heart. Get comfy because you won't be able to put this book down!"

—Sajni Patel, award-winning author of
The Trouble with Hating You

ALSO BY
SHAUNA ROBINSON

Must Love Books
The Banned Bookshop of Maggie Banks
The Townsend Family Recipe for Disaster

LAURYN HARPER FALLS APART

SHAUNA ROBINSON

sourcebooks
landmark

Published by Sourcebooks Landmark, an imprint of Sourcebooks
1935 Brookdale RD, Naperville, IL 60563-2773
(630) 961-3900
sourcebooks.com

Library of Congress Cataloging-in-Publication Data

Names: Robinson, Shauna, author.
Title: Lauryn Harper falls apart / Shauna Robinson.
Description: Naperville, Illinois : Sourcebooks Landmark, 2025.
Identifiers: LCCN 2025009148 | (trade paperback) | (hardcover) | (epub)
Subjects: LCGFT: Novels.
Classification: LCC PS3618.O3337225 L38 2025 | DDC 813/.6--dc23/eng/20250227
LC record available at https://lccn.loc.gov/2025009148

Printed and bound in the United States of America.
MA 10 9 8 7 6 5 4 3 2 1

For Matt
(even if he once doubted my love of mustard)

CHAPTER ONE

THERE IS A LIMIT TO the socially acceptable number of times you can ask someone to repeat themselves—and five fateful seconds ago, I spent my last *what*.

For most people, I stick to two. A lifetime of being deaf in my right ear has taught me that people give up when they hear one *what* too many. They'll wave it off with a *Never mind*, leaving me to stew in frustrated curiosity. For friends, I'll allow myself a third. They're usually more patient, but even they can only repeat themselves for so long before they grow self-conscious and decide no offhand remark is worth that much fanfare.

My problem: I've hit my *what* limit on someone who is definitely not a friend, and there's no way out.

I tried so hard. Dan Gorland—my boss's boss's boss, the smugly all-knowing chief strategy officer here at Ryser's DC headquarters—opened his mouth to repeat himself yet again, and I zeroed in on his every word with utmost precision. I tilted my one working ear closer to him. I tried to tune out the jazzy trumpet solo playing from the elevator speakers above us. I fixed my gaze on his lips to make out the shape of his words.

But as he spoke, he brought his coffee to his mouth, blocking my view. I could only stare helplessly at his Starbucks cup as he once again uttered an incomprehensible string of sounds. His voice turned up at the end, like a question. There was an uneasy smile on his face. His brown eyes darted strangely behind his black-rimmed glasses, flitting between me and the closed elevator doors.

I toss a glance at the doors too, wishing I had a witness. Not thirty seconds ago, I'd been talking in the lobby with Selma, the only person at this company I'd consider a friend, three-*what* status and all. While we waited for the elevator, we'd been joking about a clunky company-mandated content platform we've been trying to get rid of. If she'd been here, she could have answered him for me. But right before the elevator reached the lobby, she patted her back pocket and groaned that she must have left her phone in her car.

So, when the elevator opened its doors, I stepped inside alone—and promptly jumped when Dan materialized beside me. I covered my surprise with a smile and said hello, he said whatever mysterious thing he said, and now we're in hell.

This is why I hate in-person interactions. If this had been an email, none of this would be happening. I'd have read his words in unmistakable Calibri and known exactly what to say. Even if this were a Zoom meeting like the ones Dan calls when he doesn't feel like coming into the office, I'd still be safely tucked away in my ninth-floor cubicle, content in the knowledge that if I had trouble hearing anyone, I could just turn the volume up.

Real life, unfortunately, does not have a volume button.

"Lauryn?" Dan says. His tone is direct, prompting, like he's a teacher calling on a student who's done nothing but disappoint him. His once-polite smile is tight and frozen. I'm running out of time.

I purse my lips, considering my options.

I could ask him to repeat himself *again*, but he's already losing patience with me. I think about the presentation he gave at the office-wide meeting last month, how he barked *Next slide* twice when his assistant didn't advance the slide at the speed of light. As though he were urgently saving a life and not delivering a dull presentation about how Ryser, the food conglomerate we work for that produces everything from cereal to cat food, could boost profits by breaking into the lucrative skin-care market.

The thought of him taking that brusque tone with me makes me want to wither away on the spot. I've spent ten years carefully crafting a reputation for excellence in my slow climb up the corporate ladder. I'm not letting a sixty-second elevator ride knock me down a rung.

I could stall until the elevator reaches my floor. My gaze flickers to the top corner of the elevator, where a digital red 4 beams at me. I don't think I have five floors of stalling in me. What would I do, pretend to think it over with the world's longest *Um*? Act engrossed in the light jazz playing overhead and say, *Oh, my favorite song! There's a thrilling flute solo coming up—let's wait and listen for it?*

Or I could fall back on my usual approach: an insincere chuckle and a *Yeah*. Not foolproof, but it's gotten me through many a strategy meeting. If someone's made a joke or asked a question that can be answered in the affirmative, I'm in the clear. It's the times when it's not applicable—like when I'm at the doctor's office and the nurse asks for my date of birth, or when I'm waiting for my latte at Starbucks and the person next to me asks me if I'm in line—that it muddies the waters. But that's not so bad. They just look at me a little strangely and repeat themselves like the nurse did. Or, in the latter case, start forming a line behind me that I don't notice until it's four people deep, at which point, in a desperation to absolve myself of my newly appointed role as Official Rogue Line Leader, I flee the store before my order's called.

It's not a perfect strategy. But it *is* starting to sound more appealing.

Another glance at the indicator panel. We're still passing the fourth floor somehow, even though I feel like we've gone up and down this entire building at least three times since the moment Dan opened his mouth and asked me god knows what.

I suck in a breath and make a decision. A smile splits my face and a laugh falls out of me, all carefree and cool. "Yeah," I say.

I try my hardest to put every intonation possible into that one word. It's a versatile *yeah*. If he's asking if I'm excited for the CEO's talk at the all-staff meeting this afternoon, then *yeah*! If he's asking if I want to give an impromptu presentation at said meeting, then—well, I'd have a new problem, but at least I'd be free of this one.

This *yeah* can be anything as long as I sell it. I know from seeing myself in the corner of Dan's occasional Zoom meetings that my normal expression resembles resting bitch face—a face that once prompted Dan to ask if I had a problem with his Q2 strategy. At the time, I stammered out a denial and apologized, though I'm still not sure what I was apologizing for—having a face? If Dan had an ounce of self-awareness, he might stop to unpack why he found *my* resting bitch face threatening. Every other person on the call was also unsmiling. Selma was actively frowning; she told me once that she plays Tetris in another window during boring calls, and I assume an L block was getting the best of her again. But Selma is blond and can turn on cheer and charm like a faucet. Resting bitch face on me, a half-Black woman who spends too much time agonizing over minor interactions, must have Dan throwing me into angry Black woman territory by default.

So, I started smiling more when Dan's in attendance. It's stupid, but it keeps him from calling on me, and I've got to play the game if I want the communications manager promotion I've spent the last two years gunning for. Angry Black women don't get promotions.

Now, though, I play it up even more. I am a circus clown. I am the Cheshire cat. I won't give Dan a single reason to be thrown off by my chuckle-*yeah*. I hold my manic grin and my breath and wait for him to accept my response.

Accept it, Dan. *Accept it.*

Instead, his face falls. His eyes widen. He takes a step back, clutching his coffee cup tight enough that it bows slightly.

I step back too, bumping into the unforgiving steel wall. How could one word leave him this aghast? I feel an urge to smooth over the situation—offer up an apology, maybe. But a blind apology could backfire as spectacularly as the chuckle-*yeah*. For the thousandth time, I wonder what the hell he could have asked me.

I give up the guessing game and pivot to my usual strategy when awkwardness strikes: flee. I train my eyes on the elevator doors and wait for salvation.

The rest of the ride is silent, save for a gentle saxophone valiantly doing its best to fill the dead air. When the elevator reaches my floor, I'm ready to bolt, but Dan surprises me by stepping off first and breaking into an all-out run down the hall, even though he'd pressed the button for the fourteenth floor.

Clearly, *yeah* was the wrong thing to say.

In retrospect, there are a few important pieces of context I wish I'd thought of at the time:

1. The content platform Selma and I were joking about in the lobby is the Brand Learning Library, a hub for storing our PR guidelines. Everyone else calls it BLL, but Selma and I call it Bill.

2. We're the *only* people who call it Bill.

3. Selma and I have been plotting how to get rid of Bill, in all his sluggishness, since he was introduced last year. Specifically,

we use the term *kill Bill*. It sounds more purposeful, like we're on a mission. With Uma Thurman.

4. The language I used when talking to Selma was perhaps a little suspect to the outside observer. I was telling Selma that I'd be meeting with our boss today to propose getting rid of Bill, and that I'd gathered some statistics to support my case—but I didn't say it in those exact words. According to the formal HR report Dan submitted later that morning, I used the following phrases: *I'm finally gonna kill Bill. I'm doing it today, before the all-staff. I've got all the ammo I need.*

5. Our CEO's name is Bill Sullivan.

Twenty-five minutes later, when my boss calls me into her office with a startlingly somber expression, she tells me exactly what Dan asked me in the elevator that morning.

He'd asked, "You're not seriously planning to murder Bill Sullivan, are you?"

And I, like an absolute psychopath, had laughed and said yes.

CHAPTER TWO

I**T TURNS OUT THAT WHEN** your chief strategy officer thinks you've made a threat on the CEO's life, it's a damningly difficult predicament to come back from.

Sitting in my boss Amanda's office, feeling like a child who's been ordered to see the principal, I tried to explain. My joke with Selma, our nickname for Bill, Dan's incomprehensible syllables, my useless ear, how this was all a massive misunderstanding.

"But he asked you outright," she says, squinting at me. "You could have explained it then."

"But *I couldn't hear him*," I insist, not for the first time. I point to my deaf ear like I always do whenever she sidles up to my right side and doesn't understand why I can't hear her.

"But *you pretended you did*." She says it slowly, enunciating in full to drive home the ridiculousness of my decision. She's watching me, reading me, searching for an explanation—possibly even realizing I may not be as capable as she thought.

Amanda, I know, would never pretend to hear someone she couldn't. With her sleek, dark bob and penetrating brown eyes, Amanda is no-nonsense in a way that makes me squirm. Amanda doesn't fall into despair in basic social interactions. She does reasonable things like ask people to repeat themselves instead of spiraling into absurdity.

I've spent the last decade establishing myself as someone who *is* reasonable. More than that—reliable. Capable. Put me in a meeting and I'll ask all the right questions and suggest helpful ideas. Ask me to write a press release and I'll craft something that perfectly fits Ryser's innovative and informative tone of voice. And if I happen to leave the company holiday party early to catch up on emails (read: recover in my cubicle after exactly thirty minutes of dodging small talk like a competitive sport), that's my business. I've always been able to hide my social shortcomings behind my professional polish.

Until now.

"I know," I say. "But…well, I have a philosophy that there's a limited number of times you can ask someone to repeat themselves. Too many and it gets awkward."

Amanda's lips form a thin line of anguish. "Lauryn," she says, her words measured and pained, "I think we can safely say there are fates worse than awkwardness."

"Agreed." I chance a chuckle. Amanda doesn't smile. I play her words back, this time picking up on their ominous foreboding. "Wait, what do you mean?" The question comes out almost in a whisper, wrapped in dread.

"Well." She spends several seconds straightening the glass

paperweight on her desk. When she finally lifts her eyes to meet mine, there's a reluctance in her gaze. "Dan suggested that… maybe the stress of the last year has caught up with you. We've certainly had to put out a lot of fires lately. The child labor lawsuit. The…water situation in Pennsylvania. The *actual* fire, in Nevada. Putting out the statements, preparing talking points. It's a lot to take on."

It's hard not to wince at Ryser's laundry list of disasters. I should be able to reference them with all the same detachment Amanda uses, but it's easier to push them out of mind, focus on our team's mission to massage these incidents with deferrals, denials, distractions. It's why Amanda felt the need to implement Bill—no, *BLL*; I should really start using its actual name lest I spark another panic—in the first place: a dedicated resource detailing our strategies and accepted terms for spinning these PR nightmares.

But Amanda's gentle tone makes me want to shrink into my seat. It's as though she's trying to analyze my feelings, dig into my psyche. But there's nothing to see here. I locked my morals away in a cage when I started working here, and I refuse to let her pick the lock now. I will myself to look neutral and unbothered. Child labor for Ryser's chocolate bars, draining low-income communities' watersheds for Ryser's bottled water, all just another day at the office. Whatever it takes to get my steady paychecks and secure a promotion.

It's all part of my plan. Get promoted to communications manager within the next year. Become communications director within seven years. And then, once I'm in that role: do some good.

Instead of glossing over Ryser's wrongs, we could acknowledge the harm we caused and take a step to counteract it: partner with a nonprofit to improve labor conditions, invest in a water conservation project, fund a scholarship program, offer financial support to an affected community. Take concrete action to offset all the deferrals and denials I've played a part in over the years. Do enough good deeds to quiet the restless morals straining against the bars of their cage. Over the years, Amanda has turned down my every suggestion to add a touch of nuance to our standard response—but when I'm a communications director, with a budget and a semblance of authority, I'll be able to make a difference.

And then, the final step in my timeline: retire as soon as I possibly can. According to my spreadsheet, I only have to work here for eight more years, until I'm forty, and then I can retire early, leave the working world forever, and maybe actually feel good about myself for a change.

Or, at least, no longer contribute to a company so notorious that Wikipedia has an entire page dedicated to detailing its controversies.

Eight more years glossing over Ryser's atrocities with carefully worded statements pulled from a clunky platform I won't call Bill anymore. Eight more years living in my dark basement apartment in Brentwood for the cheap rent, even though it gets only a sliver of sunlight for fifteen minutes on a good day, my neighborhood consists of a laundromat and a perpetual construction site, and the thirty-minute commute squished against strangers in a Metro car fills me with a daily dose of dread. What's eight years in the grand scheme of things?

It crosses my mind that eight years is also the age of one of the children mentioned in the child labor lawsuit our team publicly glossed over in favor of emphasizing Ryser's "considerable progress" toward fair labor practices. But I try not to dwell on that.

"I'm sure I'm partly to blame," Amanda goes on, her tone still achingly tender. "I've probably leaned on you a little too much this year. Your work is so stellar. You always go above and beyond. But…there's nothing wrong with needing to take a step back. Dan recommended transferring you to a satellite office."

"Okay," I say slowly. This sounds all right so far. I know there's a Ryser branch in Bethesda. Not as glamorous as Ryser's shiny headquarters here in DC, but Bethesda could be a good change of pace. I piece together the positives: calling into Amanda's meetings from the comfort of my cubicle. No chance of awkward elevator run-ins with Dan. I might even find a cheap apartment that doesn't always smell damp.

"Okay," she repeats, looking pleased at how I'm taking the news.

A keen sense of satisfaction slides through me. Yes, I *am* taking this well. I am a good employee. I am hardworking and easygoing and I would never murder our CEO.

"You'll be working from our Greenstead office from now on," she continues.

That word slices through me, making me jolt upright. "Greenstead?" My mouth forms the word like a terribly familiar habit.

"That's right," she says, perking up even more, finding

something encouraging about my reaction. Mistaking my horror for excitement.

"So…" I grip the arm of my plastic chair. "I'd be running communications from there?"

Amanda grimaces. "It would be more of a support role."

"Oh." A demotion.

I want to race home to my spreadsheet, double-click it open, and run the numbers to assess what this means. A demotion means a lower salary, and a lower salary means those eight years would stretch on for longer—ten, fifteen, twenty years. Just the thought makes me feel like the walls are closing in, surrounding me in darkness.

"It's really a lovely place," Amanda tries, and I let out a loud laugh. She eyes me warily, and I'm fully aware this is not the behavior to exhibit when I've given my superiors grave reason to doubt my sanity today, but I can't help it. My mind flashes with dead, rotting fields, crumbling brick buildings, the faint smell of mustard. *A lovely place.*

"You've never been there, have you?" I ask.

Amanda tilts her head. "Have *you*?"

"I'm *from* Greenstead."

Her eyes grow large, but she quickly masks her expression with a broad smile. "I'm sure it's beautiful."

"It's smelled like mustard since the flood."

Amanda winces. "Factory malfunction," she corrects.

Ryser uses only the most sanitized language to refer to their Greenstead mustard factory's accidental tank explosion in the '90s. In the span of minutes, millions of gallons of bright-yellow mustard coursed through our small, rural Virginia town, flooding everything in its path.

I was four then. I don't remember much about it. Just that one day the world was bright and full of color and smelled like sunshine, and then suddenly fresh air was a thing of the past. The rest are snippets: A vinegar tang burning my nostrils. Endless news coverage about cleanup efforts. An unsettling feeling that nothing would ever be the same again.

"I would really rather not go," I say. It takes some effort to keep my voice even when it so badly wants to wobble. "I'd like to stay here. Please." It's a fight to keep it to one *please*, to not say the word over and over again the same way it's pulsing in my mind.

The corner of Amanda's mouth lists upward in a sympathetic half smile. "I would like that, too. But…" She shakes her head. "Dan is…rattled. This was the best I could do. You'd still work at Ryser. Just…at the charity office."

I nod slowly, resignation seeping through me.

After the flood—or *factory malfunction*—Ryser set up a charity office in Greenstead to aid in the recovery. They processed claims, issued reimbursements, oversaw repairs. But Greenstead never really recovered. Every year, the population dwindled as people took their leave for somewhere with life, somewhere that wasn't the butt of an easy joke, as if there's anything funny about your hometown being decimated in an instant.

Is this a monkey's paw situation? I wanted to do some good and now I've gotten my wish in the worst way? Going back to the town that felt like my own personal prison is a special kind of punishment. And while knowing that the charity office exists has always been a small comfort—after all, I didn't *really* abandon Greenstead if it's been in Ryser's capable hands all these years, did I?—helping out at a small-town charity office isn't quite the large-scale act of good I'd hoped to do at Ryser. No matter how many fundraisers or cleanups Ryser's charity office sponsors, Greenstead will always be a tiny tragedy of a town whose best days are far behind it.

I knew that even as a kid. I spent my childhood dreaming about leaving Greenstead at the first opportunity, and that's what I did. I left my old life in the past and set my sights on something new. I went to college at Georgetown, I got a job that paid well above market rate at the largest company in DC, and I left Greenstead behind.

And now, it seems, I'm going back.

CHAPTER THREE

GREENSTEAD DOESN'T SMELL LIKE MUSTARD anymore. Officially, anyway. After the cleanup efforts, our mayor changed the slogan on the town's welcome sign from WELCOME HOME to BREATHE IN THE FRESH, CLEAN AIR OF HOME. It was the most subtle option out of the choices he proposed.

But I could still smell it, even years later. During summer, the baking heat exposes smells that hide away in cooler seasons. I remember eating lunch at Prime Burger one sunny Saturday when I was sixteen, sitting at a table outside with Marina, my best friend until she wasn't. We'd be eating our burgers, laying claim to our preferred fries—crispy for me, soggy for her—theorizing about the true identity of Gossip Girl, when the breeze would shift and we'd smell it. A faint whiff of something sharp and sour, enough to make us wrinkle our noses and share a knowing look. We called it the ghost of mustard past. Musty, for short. Which wasn't even clever, but it made us laugh. Apparently my tendency to nickname inanimate entities goes further back than I thought.

I swear I can smell it even now, sitting in the back seat of my dad's sedan, watching Greenstead's expansive fields of nothingness pass by. I'm not sure how, since the windows are up, and the air freshener dangling from the rearview mirror is working overtime to fill the car with a fresh-cotton scent. But I swear the slightest trace of mustard is hitting my nostrils. It's fitting for late June—unless I'm losing my mind, and I might well be.

I feel like I've been transported to the past. It's strange to have shifted so suddenly in the span of three days. On Tuesday morning I was a capable professional stepping into an elevator. Now I'm an oversized child, living in my childhood bedroom, being driven around by my dad.

Up front, my dad and my stepmom, Wendy, are prattling about Greenstead's new developments since I was last here—somehow this trip to pick up Chinese food for my first dinner back home has turned into a town tour—but I'm not sure it's having the impact they hoped.

"The pharmacy on Rutledge takes credit cards now," Dad says.

I follow his outstretched arm to the building in question, a lone Wright's Pharmacy surrounded by asphalt and a patch of dirt. I try to muster some amazement at the notion of a business accepting credit cards in the twenty-first century. "Wow."

It must not be very convincing, because my dad huffs in response.

"Show her the bakery," Wendy suggests. Her chunky

bracelets jingle as she runs a hand over her short, dark curls. She turns to shoot me an encouraging look over her shoulder, like whatever they're about to show me is going to blow my mind.

I can't help but return her hopeful smile. I spent my teenage years being embarrassed about my dad's zest for the mundane, thinking he had to be the only person on the planet who enthused over every little thing—from spotting a ladybug on his lawn gnome to seeing the time on the clock match the date. (He sent me several texts when it was 1:11 on January 11.) But Wendy matches his energy perfectly.

Dad makes a turn for the bakery, and I go back to staring out the window. As we pass by Juniper Park, I crane my neck to peer at it. It's not the lush, grassy open space I remember. There's a gaping hole in the wire fence around the perimeter, and the grass is neglected and overgrown. Over by the playground, where Dad used to push me on the swings, a swing hangs lopsided, one chain broken. In the empty parking lot, an overturned trash can spills garbage across the concrete.

I swallow and look away. Every sign of disrepair is like an accusation, a pointed reminder that I don't get to mourn what this park used to be when I'm the one who left this town to work for the company that destroyed it.

Still, my mind reverts this park to the version in my memory, well maintained and bustling with people and activity. This used to be the site of Greenstead's annual apple festival, the one thing that made this town sparkle with magic, even if just for a weekend. Marina and I looked forward to it every October. We'd weave through crowds to browse the rows of booths throughout the park and load up on kettle corn and apple cider donuts. We'd snag a picnic table and split a caramel apple, eating it slice by slice as we imagined what the new school year held in store for us. We wouldn't leave until the sun was setting and the autumn air froze our fingertips. It was tradition. And though the crowds started to thin with each passing year as more people left Greenstead, we both believed we'd stick to that tradition like a vow.

We were too naive, then, to understand that even best friendships can end, even beloved festivals can be canceled indefinitely, and traditions and towns can fall apart like anything else.

"Here we are!"

I push aside the thought and look up to see a familiar tiny brick building. "You wanted to show me…Cooper Cakes?"

Dad must be scraping the bottom of the barrel if he thinks the bakery that made all my birthday cakes growing up is a new sight.

"See the new roof? Tim had it replaced last year." Dad turns to me with an expectant look.

I force a smile and try to really sell my reaction this time. "Oh, cool. It looks really good. Very sturdy."

My dad holds my gaze, trying to evaluate my sincerity. His brown eyes narrow behind his glasses. As a high school history teacher, he's skilled at sniffing out bullshit. "Bah," he says at last, facing forward with a sigh. "Well, you wanna go in, since we're here? Say hi, pick up some turtle brownies?"

"Um…" I stare absently at the bakery's smudged glass window. The flower-dotted sign in the corner is still the same, still advertising TODAY'S CAKE FLAVORS, still pretending the flavors aren't the same every day. Now that my dad's mentioned it, I *do* want a turtle brownie, shiny with caramel and studded with salty pecans.

But the thought of running into anyone who knows me—even Tim, the kindly baker who used to slip me free mini shortbread rounds when I was a kid—makes my appetite vanish. Tim, and everyone here, would know I left Greenstead to work for Ryser. Would he call me a traitor? Would he treat me differently, offer cold disdain in lieu of his usual paternal warmth? He'd probably punish me with a middle brownie, all gooey uniformity instead of chewy-crispy edges. The ultimate slight.

"No thanks," I say finally. "I'm not hungry."

Dad frowns. "Then why are we getting dinner?"

I let out a small laugh. "Not hungry for *dessert*."

"Let's just go to China Garden," Wendy says. "Lauryn's too cool for us."

"No, I'm not," I say.

"Oh yeah?" Dad retorts, putting the car in reverse. "You haven't been home in how long?"

And, yes, I have to pause to do the math. "Three years isn't that long."

I had my reasons. I didn't come home for Christmas last year because that was the year Dad and Wendy traveled to San Antonio to see her relatives for the holidays. The year before, when it was their turn to host, I got a cold. I may have exaggerated the symptoms a little, but better safe than sorry. And before that, it was another year when Wendy's relatives were hosting. It's not my fault that I'd rather lounge on the couch at home watching Christmas movies and eating frozen Trader Joe's gyoza than drive to Greenstead and watch my hometown fall apart. Or travel to San Antonio to see Wendy's family for the first time since she and my dad got married six years ago. Gyoza and *Home Alone* it was.

Besides, I see plenty of Dad and Wendy as it is. They come to DC fairly regularly—to visit the Smithsonian museums, attend the Cherry Blossom Festival, stroll around the National Mall. It's no surprise they find themselves in DC so often when DC actually has life, activity, air that smells nothing like mustard in all four seasons. The real mystery is why they—or anyone— would choose to stay in Greenstead.

And yet. When Wendy and I stay in the car while Dad heads inside China Garden to pick up our lo mein and sesame chicken, I'm struck by the way the man behind the counter greets him, with a two-handed handshake and a warm smile. I watch through the window as they chat in the empty restaurant like old friends, and I have to admit there must be something nice about walking into a restaurant and having the person behind the counter know who you are. I try to remember the last time someone besides Selma at work greeted me like they were truly happy to see me, and I draw a blank.

If I run into anyone who knows me here in Greenstead, it'll be nothing but disappointment, betrayal, or—in Marina's case—anger. And there's a strong possibility of running into her, too. I know from my occasional social media stalking that she still lives here. She works down at the elementary school as a fourth-grade teacher.

But that's fine. I won't be anywhere near the school anyway, because I'll be busy at Ryser Cares. My first day in my new role starts Monday, and I've got everything figured out. In the time it took to pack up my things and make the three-hour drive south to Greenstead, my mood shifted from disheartened to determined.

I may have been demoted, salary halved, and banished to a lifeless land, but I have a new mission: be impressive. Take initiative. Lead a new fundraising campaign, boost Ryser Cares's conversion rate, double their monthly donations, *something*. Make a memorable impact that isn't accidentally threatening an executive. Amanda will hear about all the work I've done at Ryser Cares and hire me back by the end of the summer. After going twelve weeks—one full quarter—without me, she'll be clamoring to get me back on her team in time for the start of Q4. And my brief stay in Greenstead will be nothing more than a blip. I'll go back to my apartment, my life, my eight-years-left plan.

And I'll be happier for it. Surely.

CHAPTER FOUR

R YSER CARES IS A FAR cry from the towering, eighteen-floor
building that houses Ryser's headquarters in DC. There's no
hustle, no bustle, no Starbucks on the first floor radiating
bitter-coffee rejuvenation. Just a sad, square block of concrete at
the corner of an abandoned strip mall.

Standing outside my car on Monday morning, I can only stare
across the nearly empty parking lot at the gray one-story building
that awaits me. The words RYSER CARES appear above the door in
a blocky, outdated font. My eyes scan the vacant storefronts next
to it, superimposing my memories over the emptiness. The one
directly beside Ryser Cares used to be an antique furniture store.
Beside that was the stationery shop where Marina and I used to
hunt for unique erasers to add to our collection. Then there was the
fresh foods market that had the good granola you couldn't find at
Food Lion, crunchy and teeming with toasted pecans and pepitas.
All of them gone.

A pang runs through me at seeing so much nothing in place of the spots that live on in my memory. But Greenstead has been declining for as long as I can remember. There's no point in mourning what I've always known.

A flicker of movement through the window of Ryser Cares snaps me back to attention. Right. My first day of work in my new role.

I take a steeling breath, grip the strap of my purse, and stalk toward the entrance with purpose.

I get within six feet of the door when a goose pops out from behind a tall planter and makes a beeline for me, flapping its wings and honking menacingly. I let out a yelp and scramble toward my car.

After a pause, I turn around cautiously, my heart still hammering. The goose stands at the curb, its dark, beady eyes trained on me. I gather my resolve and take a careful step forward—and then another goose emerges from behind the planter. This one's calmer, more assured. Which is somehow even more menacing. Like it knows precisely how to tear my limbs apart but can't be bothered just yet.

I reach into my purse. I'm tempted to grab my phone and call out of work for the day, though I have no idea what I would say. Whining to Amanda that *I can't come in today because of the geese* seems counterproductive to my plan. Plus, if Dan got word of it, he'd take it as more evidence that I've lost my mind.

Actually, I don't even know if Amanda's the person I would call. She's not my boss anymore. My new boss is… Well, I don't know who my new boss is, but I assume it's someone in that building there. Past the geese. I just need to…get inside.

In all, it takes me twenty minutes to enter the office. I tried a variety of tactics, from slowly stepping forward, to approaching the door at an angle, to finally screeching and making a run for it as both geese nipped at my heels.

Once inside, I slam the door shut. I stand there, breathing raggedly, my purse falling off my shoulder, still gripping the door handle like a lifeline, even though the geese have now smugly sauntered off.

"Can we help you?"

Slowly, I turn. Two men stand at opposite ends of an air hockey table, watching me with apprehension. One is a Black man in his fifties, with graying beard scruff and a wrinkled Pink Floyd shirt over his faded jeans. The other looks closer to forty. His dark hair is coiffed and shiny with gel, but he's also wearing an outfit too casual for the Ryser office, screamingly bright colors that stand out against his brown skin: a tropical shirt in vibrant hues of blue and yellow, and striped yellow-and-orange shorts in a strangely shiny material. They look like swim trunks. But no one would wear swim trunks to an office. Though it is oddly warm in here.

Now I feel silly for spending half an hour this morning putting together the outfit I thought would help me make a good first impression. My hand runs to the waistband of my dress pants. I feel an urge to untuck the hem of my satin blouse, rip off my sensible cardigan, yank the headband off my neatly wrangled curls, not feel like the odd one out five seconds into my new job. But I fight off the impulse. My hand drops to my side. I'm here to impress, I remind myself. Not to blend in.

"Are you here to fix the AC?" asks Maybe Swim Trunks.

"No, I…" I scan the office for a sign of Ryser. It's an open floor plan, about half a dozen desks scattered throughout. A blond white woman in her fifties sits at a desk near the back, crocheting a top of some kind while staring at her computer screen. A Black woman who looks closer to my age perches on a desk by the window, engrossed in her phone. "I think I have the wrong place," I conclude. "I'm looking for Ryser Cares. Have they moved, or—"

"This is Ryser Cares," the Pink Floyd man confirms. He furrows his brow, taking me in. "And you're sure you're not here to fix the AC?"

I shake my head, less an answer to his question and more a sheer inability to process what I'm seeing. I've heard about Ryser Cares all my life. Ryser ran a local ad here nonstop after the flood, bragging about their efforts to clean up Greenstead, inviting residents to stop by the charity office if they needed anything. Every Halloween, at least one kid in my class dressed up as the spokesman from the Ryser Cares ad. All they needed was a blue sweater vest, a bow tie, a pair of khakis, and a broom, and they'd be instantly recognizable. Ryser Cares hosted food drives every Thanksgiving, charity 5Ks every spring. Their entire personality as Ryser's charity division was their devotion to helping Greenstead.

Ryser Cares can't be…this. An empty office, an air hockey table, stale air, and crocheting? It doesn't make sense.

"I thought Ryser Cares would be…" I look around again at the sparse office. "Busier."

"How can we help you, hon?" the crocheter in the back pipes up.

I set my confusion aside and put on my best I-am-a-professional smile. "I'm Lauryn Harper. I was transferred here from DC. You should have gotten an email?"

Maybe Swim Trunks makes a sympathetic noise at the word *transferred*, while Pink Floyd says, "I haven't checked my email this week."

I let out a quiet laugh. But as he keeps looking at me with polite curiosity, it dawns on me that he isn't joking. My mind returns to its frantic whirring.

"What'd you do?" the woman leaning on her desk asks, finally glancing up from her phone. She's dressed casually like the others, in a loose yellow tank dress. Her microlocs sit in a knot atop her head, gold hoop earrings sparkling. A plate of what looks like homemade granola bar squares sits on her desk. "Oh, do you want a date bar?" she asks, following my gaze.

"No. Uh, thank you, though," I say as Maybe Swim Trunks grabs two. "What do you mean, what did I do?"

"To get *transferred*." She raises her eyebrows when she says it, like it's code for something.

"Oh." I fiddle with the strap of my purse, straightening it with too much care. "It was just a…misunderstanding."

This earns a chuckle from her and a full-on guffaw from Pink Floyd. "Misunderstanding, mishap, mistake," he says. "It's all the same, in the end."

That's not ominous at all.

"What do you mean?" I ask.

"Well, for instance…" The woman sets her phone down and swivels to face me. "I used to work in Ryser's R&D department. I developed a Parmesan ranch salad dressing for our partnership with Kraft. Everyone loved it, it passed all the testing, it hit the shelves, and then…"

"The dressing turned green," I finish in a murmur. The details come back to me now: Overnight, the salad dressing transformed from a creamy off-white to an unsettling chartreuse. Testing revealed that the product's pH was conducive to bacteria growth—a perfect recipe for botulism. No one got sick, but Ryser had to do a recall.

Product recalls are fairly common, but this one cost us a partnership. Our SVP had spent over a year wooing Kraft, periodically giving updates in all-staff meetings about how securing a partnership with Kraft would help us tap into the Cheese Youth market. And now I come to meet the person responsible for losing it.

"Yep," she says. "Ryser lost the partnership, and millions of dollars, so…they transferred me to the Flop House. Just like you."

"No," I insist. "They didn't transfer me to the…" I can't even say it. "This is just temporary. I'm going back."

"Okay." She holds up her palms in surrender, then returns to her phone.

I can't resist asking, "How long ago was that? When you were transferred?"

"About four years ago. Or five."

The air leaves my lungs. My head swivels to the others in the office, still looking on curiously. "And were you all…transferred? For messing up at Ryser?" When they all nod, I ask, "And you've been here ever since?" They nod again.

"My theory is they think we know too much, and that's why they haven't fired us," the crocheter says. "So…they sent us here instead."

"What do you mean, know too much?"

The crocheter shrugs. "I worked in social media management. I handled a lot of crises Ryser wouldn't want me talking about."

The word *crises* sends a sense of foreboding rippling through me. I've certainly dealt with my fair share of those. But I don't belong in the *Flop House*, as the ex–research specialist so horrifically put it. I'm not here because of what I know. I'm here because Dan Gorland overreacts to misunderstandings. I belong in DC. I have work to do there. An eight-year plan to carry out. A difference to make.

"What else?" I ask.

"From my time in R&D, I know that a lot of the ingredients Ryser says are sustainably sourced are…very much not," the ex–research specialist says.

The child labor lawsuit for Ryser's chocolate springs to mind, but I don't let myself wonder how many other ingredients she might be talking about. I shove the thought aside and fix my gaze on Maybe Swim Trunks, hoping he'll break the pattern.

Maybe Swim Trunks, still chewing his date bar, says, "Probably just nepotism in my case. The COO's my dad."

"Your dad's Sujay Sharma?" I ask, and he nods. It's hard to picture the man in front of me sitting down to a family dinner with Sujay Sharma, who would probably wear a suit and tie to a pajama party. But nepotism would be a solid reason to resort to a transfer over a dismissal. Not that my transfer is anything like theirs.

"What about you?" I ask Pink Floyd.

Pink Floyd stares down at his feet. "I don't know what I know."

"What?"

He sighs and looks up, reluctance on his features. "In the '90s, I worked in the mail room at Ryser. I used to sneak up to the bathroom on the sixteenth floor sometimes, when I wanted to read on the clock. It was the nicest bathroom in the building," he explains. "One day, I was doing my secret reading routine—the first *Song of Ice and Fire* book had just come out, and I was close to finishing it. At some point, people came in and started talking, so I plugged my ears so I could concentrate. When I finished the book, I came out of the stall and saw our CEO and head of legal looking…shocked to see me. I guess they didn't realize I was there.

"They went out of their way to be nice to me after that. I kept getting promotions that didn't make sense. I made it all the way up to office manager. And when I fell for a scam email that I thought was from a vendor, and I lost the company over a million dollars, they still didn't fire me. They just sent me here. I've always wondered if it had something to do with whatever they thought I heard in that bathroom. I figure it must have been important."

I can only blink. "Okay, but…that doesn't have anything to do with me."

"What was your job, before they sent you here?" asks the ex–research specialist.

Was. That hurts.

"I work in PR."

"Okay," the crocheter says, setting her hook down. "And in your time working in PR, did you maybe…learn some things about Ryser that they might not want you to share publicly?" Her tone is annoyingly gentle.

And, fine, it's not like I have to think about it. I know full well how much Ryser glosses over its controversies. When spinning the story about the fire at our corn chip factory in Nevada, we covered up the fact that our director of manufacturing insisted everyone return to work immediately after the fire, leading to complaints about smoke inhalation and toxic fumes that we quietly buried. Or how draining that small-town Pennsylvania watershed for our bottled water happened partly because Ryser extracted more water than they'd been legally permitted, a fact that never made headlines. That's the whole reason Bill exists, so we know exactly what we're supposed to say about these incidents—and what to keep quiet.

"Sounds like a yes to me," the ex-specialist says, sharing a look with the crocheter.

I emerge from my haze and try to arrange my face into something that's not *recalling the horrors.* "Okay, yes, I'm…privy to certain information," I admit. "But I—" I don't know how to politely say *I'm not like you.* "My situation's different. It'll blow over. They're gonna want me back."

"Remember when *I* thought I was going back?" The ex–research specialist turns to Maybe Swim Trunks, who laughs.

"She just needs some time," the crocheter says, and Pink Floyd agrees. There's something pitying in the way she smiles at me.

"It's not so bad," Pink Floyd tries, setting his mallet down on the air hockey table. "It's relaxing."

"But…you shouldn't be relaxing. We should be working. That's how we can show them we deserve to get our jobs back." I rifle through my mind for the charity events I remember Ryser Cares throwing when I was a kid. "What are you working on now? You usually do a community cleanup in the summer, right? I could help with your publicity campaign."

"Oh, they stopped with all that *years* ago," the crocheter says, eyes still on her crocheting. "The board decided it wasn't needed anymore. Not enough ROI."

My head cocks to the side. "I'm not sure charity is supposed to have any ROI."

"Try telling that to the board," Maybe Swim Trunks mutters.

"So…what do you do here?"

"I've been rewatching *Love Island*," the crocheter says. "I'm up to season five now." She lifts her head, sees my expression. "And we process claims," she adds reassuringly. "When someone comes in with one."

"Yeah, we got two whole claims last month," the ex–research specialist says. "It was thrilling."

My mind scrambles as my expectations keep finding new depths to sink to. Ryser Cares is an ironically named front. The likelihood of impressing Amanda from afar rapidly shrinks from an achievable goal to a pipe dream. My time in Greenstead is looking less like a stopover and more like an eternity. I'll never be able to rise up the ranks to make enough of a difference at Ryser to offset all the questionable things I've contributed to over the years. I did all that planning just to wind up here, at a dead end, with a stain on my conscience that I'll never be able to erase?

Hell, I can't even make a difference on a smaller scale here at Ryser Cares. This isn't a charity office; it's the Flop House. All the years I spent working at Ryser, assuming Ryser Cares was doing right by Greenstead, and it's a lie. All the more reason for Greensteaders to hate me.

Something on my face must reveal my despair because Pink Floyd wheels a chair over and motions for me to sit down. I obey, concentrating on breathing in and out.

"You'll get used to it, hon," the crocheter says. "I hardly ever smell the mustard now. And when I do, it just makes me want a pretzel."

They mutter in agreement about the deliciousness of pretzels while my brain races to comprehend what's happening. Pink Floyd offers to pick up a round of pretzels for everyone. When he opens the door, I lift my head weakly to warn him about the geese, but they leave him alone as he walks past, completely unbothered.

Traitors.

CHAPTER FIVE

M Y FIRST WEEK AT RYSER Cares passes in monotony, punctuated by the decisive strikes of air hockey mallets and overdramatic dialogue from whatever episode of *Love Island* Jen, the crocheter, is watching behind me.

The start of my day is a solitary one. I quickly learned that the only reason my colleagues were in the office so early on my first day was because the AC repairman gave them an early-morning time slot. Once he fixed the AC, they returned to their usual schedule of midmorning arrivals.

But I still show up at 8:30 a.m. each day, just like in DC. From my desk behind Tessa, the ex–research specialist, I doggedly turn on my laptop each morning and begin my routine of reading through the industry newsletters in my inbox while my coworkers slowly trickle into the office.

Then I hunt for a project to work on, which always goes nowhere. Asking Jen for an email list of Ryser Cares donors elicits a sympathetic shake of her head. When I ask Randy (the actual name of the Pink Floyd shirt–wearer) what media contacts Ryser Cares is in touch with, he winces, shrugs, and goes back to his book. One morning, I catch Arun (who *was* wearing swim trunks, I discovered; he left early that day to take his niece to a water park in Falls Point) staring at his computer in concentration. I race over and offer to help with what he's working on, only for him to tilt his monitor toward me and ask if I think the sunglass frames in Electric Tangerine or Pink Lava would suit him more.

Then, with nothing else to do, I put on my headphones and make my way through the backlog of professional development recordings I'd bookmarked but never gotten around to watching. Though they can never fully drown out all that swirls around me, air hockey and *Love Island* and pleasant chatter that has nothing to do with work.

Every so often, a cheery chime breaks up the sound. It always makes my heart thump. When I hear it for the first time this morning, a muggy and overcast Tuesday, I sit up straighter, minimize the window I have open to a webinar on evaluating the effectiveness of PR campaigns, and click over to my inbox. Maybe this time it's Amanda, begging for me to take my old job back.

Donuts in the 12th floor kitchen!

I breathe out a disappointed sigh through my nose. Being on the DC office email list is a special kind of punishment. Every office-wide announcement salts the wound of my exile.

I go back to slouching and return to my webinar. As the presenter dives into engagement metrics, my mind wanders to the dismal prospect of being stuck here with no end in sight.

I could make a drastic move, quit and get a new job. But then what would have been the point of the last ten years of my life, my plan to get promoted, do good, and retire early? What would have been the point of my dreary apartment, my sense of morality screaming from its cage every time I wrote the words to gloss over Ryser's latest catastrophe? How could I shrug and accept the fact that leaving Ryser now, with my mission incomplete, means I'm every bit the hypocrite this town—and Marina— undoubtedly thinks I am?

Quitting isn't an option. I can get my old job back if I try hard enough. It's why I haven't asked to be taken off the DC office email list, why I'm still holding onto my apartment in DC. Some part of me is certain I'll be back there soon enough once this whole misunderstanding is sorted out.

But that does little to assuage the way I feel now: utterly aimless and hopelessly stuck.

My mom used to talk about feeling stuck a lot. She saw the way Greenstead had been steadily shrinking since the flood, and she wanted to get out. But she had my dad, who was happily employed as a high school history teacher and unbothered by Greenstead's slow pace. She had me, who, at ten, wasn't all that interested in the idea of moving unless I could take my life with me: my best friend, Marina, the toy store that special ordered gradient puzzles at my request, our neighbor's affectionate poodle mix who I got to walk sometimes.

My parents started arguing, a lot. I spent more weekends sleeping over at Marina's to escape it. When I was twelve, my parents divorced and my mom took off. She moved to New York, started working as a flight attendant, and began a new phase of her life. She'd zip around the country, call me every couple of weeks, send postcards imprinted with Hawaiian palm trees or the Space Needle. She sounded happy when I spoke to her. Free.

It made me start rethinking my own life, wonder whether the itch beneath my skin was just the typical adolescent feeling that I didn't belong, or if it was something more, that stuck feeling starting to take root. I may take after my dad physically, from the brown skin and high forehead all the way to the string-bean-like physique. But did I inherit my mom's restlessness? I'd stare at the postcards on my wall, then I'd look out the window at our front yard with its patchy grass that never grew back right since the flood, and I'd tell myself my best chance at happiness was leaving.

An acceptance email from Georgetown University was my ticket out. I soaked up DC's bustling pace with bliss. At the end of my freshman year, when Ryser called to offer me an internship, I leapt at the chance. Never mind that it was technically my first day interning for a dull accounting firm in Greenstead. Ryser's busy atmosphere and promise of opportunity felt like Greenstead's antithesis. I accepted the Ryser position with relief and quit my Greenstead internship on the spot. It was a decision that made my dad raise an eyebrow, but he didn't comment on it. My mom, of course, understood the necessity of taking a drastic step to escape Greenstead.

I told myself it was just a summer internship, that I'd work for a place that didn't make me feel like a hometown traitor once I graduated. But as graduation loomed ever closer, that last semester a blur of cover letters and job rejections, hearing my classmates talk about needing to move back home scared me into deciding I'd do whatever it took to put Greenstead behind me. I couldn't be picky, I reminded myself. I'd apply for every listing I remotely qualified for and take the first job I was offered. And when a Ryser recruiter called to tell me I'd gotten the job, that was it. I accepted in an instant.

I carved out a life for myself that gave me everything I needed: a well-paying job, a city that was growing instead of shrinking. I'd see Mom whenever she had a layover in DC. And I was close enough to see Dad throughout the year—mostly from the comfort of my new life in my new city, where I could forget all about my decaying hometown.

And here I am again.

My gaze flickers when something moves in my peripheral vision. It's Tessa, passing by with a plate of muffins. Our eyes meet, and she stops, a flash of alarm passing over her. No doubt worried I'm about to hound her with questions about community impact statistics like I did yesterday. As if to distract me, she shoves the plate of muffins in my face.

I pause my webinar and take off my headphones in time to hear her say, "Blueberry muffin?" As I consider them, she peeks at my monitor, showing a graph from the webinar, and lets out a relieved sigh.

"What?" I ask.

"Just checking that this isn't a *The Shining* situation." When

I blink at her, she gives me a playful smile and adds, "Arun said if we see you typing 'All work and no play makes Jack a dull boy' over and over again, he's hiding the scissors."

I force a hollow laugh and grab a muffin. As she takes her leave, I remind myself she was just teasing, but a lonely feeling grips me at the image of Tessa and Arun joking about me behind my back. Even if it's good-natured, even if it means nothing, it's another reminder of how out of step I am with the rest of the team here. But I have to be, if I have any chance of getting out.

I watch Tessa head toward the back of the office with the others. Arun leans against Jen's desk, gesturing animatedly with a blueberry muffin in hand as he talks. Randy emerges from the kitchen and hands them paper towels; only then does he unwrap his muffin and join the conversation.

I don't get up to join them, but I don't put my headphones back on, either. I bite into my muffin—which is as moist and flavorful as it looks—and listen to their chatter. Arun's passionately explaining why Jen should give the Fast and the Furious franchise another chance. Tessa delights in pointing out plot holes ("Okay, but they're *family!*"), and Randy eventually interrupts their banter by asking who wants tea.

They seem so…*happy* here. They've been demoted and sent to a dying town to sit in an empty office where nothing happens, and they couldn't be more content.

If I weren't so afraid of becoming them, I'd feel for them. This is what happens when you're stuck. You fall into quicksand, and you don't realize you're sinking until it's too late. It's why Mom left when she did. She saw the signs and knew she had to save herself, even if it meant breaking up our family in the process.

If I continue to stay here, what will happen to me?

My dad seems pleased to have me back home. He's been cooking all my favorite childhood meals: chicken and dumplings, tortellini in Alfredo sauce, spaghetti and meatballs. Then we go around the table talking about our days, and he seems blissfully unaware of how dull it is to live here. He recaps the events of his morning run, which, at its most thrilling, includes waving to more than one neighbor. Wendy shares an anecdote from her job at the dental office downtown. Yesterday, it was her observations on which of their new polishing paste flavors, piña colada or fruit punch, is more popular.

Then they turn to me and ask how my day was, and I have to sort through the day's nonevents and find something to… embellish. Randy brought in more donations than Arun in their telephone fundraising competition. (Translation: Randy beat Arun in air hockey.) Jen's making excellent progress on her clothing drive. (She moved on to the sleeves portion of the woven top she's crocheting.) Tessa's brainstorming new community outreach projects. (She cracked her daily sudoku puzzle before lunch.) I'm spearheading a cleanup campaign. (I wiped the kitchen counters while waiting for the kettle to boil.)

Dad and Wendy don't ask how Ryser Cares could be working on all these charity projects when the office hasn't done anything of value in years. They don't challenge me or press for details. They nod encouragingly and tell me that's wonderful, how lovely, they're happy I'm happy. And I want to scream.

My mom, on the other hand, understands the terrors of returning to Greenstead. When I texted her with the news of my transfer, her reply was sympathetic.

Oh, I'm so sorry. I wouldn't go back to that place for anything. I hope you can get out soon.

The urgency in her words makes sense. She knows I've entered a colorless void where every day is the same. Wake up, sit in this office trying to be productive, go home, make pleasant conversation over dinner with Dad and Wendy, go to my room and work on a puzzle until it's time for bed, and then everything repeats all over again.

If I spend a minute too long here, the tedium will swallow me whole, and then I too will be perfectly content to sit here and waste away for eternity. I'm starting to wonder how long I can hold out.

The door swings open with a loud creak. I look up, figuring it's Randy going on another pretzel run. Instead, I meet the bewildered expression of my ex–best friend Marina Ramos.

Seeing her transports me back to our bitter argument at the last ever apple festival. Snippets of it hit me like punches in the gut, one after the other. Our raised voices, the sweet smell of kettle corn, the anger flashing in Marina's eyes right up until she stormed off for the exit.

I wonder if she's thinking the same thing, because she freezes in place, eyes wide. I straighten my spine and square my shoulders, but good posture doesn't help me look put together when

I'm still gaping at her in confusion. Behind me, the conversation comes to a halt.

"Hi," Marina ventures, her dark brows dipping slightly. I'm busy trying to reconcile this early-thirties Marina with the teenager I once knew. Her dark brown hair was long and frizzy, and now it's shoulder-length, shiny, and neatly tamed. She's grown out her bangs, and it suits her. In a red cap-sleeved sundress and flip-flops, it's like she and the Ryser Cares group all got the same casual-dress-code memo. Then there's me, all dark colors and sharp angles in my pleated black pants and navy collared blouse, dressed to impress someone who isn't even here.

"Hi," I say. "Um." I stand, not sure what the proper protocol is for greeting someone who used to be your best friend, before you got into a shouting match near the cotton candy stand. I glance behind me at the Ryser Cares group, still congregated at Jen's desk. From the uncertain looks they're exchanging, they weren't expecting her either.

"What are you doing here?" Marina asks.

"I work here?" I can't help the way it comes out, nor the way my face scrunches in uncertainty. It does feel more like a question than a statement.

"Since when? I knew you worked for *Ryser*, but I thought you were in DC." Her eyebrow lifts in disdain when she says the company's name.

Her tone makes me bristle. We used to make fun of those Ryser Cares ads, but my jabs were always more lighthearted than hers. I'd mimic the spokesperson's stilted voice, but Marina, even at ten, would say what a joke it all was, how this was basically the equivalent of Scar from *The Lion King* boasting about improving Pride Rock, as if he wasn't the reason it declined in the first place—except worse, she'd say, because at least Scar had a cool accent and a catchy villain song. I'd agree and nod along with her, but I'd think to myself that Ryser couldn't be that bad if they were here, cleaning, caring. In retrospect, I was probably a little too susceptible to their ad campaign.

It's no surprise that Marina takes issue with me working at Ryser. She's not capable of nuance, and that's her loss. I could tell her about my eight-year plan, the career track, the good I'll do once I get my promotion, how once I'm forty I'll take my money and run and never have a single thing to do with Ryser ever again. How I'm going to buy a town house in a neighborhood with sidewalks and walkability and *life*, where I can walk to cafés and restaurants and enjoy the small pleasures Greenstead could never give me. How I'll adopt a dog and give it the life it deserves: a living space that isn't a sad basement apartment, a backyard to play fetch in. Live out the rest of my days far away from endless controversies and unethical business practices. But there's no point telling her any of that, because she wouldn't listen to anything I said after *Ryser*.

Early retirement became my goal after my first Ryser scandal a year out of college. An environmental organization published a report revealing that Ryser's palm oil supplier was destroying rain forests and orangutan habitats to source the oil. I robotically did my job helping Amanda spin the narrative in Ryser's favor, but I spent my downtime clicking through pictures of sad-eyed orangutans and feeling like a monster. I briefly went on the job hunt, but the listings I came across gave me pause. A pay cut, only two weeks of PTO, *and* no free snacks in the office kitchen? Just to win the approval of some orangutans on the other side of the world? It was then that I learned my morality is more flexible than I was willing to admit.

So, I came to a new conclusion: I'd keep my job, but I'd appease the orangutans another way, and thus my plan was born. I read up on the FIRE movement—Financial Independence, Retire Early—I cut unnecessary expenses, I left my apartment in the heart of the city for a cheaper place in a less lively neighborhood. I focused on putting my head down, working toward the next promotion, saving my money to the extreme. When I turn forty, I will become someone the orangutans approve of.

Though I doubt I'll ever win the approval of anyone in Greenstead.

"Well, I *was* at Ryser in DC, until a couple of weeks ago." I take a breath, trying to figure out how to explain why I work for Ryser and how to spin the demotion without making Ryser look bad. But when I open my mouth, the excuses die on my tongue. I don't owe her any explanations, I remember. We're not best friends anymore.

"Long story," I say with a wave of my hand. "I'm just…here to help out. It's temporary." Blessedly, the Ryser Cares folks don't correct me.

"How generous," she says dryly.

I dig my nails into my palm. I haven't forgotten what she shouted at me during our fight. The words *You're fucking selfish* always come back to me at the oddest times. After a glowing performance review from Amanda. After transferring my annual bonus to my savings account. Marina and I went a decade without speaking, and still I could never escape her judgment.

She shouldn't get to haunt me like this. She's not my friend; she's just a woman who's walked into my place of business. A prospect or a potential business partner. Business partners I can handle.

"So…" I say, slipping into my self-assured Business Partner voice. I clap my hands together with a grin. "How can we help?" I realize as the question leaves my mouth that I actually have no idea how to help. No one here has trained me on anything. But Business Partner me is an excellent performer.

"Marge suggested I come here," she says. Seeing my blank expression, she clarifies, "Randy's wife?"

As I'm about to dig myself deeper and pretend to be intimately acquainted with this Marge, Randy steps forward. "Marge sent you?" he asks.

"Yeah. She thought you'd be able to help save the community center."

"Save the community center?" I echo, Business Partner voice momentarily forgotten.

It's never once occurred to me that the Greenstead Community Center could ever need saving. That large, redbrick building sits in my memory as a permanent fixture. Home to the only public swimming pool in Greenstead, it's where Marina and I went swimming most summers when our parents weren't willing to take us to the water park in Falls Point. We'd receive its program guide in the mail at the start of every season, advertising its offerings: after-school programs, art classes, group exercises, book clubs, planned hikes along the Echo Hill trail. My dad met Wendy on one of those hikes.

Marina and I took a watercolor painting class there one summer, when we were twelve and her mom was sick of us loafing around on her living room couch watching *The Proud Family* reruns. We learned that neither of us had a burgeoning talent for art, but it gave us something to do, and we had fun exploring the community center afterward. We played Battleship on the ancient set in the rec center while seniors played chess nearby. We sat outside by the basketball courts, making bets on which kid would sink a basket next. The mountain landscape she painted for me in that class still hangs in my childhood bedroom. Now I have to stare at it every day, that physical reminder of how close we were then and how nothing we are now.

Marina throws me a begrudging glance. I know that look. No matter who she's talking to or what grudges she's holding, she can never resist launching into a rant.

"The town can't afford to keep it open anymore," she says. "They're talking about selling the building. But my students need it. For a lot of them, it's a safe place where they can go after school until their parents get off work. And it's not just kids. The computer class I teach at the community center is for adults, and they need it, too. It's one of the only places left where people can get together. We've already lost the Powell Market and the bowling alley. I'm not losing the community center, too. So, let's save it."

Let's save it. Like it's that simple.

Ever since I've known her, starting from that first day of third grade when we were sat next to one another and instantly bonded over how our erasers made a perfect pair—my miniature burger to her tiny carton of fries—Marina has always been endlessly optimistic. She believes in goodness, fairness, that right will always prevail over wrong.

Two months into third grade, she found a nickel on the playground at recess and took it to the yard supervisor, who chuckled, patted her on the head, and told her it was hers to keep because no one would miss it. And Marina, who didn't like the idea of holding on to money that didn't belong to her, asked our teacher to see if anyone in our class was missing a nickel when we got back from recess. Sure enough, the messy-haired kid two rows in front of us started counting the coins in his pocket and realized his lunch money was five cents short. As a reward, our teacher let Marina pick a sticker from her coveted sticker drawer.

I felt a strange sort of jealousy at the time. Not about wanting the holographic rainbow sticker Marina chose, but because Marina had an instinct for goodness that I was missing somehow. Because when Marina had taken that nickel to me, I'd told her to keep it. If it were up to me, that kid would have gone hungry and I would have dropped that coin into my piggy bank without a second thought.

The doubt on Randy's face tells me he's also at a loss against Marina's sky-high optimism. "I would love to save it, if I could. I know how much Marge loves teaching her boxing class over there. But…I'm not sure what we could really do."

"I was thinking we could revive the Greenstead Apple Festival," Marina replies.

"Apple festival?"

Apparently my only contributions to this conversation are repeating Marina's words like a dumbfounded parrot. It's whiplash-inducing, being inundated with a flood of memories every time she speaks, blinks, exists. Now I'm back at the apple festival, one of the years before our fight, sinking my teeth into a caramel apple, leaves rustling at my feet, Marina by my side.

"We could bring it back and set up a way for people to donate," Marina says. "Maybe it would raise enough money to save the community center."

"Fun!" Jen enthuses. I turn to see she's drawn closer, coming to stand beside Randy. Arun and Tessa, too, have moved forward, standing in the aisle by my desk.

A tentative ray of hope lights Marina's eyes. "So you'll help?"

Jen's face falls into uncertainty. "Oh, I didn't mean… I think it's a wonderful idea. I'm part of the community center's crochet circle; I'd hate to see it go. But…there isn't much we could do."

"I play racquetball at the court over there almost every weekend," Arun says. "I could make a personal donation. How much do you need?"

Marina chuckles wryly. "My best guess? At least a hundred thousand dollars."

Arun's shoulders droop. "Oh. Um…have you tried seeing if the town council will help? Get it on Mayor Bradley's radar?"

"I think I'd have a better chance of calling up Bigfoot,"

Marina replies, and the office breaks into titters. I fake a laugh too, pretending to get it.

"So there's nothing you could do?" Marina asks Randy. "Marge said maybe you could—"

"I think Marge may have overestimated my abilities," Randy says, rubbing the back of his neck. "I can't speak for the rest of us, but…I wouldn't even know how to help. I'm no good with… any of that stuff."

"What stuff?" Marina asks.

"*Everything*. It's why I'm here."

"It's why we're all here," Tessa says quietly. "Flop House."

"What was that?" When Tessa waves it off, Marina sighs. "I guess that's typical. I should know by now how pointless it is to ask Ryser for help."

Marina's gaze falls on me when she says this. Her eyes narrow just enough to make it abundantly clear that this is really an insult meant just for me. She's trying to convey how enlightened she is, how *right* she is for knowing Ryser would never lift a finger to help anyone, while I'm just the useless corporate lackey who sold my soul for a paycheck.

I imagine the satisfaction of telling Marina, *No, actually, you don't know everything, we will help.* Her self-righteous veneer would buckle on the spot.

I don't know how to throw a festival, but it would be glorious to play the part, save the day, shatter her expectations and come out on top. Then she'd see I have a heart. I'd get to feel like the superior one, like I finally did something right, followed that instinct for goodness that's always escaped me.

Somewhere along the way, the fantasy starts to feel more possible. This isn't that sweeping act of good I'd planned to do as communications director, but it's something, isn't it? It's a way to help out Greenstead. It's something to do while I'm here, instead of wasting away watching professional development webinars, peppering my new colleagues with questions they can't answer, and lying to Dad and Wendy about what goes on here.

The idea grows larger in my mind, glittering with promise. This could even help me get my old job back. Throwing this festival would be a PR boon for Ryser, earning them the goodwill they desperately need after the last year of press disasters. They could plaster their website with pictures of smiling children holding sugar-dusted apple cider donuts, a crowd of grateful Greensteaders cheering in front of the newly reinstated community center, the mayor of Greenstead raising an apple cider toast to Ryser Cares. Amanda will thank me sincerely, realize how much she needs me on her team, and summon me back to DC. Maybe she'll even promote me on the spot. And I'll float back home, my early retirement plan back on track, leaving Greenstead behind a better place and proving that I'm a good person once and for all.

And somewhere in there, a thought so small I'm reluctant to acknowledge it: I wouldn't mind another caramel apple. I wouldn't mind replacing that jagged, hurtful memory of fighting with Marina at the last festival with something happier.

"We can help," I say.

Marina blinks once, twice. "You can?"

"We can?" Arun says. Beside him, Randy bites his thumbnail.

Jen looks conflicted, like she's fighting the urge to correct me. Tessa winces in the way one might when they're watching a car skid off the road.

"Yes," I say. It feels good to return to the poise of Business Partner me. "Ryser's one of the biggest food suppliers in the country. Our entire mission is about empowering people through food. We absolutely have the resources to support an apple festival."

"Really." Marina's voice is dripping with doubt. Her gaze shifts from me to the rest of the Ryser Cares team.

I keep my head high. "Really." I reach for my wallet and pull out my business card. "Here's my card. Let me know when you want to set up a meeting. I'm looking forward to collaborating."

My genial Business Partner smile seems to catch her off guard. Marina slowly takes the card, stares at it, tucks it into her purse. "O…kay." With one last wary glance at me, she turns for the exit.

When the door swings shut with her departure, I'm acutely aware of four questioning pairs of eyes on me.

"How are we supposed to throw a festival?" Tessa asks.

"We'll figure it out."

They keep staring, but I turn to look out the window, watching Marina get into her car, feeling like I've won a chess match.

I still need to get my colleagues on board, and there's the small matter of figuring out how one throws a festival, but I'll find a way. The way I'm feeling right now, anything is possible.

GREENSTEAD
APPLE FESTIVAL

OCTOBER 2001

THE FIRST APPLE FESTIVAL MARINA and I attend together feels like a new beginning. Not just the usual start-of-the-school-year new beginning, all the potential of unsharpened pencils and blank notebooks. Not the new beginning of Greenstead's tentative return to normalcy just a few years after the flood. This is something more: our first time hanging out off school grounds after becoming fast friends on the first day of third grade just a month ago.

Fast friends is what my mom calls it, a term I never quite liked. Like fast food, it makes me think of something cheap, artificial. Our friendship may be new, but I know it's something real.

I revel in the satisfying crunch of leaves beneath my feet as Marina and I trail after her mom and two older sisters through the crowded festival grounds. We make a game out of finding the biggest, crunchiest leaves to stomp on, weaving through the booths and turning the entire park into an elaborate game of hopscotch. When we bump into Marina's twelve-year-old sister, she rolls her eyes and calls us immature. Marina and I share a grin like we know a secret: Life is way more fun inside our bubble of friendship. It's so much better to be immature and together than aloof and alone. How sad, I think to myself, that her sister doesn't know that.

When we line up at the hot apple cider booth, I spend the entire time fingering the folded twenty-dollar bill in my pocket. I'm ready to pay for my own, but Marina's mom, a woman with big wavy hair and large brown eyes, hands the first cup of cider to me. That gesture makes me feel like I've been formally accepted into the Ramos family, my friendship with Marina blessed and certified.

At the Lettie's Confections booth, we discover that the caramel apple Marina and I both want—coated in crushed peanuts, drizzled with milk chocolate—is the last one left. I tell Marina she can have it (I did receive the First Cup of Cider, after all), but she insists we share it. Lettie, a grandmotherly Black woman with a gap-toothed smile and a short tuft of hair, runs it through her apple slicer and hands over a paper tray of peanut-chocolate-caramel apple slices in all their glory. We sit at one end of a picnic table savoring our sweet, sticky apple slices while Marina's eldest sister sits at the other end, daintily nibbling her plain caramel apple and pretending not to know us. In the age of cooties, there's something intimate about Marina and me eating from the same tray. It feels like something fast friends don't do.

I've had friends before, of course, but the two of us click in a way that feels new to me. There's an ease to our rapport; I never feel like I'm constantly searching for the right thing to say. The focused way Marina talks to me makes me feel like she's interested in *me*, not which Little Debbie snack cake I have in my lunchbox or whether my golden retriever Lisa Frank folder is cool enough. Whether we're trading erasers from our collections or sitting on the edge of the playground joking about our favorite *Recess* characters, time always flies by when we're together.

That cider blessing doesn't feel like enough anymore. I need confirmation, right from the source, that this friendship matters as much as I feel it does. When we are down to the last two apple slices, I blurt out the question.

"Are we best friends?"

Marina stops chewing. She tilts her head to the side, considering my question with all the gravity it requires. She resumes chewing, swallows, and says, "I think we are."

Blissful relief spills through me. "Me too."

And so it's decided. We each raise our last apple slice in the air, a toast to ourselves and each other and the traditions we've unknowingly started today. I think we both know, even now, that our toast marks only the beginning of so much more to come.

CHAPTER SIX

WHEN I CROSS THE PARKING lot the next morning, my gait is steady. I train my eyes on the front doors that I'm definitely going to make it through without any goose-related interruptions.

Marina's coming by this afternoon for our first festival planning meeting. I'm sure it'll mean more pointed Ryser digs with her usual air of superiority, but I can't even dread it. For the first time since coming here, I have a project to work on. I have *purpose*.

My colleagues are less enthused. Yesterday, I forwarded them the meeting invitation Marina sent me, but no one checked their email. The mood in the office was subdued after Marina left. Jen took up her crocheting, but she didn't make much progress; every so often, she'd mutter about missing a stitch and unravel some to correct it. Tessa took longer than usual to finish her sudoku puzzle; she kept looking up from her phone, deep in thought. The air hockey table and Randy's book went untouched; he was intently typing something on his phone, making me suspect he was texting his wife to ask how on earth she could do something as appalling as believe in him. And Arun spent a good twenty minutes staring at nothing, clicking and unclicking his pen in rapid succession until Jen had to ask him to stop.

When we meet with Marina today, they'll see this isn't anything to worry about. I'll ease them back into the world of productivity slowly, gently. I even stopped by the bakery on my way here and picked up bagels and cream cheese for the office. They seem to like carbs. Maybe I could lay out the bagels in the conference room behind the kitchen. No one's used it since I've been here, but that'll change today. I never thought I'd be so excited for a meeting.

That's when a goose runs at me, wings flapping wildly.

I scream and drop the box of bagels, then turn on my heels and run. It's honking now, the flapping sounds getting closer and closer until I feel air fanning the back of my neck and realize with horror that it's flying after me. I sprint across the parking lot, expecting any second for the feather-wind on my neck to be replaced by the puncture of a pointed beak. Already, I'm mourning my untimely death by goose. How tragic, to die here in the town I spent my life trying to escape. Geese must love irony.

I reach the end of the parking lot, veer left, and keep running. The honking subsides, and I can't hear the flapping anymore, but I don't stop until I've done a full lap around the parking lot. Only then, with heaving breaths and a stinging pain where the backs of my flats dug into my ankles, do I check to see if it's safe.

I spot the goose about twenty yards away, side by side with its mate, who must have been enjoying the show from afar. The pair strolls confidently past the old stationery store. I don't think they could get to me before I reach Ryser Cares, but still I bolt toward the office, pausing only to snatch the box of bagels. The geese continue their slow walk, benevolently allowing me to reach the office alive.

Once inside, I check the bagels for damage. The bottom corner of the box is dented, but the sticker seal is still intact. The bagels, nestled beneath a layer of wax paper, are safe from harm. At least one of us is.

"That was cute," a voice comments. I startle, almost dropping the bagels a second time. Marina sits at my desk, a book in her hands. She gestures toward the window, where she had a perfect view of me running for my life from a twelve-pound goose. "Is that like a morning routine?"

I pause to catch my breath, still ragged from the goose attack. "No," I say. But when Marina narrows her eyes at me, I fold. "Yes," I grumble, and she snickers. I drop the bagels on the desk in front of her. "They don't bother you?"

"No," she says with a shrug.

"And you didn't want to help me out?"

She shakes her head like the answer is obvious. "The first rule of any nature documentary is not to intervene."

I sigh. "What are you doing here? I thought we were meeting at two."

"We *were*, but I moved it up. I called the county Chamber of Commerce this morning to float the idea of the festival and see how we could get vendors involved, and they said we needed to present the idea at their next meeting. Then they told me *when* their next meeting is." She lowers her chin and waits for me to do the math.

"It's today?" I guess, dread turning in my stomach.

"At four thirty. Their next one isn't for another month, so... today it is."

I sink into a chair beside my desk. "And when you say *we* need to present it, you mean..."

"You and me." Confusion clouds her face, as though she's trying to understand how I've forgotten the meaning of basic pronouns. "And the rest of the office, if they're up for it."

I imagine standing before every business owner in the county, declaring myself a Ryser representative. A sea of disappointed faces appears in my mind. Tim Cooper of Cooper Cakes. Rosie Lee, who owns the farm-slash-petting zoo where we used to go on field trips. Her pigs, my favorite part of the field trip, join the fray too, snorting at me in disgust. Even Mayor Bradley enters the picture. After Marina's Bigfoot comment, I asked my dad about Mayor Bradley at dinner last night, and he told me he's notoriously reclusive. In his five years as Greenstead's mayor, he's held exactly one press conference, and that was just to announce he does not answer phone calls and would communicate over email only. But sure, let's throw Mayor Bradley into the mix too, coming out of hiding just to declare me an official traitor. I imagine boos. Tomatoes hitting my chest and landing at my feet with a sickening plop. The idea of publicly putting myself on display just to be called a disappointment makes me want to plod right out the door and submit myself to death by geese. It would be less painful.

But I don't know how to express any of that to Marina. She'd just confirm my fears and list all the reasons she and everyone else in town are disappointed in me. Just like yesterday, I need to stop seeing her as my ex–best friend and see her like a prospect. It's easier that way.

"I think you'd be better suited to take the reins," I say, tapping back into Business Partner me. "This is your idea. Your perspective will really resonate with everyone."

Marina frowns. "You said you'd help."

"Of course. I just think I'd be of more value…behind the scenes."

"What if they ask about Ryser's involvement? I don't even know what that means. But *you* do."

Her eyes are serious. I can see frustration starting to build beneath the surface. It *is* a reasonable assumption, that I might know how the hell Ryser will be supporting this festival I agreed to help with.

There's no getting out of this, unless I'm willing to admit the truth.

I swallow my anxiety and give her my best fake smile. "You're right. I'll present with you."

A satisfied smirk crosses her face. "Good."

"Good."

That settled, Marina leans back and surveys the empty office. "Where is everyone?"

"They usually get in at around ten." On a good day. When she looks less than impressed, I add, "Ryser encourages flexible schedules."

I ignore her skeptical scoff, turn on my laptop, and say we should get started on the presentation. A concept that definitely doesn't make my stomach curdle.

Working on the presentation with Marina reminds me of the times we spent working on projects together in high school, but in a parallel universe sort of way. None of that warmth, our shorthand, the research rabbit holes we'd go down. Now, we sit several feet apart, just close enough to reach the laptop. Our words are reluctant and focused only on the task at hand. We avoid eye contact whenever possible, talking at the laptop instead.

But there are little moments that feel like déjà vu. The way she spends ages scouring PowerPoint templates to find the right one, ignoring the ones I point to as my patience dwindles. The excitement that lights her eyes when she gets a burst of inspiration. The pieces are there, but they don't fit the same way anymore. It makes me wish I could snap my fingers and get our easy dynamic back, when we fit together and made sense.

"What's that?" Arun asks when he enters the office, nodding his chin at the PowerPoint slide on my computer screen.

I toss a wary glance at Marina, then silently pray Arun has gotten over his reluctance about reviving the apple festival. "We're working on a presentation for potential vendors. We have to present it at the Chamber of Commerce today."

His brow pinches like I'm speaking another language. "Oh," he says, which is probably the best I can hope for. "I actually wasn't asking about that; I was asking about…" He points to the box at the edge of my desk.

"Bagels and cream cheese," I say through a quiet sigh. I don't bother checking to see how Marina's taking in Arun's uncooperativeness. "Have some."

"Sweet. Thanks."

We watch Arun help himself to a cinnamon-raisin bagel and apply cream cheese to each half with artful intensity.

"You wanna grab a chair?" Marina offers. "We're putting together a list of the ways vendors would benefit from exhibiting at the apple festival."

Arun smiles grimly. "I'm no help. Sorry. I just…make things worse."

It's a surprisingly glum response from someone wearing a bright-green shirt covered in cartoon bananas. Arun lifts his bagel at us in thanks, then wanders off to the kitchen in the back.

"Arun knows his boundaries," I say sunnily.

The rest of the team responds similarly when they trickle into the office and stop by my desk. They laud our progress in a detached sort of way, but when I ask if they'd like to help, they shrink away and mutter an excuse. At first, I think it's laziness— they're used to spending their days at their leisure, after all—but more than once I spot Tessa looking up from her phone to peer at us, Jen pausing her show for minutes at a time like she's listening, Randy chewing his lip in thought. Arun strolls past our desk once, twice, then finally stops.

I stop typing, waiting for him to just come out with it and ask for a second bagel.

"I think your vendor minimum might be too low," he says. I almost fall out of my chair. "What?"

"You have to assume every vendor's going to bring in a dollar figure, right? Pay a participation fee to cover your festival costs?"

"I thought Ryser would cover the festival costs," Marina says.

"Our budget's been almost nonexistent for years," Tessa replies.

"Barely enough for a decent Christmas party," Randy says mournfully.

"Oh." My chest deflates like a popped balloon. Their uncertainty yesterday starts to make more sense. I glance at the slide deck Marina and I spent all morning working on. "So...we can't afford to throw a festival? Is that why you don't think it's a good idea?"

"I didn't say it's not a good idea. You *can* afford it." Arun pulls a chair from the desk next to us and scoots in. "That's what I was saying about the vendor minimum. If you get enough vendors, their participation fees will cover the festival costs. Things like applications, permits, table rentals, tents, liability insurance—"

"Insurance?" Marina repeats.

"How do you know all this?" I say with an incredulous laugh.

"I used to help run events," he says. "Back at the DC office. But...that was a while ago, before they transferred me. I'm sure you've already thought of all this." That note of morose self-deprecation has returned to his voice. He starts to inch his chair away.

"No!" Marina and I both shout. Arun does a double take, looking back and forth between us.

"We could really use your help," I insist.

He eyes us almost sternly, like he thinks we're playing a joke on him. "The last event I ran for Ryser, I took a chance on a new caterer and ten thousand people got food poisoning."

"*Oh*," I say as the memory washes over me. "I remember hearing about that." It happened while I was interning at Ryser in college. I'd been interning for a different department—marketing—but I remembered Amanda looking particularly frazzled when our paths crossed. The event made headlines and spurred our CEO to email all employees with somber assurances that the problem had been dealt with. Arun, apparently, was the problem.

But he's also our best hope.

"Is that why you didn't want to help?" I ask. "You think you'll screw it up?"

"Well, yeah. I have a pretty good track record for screwing up. No sane person would let me—or any of us—near their festival."

I wait for the others to refute his claim. But the office is silent. Randy, Tessa, and Jen are avoiding eye contact. "You don't agree with him, do you?"

Jen shrugs. "I accidentally live-tweeted *all* my thoughts on the *Bachelorette* finale from the CEO's account instead of mine," she says. "I used some…phallic GIFs. Not something anyone wants in a social media manager."

I clamp my lips together to suppress a smile at the mention of *phallic GIFs*. But there's nothing funny about the shame on Jen's face. "Do you all feel this way?" I ask. "Like you can't contribute anything?"

"I put botulism in salad dressing and blew up a multimillion-dollar partnership, remember?" Tessa reminds me.

"Don't forget me losing a million dollars in a phishing scam," Randy says.

Marina's head swivels from one person to the next, taking in these revelations. I wonder if she's having doubts about coming to this group for help. But their dejected faces pull at me. No wonder they're so content to stay here, wasting away in this useless office in a comatose town. They think they're not capable of achieving anything better. They're afraid of repeating history.

"So what?" I say. "I threatened to murder the CEO." I meet their confused surprise with the full story, detailing the elevator incident, my deaf ear, Bill. "Security had to escort me from the building."

A silence follows. I've never told anyone the story until now. I'd glossed it over as a misunderstanding, put on my headphones, and shut out the world. But it's occurring to me now that, no matter how superior I felt, with my stiff blouses and my webinars and my stubborn refusal to be one of them, I *am* one of them. It's why I've been hiding away in my childhood bedroom since I've been back, afraid of running into anyone who knows me. It's why the thought of facing an assembly of local business owners this afternoon makes me break into a sweat.

But I can't let that fear rule my life. None of us should.

"Damn," Tessa says, giving me an amused once-over. "They must really not give a shit about us if they sent us a whole-ass murderer."

Arun's laugh lights up the room. Jen's comes next, then Randy's deep rumbles of laughter.

"The geese were trying to warn us!" Jen exclaims.

I sit there, smiling the widest I can remember in months, feeling so exposed I want to throw myself under my desk. But what stops me is this camaraderie I've tapped into. I didn't realize how good it would feel to share a part of myself with them.

I turn to Marina, curious to see how she's taking it. She's looking distant. Thoughtful. Almost like she's reconsidering her idea to work with us.

"What?" I ask her, resignation seeping into my voice. Already I'm bristling at the thought of her taking issue with our mistakes just as I've started to get the others to loosen up.

"I almost burned the school down," Marina confesses. That gets everyone's attention. "When I was a student teacher, they had a bearded dragon for a class pet. I was cleaning its tank, and when I finished, I forgot to put the heat lamp back over the tank. So…overnight, the heat lamp burned a hole in my boss's desk. The bearded dragon was fine!" she adds when Jen gasps. "But the classroom smelled like smoke for a week." She glances at me. "If you're a murderer, I'm an arsonist."

A surprised laugh leaves me. "I guess we make a good team," I say, then regret it immediately. Is that too forward? Too trite? Too reminiscent of the years when we very much *were* a team?

But Marina just smiles, and I feel the distance between us lessen the tiniest bit. It emboldens me to turn to face the others. "Now that we've established none of us can be trusted to do anything…do you want to try anyway?"

The looks that go around the office aren't doubtful this time. They hold interest. Curiosity. Maybe even excitement.

The ideas start pouring out. Tessa proposes diverting our paltry claims budget to the festival, adding that hardly any claims meet Ryser's increasingly strict criteria anyway. Randy offers to contribute all fifty dollars from the Christmas party budget toward the festival costs. For the rest of the day, our presentation prep is more cooperative, with all of us brainstorming out loud, tossing out ideas for winning over vendors. Arun suggests offering free advertising space on the festival website. (We make a note to create a festival website.) Jen offers to set up social media accounts promoting the festival and highlighting vendor goods (and assures us there's no chance she'll repeat her account mix-up mistake, because now she exclusively uses Twitch to discuss her *Bachelorette* opinions, and I need a minute to conceive of this sweet, fiftysomething woman as a Twitch streamer, of all things).

Their suggestions turn from logistics to things they'd like to see at the festival. Arun wants an apple cider dunk tank. Tessa muses that a pie-baking contest could be fun. Randy asks if live music could be a possibility. Jen says a history-loving friend in her crochet circle would probably love to do a display on the history of Greenstead. I write down every single idea, getting lost in the fantasy that this just might work.

Four o'clock arrives just as we're finishing up the final slide. The energy in the room intensifies as people start gathering their things. Arun's telling Marina we'll easily reach the minimum number of vendors he thinks we need to participate—thirty-five—and Jen and Tessa toss out higher numbers, forty, fifty, one-upping each other in optimism. Randy offers to drive, jingling his car keys on his way to the door.

I stare out the window as Randy drives us through Greenstead's barren fields, down a stretch of highway, and into the exquisitely manicured downtown area of Falls Point, the next town over. Every time that Chamber of Commerce scene I'd imagined earlier passes through my mind—jeers, boos, tomatoes galore—I need only to look around me to assure myself we can do this. My new colleagues have the good ideas, Marina has the passion, I have years of experience giving presentations. We'll win over the vendors. We'll get the thirty-five we need to participate so we can afford to throw the festival. We'll save the community center, I'll prove I have a heart, I'll get my old job back, and the world will keep on turning.

Still, when we step out of Randy's van and head up the stairs toward the Falls Point Civic Center, a modern, two-story building with large windows, I feel my resolve slipping with each step I climb. But when Jen tosses me a nervous look, I shoot her a reassuring *we got this* grin.

And if that smile succumbs to doubt the second we pass through the civic center doors, no one needs to know.

GREENSTEAD APPLE FESTIVAL

OCTOBER 2006

B Y THE TIME WE'RE THIRTEEN, the apple festival isn't cool anymore.

For most eighth graders, anyway. Our classmates deem the festival babyish, preferring to spend their weekends at the movie theater, the bowling alley, or the strip mall on Kent Street that's more strip than mall.

But for Marina and me, it's a sacred tradition. In our thirteenth year, it's something else, too: freedom. For the first time, we're old enough that we don't need parents hovering around us. Our parents drop us off at Juniper Park, we meet up at the tall stack of hay bales by the festival entrance, and we enter the park feeling like the entire world is ours for the taking.

With no parents or judgmental older sisters in earshot, we're free to say and do whatever we please. We take our time trying on scarves at a knitwear tent, meticulously considering whether burnt orange or emerald green would complement our wardrobes better. We walk down the rows of booths talking freely, without looking over our shoulders to check who's listening—last night I dreamed I was married to our algebra teacher; Marina wants to try out for choir; my mom hasn't called as much as I thought she would since she moved to New York; Marina's older sister had a pregnancy scare.

As tradition dictates, we buy one milk chocolate peanut caramel apple from Lettie's Confections and sit at a picnic table to split it, slice by slice. Unlike that first time, there's no need to define our friendship. With that matter settled long ago, we engage in the important work of people watching. Kids throw tantrums over balloons and cotton candy, and we marvel over how we could have ever been that juvenile. Young women walk by and we catalog their outfits, noting our favorites. (Marina's partial to colorful dresses over muted tights, while I'm fascinated by the way a simple pair of brown leather boots can go with any outfit.) When young men pass by, we confer over who qualifies as a Jack. This is a term we coined after going through her dad's old high school yearbooks one night and coming across a picture of a sophomore named Jack. With his impish smile, deep-set dimples, and eyes that sparkled with intrigue, *Jack* soon became our shorthand for any cute boy.

"He's a Jack," I say, pointing at a rosy-cheeked teen cooing over a goat at the petting zoo.

"Definitely," she agrees.

More people pass. I keep eating, observing, looking out for

Jacks and leather boots. It's when I reach for another apple slice that I realize Marina hasn't eaten one in a while. She's staring ahead, but her eyes are roving with thought.

"What are you thinking?" I ask.

"What if…"

"Hmm?" I nudge her with an elbow.

"What about her?" she asks, jutting her chin up ahead.

I follow her direction to see a girl of about fifteen kneeling by the jewelry booth to tie her shoe. She's dressed in a simple white sweater, jeans, and Vans. Marina normally likes outfits with a pop of color, but there's appeal in simplicity too. "You like her sweater?"

"No." Marina hesitates. "What if I think she's a Jack, too?"

It takes me a moment to parse out her meaning. I glance at the girl again, looking for what Marina might see. The concentration on her face as she inspects a necklace. The way her wavy brown hair tumbles down her shoulders. The shy smile she gives the booth attendant who comes to speak to her.

"Then she's a Jack," I say. "Or…Jill?"

Marina grins, tipping her head to the side as she thinks it over. "Jordan," she decides. "Works for anyone."

"Jordan," I agree.

And it's settled. Marina goes back to our apple slices. We return to people watching and commentating. And with every minute that passes in this new, supervision-less life, every word we utter that our parents aren't around to eavesdrop in on, every Jordan Marina shyly points out to me, I feel our world growing brighter, wider, stretching out before us with possibility.

CHAPTER SEVEN

A s the **Walnut County Chamber** of Commerce meeting is called to order, I find myself playing a stealthy game of peekaboo with the fifty or so business owners in attendance.

Most I don't recognize, either because they're from Falls Point, the only other town in Walnut County, or because I've been gone too long to know who lives in Greenstead anymore.

But there, in the fifth row, sits Tim Cooper, the man who baked all my birthday cakes growing up. He looks the same in some ways, tall and dark-skinned, always dressed in plaid, even in the summer. But his neatly trimmed mustache is gray now, and extra lines crease the corners of his eyes. I wonder how he'll react when he sees me here, how I've grown from the little girl who loved corner brownies into a Ryser shill. Then he yawns into the crook of his elbow and his head shifts a few degrees my way, and I turn sharply to face another direction.

"What?" asks Marina when I accidentally jostle her in the process.

"Nothing."

She gives me an odd look but returns her attention to the front. At the head of the room, six Chamber of Commerce board members sit at a long folding table, five sleepily listening while one recites extremely detailed minutes from last month's meeting. I'm sitting with Marina and the Ryser Cares group in the seats designated for presenters, uncomfortable wooden chairs lined along the side wall.

As the secretary drones on about a discussion regarding what type of ribbon to use at a ribbon-cutting ceremony for a new smoothie shop in Falls Point, I roll the dice and peek at the audience again. I spot Meg Gordon, a short white woman with a pink pixie cut who owns the one pretzel shop in town. My family didn't frequent her shop as much as we did Cooper Cakes. She might not remember me. She might not call me a traitor.

I blink to attention when the secretary finishes speaking and another person, a Black man in a cream-colored cardigan, introduces himself as Ben, the president of the Walnut County Chamber of Commerce, and begins running through the agenda. We're last on the docket, which gives me about one second of relief before I realize that just means I get to be nervous until it's our turn.

"First up, Jaclyn Haynes?" Ben says.

An older woman slowly rises from her front-row seat. It's not until she starts speaking that I recognize her. "My daughter thinks selling CBD oil in my boutique will help me bring in new customers."

That croaky voice transports me back to being ten years old and boredly following my mom around as she shopped in Jaclyn's body care boutique, a cramped place that smelled like what would happen if a pine tree rolled around in baby powder and cinnamon before falling into a vat of vanilla extract. While Jaclyn chatted to my mother about lavender body butter, I'd sniffed shelf after shelf of sample lotions until I had a sneezing fit.

"Okay," Ben replies warily.

"I don't sell a product unless I've tried it. I've never done... you know...before." Her hand nervously toys with the hem of her floral blouse.

"CBD oil?"

Her voice drops to a whisper. "Drugs."

"CBD oil is not drugs," interjects a woman beside Ben. She's dressed more casually than the other board members, in a knit, halter-style crop top.

"Oh, you know what I mean." Jaclyn waves her off. "Anyway, everything I've read on experimenting with drugs says you should do it with a more experienced person who can keep you safe. I believe it's called a 'trip sitter.'"

A few seats down from me, Arun lets out an exhale that sounds suspiciously like a suppressed laugh. Randy nudges him with his elbow.

"How is this Chamber of Commerce business?" Ben asks with a sigh.

"I can't sell it in my store until I've tried it. My daughter moved to Atlanta, and my husband's never done it. This is my first drug experience, and I need someone to guide me through it."

I can see the wheels turning in Ben's head as he considers Jaclyn's request. The reluctance in his eyes suggests he wants no part in entertaining this, but his features soften as he looks at her. "All right. Who wants to watch Jaclyn do drugs?"

"I got you, Jaclyn," says the crop top woman.

"Thank you, dear." Satisfied, Jaclyn takes her seat.

"Elise will watch Jaclyn do drugs," the secretary recites slowly as he types the meeting minutes into his ancient laptop.

Arun strangles another laugh. Then a few others express interest in trying CBD oil, and before long Elise has turned it into an open-invitation house party. Jen raises her hand and adds herself to the list while Arun and Tessa share looks of amusement.

Once the secretary enters the details of Elise's house party into the record, the agenda moves on down the list, putting me one step closer to standing before these people and opening myself up to their judgment. They'll be the ones to decide my fate, whether I'll be moving forward with the festival and making progress toward returning to my old life in DC—or if I'll be doomed to waste away in Greenstead for all eternity.

The next item concerns a grand opening for a new olive oil shop in Falls Point, leading a few Greensteaders to gripe about Falls Point's annoyingly stable economy and wonder whether anyone really *needs* a store that sells nothing but olive oil. The Falls Pointers accept these comments with polite annoyance.

Next up, Ben calls on Jess Kang. A tall, tan-skinned Asian person with an artfully messy mop of dark hair stands and makes their way past us. I think they're staring at me as they pass, until I realize they're actually looking at Marina. Marina pointedly averts her gaze, but as soon as they pass us and head up to the front, Marina lets herself stare. When Jess stands to face the room and clears their throat, their eyes go to Marina, and Marina shifts in her seat. I feel a fleeting impulse to lean over and whisper to Marina that Jess must clearly be a Jordan, but I let it wither. She probably doesn't remember our language anymore.

"I wanted to talk to you about a proposal," Jess begins. I'm not sure why there's an edge of dread in their voice until they say, fast like ripping off a Band-Aid, "From Solar Summit."

At once, several loud groans ring throughout the room.

I bite back a smile. Some things never change. Solar Summit, an amusement park in Falls Point, makes so many people here furious. I've never understood the hate. I loved going to Solar Summit as a kid. Finally growing tall enough to ride the Avalanche, its flagship coaster that boasts five inversions and speeds of sixty-plus miles per hour, was truly one of the greatest accomplishments of my childhood. Marina and I went to its adjacent water park, Splash Planet, multiple times every summer. Solar Summit is a Virginia staple.

But a lot of Greenstead residents, especially the older generations, wax on about how much better life was before Solar Summit came along. They said the Industrial Expressway, the one road in and out of town, used to be wide open and accessible instead of clogged with enough tourists to make commuting a living nightmare. They said the fields along the expressway used to be pristine rather than covered in litter from road-tripping tourists who couldn't be bothered to dispose of their garbage properly. Personally, I've always thought they just can't stand the idea of Falls Point being so successful when Greenstead is anything but.

"Solar Summit," Jess says, raising their voice to be heard over the groans, "has proposed building a resort hotel in West Greenstead, and I think it's a great idea." Amid the grumbles, Jess outlines the resort features Solar Summit is planning on: a mini-golf park, an arcade, a movie theater, a shopping center.

It certainly sounds like an improvement to me. I'd probably have been happier growing up in Greenstead if there were more places like this, somewhere with a little more life than a bowling alley where half the lanes were always out of order. And giving more people a reason to come to Greenstead sounds like an automatic win.

Jess explains that Solar Summit would even provide a service to shuttle tourists to and from the amusement park—which should, they say pointedly, help cut down on the traffic everyone loves complaining about. "It would also bring a lot of tourists to Greenstead," Jess says. "Which I think we can all agree would be beneficial."

"We don't need *their* tourists," says Jaclyn.

"I think you'd be lucky to have our tourists, actually," says a blond woman sitting next to her. "Isn't that why you want to start selling CBD oil? So you can bring in more business?"

Jaclyn crosses her arms. "That's different."

"How is that different? More business is more business."

"It's different," says Tim Cooper, sitting up straighter, "because bringing in Solar Summit means once again being overly reliant on someone else, which sets us up to fail if something goes wrong. We loved the jobs Ryser's mustard factory brought to Greenstead, didn't we? And what happened there?"

The woman falls silent. Once someone's pulled the mustard card, it's hard to argue back.

"I'm not sure we should let fear hold us back from something that could really benefit us," Jess says carefully.

"I'd rather be afraid than covered in mustard," says Elise, and a few Greensteaders break into scattered applause at this nonsensical statement. Someone suggests turning it into a bumper sticker. The secretary adds this to the agenda for next month's meeting.

Jess's presentation flounders after that. They hold up a clipboard and say they'd love to get the endorsement of local businesses—especially any Greenstead ones, they emphasize—before they take the proposal to the mayor. But the mention of the mayor raises more grumbles.

"Like Mayor Bradley's gonna do anything," Elise says. "I'm still waiting for that community development grant money he promised us."

Jess squirms, lowering the clipboard. "That's proven... more difficult than he imagined. It turns out that grant is only available for towns of a certain size, and our application was rejected because the federal government classifies Greenstead as, uh—well, the term they used was 'unincorporated shamble.' But he's working on it!" Jess's smile falters amid the group's mutterings. "Anyway," Jess says, raising their voice, "I think this initiative would also do a lot for community development. Who wants to sign?"

Jess waits patiently, circling the room and holding the clipboard out. A few people sign it, but none of the Greenstead complainers show the slightest interest. The audience breaks into idle chatter, and Jess leaves with disappointment etched all over their face.

Not the most promising omen for our presentation. I swallow and exchange looks with my coworkers, who all seem much less motivated than they were ten minutes ago.

"Marina Ramos?" the president calls, reading off his agenda. "You're next."

This is it. I take a deep breath, straighten my blazer, and rise to my feet. When we reach the front, Marina takes out her laptop and fiddles with the display cables. I chance a glance at the faces in the crowd. The second Tim catches my gaze, I look away.

Marina launches into a speech about the important role the community center plays in giving Greenstead kids and adults alike a place to gather and connect. Jaclyn, Elise, Tim, and a lot of the folks who'd groused about Jess's proposal start nodding. When Marina raises the idea of bringing back the apple festival to boost tourism and raise funds for the community center, the looks range from doubtful to intrigued. But then she says, "Ryser Cares has agreed to support the festival," and the protests burst forth.

"Next you'll say you've got Solar Summit's support," Elise grouses.

"That wouldn't be a bad idea," Arun mumbles, but Randy nudges him.

"What support could *they* offer, really?" Elise continues. "Free mustard?" The room breaks into titters.

Marina looks helplessly to me. I clear my throat and force myself to make eye contact with the audience.

"We'll assist with advertising, and we'll offer some monetary support," I say. *Some* is an extreme understatement, but they don't need to know that.

"Aren't you Darren Harper's girl?" Tim Cooper says, squinting in my direction.

My cheeks instantly heat up. "Yes," I say tentatively. Recognition dawns on a few of the faces trained on me.

"What are you doing working for Ryser?" he asks. His voice is filled with genuine bewilderment. There's an almost paternal concern in his eyes, as if he thinks maybe I was kidnapped and forced into indentured servitude. In his expression, I see birthday cakes through the years, my name in sugary pink script.

"Well, I…" I let out a breath. "I've worked for them since I graduated from college. I interned there." I'm aware that none of this answers his question.

"I know; Darren told me. But why?" he presses.

I hesitate for a beat too long. His question feels enormous suddenly, impossible to answer. I scramble for something, anything to say about Ryser. "Ryser is devoted to empowering people through food."

Still not an answer, but it's a sentence, at least.

"Which is why we're honored to lend our support," Arun says, taking a step forward. I shoot him a grateful look. Tim's face is still tight with doubt, but he doesn't press me any further.

"What does 'support' mean, exactly?" asks Ben. "It can't be much. We know Ryser Cares hardly does a thing these days."

My colleagues and I exchange glances. Not one of us can disagree with him on that.

"If you really want vendors, you'll have to put your money where your mouth is," Ben says. "Cover the participation fees, and then maybe you'll get some vendors. Does that sound fair?" He looks out to the audience.

"Sounds fair to me," Tim says. "I'd sign up if you waived the fee. I don't see why we should have to pay to have a booth at a festival y'all basically killed in the first place."

While others murmur in agreement, I turn to Arun, our events expert. Looking remorseful, he subtly shakes his head.

My stomach sinks. All the hopes I'd fastened to this festival start collapsing around me. This festival was supposed to be my purpose while I'm stuck here. My path back to DC. A chance to do something good through Ryser. A way to save one of the last remaining pillars of our town and prove to Marina that I'm not the soulless sellout she sees me as.

And then there was that small inkling I felt yesterday, that pull toward the idea of attending another festival and replacing our argument with a happier memory. That festival was so intertwined with my childhood, my friendship with Marina. I can't imagine standing before our younger selves and telling them the festival is dead, our friendship over, and I didn't try my hardest to save it. My friendship with Marina may be beyond repair, but I owe it to those versions of ourselves to do everything in my power to make this festival happen.

"Ryser will cover all vendor participation fees," I announce. My words come out steady, certain, masking the knot growing larger in my gut. Arun nudges my elbow, his eyes wide in a mystified question, but I ignore him. "All you'll have to do is show up. As Marina said, we're expecting a lot of tourists. This is gonna be big, and you can be part of it for free. Who's interested in participating?"

The hands that fly up make my false promise worth it, if only for a second. We've won over Tim, Meg, Elise, Jaclyn, and at least three-quarters of the room. By my quick math, we've exceeded the thirty-five minimum we'd set. Our skeleton frame of a festival has vendors, if nothing else.

I just need to figure out how to convince Ryser to sponsor a festival.

CHAPTER EIGHT

Τ HE MOOD ON THE DRIVE back to the office is…mixed, to say the least. Our group's joy at getting the support of local businesses is muddled by confusion as to why I would pledge money we don't have.

As Randy pulls out of the parking space, I see him eye me in the rearview mirror, but he doesn't speak.

Marina does.

"What was *that*?" she asks sharply, turning to face me. We're tucked in the back seat of the minivan, and when she speaks, four sets of eyes—Tessa and Arun in the middle row, Jen in the passenger seat, Randy through the rearview mirror—fall on us. "Where's that money coming from?"

"I—" I shake my head. "We needed vendors. Now we have vendors."

"Not if we can't come up with the money."

"We will." I fiddle with the strap on my seat belt. "Ryser is worth billions of dollars. In the communications department alone, our budget is…ridiculous," I say, thinking about the money Amanda has been willing to shell out for splashy ad campaigns, unnecessary AI tools no one knows how to use, *Bill*.

"You don't work there anymore, dear," Jen reminds me.

"I know." My voice comes out small, unsure. I play with a button on the sleeve of my blazer, trying to think. "Arun, how much would we need? How much does it cost to throw a festival, if we can't rely on vendor fees?"

Arun lets out a low chuckle. "If you want the most ballpark of ballpark figures, I would say a bare minimum of at least ten thousand dollars."

My breath leaves my lungs in a subdued sigh. "Oh."

"We still have our claims budget," Tessa offers, which makes me perk up a little.

"I'm saying ten thousand in addition to the claims budget," Arun says.

"Oh," I say again.

"You *could* do it for cheaper," he says. "But…it would be a much smaller festival."

"Maybe we go smaller," Marina says, staring at her hands in her lap. "Some tourists are better than none, I guess."

Scaling down feels wrong. This festival is supposed to generate excitement, bring people to Greenstead, save the community center. It's supposed to be big enough to make Amanda take notice.

"No," I say. "We'll get the money. Just…let me think about it." Tessa and Arun exchange a doubtful glance as they face forward, but I don't dwell on it. Ryser pulls in revenue by the billions. There has to be a way to convince them to allocate a drop of their profits to their charity division. Charity does wonders for PR, doesn't it?

My phone vibrates in my pocket, the triple-pulse notification I'd set for work emails. Out of habit, I pull it out and check my email.

Announcement: Massage Mondays are back!

My shoulders slump. I'm so glad the DC office is living it up while we're packed in a van sulking over a festival we may never get off the ground. If anyone could use a massage, it's us.

I scroll through the rest of the unread emails that came in while I was distracted with festival planning today. Nothing from Amanda, as usual. Just another slew of DC office alerts.

Leftover sandwiches on 12

Reminder: All fridges will be cleared on Friday

Don't forget! Ryser Inspire Awards Night happening tomorrow!

At first, my eyes gloss over them all, these reminders of more things I'm missing out on. The Ryser Inspire Awards were pretentious and self-congratulatory, but I still went every year. Mostly because Amanda encouraged attendance and I thought showing up might increase my chances of getting a promotion—or winning an award myself. At least the food was a highlight, plentiful and delicious. I must have eaten at least six truffle risotto balls at last year's event, not to mention half a plate of mini fruit tarts from the dessert bar. But I'm not part of the DC office anymore. Although…

I double-click the email, scroll through it.

What's stopping me from showing up anyway?

It's not my fault they've forgotten to take me off the DC email list. I submitted my RSVP two months ago when the invitations went out. I can still show up, can't I?

I think back to awards shows past, which were always held at a hotel a few blocks over from the office. Someone in HR mans the doors, checking names off a list. My name would probably still be on there. The demotion was only recent. I could talk to Amanda, remind her I exist, tell her about the festival and its value for PR, ask if she can allocate some money from the communications budget toward the festival. It's not begging; it's strategizing.

My heart flutters with hope. This isn't over yet.

"I know how to get the money," I announce. "I'm going to the Ryser Inspire Awards tomorrow."

Tessa tosses me a skeptical look. "Are you invited to that?"

"I *was*. Before the transfer. They probably haven't taken me off the list."

"What are the Ryser Inspire Awards?" Marina asks reluctantly.

"Bullshit," Tessa says, just as Arun says, "Really good coconut shrimp."

"I don't remember any awards coming with ten thousand dollars," Randy chimes in from the front.

"No, but I can talk to my boss and try to convince her to divert some money from her budget. It would be good PR."

"Good PR *is* all Ryser cares about," Marina mutters. I ignore her.

"I feel bad that you're going on your own," Jen says. "I feel like one of us should go with you."

"That's okay. I'm fine."

I hold back from admitting how excited I am at the thought of getting in some face time with Amanda after the brick wall of silence I've gotten from her. I've sent her a few emails over the last couple of weeks, sharing some thoughts and ideas about campaigns I was working on at the time of the elevator incident. Those emails all went unanswered. But she'll have to acknowledge me when I'm there in person. Surely things have subsided now that Dan's had some time to calm down. Amanda will see me there looking cool, collected, and capable, and she'll ask herself how she could have ever let Dan demote me.

"Why don't we go?" Arun suggests. "All of us?"

My eyebrows shoot up. "All of you?"

The image I'd conjured in my head of impressing Amanda did not involve the entire Ryser Cares office trailing after me. I picture Arun stuffing coconut shrimp into the pockets of his swim trunks, Tessa sarcastically slow-clapping for every award winner, Jen dancing a bit too enthusiastically to the music, Randy hiding behind the curtains to read. Not to mention the logistics of trying to scrounge up invitations for four extra people. Tickets run out quickly—even if the awards are dull, free food and an open bar go a long way. If anyone hasn't submitted an RSVP by the deadline, the tickets become available for plus-ones so people can bring their spouses.

"Yeah," Arun says. "Jen's right; you shouldn't have to go alone. Weren't you just telling us earlier today that we should stop being afraid of things?"

Damn him for using my own inspiring words against me.

"Yes," I admit.

"I'm not sure I'm *afraid* of the Ryser Inspire Awards," Tessa says. "Afraid of how boring they are, maybe."

Arun gives Tessa a playful shove with his shoulder. "You know what I mean. Not the awards, but…being back there, around our old bosses. The people we failed in front of. The people who told us we're screwups and sent us to Greenstead. We have to face them sometime, don't we?"

"Not if we don't want to," Randy mumbles.

"But maybe we *need* to," Arun says. "We'd have a better shot at getting the money if we all split up and ask our old department heads for it, right? Five chances are better than one."

And now he's weaving math into his argument. It's hard to argue with the cold, hard logic of numbers. I stay silent, waiting for someone to disagree.

"That's true," Jen says. "We might even have a better chance than Lauryn. Not that I don't think you'll do a wonderful job," she adds, turning to face me, "but it's been years since we were transferred. Our…mishaps…won't be as fresh in everyone's minds."

No counterarguments, just more logic. Wonderful.

"You're in?" Arun asks her.

"I am," Jen says. "Randy?"

Randy sighs. "Fine."

Now Arun and Jen turn their eyes on Tessa, who groans. She sweeps her microlocs back and releases them, letting them cascade over her shoulders as she thinks. "Most of those people haven't seen me in almost five years."

"I know." There's a gentle understanding in Jen's expression.

"You don't have to go if you don't want to," Arun says.

"Maybe it *would* be good, if I go. The longer I go without seeing them, the more I'm gonna feel like I'm…hiding. I don't want to hide." She tosses a glance toward Marina and me in the back seat. "I transitioned after I was transferred to Greenstead. No one at the DC office has seen me since. But…they should," she decides, turning to Arun with a decisive nod.

Arun beams. Jen bursts into quiet applause. I selfishly think it's rather annoying that Tessa has given me yet another reason why I can't say no to bringing four extra people to the awards night.

"Are you coming?" Arun asks Marina.

I have to suppress a sigh. Another party crasher, sure. So Marina can judge me and my employer some more.

"Me? I don't work for Ryser."

"Yeah, but you could be our Greenstead representative," Tessa says, inspired. "Our secret weapon. You could talk about the community center, why Greenstead needs the money—"

"A few tears wouldn't hurt," Arun adds.

"And they'd have to say yes," Tessa finishes.

"Plus the food is awesome," says Arun.

Marina laughs. "I don't know." But she's smiling, clearly interested in the idea. Slowly, almost self-consciously, her gaze falls on me. Like she's waiting for me to weigh in, expecting me to say no.

I could say it's not a good idea. I could point out the logistical nightmare of sneaking yet another person—a nonemployee, no less—into a stuffy awards ceremony.

But there's a spark of interest in her eye. Arun seems to have his heart set on all of us going as a unit. Or…team? Are we all a team, Marina too? Despite the distance between Marina and me, we did still spend the day working on the presentation together. We did all show up to the Chamber of Commerce and convince a room of business owners to exhibit at our festival. And though I've only been at Ryser Cares for a week and a half, I do feel a strange sense of camaraderie with these people that I've never felt with the communications team I've worked with for the last decade.

We just might be a team. And teams leave no man behind.

"The food *is* really good," I say, glancing at Marina. "You should come."

Marina breaks into a shy smile. "Okay. I'll come."

Arun lets out a cheer. The conversation turns to what time we'll head out tomorrow, how we'll get there (Randy volunteers to drive), what persuasive strategies to employ to ask our old colleagues to finance the festival. The initial thrill I feel at making them happy is quickly replaced by the same trepidation that's been building inside me for the last few minutes.

I chew on the inside of my lip and stare out the window. Sneaking my ex–best friend and a gaggle of self-professed screwups into a swanky event is a long shot. And I have less than twenty-four hours to hatch a plan for how the hell to pull this off.

CHAPTER NINE

P ASSING THROUGH THE MARQUISE HOTEL'S revolving doors
feels like traveling back in time to just a few weeks ago, when
I was a stellar employee who would never be associated with
murder.

The hotel lobby is teeming with Ryser employees in their stiff
and shiny business formal best, filling the space with chatter. My
gaze bounces around the room, from one familiar face to another,
drinking in these figures from my other life at the DC office. The
fast-talking guy in IT, the sales exec who speaks only in clichés,
the—

A force from behind pushes into me, making me stumble
forward in my heels. A hand steadies me, gripping my arm until I
regain my balance.

"Why would you stand still in front of a revolving door?"
Marina snaps once she lets go of me.

"Sorry." I step to the side and glance behind me at the pileup

I've caused. Tessa's rubbing her shoulder while Arun raises his palms in innocence; behind them, Jen stands trapped in the revolving door, her hands pressed against the glass like a forlorn mime. And Randy has skipped past the mess entirely to enter through the side door next to it.

After we make enough room to release Jen from her prison, I motion for them to follow me somewhere less obvious to regroup. I lead us past the RYSER INSPIRE signs, down the hall, and around the corner. At the entrance to Ballroom A, a figure stands in front of a high-top table, a piece of paper in hand.

"That's who we need to give our names to," I say, keeping my voice low. I stop at a cushioned bench by a window and turn to face my group. "Does everyone remember who you're supposed to be?"

It hit me yesterday evening that assuming identities might be the best way to sneak everyone in. I've been to enough of these things to know who shows up and who doesn't. And if we're already racking up crimes, between my alleged murder attempt and Marina's arson, then we may as well add identity theft to our collective transgressions.

If nothing else, our group looks transformed. My blouse and dress pants are nothing new, and Marina's plum-colored wrap dress is similar enough to the outfit she wore yesterday. But the Ryser Cares team has made an effort to step out of their casual comfort zone. Arun's blue button-down is tucked neatly into the waist of his gray dress pants. Tessa's in heels and a striped blouse tucked into a pencil skirt, Jen's sporting a sparkly black cardigan and slacks, Randy's in a jacket and tie. They all look the part. They just need to play their roles.

"I've got it down," Tessa says, assuming a silky voice and pretending to tuck her hair behind her ears. "My name is Selma Blackwell."

I'd texted Selma last night to ask if she'd be attending the awards tonight, and she'd replied to say she was skipping it because it wouldn't be fun without me there. Her response tugged at my heart, made me feel guilty for not reaching out to her since my demotion. I'd always thought of us as nothing more than work friends by default, people who got along well and enjoyed grabbing the occasional lunch together but would never hang out outside of work.

Besides, we may work for the same problematic company, but Selma makes up for it in ways I don't. She's a vegan. She volunteers at a hospitality house. She donates to food banks. All the good she does cancels out the questionable things we do at Ryser. While I, with my love of pork gyoza, my staunch avoidance of social interactions, and my hoarding every penny for early retirement, am nothing more than questionable.

Selma's text gave me an impulse to reciprocate, tell her she made the awards more fun too, fill her in on life in Greenstead and my absurd plan to sneak the Ryser Cares office into the awards event. But, deciding that might be too much, I responded with a heart emoji and told myself I'd text her later.

At least I could count on Selma to not show up and throw off our plan. The other names we're using are less of a sure thing, however.

Randy clears his throat. "I'm Dan, uh. Gorland. Dan Gorland."

Just hearing the name sends a spike of annoyance through me. But as much as he's thrown my life off course recently, I think I can count on him to not show up tonight. Amanda has talked before about how Dan hates going to Ryser's awards events, opting to skip them whenever he can. Though using his name comes with a risk: he's the most senior of the identities we're faking tonight, which means the young woman at the door might know Randy's lying. But she doesn't look like anyone I recognize—which could, I hope, mean she's new.

"Sharon Bhatt; how do you do?" says Jen. She holds out her hand, palm down, like this is something out of *Bridgerton*. Arun plays along, taking her hand with a formal bow, and I have to glance around to make sure no one's staring at us.

Contrary to whatever Jen may have decided, Sharon Bhatt is not a Regency-era royal but a data engineer. She's usually working late, putting out fires. Last year, she showed up halfway through the event because her team had to stay late to deploy a critical website update. The fact that she always shows up eventually means we'll have to make the most of our time tonight. We'll have to get in, talk to our targets, and leave before Sharon arrives.

"Colby Yates, charmed to make your acquaintance," Arun says to Jen.

As a sales rep who's worked for Ryser for less than a year, Colby doesn't technically *have* a record of attending or skipping Ryser's awards night. But he didn't show up to the Pi Day party in March despite signing up to bring a key lime pie, nor the holiday party last year, even though I got his name for Secret Santa. I have to believe his streak of false promises will continue.

"Mary Forrester," Marina says, sounding uncertain. "I… work for Ryser. I love…exploitation."

"Perfect," Tessa replies, making her smile. "So natural. No notes."

I don't know much about Mary, but I know she won an award last year for helping transition our ticketing system to a new platform, and I know she works under Sharon. I'm hoping that whatever keeps Sharon staying late keeps Mary busy, too.

"Okay," I say. I glance toward the doors of Ballroom A, where a twentysomething woman with frizzy red hair is using a pen to check someone's name off the list. I may not have seen her around the office before, but there's a Ryser lanyard around her neck. She must be the new HR admin they hired last month. I watch as she gestures for the person to enter the ballroom. I breathe in, summoning my courage. "Let's go."

Randy and Marina exchange uneasy looks, but they join me in approaching the doors. I linger behind, waiting to go last. If any issues arise, I should be the one to deal with them. I am the only invited person here, after all. Though I'm not sure what I'd do to handle said issues. Just the thought is enough to make my palms sweat.

Tessa goes first. She steps up to the front and utters Selma's name in that same honeyed voice. The redhead runs a pen down her list, checks something off, and cheerfully tells her to have a good night. Tessa tosses a quick glance over her shoulder at us before she glides into the room and disappears from view.

Jen and Marina go next. Jen stumbles over her fictitious last name, and Marina mumbles to her shoes and is asked to speak up before the redhead understands what she's saying. But the names are crossed off, the redhead smiles, and they too pass through without issue.

Next up, Arun gives Colby's name. As with the others, my breath halts in the agonizing moments as the woman runs her finger down the list. When she reaches the bottom and frowns, my pulse races. Did Colby not RSVP? He really picked *now* to abandon his dependable undependability? No one likes inconsistency, Colby.

She flips to the next page, and the next, poring over each one. Arun gives me a worried look, and I vow to find Colby's address and key-lime-pie his house for showing me up—but then, miraculously, the crease in her forehead disappears and a grin takes over her face.

"Colby *Yates*," she says victoriously, crossing it off with a flourish. "I'm sorry. I was thinking *Gates* for some reason." She beams at Arun. "You're all set. Have a great night."

"Don't worry about it. Happens all the time." Arun winks at her on his way in. Randy and I share a look over his newfound swagger and stifle a laugh.

My breathing steadies. We're almost home free. I can practically taste the truffle risotto balls. It's just Randy and me to go now. True, Randy's the biggest risk since he's assuming the identity of one of Ryser's highest-ranking executives, but the HR assistant seems easygoing enough. If she was the one they hired last month, she wouldn't have any reason to recognize Dan.

Randy seems to think so too, going by the way he puffs out his chest when he steps forward. "How're you doing?" he asks, speaking an octave deeper than his usual voice.

Before the redhead can respond, a short, thin-faced woman I recognize as Janet, our head of HR, ducks out from the ballroom and taps her on the elbow. "I'm having trouble getting the laptop set up. Would you mind taking a look?"

Randy and I watch in horror as our perfect, friendly redhead excuses herself and flits into the ballroom.

"Sorry about that," Janet says. "We're still getting everything set up. I can never remember which cord plugs in where."

I laugh nervously. "Yeah, me neither."

"Name, please?"

"Da—"

"Lauryn Harper," I interrupt, stepping on Randy's shoe. He frowns at me, and I widen my eyes in a warning before turning back to Janet with a too-big smile.

"Lauryn Harper," Janet murmurs, going down the list. "*Oh.*" She stops suddenly, her head snapping up. "You're the one we… transferred. Dan told me."

My hands start to fidget at the reminder. She could act a little less like I'm wanted for murder. Though I guess that's not too far off from what Dan has probably told her. "Yes."

She studies me carefully. "Are you feeling okay?"

"*Yes.* It was a misunderstanding."

She gives an unconvinced hum. "Is that your purse?"

I follow her gaze to the compact black bag hanging on my shoulder. "Yep." A long pause unfolds as she stares at it. I imagine she's weighing the odds that I've brought a weapon with me, now that I'm on record as an attempted CEO murderer. "Do you… want to go through it?"

She blinks once, twice, then shakes her head. "No, of course not." Janet crosses my name off the list and gestures for me to enter the ballroom. I hesitate, casting an uncertain glance at Randy. I can't abandon him here.

"Name?" Janet prompts him. Randy opens his mouth, then closes it.

I move between them and shove my purse at Janet. She takes a step back, and my purse lands on the table in front of her. "I'd feel better if you took a look," I say. "I couldn't enjoy my night if you thought I was up to anything weird. Here, please." I make a show of unzipping it, and I push it toward her with just enough force that both the purse and the list underneath fall to the floor. "Oh, I'm so sorry!" I exclaim.

I bend down and snatch the list before Janet can get it. She gingerly picks up my purse, along with the spare tampon and half-empty package of tissues that fell out of it. I scan the front of the list, desperately searching for a male name I can latch onto. The first one I see is Ron Barker, and I have no idea who that is or whether Janet knows him, but it hasn't been crossed off yet, so it's the best hope we've got.

"That's all right," Janet says with a nervous titter. She places the tampon and tissue pack back in my purse, taking a few seconds longer than necessary. When she seems to feel that there isn't a weapon hiding at the bottom, she breaks into a relieved smile and hands it back to me. "I don't need to go through it, but it was kind of you to offer. Have a wonderful night."

My smile stretches my face, wide and saccharine. "Thank you. I'll wait for you to check in my friend. Ron Barker." I hoist my purse over my shoulder and toy with the strap as Janet looks Randy up and down. I silently will Ron Barker to have a forgettable face, to do mediocre work, to have given Janet absolutely no reason to know he exists.

"Of course," Janet says easily. She strikes his name off the list, and we're free. Randy and I speedwalk our way inside the ballroom and immediately dodge to the right, out of Janet's sight. He lets out a sigh of relief. I sink my back into the wall and let my tense muscles relax.

"Quick thinking," Randy says.

"It got the job done," I say with a satisfied nod. "But I have no idea who Ron is or when he'll show up, so...we should act fast."

Randy sets off in search of his old coworkers. I stay where I am for a minute, surveying the room. As usual, this large ballroom is the picture of elegance. Cream-colored tablecloths are draped over round tables, a vase of fresh flowers in the center of each one. People wearing sharp blazers or silky blouses congregate around the open bar at the back of the room, or they sit at tables making conversation. Hotel staff dressed in black and white circle the room with trays of appetizers. I take a shot glass of crab bisque when it's offered to me and sip on it, savoring the velvety texture and sweetness of fresh crab as I search the room for Amanda.

"Hi." Marina sidles up next to me in a way I don't expect. People always seem to gravitate toward my deaf side in social situations, requiring me to do gymnastics to subtly reposition myself to get them on the side of my hearing ear, all while nodding politely to garbled gibberish. But Marina comes right up to my hearing side in a way that I don't think is coincidence.

She used to tell me I basically trained her that way, how in those early days when we'd walk to our third-grade classroom together, half the time she'd turn to see that I'd disappeared, only to appear suddenly on her right. It wasn't long before she memorized what side she needed to be on to negate the need for my stealthy maneuver. As soon as she figured it out, she always made sure to be on my hearing side. In a world where I always have to make the extra step just to hear people, where I'm always the one switching places, changing sides, craning my neck for scraps of sound, seeing Marina take that work upon herself felt so freeing. Like I could just *be*, and she would move her world around to accommodate me.

I don't have a lot of people in my life like that now—except maybe Selma, who does check with me about what side she should sit on before she takes a seat, when she remembers. It's just not as deeply ingrained in her like it was (or still is?) with Marina. I push the thought down.

"Hi," I greet her back. "How's it going?"

"Good so far. Arun and Tessa are chatting up some people. Jen's still circling around. I haven't had to whip out the sad eyes yet."

"That's a superpower you should conserve, anyway," I joke, and she surprises me with a small laugh. A server passes by carrying a tray loaded with coconut shrimp. He pauses to offer us some. I take one, but Marina declines.

"I guess now I know why Ryser couldn't restore Greenstead,"

she says. "They need to pay for seven tons of coconut shrimp for their stupid awards night."

The remark digs at me, but not enough that I feel bad about holding one of the offending appetizers. "Honestly, it might be worth it. They're amazing." I shove it in my mouth, bite off the tail, and face Marina, chewing obnoxiously.

Marina gapes, and I worry she might take my joking remark the wrong way, but she just laughs, louder this time, and I smile even with my mouth full. It can't be a pretty sight, but she's seen me do worse.

Just then, I see a familiar figure in a flowy black dress pass us and head toward the bar. Her hair is short and dark, just like Amanda's. I watch her back as she speaks with the bartender. When she turns around, a clear drink in her hand, I straighten.

"What?" Marina says.

"That's my boss."

"*Oh.*" Marina glances from me to Amanda, then back to me. "Shouldn't you...go talk to her?"

I rotate the plastic cup of crab bisque in my hand. I know I should approach Amanda, but I can't seem to move my feet. The memory of sitting in her office, hearing her demote me, and being struck with powerlessness pops vividly into my mind.

Amanda crosses the room with her drink. A server offers her a tray of canapés. She takes one and stands alone, chewing and sipping, easily approachable. But Janet's expression crops up in my mind next, that bewildered shock and concern. Like I was erratic, unpredictable, something to be feared.

I don't want to see that on Amanda. I don't want a repeat of what happened in her office. I need her to see that I'm capable, reasonable, and—ideally—fully deserving of getting my old job back.

And I need her to give me ten thousand dollars. Can't forget that.

I bolt down the last of the crab bisque from my cup like it's a shot of whiskey. "I am," I say to Marina. "I'm going now."

Amanda's checking her phone now, the canapé long gone, and it's not until I get within a foot of her that she looks up and startles. Recognition flashes in her eyes. How wonderful that *deer-in-headlights* is my default greeting from Ryser folks now.

"Lauryn, hi," she says. "I didn't expect to see you here."

"Yeah," I say with an awkward laugh that I hope sounds more carefree than hysterical. "I got the reminder email yesterday, and I thought, why not?"

"Oh," Amanda says again, this time drawn out with a hint of suspicion. "It's good to see you." Her remark doesn't quite end in a question, but it's not entirely a statement either. "How have you been?"

"Good," I say, if only because it's what people say. "How about you?"

"Oh, the usual."

It's a little insulting that she's down one of her best employees and yet life is *the usual*, but it's fine.

"How are things in Greenstead?" Amanda asks, after taking a long drink.

"Lovely," I say, repeating the word she'd used to describe it during the demotion. But if she picks up on the reference, she doesn't let on. She just gives me another placid smile and looks around the room as if hoping an escape portal might materialize.

"I love bruschetta," Amanda says, stepping around me to wave down a passing server. I grab one off the tray too, to have something to do.

But now that she's moved, Amanda is standing on my deaf side. Which she should know; I've told her about this several times. But it's always me who has to do the maneuvering to hear her.

I start the process by taking a step to the side, but then she says something I don't quite catch and pulls up a chair at the nearest table. The seat on her right is taken by a purse, so I reluctantly take the chair on her left, putting her once again beside my deaf ear.

She takes a large bite from her bruschetta. This seems like the best opening I'll probably have.

"I'm actually working on throwing an apple festival this fall through Ryser Cares," I say, the words falling out in a rush. "Greenstead's apple festival started to peter out in the years after the"—I pause—"*factory malfunction*. Someone came to the office with a proposal to bring it back. They're hoping it will raise enough money to save Greenstead's community center."

Amanda gives a hum of acknowledgment, still chewing.

"It got me thinking about what good PR it would be for Ryser to sponsor the festival," I press on. "To show how committed we are to helping Greenstead get back on its feet."

"Okay," Amanda says, wariness tinging her voice. "What jewel heaven blind?"

Well, that can't be right.

When I can't fully hear someone, my brain replays the audio of their words over and over, trying to match the sounds to words, then shuffling through options to find the combination that makes the most sense for the context. I pause to work through the permutations until I settle on *What did you have in mind?* It's the most logical option. That or she wants me to solve a riddle about unholy gemstones—which I'm not above taking a crack at if it gets us that festival money.

"It would be great if Ryser could provide the money we need to get the festival off the ground," I say. "About ten thousand dollars or so."

"Ten thousand dollars?" she says, her voice growing louder.

"Give or take. By our estimates, that's what we'd need for the festival to be a success, and of course we *want* the festival to be a success."

She purses her lips. "I'm not sure that's the best idea."

"It would be great publicity for Ryser—which we could really use," I add. I don't need to remind her about the last year we've had, rushing out official statements, updating Bill with new euphemisms for the company's latest atrocities. "And a lot of our competitors are getting involved in community projects like this. Did you see that Hatchley Foods sponsored a community garden in a food desert last week?" I ask casually. After all those industry newsletters I've read in full to pass time in the Ryser Cares office, I could rattle off every minor occurrence in the food and beverage world from the last two weeks.

Amanda grows pensive, staring into her drink. I bite into my bruschetta to give her time to mull it over.

"It might be a good move," she concedes, bobbing her head to the side as if weighing the pros and cons.

I have to rush to finish chewing the bruschetta, worried she might change her mind if I don't speak quickly enough. I hastily swallow a jagged piece of crust and ask, "Does that mean you'll do it?"

Amanda takes another bite. As she chews, she covers her mouth with a hand and utters a string of words I can't make out. I hear *hazmat inner rocket* and *Lee done scatter bee*, and my brain whirs into action trying to parse together soundalike phrases that make sense. But it can't crack the code fast enough, because then she swallows and says, "Does that work for you?"

"What?"

"Does that work for you?"

I hate when I ask people to repeat themselves and they say only the part I've already heard. "What did you say before that?" I try again.

"I said we should have room in the budget for it, and—" She leans in toward my deaf ear to say the rest, which is about as useful as whispering into my shoe. She pulls back, looking at me expectantly.

Well, I've hit my two-what maximum. But I've learned my lesson about agreeing to something I haven't heard. "I'm sorry, I didn't hear what you said," I confess.

She stares at me, a frown pulling at her mouth. Then she tips her head back and laughs. I can only sit there, feeling silly and stupid and baffled as to how hilarious a hearing impairment could really be.

"You had me," she says when she's composed herself. "It's good that you can joke about what happened with Dan. That's a good sign." She squeezes my arm.

She thought I was putting on an act. Making light of the Dan incident by pretending not to hear her. I open my mouth to correct her, then close it. What does *That's a good sign* mean? I'm one step closer to getting my job back? I glance down at her hand on my arm. Is this a reassuring gesture, a sign that she's still on my side? What if correcting her undoes whatever *good sign* I've unwittingly sent her?

Before I can make up my mind, someone calls her name and beckons her over to their group. Amanda gives them a wave, then rises from her seat. "I'll update our budget tomorrow," she says. "I think we can manage diverting ten thousand to the festival."

With that, she takes off, leaving me to stew in confusion-tinged relief. Whatever just happened, I got the money. And Amanda thinks I'm funny. Which is a nice bonus, really.

I scan the room, curious about how the rest of my team is doing. That's when I catch sight of the redhead entering the ballroom, mouth turned down in a frown. Her head moves from side to side, like she's searching for something. Or someone. Beside her is a tall Indian woman who looks confused and a little outraged.

The real Sharon Bhatt has arrived.

Going by the looks on their faces, I have a minute or less to gather my group and escape before they realize what we've done.

I don't know what they'll do—publicly reprimand us, kick us out, send us to a place even more lifeless than Greenstead. But I'm not waiting around to find out.

Keeping my eyes on the carpet to avoid the redhead spotting me, I stand and make my way through the room.

I see Marina first, still standing by the wall. I widen my eyes and point to the exit, and she catches on immediately, peeling off to grab the others. I spot Arun near the front of the room, talking to an older man with long, white hair tied in a ponytail.

I wave at Arun from behind the man. When he notices me, I jerk my head in the direction of the door. He excuses himself, stepping backward and bumping into the table full of Ryser-branded aluminum water bottles. They start to wobble, and Arun dives to catch the ones that fall off the edge. Now holding three water bottles to his chest, Arun joins me in covertly speed-walking through the room.

It's then that the redhead and the real Sharon Bhatt begin walking toward us. I grab Arun's arm and dodge to the right, then let out a relieved sigh when I realize they're approaching the front of the room. But seeing them make their way to the microphone sends panic through me all over again. Are they going to give an announcement to make a spectacle out of ejecting us? Right after I made my hilarious *good sign* impression on Amanda? My heartbeat thunders in my ears.

"There's Tessa," Arun says, gesturing toward the bar. Tessa stands with a highball glass in hand, throwing her head back in laughter with a few people I vaguely recognize from the research department. Arun edges toward the bar and subtly nudges Tessa's elbow.

She turns around. An understanding passes over her at the sight of us both. "It's been great catching up," she says, still using that silky voice she put on earlier, "but I've got to step out for a minute." She sets her drink down and follows us to the door.

I look around the room frantically, searching for any sign of Marina, Jen, or Randy. "I don't see the others," I say, panic rising in my throat.

"Maybe they already left," Arun says.

I'm doing another visual sweep of the room when my gaze locks onto the redhead. Her eyes narrow, and I can see her mind piecing it together. She makes a beckoning motion with her hand, imploring me to join her and explain myself.

I nod in her direction, slow and exaggerated, trying to look obedient. Then, through gritted teeth, I say, "Run."

And Arun, Tessa, and I take off through the ballroom doors at lightning speed.

CHAPTER TEN

AS WE RACE OUT OF the ballroom, I catch sight of Marina, Jen, and Randy standing by the cushioned bench where we'd all lingered awkwardly less than half an hour ago.

"We're running," I say breathlessly, as if it isn't obvious. I'm not even sure it's necessary anymore now that we've left the ballroom, but they join us. Marina lets out a giddy laugh and Randy mutters "Why?" under his breath as he starts speedwalking behind us.

We run toward the lobby, and straight ahead is the revolving door where I caused a human traffic collision on my arrival. I veer toward the manual door beside it, pushing it open and sprinting outside. Only when I've gone another half block do I stop and bend over, hands on knees, lungs burning, struggling to catch my breath, yet feeling strangely light and fizzy inside.

"What was—what *was* that?" Randy lets out through a gasp.

"The real Sharon Bhatt showed up, and I panicked." I look past the group, back toward the hotel entrance. There's no sign that Sharon, the redhead, or hotel security have come chasing after us. "But I think we got away with it," I say.

"I would have worn different shoes if I'd known there was a track component," Tessa says, glancing down at her heels.

"Sorry," I say, but Tessa just laughs and waves it off. Leaning against the brick wall of the café behind us, still panting but with a wide smile on her face, Tessa looks so much more relaxed than she did on the car ride here. I think we're all awash with relief that the hard part is over.

Once I've caught my breath, I ask, "So, how did everyone do?"

"They're letting us use their corporate discount at the print shop," Randy says. "Any flyers, banners, or signs we need will be a little less expensive now." He gives an apologetic shrug, but no victory is too small to discount. Not when I know how easy it would have been to leave empty-handed.

"That's great," I say, clapping Randy on the back. "We needed banners."

His gaze slips to the floor and he smiles with something like pride, and I wonder how long it's been since anyone at Ryser Cares got to feel like they accomplished something.

"My old colleague's letting me promote the festival on Ryser's social media accounts," Jen says.

"Another win!" I reach over to high-five her. "Arun?"

"I got the equipment rental hookup," Arun says, satisfaction entering his voice. "Tents, tables, chairs, at a pretty good discount. And hey," he adds, looking down at the three Ryser water bottles he accidentally took on his way out, "free water bottles."

"Yes!" I cheer.

"My friend in R&D's gonna mail me some of our limited-edition products that haven't released yet," Tessa says. "I don't know what we'd do with them, but we'll have wasabi ginger potato chips for days."

"Exactly what we needed," I say.

"I could see us using that for raffles or giveaways," Jen volunteers. "People love exclusive stuff." Seeing the gears turning in her social media brain makes my heart swell with appreciation.

"How'd you do?" Tessa asks me.

I look around at their eager faces, giddiness rising within me. "I think I got the money," I reveal.

Arun gives a disbelieving laugh, and Randy breaks into a round of golf claps. And, god, how do I feel so much more accomplished here and now than I can ever remember feeling at work? I've drafted press releases that needed zero edits before being sent out to the public. Our senior communications director, Amanda's boss, has personally thanked me for talking points I helped craft for him before an interview with MSNBC. But this moment of shaking down my boss for money and then sprinting out of a hotel like an outlaw somehow feels a thousand times better than any of that.

"I didn't have an assignment," Marina says, "but I put, like, twenty coconut shrimp in my purse."

My laughter comes out confused, like she's told a joke with a punchline I can't figure out. Until she lifts her purse off her shoulder and holds it open. Sure enough, I'm greeted with a mountain of golden fried shrimp and the sweet smell of coconut.

"You were right," she says. "They really were delicious."

Looking from the bulging bag of shrimp to Marina's earnest expression, I burst into giggles. Soon we're all laughing, standing in the middle of the sidewalk. Pedestrians weave around us, and the city street traffic rumbles on, and the setting sun is telling us to wrap it up. Our laughter is drunk with the absurdity of tonight, the loose-limbed relief that the hard part is over, and a sense of togetherness threading us closer.

I realize in an instant that I don't want this moment to end. My off-work hours and weekends are filled with solitude, with puzzles and TV shows and rarely stepping foot outside. I don't want to get in the car and start the drive back home to sit alone in my childhood bedroom and work on the half-finished puzzle at my desk. I want more of whatever this is.

"Does anyone feel like getting a drink?" I ask.

We wind up in a dive bar, a place I've passed about a thousand times on my way home from work. I've never once gone in. I've never had a reason to, until now. We scoot into a booth tucked away in the corner, and Marina empties the contents of her purse onto a pile of napkins we fan out on the table.

Our server doesn't even blink at our mountain of shrimp; he hands us sticky menus and leaves us to deliberate. We place our orders, and when our drinks come, we toast to ourselves and each other. My pale ale tastes like victory.

"I still can't believe we pulled it off." Arun bites into a shrimp and deposits the tail on one of the plates our server brought us. "Correction, *you* pulled it off," he says, pointing at me.

My lungs swell with pride. "It was all of us. It was your idea to have everyone come. I couldn't have done it without any of you."

It is strange, now, to think about how it might have gone if I'd gone alone like I'd originally planned. I wouldn't have had the hassle of sneaking them all in, but I also wouldn't have this moment now, the six of us sitting in a bar, making our way through a pile of stolen shrimp. I'd still be at the event, nodding and clapping my way through jargon-filled speeches from Ryser executives.

"You could have done it without me," Marina says. "No one needed my Greenstead guilt."

"But we needed sustenance," Tessa says, grabbing a shrimp. "We would have starved in the streets without you."

"And this whole festival was your idea," says Jen. "You gave us a reason to…" Her voice trails off. "Feel useful."

"Of course you're useful," Marina says easily, casting Jen a sideways glance. Jen smiles with a feeling I know well, the tickled pleasure of unexpected pride.

Marina was great at that, building people up. I think back to pep talks before presentations, the fierce protectiveness in her eyes. How I'd once sobbed about my tenth-grade crush rejecting me, and she'd rattled off over a dozen reasons why I was better than him.

I don't think I appreciated enough how good that felt, being the subject of Marina's praise. Now, I'm lucky if she withholds a snippy remark.

I take another sip of my drink and turn to Jen. "Why do you stay? If being at Ryser Cares, in Greenstead, makes you feel useless?"

It's what I've been trying to figure out. I've been plotting my escape ever since I was thrust back to Greenstead, yet they seem so perfectly complacent. They *must* want more. Tonight, they radiated excitement and triumph. They can't be content to stay in exile at the Ryser Cares office forever.

Jen taps her lavender acrylic nails on the grooved wooden tabletop. "I didn't realize how much I hated my old job until I left it," she said. "The stress of running Ryser's social media accounts, working on the weekends, having to be ready any moment with a response. When I moved to Greenstead, I was free of all that. I don't think I want all that pressure. I don't want to mess up again."

Randy nods, his expression pensive. "Exactly. Not that my job was high-pressure or anything, but falling for that stupid phishing scam made me never want to be in that position again. I don't trust myself. Christmas parties are about all I let myself handle at Ryser Cares. Staying in Greenstead means my job is as low-pressure as I can take. And I have a life here now. It's where I met Marge, on one of those hikes the community center organized. It's where we got married, bought our house, became foster parents. I can't imagine leaving."

I lean my head back against the vinyl cushioned booth. Setting aside the fact that Randy met Marge the same way my dad met Wendy—are community center–planned hikes the Greenstead equivalent of Tinder?—I can't stop turning his words over in my mind. I don't know how it is that he can't imagine leaving, and yet that's exactly what my mom did. Like Randy, she had a life here, a spouse, a kid. It wasn't enough for her to stay. Yet for Randy, somehow, it is. Seeing his soft smile when he utters his wife's name, I can't imagine him ever saying he feels stuck. My mind can't make sense of it.

"And," Arun says, "when you're the laughingstock of the company—and your family, because your dad's the COO—you start to lower your expectations about yourself. They said Ryser Cares is all I can do. So, Ryser Cares is all I do. I'm not gonna look for another events job when the last one I threw was a disaster. I used to think maybe I was good at my job, but…" He stares into his glass. "I think I just deluded myself into thinking I had any real skills. I had that job because of nepotism. That's all there is to it."

"You're wrong," Jen says. There's a note of patience in her tone, like this is a conversation they've had several times.

"My dad likes to say I'm living proof of why you should never hire your family."

I wince, and Randy makes a disapproving grunt.

"Your dad's a dick," Tessa mutters, bringing a smile to Arun's face.

"Oh, I know," he replies, and we all laugh. "As much as I miss DC sometimes…I do love that being in Greenstead got me the hell away from my dad. And my sister's in Charlottesville, so I get to see her and my niece more."

"And Greenstead was the first place where I was fully…me," Tessa says. "I'd been wanting to transition for a while. When I heard I was being transferred, I was *pissed*, but then I thought… no one in Greenstead knows me. I could just show up as *me*, as Tessa, and that's all they'll know me as. So I did." Her proud smile grows pensive. "But it'd be nice to move to Richmond eventually. I'm there a lot to see friends, hang out, explore. I love the food, the…vibrance. And the sidewalks," she adds with a dry chuckle.

I force a laugh in return, even though I can't fully relate. I loved starting college in DC, where I could step outside my dorm and just start walking, passing libraries and shops instead of dirt roads and ditches. It felt like my world opened into new dimensions. But the neighborhood I moved to once I went all in on my FIRE plan doesn't offer any of that. Laundromats and construction zones aren't quite the city life I'd imagined. But with so much of my money going to savings, that was all my carefully allocated rent budget would buy me in a city with one of the highest costs of living in the country. Somehow, my new city life left me feeling just as constrained as before.

"You're not a fan of Richmond?" Tessa guesses, trying to read my expression.

"Lauryn has a whole thing about Richmond," Marina says. When I turn to her in surprise, she stiffens and reaches for her drink. "Or—maybe that's changed. I don't know."

I have to sit with that for a moment, the knowledge that Marina remembers minute details about me, that they can come slipping out without thinking. That I'm not alone in remembering everything our friendship was.

"I wasn't even thinking about that, but she's right," I tell Tessa. "I've always kind of…avoided Richmond. I just think of it as the place where I had to get my hearing tested every year, which…wasn't fun."

I was four when my parents realized I was deaf in one ear, after giving me the phone to talk to my grandma left me crying that I couldn't hear anything, until they switched it to my other ear. That prompted a series of appointments at a fancy hearing center in Richmond, all to conclude I must have lost my hearing as a toddler, maybe from a virus or an ear infection. Then came the annual hearing tests, the powerlessness I felt every time I sat down for a test I was guaranteed to fail. I came to resent that hour-long car ride to Richmond. It left me with no interest in seeing what the city had to offer besides stiff waiting room chairs and *Press the button when you hear the beep*. But Tessa seems to take this as a challenge.

"I go to Richmond like every other weekend," she tells me. "You're coming with me next time. I promise there's fun stuff there."

"Okay." I don't expect to feel such a thrill at this. I have to sip my drink to make a show out of being casual. I just can't remember the last time I made weekend plans with anyone.

"You go that often?" Marina asks, leaning forward on her elbows. "What's stopping you from moving there?"

Tessa shrugs. "I keep going back and forth on what my next move should be, job-wise. I spent so much time working toward R&D. And now…I don't think that's what I want. Not just because of the salad dressing thing. I wasn't ever really passionate about it. But I'm still paying off loans from my food science degree. Pivoting to something else is a risk. It's easier to just… get a little too comfortable staying where I am."

"I know what you mean," Marina says.

I jerk my head toward her in surprise. In all those years we spent talking about our hopes and dreams, never once did she mention wanting to leave Greenstead. And clearly that hasn't changed. She's still throwing her whole heart into goodness, searching for a way to salvage the deteriorating town she loves so much. She couldn't possibly relate to Tessa.

"I know what *all* of you mean," Marina says, sending me into another spiral of surprise. "I feel like all I do lately is mess up."

I may as well be on the floor at this point. Marina doesn't mess up. That accidental arson story she trotted out was years ago, when she was a student teacher. She's been nothing but successful since then.

We may not have had a real conversation in over a decade, but I still know Marina. I've seen her social media posts about her life as a fourth-grade teacher. I've seen the hand-drawn cards her students make for her, not even for Teacher's Day or her birthday, just handmade cards on a random Thursday, just because they love her that much.

Her posts exude happiness and fulfillment in a way that makes me feel empty and maybe a little bitter, which is why I haven't looked up her account in a while. But now I'm starting to realize I can't remember the last time I did.

"I can't see you messing anything up," I say, hoping she'll fill in the blanks. But she just gives me a closed-lipped smile and drinks her beer.

We stay in that booth for another two hours at least. It feels like a place outside of time and geography. No stuffy Ryser office politics, no faint mustard must of Greenstead, no drowning in lowered expectations at the Ryser Cares office. Here in this booth, in this bar, we've found a place that is entirely ours. Randy shows us a picture of him and Marge on a ski trip they went on last winter. Jen walks us through a play-by-play of the latest season of *Love Is Blind* and the jokes her online community has spun from it. Arun shows us a video of his four-year-old niece shrieking with excitement the moment they entered Solar Summit's water park in Falls Point.

Tessa tells us about how she keeps talking herself out of getting an annual pass to Solar Summit. "I mean, I'm thirty-nine years old," she says. "That park's for kids, right?"

"No," Marina and I say firmly.

Our eyes catch across the table, and I know she must be thinking about all the trips we've taken there. They're certainly running through my mind, anyway.

"Get the annual pass," Marina says, turning back to Tessa. "Your future self will thank you."

"I would," I agree. "I mean, I *won't*, because I'm moving back here when I get my job back," I correct myself. "But if I *were* staying in Greenstead for the long term, I would."

Randy, Tessa, and Arun exchange looks. Jen nods brightly and says, "Of course you will, hon." But there's something off about her smile.

Marina looks… I can't place it. A little wounded, maybe.

"Not that Greenstead isn't great," I rush to say. "I just, I mean, I'm still paying rent on my apartment here, so I've got to come back." I end on a nervous chuckle that dies in my throat.

"I know," Marina says, but her expression is unreadable and closed off now.

I stew in the awkward regret of feeling like I've killed the moment somehow, but the conversation floats on. I drain the rest of my drink as the others talk, and little by little, that regretful feeling eases out of me.

Marina and I exchange a look when a Destiny's Child song that we'd devised a whole dance routine for plays over the jukebox. She doesn't comment on it, and neither do I. But that small acknowledgment is enough to take root in my gut, make me feel like we've smoothed over whatever that moment was.

We applaud when Tessa eats the last coconut shrimp, and we take that as our cue to head out. After we throw away the grease-soaked napkins and pay the tab, we step outside into fresh air, a dark sky, and glittering city lights.

The car ride back is filled with chatter as we pick up the conversations we left off in the bar. Randy and Marina swap book recs, Arun talks about wanting to take a trip to Colorado and Jen recommends an inn she once stayed at, Tessa shows me a crossword app she likes after she hears about my love of puzzles.

Every now and then, I glance Marina's way, overcome with an urge to say something. To ask her why she feels like she screws up, to apologize for my eagerness to leave Greenstead, to ask if she ever got an annual pass to Solar Summit like we used to dream about.

I don't find the courage to, tonight. But I do think to myself, with a floaty sort of hope, that maybe next time we can have those conversations. I feel like we opened a door to something tonight—and I'm only just now realizing how badly I don't want to see it close again.

GREENSTEAD
APPLE FESTIVAL

OCTOBER 2010

AN UNDERCURRENT OF CHANGE WEAVES through the apple festival of our seventeenth year.

Beyond the usual change fall brings—leaves transformed to shades of honey, a flurry of pine cones and acorns at our feet—a truth hangs over Marina and me as we traverse the festival grounds. The start of our senior year of high school means we don't know how our lives will look by the time next year's festival rolls around. The concept of college looms over us, a reminder that the life we're used to will soon come to an end.

For the first time, it hits us that the festival is emptier than it's been in years past. Its attendance likely dwindled little by little over the years, as more people moved away from Greenstead and fewer tourists took interest in visiting. But we don't notice it until now. The line at the apple cider booth used to stretch across the aisle, requiring us to carefully sidle through it on our way past. But now it's just three people deep. The booths used to extend from one end of the park to the other, offering a bountiful assortment of foods, drinks, jewelry, clothes, artwork, crafts, and more. Now, the selection seems sparse, with a vast expanse of extra space between the booths.

There's one booth in particular whose absence we feel the most.

"Lettie's isn't here?" Marina asks when we reach the end of the aisle. "Did we miss it?"

"We couldn't have," I reply.

We never fail to take note of Lettie's Confections on our first walk around the festival. Lettie's smiling face and her table full of caramel apples are a constant. We've joked before that everything we do at the festival is just marking time until we're ready to begin our ritual.

We do another walk down the aisle just in case, but all it does is confirm that Lettie definitely isn't here this year. The realization rings a note of unease somewhere in my brain. Not so much about Lettie herself—we learned at the donut booth that she retired and moved to Florida over the summer—but what she's come to represent. We built a tradition around this woman's caramel apples, and she went and took that tradition to St. Petersburg. It's a reminder that change is inevitable, that reality will always win out over rose-colored fantasy. It's a reminder that no matter how much Marina and I say nothing will change next year, nothing is certain.

And yet.

Marina and I forge a certainty out of the unknown anyway.

After we've had our fill of the festival, we buy a bag of apples from the Mason Farms booth and spend our evening in my kitchen, standing over a hot stove, apprehensively waiting for our homemade caramel to resemble the picture from the recipe on my laptop. It doesn't, not completely. It's a little too thin, sliding off the apples in stubborn resistance. But that doesn't stop us from sitting at the kitchen table and dipping apple slices into our runny caramel, one after the other, crunching into sticky sweetness with satisfaction. Just like that, our tradition continues.

I'm certain, then, that nothing can challenge our friendship. Whatever change the next year brings, we'll weather it. We'll adapt. My heart beats with a sentiment that my brain knows is naive but feels too true to deny: This friendship is forever.

CHAPTER ELEVEN

RUE TO HER WORD, AMANDA emails me the next morning with confirmation that she'll allocate ten thousand dollars from her PR budget toward the festival. We can put any festival-related expenses up to that amount on the Ryser Cares corporate card, and I'll just have to submit expense reports detailing our festival spending.

Reading her email with the expense report instructions, I grow certain that these logistical details must be what she was referring to on awards night. She probably wanted to make sure I was okay with submitting tedious paperwork. And I am. I put the matter out of mind and move on to sharing the exciting news with my team: we officially have our funding.

Marina comes by that afternoon to start planning. The three of us sit around the oval table in the office's one meeting room as Arun patiently walks us through the logistics of planning an event on public property. He points us to Greenstead's Parks, Recreation, and Tourism Department website, a dubious-looking page with nearly impossible-to-read white text against a gray background. We squint our way to its permits section and click on the application for throwing a large event.

We select Juniper Park as the location, both because it's where the apple festival has always been held and because there aren't many other options. Juniper Park is the biggest park in Greenstead, boasting sixty acres of open space. Somehow the idea of throwing a festival in the second-largest open space in Greenstead—a supermarket parking lot—doesn't quite have the same appeal.

For the festival's date, we enter the second weekend of October. It's when the festival used to be held, right during Greenstead's peak apple season. It's when our vendors have the most availability. It's just within the ninety-day advance-notice period the application requires for festivals and events—which is for the best, since it's going to take us at least that long to learn how to throw a festival, even with Arun's tutelage. And it won't compete with the Halloween events we know Solar Summit runs from mid-to-late October. Never has there been a more perfect date than the weekend of October 11, we decide, entering it on the application.

Until the page flashes a bright-red banner in our face to announce that October 11 is taken.

"How is it taken?" Marina says, pulling back like the page has personally insulted her. "Greenstead doesn't even *do* events anymore."

Next to her, Arun pivots the laptop in his direction and tries selecting the date again, to no avail. "Someone must be doing something on the 11th," he says.

"Can we pick a different day?" I ask.

"We *could*, but it wouldn't work as well," he replies, running a hand through his hair. "If we go later, we're competing with Solar Summit's Halloween events. If we go earlier, we're competing with the state fair—and losing all the vendors who're gonna be exhibiting there. Any earlier than that and we won't have enough time to plan it properly."

Between us, Marina crosses her arms, glaring at the screen. "It can't be possible that someone else is throwing an event in Juniper Park on October 11. Every vendor in the county is wide open that day. What could it be?"

I slouch in my seat. Is this the curse of Ryser Cares? Even when we think we're doing something good, making a difference, some embittered whisper slinks from the drab walls of this office to remind us we're destined for failure?

Arun doesn't seem to think so. He pulls out his phone and calls the number at the top of the application, determination in his eyes. We listen as he gets through to someone, explains our predicament, and asks about the October 11 slot. He listens and nods. I can only stare at the bioluminescent jellyfish on his shirt and implore them to bring us luck. After a long pause, he hangs up with a resigned sigh.

"They said Juniper Park is booked for an event that day, but they won't say what."

"Like there's any reason to keep it that top secret," Marina grumbles.

"What now?" I ask. The application page flashes a new color at us—a pastel-yellow this time—and threatens to time out. We all watch it forlornly without making a move.

"We could try a different date?" Arun suggests. "We wouldn't have as many vendors, and not as many people would come, but…"

"No," Marina says, sitting upright. "We're getting the eleventh."

"How?" I ask, but she's already pulling her phone from the pocket of her dress. She brings the phone to her ear, eyes blazing. When no one seems to pick up, she huffs through her nostrils.

"Fine," she says, standing up. "I'll go in person."

"I'll go with you," I say, mostly out of curiosity. It's kind of refreshing, not being the subject of Marina's ire. Even if I'm just an onlooker and not the sounding board I used to be, it's a nice change of pace.

Greenstead's town hall is a two-story building with grimy, off-white pillars descending to the ground like jail bars. Marina marches inside, and I have to jog to catch up. Once we enter the building, I catch a glimpse of the words PARKS, RECREATION, AND TOURISM and 1ST FLOOR on a sign that looks like it's from the '70s, but Marina heads straight for the elevator.

She pushes the button for the second floor, then stares right ahead, her jaw set. I have to fight the urge to ask where the hell we're going. Instead, I remain silent and let the elevator groan its way to the floor above.

On the second floor, Marina expertly weaves through a maze of corridors until we reach an open set of weathered wooden doors. The words MAYOR'S OFFICE hang above the doors in bronze lettering—except the R is missing, with just a faded outline of where it used to be.

She enters through the doors and moves past the receptionist sitting at the first desk, who doesn't look surprised to see her. Marina doesn't stop until she reaches a desk against the back wall. I recognize the person sitting there, head down as they scribble notes in the margins of a document. It's Jess from the Chamber of Commerce meeting, whose Solar Summit proposal was met with unwarranted ridicule.

"Hi," Marina says. The word is reluctant yet full of determination.

Jess lifts their head, blinking in surprise. "Hey." Their eyes flit from Marina to me, then back to Marina, like they're trying to solve a riddle.

"I need to ask a favor." Marina pulls out one of the wooden chairs in front of Jess's desk and takes a seat.

I take that as my cue to sit down, too, even though I'm still trying to make sense of what's happening. Clearly they know each other, but Marina's normally…friendly to people she knows.

Jess's eyebrows lift slightly, and the corners of their mouth perk up. "Okay," they say slowly.

"Someone booked Juniper Park for the date we need it for the apple festival. I need to know who it was."

"The parks department's on the first floor," Jess says.

"They won't tell me anything. So I thought…" Marina lifts a brow.

Jess lowers their chin. "You need to stop making me butt in

on other departments' stuff. Roberta in the Treasurer's Office stopped bringing her biscotti up here after I waived your late fee for you."

"I shouldn't have to pay a late fee if she sent my tax bill to the wrong address!" Marina protests.

An easy smile slips onto Jess's face, like this is ground the two of them have tread many times before. "All I know is I haven't had pistachio biscotti in over a year, and I'm not trying to piss off Alex in Parks. He has the good Post-its."

"Okay, but…" Marina tilts her head toward Jess's computer. "You *could* look it up, though, couldn't you? Theoretically?" Her voice is innocent, teasing. "I'm not asking you to *tell* me. You could just…look it up, and maybe I could figure it out on my own."

Jess smirks, their brown eyes sparkling in amusement. I don't know how we've shifted from annoyance to flirting so quickly, but I'm starting to feel like a third wheel.

"It'll be a bit," they say. "The parks database is…slow."

"Shocking," I say. "Their website was so state-of-the-art."

Jess turns to me, as if surprised I'm still there, but their lips curl into a smile. "Don't get me started on their website."

A phone nearby rings, faint yet shrill. I scan the room, searching for the source—a fruitless endeavor since I'm not actually capable of identifying where sound is coming from. Marina used to joke about how, whenever she'd call my name to get my attention in the cafeteria or on the playground, I'd spin in circles like a dog chasing its tail. My one hearing ear can't locate sounds by itself, so the only way for me to source a sound is to see it—see the lips forming my name, see the phone lighting up with a call. I look down at the phone on Jess's desk, then turn around and peer at the receptionist's. Neither of their phones are ringing. But still the sound continues.

And still Jess and Marina sit without talking. The longer their silence draws on, the more compelled I feel to fill it.

"I liked your Solar Summit proposal," I say. "It sounded like a good idea."

"Thank you," Jess says, their brow wrinkling in surprise. "You're about the only person in Greenstead who thinks so."

I glance at the door to our right, where gold letters on frosted glass spell out MAYOR ANDRE BRADLEY. The door is closed, but light filters through the glass. I wonder if the ringing phone belongs to him. "What about the mayor?" I ask, lowering my voice.

Jess lets out a wry chuckle. "I'm waiting for the right time. He's still busy working on trying to get the community development grant, but...it's not going well. He drove up to DC yesterday to meet with some people about it. And now he needs a week to recover."

"From what?"

"People," Marina says, giving Jess a knowing look.

"Exactly," Jess replies. "He hates meetings. And calls. He tolerates *me*, because I help him avoid people, but I'm not pitching him the Solar Summit thing until it's really solid. If I'm forcing him into a meeting, I want to make it count."

"Huh." Mayor Bradley sounds like my kind of guy, really. You can't have awkward mishearing incidents if you avoid people at all costs. "Well, I think your Solar Summit idea is smart. It would bring in tourists. And West Greenstead is so run-down anyway."

Marina scoffs when I say this, though I'm not sure why. As the residential area of town closest to the mustard factory, West Greenstead was hit hardest by the flood. Property damage, flooded basements, structural issues. The cleanup efforts immediately after the flood couldn't prevent the long-term impacts that manifested as massive surprise problems years later: rotting frames, mold, foundation upheaval. I knew a few classmates in high school who lived in West Greenstead, and it always went the same way: worsening damage, failed attempts to sell their homes, foreclosing, moving away. I can't imagine things have improved.

"All true," Jess says. "But, you know. A lot of people don't trust it. They don't want another outsider putting roots in town in case history repeats itself." Jess shrugs. "Anyway, it doesn't matter. There's a homeowner in West Greenstead who refuses to sell their house, so the proposal's at a standstill anyway, even if I could get support."

I consider this, trying to think back to the updates my dad's given me on our semiweekly phone calls over the years, all the people who have left town. At this point, it doesn't feel like there's anyone left in West Greenstead.

"Who?" I ask.

Jess tilts their head toward Marina. I turn to her in surprise. When did she buy a house?

Marina ignores me. "Has the database loaded yet?"

Jess returns their gaze to their computer. "Yes," they admit. "What was the date you wanted?"

"October 11."

Jess hits a few keys and stares at the screen, frowning in concentration. Suddenly, they break into a grin.

"What?" Marina asks, leaning forward to see the monitor.

"This is classified, remember?" Jess tilts the monitor away from her. "We said I wasn't gonna tell you. Cat-shaped Post-its are at stake."

"Okay…" Marina studies Jess, thinking. "But it's someone you know."

"Yes, kind of."

"Someone I know?"

Jess laughs. "*Yes*. You go way back."

Marina smiles automatically, and they're falling back into flirtation again. It leaves me scrambling to make sense of these new facts I'm learning about Marina. She's a homeowner. She has some kind of history with Jess. She feels like she's always messing up. Without the context, though, it's just a collection of facts I can't piece together.

Being a curious onlooker doesn't quite feel fun anymore. Just lonely.

"I'm getting the sense I don't like this person," Marina says.

"Oh, you super don't." Jess leans back and laces their fingers together over their stomach, watching Marina with delight.

"Well, the first person who comes to mind would be…" Marina frowns at Jess, which only makes them grin harder. "It's not Nancy Fletcher?"

The name is like a time machine. In an instant, I'm pulled into the halls of my old high school, Nancy's thoughtless remarks and high-pitched giggle, the smack of her gum, the sickeningly sweet odor of her cotton candy body spray.

Jess nods emphatically. Marina groans and slouches against the back of her chair.

"Nancy fucking Fletcher?" I say.

Jess looks at me quizzically for a moment before they catch on. "You went to high school with her too," they say, piecing it together. "What a beautiful coincidence."

"Don't act like you don't hate Nancy too," Marina says.

"Oh, I can't stand her. But I'm not the one who needs to use the park she booked."

"I hate you," Marina says, but she's smiling.

"Tell Nancy I said hi," Jess quips.

Marina and I ride the elevator down to the main floor in silence. Once the doors whine open, Marina sighs but makes no effort to move.

"Well," she says. "I guess we're talking to Nancy."

CHAPTER TWELVE

H OW TO DESCRIBE NANCY FLETCHER...
It's not that she's a bully. She is just so deeply enamored with herself that everything and everyone else are simply inconsequential.

When Marina and I were tasked to work with Nancy on a group project in our ninth-grade geography class, Nancy's one contribution was spending forty-five minutes picking a font that would make her name look the prettiest on the title slide. *You don't understand,* she said when we tried to pull her focus to the actual assignment. *Your last names don't start with F. Your names look boring no matter what.* Her tone was bizarrely matter-of-fact, like we couldn't possibly understand the burden—the *responsibility*—of a surname as regal as hers. Then, once she did settle on a font—Edwardian Script, like her name was going on a monogrammed towel and not a PowerPoint presentation about plate tectonics—she announced that she needed a Frappuccino and abruptly left.

Nancy always believed—and told us, repeatedly—that she was destined for better things. Her big break came when she was cast on a reality dating show right out of college. Nancy got highlights, flew out to LA, and showed up on set ready to be the star.

I never watched the show, but I remember looking up articles about it from my apartment in DC, eager for hometown gossip. She was eliminated toward the end of the season, so she made it pretty far, all in all. But little else resulted from her time in LA. All I know is that she eventually moved back to Greenstead and leveraged her brief flash of fame for a job hosting a morning show on Greenstead's local news channel. I'll never forget coming home to visit my dad for Christmas one year, turning on the TV, and seeing Nancy's smiling face like a jump scare. It turns out my dad and Wendy love tuning in to Nancy's show every morning. They say she's funny, and not even unintentionally, which I refuse to believe.

In the town hall parking lot, Marina and I sit in her car and look up Nancy on our phones. Her website is a sea of headshots, stills from her morning show, and even grainy stills from her reality show appearance.

I fill out the contact form and write a polite message asking to get in touch with her about a schedule conflict. Then I scroll up and down the page, searching for the submit button.

"I think it's her face," Marina says, pointing to an icon-sized photo of Nancy beneath the form. I press it and, sure enough, the form is submitted.

"People in this town really need to take a web design class," I say, and Marina lets out a wry laugh.

Nancy gets back to me within the hour, informing me that she can squeeze us in for lunch this weekend. Her email sign-off is *Ta-ta, Nancy Fletcher*, all written in Edwardian Script, of course. Below her name is a picture of her face. I don't know why I'd expect anything else.

Two days later, Marina and I make the drive to Falls Point together to meet Nancy. I have to circle the area in search of street parking, and I finally find a spot by an ice cream shop with a line of people waiting outside. Marina politely doesn't comment when I realize I'd pulled into the spot from the wrong angle and have to pull out to redo my parallel parking job.

"Why is she making us come out here?" Marina grumbles as I move two inches back, one inch forward for the tenth time. "We're all in Greenstead. We could have just met there."

I look around at Falls Point's idyllic downtown. The towering trees, the shops with no sign of disrepair, the bustling activity of pedestrians walking along the sidewalk. I refrain from pointing out that Greenstead doesn't have a downtown as lovely as this. Not anymore, anyway.

We meet Nancy at a modern-looking café. She's sitting outside at a small round table, a large pair of sunglasses perched on her dainty nose. Her light brown, shoulder-length hair is shiny and sleek, streaked with blond highlights throughout, and her patterned blue dress is perfectly pressed. The fabric looks heavy enough to be stifling on a 90-degree day like today, but there isn't a drop of sweat to be found. Meanwhile, even in my sleeveless linen top, I'm sporting a ring of sweat where my belly button meets the fabric.

"Hello," Nancy says, standing when she sees us. When she approaches, I think she's going in for a hug, and I start to open my arms, but instead she does the European cheek kiss thing that I've never understood.

"O-oh, hi," I stammer as she presses one cheek against mine, then the other. "Am I supposed to…?" But then she's moving on to Marina, who looks about as flustered as I feel.

"So good to see you," Nancy coos. "Sit, sit!"

Marina civilly asks Nancy how she's doing, which leads Nancy to chatter for ten minutes about her new obsession with celery juice, her kayaking plans for next weekend, and her Scottish terrier, who, I have to admit when she shows us a string of photos, is adorable.

Nancy finally stops to take a breath when our food arrives. Our server delivers Marina's quinoa salad and my caprese sandwich first and tells Nancy her chicken pesto wrap will be right out. Nancy thanks her, but her expression is tight. I know she wants to complain about the injustice of being served last, but she holds her tongue and turns to us instead.

"How have you been? Are you still working at that tragic school?"

Marina's pleasant smile stiffens. "Longview Elementary is not tragic."

"I heard there was asbestos in the gymnasium," Nancy comments, checking her Apple Watch.

"That was a rumor *you* started!" Marina huffs out a breath. "If you see white powder at a science fair, a reasonable person assumes it's baking soda for a volcano. You don't turn what was supposed to be a nice segment on kids in science into an exposé about the hidden dangers of public school. A parent pulled their kid out of class because of you."

Nancy nods patiently. "The realities of journalism can be hard for some people to understand. I just report the truth."

"No, you don't!" Marina barks back. "You report on whatever gets you the most attention."

I fake a cough. Marina turns to me, and I raise my eyebrows to remind her that maybe attacking the person we're asking a favor from isn't the way to go.

"You haven't been in the Longview Elementary gymnasium recently, have you?" Nancy asks, eyeing me like I'm a leper.

"I was just clearing my throat," I say brightly, but Nancy doesn't seem convinced.

A silence settles over us. Our server returns to place Nancy's order in front of her. Nancy asks if the arugula salad on the side is organic, because it doesn't look organic. After the server assures Nancy of the integrity of their arugula—and Marina rolls her eyes at Nancy's doubtful hum—I decide to ask for our favor now, before Nancy and Marina get into another spat.

"So," I say, "Marina and I are trying to bring back the Greenstead Apple Festival to raise funds for the community center, but you have Juniper Park booked for the day we need it."

A petite wrinkle forms in Nancy's brow. "Do I?" She sips demurely on her Bloody Mary.

"On October 11," Marina prods.

"Ah. Yes, that's for my Nancy convention."

Marina and I share a look.

"Your what?" I say.

"It's for the fans," Nancy says. "They love getting to meet with me in person, take photos, have me sign autographs. It really means a lot to them."

"The fans," I repeat.

"Of course. From watching me on *Love Quest* or *Wake Up with Nancy*. My Nancies."

"Your…" I share another glance with Marina. "Your fans are called Nancies?"

"And that's not confusing?" Marina asks.

"No," Nancy says breezily.

Marina's fighting a smile. I have to take a long drink from my ice water to keep from laughing.

Marina clears her throat and takes a bite of her quinoa salad. "And it *has* to be at Juniper Park?" she asks.

"I like open spaces," Nancy says. "I'm very outdoorsy."

At this point, Marina and I have to avoid eye contact, because it's the only way to make sure we don't laugh. There's no way this woman needs a sixty-acre park to meet with her alleged fans.

"And it *has* to be October 11?" Marina asks. "You can't do another day?"

"Eleven is my favorite number," Nancy says, frowning at us.

"Isn't there another open space you could do it in?" I ask. "Like Mill Park?"

"In West Greenstead?" Nancy asks, her voice lowering like she couldn't be caught dead even uttering the name.

I sneak a glance at Marina, whose lip is curling in annoyance.

"I need somewhere pretty for the pictures," Nancy says. "Only the best for my Nancies!"

I take a bite of my caprese sandwich and try to think of a new angle. "How many…Nancies…are coming?" I ask. "Does it really need to be at the biggest park in Greenstead?"

Nancy falters. She plays with the straw in her drink. "Twelve so far," she admits. She lifts her chin. "But I'm expecting more RSVPs. They're…still getting organized."

"We're expecting at least three hundred people at our festival," I say. "Juniper Park is the only place where we can do it, and October 11 is the only weekend that works. Would you be willing to move yours? I could help you find another location or work out a different date."

Nancy glances from me to Marina, considering. She takes another sip of her Bloody Mary, then checks her Apple Watch. While she swipes and taps at the screen with a concerning level of concentration, I wonder if she's sending out some sort of signal to sic her Nancies on us, if five minutes from now an army of white women with Karen haircuts will come stampeding down the sidewalk ready to attack.

"Here's what we'll do," Nancy says, folding her hands on the table. "You'll section off a part of the park where I can hold my Nancy convention. You'll provide me with a stage and seating for my Nancies. You'll set up a greenroom for me. And you'll include my show and my Nancy convention in festival promotional materials."

"You want us to…have the Nancy convention at the festival?" Marina asks.

"I don't see why my Nancies should have to suffer just because of your poor planning."

I bite my lip. A joint apple festival/Nancy convention is not the nostalgic festival comeback we'd envisioned. Juniper Park was supposed to be filled with apple festival vendors from one end to the other, not have a weird roped-off section to the side where Nancy could hold a glorified meet and greet with her so-called fans.

Plus I'd sold this event to Amanda as an easy PR win for Ryser. Ryser helping Greenstead revive its apple festival is a straightforward, uplifting story. Ryser helping Greenstead revive its apple festival and hold a fan convention for a local TV personality is... confusing. I'd been planning to send Amanda weekly updates of our festival progress (partly to remind her how hardworking I am; partly out of paranoia that this was the unheard thing she'd asked for when she agreed to supply the funds). I'm not quite sure how I'd spin the Nancy convention component.

"Unless you don't want to," Nancy singsongs, cutting a perfectly round slice from her wrap. "You could always hold your little festival in Mill Park."

I exchange a look with Marina. She's grimacing, but she gives a tiny shrug. We need Juniper Park, even if it comes with Nancy strings attached. And at least Nancy will now be promoting the festival on her show whenever she mentions her convention. I could easily add a bullet about that in my update for Amanda: *Secured media coverage on a widely watched local morning television show.*

"Okay," I say. "We have a deal."

"Good. I'll have my team send you my rider." She pauses and sets her knife and fork down. "Oh, you're probably not used to working with celebrities. A rider is a list of—"

"We know what a rider is," Marina interrupts, but that doesn't stop Nancy from talking over her anyway.

At the end of the meal, Nancy insists on paying, and we don't fight her on it. She *is* the celebrity, after all.

"Well, that was wild," I say once we're back in my car. In the passenger seat, Marina gives a distracted laugh, but she's occupied with her phone. "I can't believe we got roped into throwing a Nancy convention," I continue, pulling out of the parking space.

Marina hums in response but doesn't speak. I guess whatever had us exchanging looks and stifling laughs a few minutes ago has dissipated with Nancy's absence. It was just temporary Nancy-induced solidarity, and it's over now. What a sad thought, that our friendship needs Nancy Fletcher's presence to get us back on our old footing.

As Marina stays buried in her phone, I quash my disappointment and turn the radio up to fill the silence. I keep my eyes ahead, willing myself to focus on following the road back to Greenstead instead of sitting in the whiplash of Marina and me laughing at lunch one second and switching back to strangers the next.

But a minute later, Marina reaches over to turn down the radio and says, "Nancy's season of *Love Quest* is on a streaming service called Lurv Plus, and Jen just gave me the password to her account." She holds up her phone. "Do you want to watch Nancy look for love?"

"God, yes." Remembering our sleepovers spent binge-watching rom-coms and *Gossip Girl*, I add, "If we want to do this right, we're going to need a large cheese pizza and an order of cheesy bread from Pirate Pizza. And a two-liter of Dr Pepper." I hesitate when I realize reciting our sleepover staples might be taking it too far.

The corners of her lips turn down. I brace myself for disappointment. "Pirate Pizza closed down a few years ago," Marina says. "But Top Slice's cheesy bread is pretty good."

I break into a smile. "Perfect."

"We should also get Häagen-Dazs," Marina says.

"And Cool Ranch Doritos."

"Sour Skittles."

"Raisinets."

It doesn't even matter that we've just had lunch. No movie night is complete without our favorite foods. Already my mouth is watering for pizza, cheesy bread, and those coffee almond crunch ice cream bars we love.

"Are we watching it at your house?" I ask.

"Oh." She makes a face.

"It'd be cool to see your place," I say. "Plus it's Sunday, which means my dad and Wendy are taking over the living room to watch whatever they're bingeing. Lately it's *The Crown*."

I joined them on the couch for an episode last weekend while I was waiting for my Bagel Bites to heat up, and I made a mistake by asking a question about the Suez Canal. My dad paused the show, shocked that I hadn't heard of the Suez Crisis, then spent the next twenty minutes alternating between delivering a detailed history lesson and bemoaning the state of the American educational system. I refrained from pointing out that perhaps, as my eleventh-grade history teacher, he might be partially to blame.

Since then, I've tried to keep my distance when they're watching TV. I relay this to Marina and fix her with imploring eyes.

"Okay," Marina agrees. "We can go to my house."

I'm not sure what's driving that hesitation in her voice, but I know her house can't be worse than my tiny, dark basement apartment in DC. Or an afternoon of history lessons with my dad.

The closer we get to Greenstead, the more energized I feel. We might be starting to fall back into step, at long, long last.

GREENSTEAD
APPLE FESTIVAL

OCTOBER 2012

TENSION PRICKS THE AIR AT the apple festival Marina and I attend during our sophomore year of college.

Like last year, I take the bus down from DC for the weekend. But this time, Marina and I aren't prattling about our new college lives. She's not giving me a detailed breakdown of her dorm mates' drama at William & Mary like she did at the last festival; I'm not recapping my first (and last) frat party experience. This time, we're quiet as we stroll the booths. Even fewer vendors and attendees have shown up this year. The sky is overcast, a cold, angry wind whistling through the park. There's less laughter, music, and excitement around us. It feels more like a funeral than a festival.

I don't have to mention this past summer to know that's what's hanging between us. A few months earlier, during one of our regular walk-and-talk calls, where we'd walk around our respective campuses and catch each other up on what we'd been up to, Marina told me about getting an internship doing administrative work at an accounting firm in Greenstead. After a couple of weeks of feeling down—first being rejected for the counselor job she'd applied for at a music camp in Norfolk, then discovering her closest dorm mates were planning a summer trip to New York without her—the Greenstead internship was just enough of a consolation prize to lift her spirits. Then she asked about my summer plans, and I replied that I didn't have any yet.

What I hadn't told her was that I'd applied for an internship at Ryser. I'd come across the listing while looking for summer jobs, and while I understood Ryser's storied history with Greenstead, I was desperate to not have to return home for the summer. An internship with Ryser would mean staying in DC, enjoying my new city, and making some money at a place that, going by the job description, actually sounded kind of fun. I liked free snacks. I liked ice cream socials. I liked the sound of *a dynamic, fast-paced environment.*

I applied, and I decided I'd figure out how to tell Marina about the possibility of interning for our town's collective enemy later. After all her rants whenever a Ryser Cares ad came on, and her ongoing boycott of Ryser products—she was the only third grader I knew who'd ever boycotted anything; in fact, she was the reason I learned the word *boycott* as an eight-year-old—I knew she wouldn't understand.

But, while they'd called me in for an interview, I ultimately didn't get the internship. I tucked away my disappointments, reminding myself that at least this meant I wouldn't have to tell Marina I was a sellout.

"What if you applied, too?" she asked when I told her I didn't have any summer plans. "They asked if I knew anyone else who could intern. It would be so much more fun if you were there. We could spend the summer working together!"

After a year in DC, I'd been dreading the prospect of returning to Greenstead for the summer. But interning with Marina would make the idea more tolerable. Fun, even. I quickly agreed and submitted an application the next day. After a phone interview that consisted of three questions about how I liked college, how my dad's triathlon training was going, and when I could start, I was offered the internship. My conversations with Marina turned to the summer we'd spend together, how we'd work during the day and have evenings and weekends to ourselves. We talked about spending a Saturday at Solar Summit, going tubing in James River, maybe road-tripping to Virginia Beach for a weekend. Our summer was shaping up to be our best one yet.

Then two things happened.

First, our internship began. Marina and I toured the small office, with its dim fluorescent lighting that cast everyone in a sallow hue, the three employees yawning at their desks, the gray walls and cubicles, and the unpleasant smell emanating from the tiny office kitchenette, like fish-flavored popcorn. It was so different from the Ryser office I'd seen during my interview, where colleagues chatted in halls, people had important-looking meetings behind glass doors, innovation rooms held beanbags and flip charts scribbled with ideas, and the kitchen smelled like fresh coffee and donuts.

Second, three hours into the internship, the marketing manager who'd interviewed me at Ryser called with a last-minute offer. The candidate they'd hired had a family emergency and dropped out of the program, they said. Was I available to start interning for them tomorrow?

It felt like a lifeline. I was being handed an out from toiling away in this dead, quiet, fishy office. An out from languishing in Greenstead and getting stuck in the same quicksand that had grabbed hold of everyone else in this town. Now that I knew what life outside Greenstead was like, being back there felt like a prison sentence.

I could find some sort of summer housing in DC to make this Ryser internship work. My old roommate had mentioned renting an apartment as a subletter for the summer; I could probably crash with her. Hell, I'd get up at 5:00 a.m. and commute from Greenstead to DC each morning if that was what it took to escape this wasteland.

I choked out a yes without a second thought.

My supervisor was unfazed when I handed in my resignation, as though it was common for interns to run screaming within hours of starting.

Then came the task of telling Marina.

"So…it turns out there was a mix-up," I said, staring just past her at a lone pushpin stuck in her cubicle wall. "I just found out I won't be getting college credit for this internship, so I have to switch to another one, in DC. I start tomorrow."

"Oh." Marina's brow dipped. I could see her trying to piece together how this could have happened in the last three minutes. "Wow. You…have another internship already?"

"Yeah. Their first choice left, so now they want me."

"Okay," she said slowly. Still her mind was puzzling. "Where is it?"

I hesitated for several long seconds, then got out the words as quickly as I could. "Ryser. My degree program, um, made me apply."

Something flashed across her face. "Why didn't you tell me you applied?"

"I forgot." Seeing the suspicion in her eyes, I changed course. "I mean…I got busy all of a sudden. It's…it's not important. But I'll come back on the weekends. We can still do everything we planned. Are we still on for Solar Summit this weekend?"

Her response came after a long pause: "Yep." She spoke without emotion, but her smile was the signal I needed that this was fine. *We* were fine. I bolted in such relief that by the time I asked myself whether there was something strained about her smile, I was already on the bus back to DC.

I thought—hoped—that this wouldn't change anything between us. But in a single text a few days later, she canceled all those summer plans we made. I got busy all of a sudden, she texted. And I couldn't bring myself to call her out on using the same exact lie I'd fed her.

Now that we're together in person for the first time since that awkward moment at the accounting firm, I don't know what to say. I briefly consider apologizing again before deciding that would be overkill. Instead, I ramble to fill the silence.

"I went to the DC state fair last month," I say as we pass a booth selling art prints. "They had so many art booths. They also had an art contest. And a pie-eating contest, and a million other contests."

Marina says nothing.

"They had a huge animal adoption booth," I continue when we pass the empty space where the petting zoo used to be. "I petted four dogs and it was amazing. Oh, and there was a West African food truck. I got to try jollof rice."

"Sounds fun."

I shove my hands in the pockets of my jacket, racking my brain for something else to say. I just need to keep talking, and this moment will pass, and she'll be back to her old self. "Do you think Musty's started sticking around in the fall, too?" I ask. Referencing our old name for Greenstead's faint mustard smell will get me some nostalgia points, at least. "I feel like I can still kind of smell him. But maybe being in DC has spoiled me. A summer without breathing in Musty was pretty refreshing."

"You can just go, if you hate it here so much," Marina snaps, coming to a stop. "If you want to ditch me like you did at the internship *I* recommended you for, go ahead."

I stop dead in my tracks. "I wasn't ditching *you*. I told you, there was a…mix-up."

"Was there really?" she presses. The way my eyes fall to my boots is response enough for her. "I guess you'll do anything to get the hell away from here."

I let out a frustrated sigh. "I'm sorry I left the sad, boring office in a town where everyone's stuck. I'm sorry I took a paid opportunity in a place where people haven't given up yet."

Her laugh is hard and sarcastic. "So you think I'm stuck? You think every single person here"—she gestures to the people scattered around the park—"has just given up?" She's speaking loudly enough that a woman at the cotton candy booth behind her takes notice, frowning at me as if I've insulted her directly.

My face warms. "I didn't mean that. I just—"

"Well, I'm not stuck," Marina continues on, crossing her arms. The wind whips her hair across her face and she doesn't bother to move it. "I actually give a shit about the place where I'm from, which is more than I can say for you. If I'm stuck, then you're fucking selfish."

Wind flies through my jacket, stinging me with cold, but it's nothing compared to the punch-in-the-gut feeling of my best friend calling me selfish. It pierces my sense of self like an arrow. *Am* I selfish? Have I always been, and I just never noticed it until now? Is that what's wrong with me, why I couldn't wait to leave Greenstead while everyone else is content to stay here and support each other?

But how is it selfish to want a different life for myself?

Doubt gives way to anger, cold transforming me into steel. "Fine," I spit. "Let's say I'm selfish. I'd rather be selfish than naive and self-righteous. It's exhausting trying to live up to your standards."

Her jaw drops. For a moment her eyes shine with tears, but she blinks them away and shoots back, "I didn't realize not wanting my best friend to lie to me is an impossible standard."

I roll my eyes. "Oh, come on. You're not mad because I lied. You're mad because I took an internship that doesn't abide by your stupid Ryser boycott."

"You don't get to tell me what I'm mad about!" Marina shouts, causing a few passersby to turn their heads. "And if that's what you think, you don't know me. And *I* clearly don't know *you*."

I hate the way she's looking at me. Like I'm some monster she doesn't recognize. It makes me want to hurt her right back. "I only lied because I'm sick of the way you judge me. Did you ever think maybe the reason your dorm mates planned that trip without you is because no one wants to be around a judgmental buzzkill? I'm not putting up with it anymore. I give up. I'm done."

Marina's face is a stone wall, her expression unreadable. "Fine. I'm done too."

With that, she stalks off toward the parking lot.

I remain rooted to the spot, still reeling from her anger. It's then that I notice the wary looks from the vendors and attendees in earshot. I cast my eyes down and plod to the exit, eyes stinging as I blink back tears against the wind.

On the long bus ride back to DC that evening, it occurs to me that for the first time in our eleven years of attending this festival together, we didn't end it with a caramel apple.

It's this realization that makes our fight feel bigger than any of our past arguments. It's then that I know there will be no apologies, no amends. How can there be, when we don't live in the same town anymore, when we don't see each other at school every day? When I'm a selfish monster and she's a self-righteous saint?

With every mile I draw closer to DC, I feel like I'm pulling further away from our friendship. I could get off at the next stop, I tell myself, turn around, show up at her door, talk it out, make it work. But I stay seated. She could also reach out, if she wanted to. This isn't just on me.

And when I step off the bus and check my phone to see no missed calls or texts, I know something I shouldn't yet know. Even though it's only been a few hours since our fight, and there's still a chance we could make up later tonight, or tomorrow, or when I'm back in Greenstead for Thanksgiving or Christmas, I feel a truth somewhere deep in my gut.

Our friendship is over.

CHAPTER THIRTEEN

A N EERIE SILENCE HAUNTS MARINA'S neighborhood.
When I pull into her cul-de-sac, I see no cars in driveways. The vinyl siding on all the houses is worn and discolored, grass knee-high and sickly yellow. An overturned mailbox lies on a lawn, mouth open in an eternal scream.

Marina's house, a two-story colonial painted a shade of blue that's seen better days, is the only one that still looks lived in: green plants hanging on the porch, her car in the driveway, shades over the windows. I think back to what Jess said about Marina being the lone holdout, preventing Solar Summit from paving over her neighborhood to build a resort hotel here. It starts to make sense why Marina had insisted we meet at the Ryser Cares office today before heading out to lunch with Nancy. I don't think she wanted me to pick her up here and see the lonely state of her neighborhood. Even after she agreed to let me come over, she tasked me with going to Top Slice for pizza and cheesy bread first. She said it was for efficiency's sake, and that she'd be going to Food Lion for snacks and drinks. But now, as I ring her doorbell with two pizza boxes in hand, I wonder if she was stalling.

"Hey," Marina says, a little breathless when she answers the door. "I was just cleaning up."

"You don't have to clean for me." Except I realize as I say it that it's not really true. Close friends can see your place in any state, but that's not what we are anymore.

"I can put those in the kitchen." Marina takes the boxes from me. "I'm just setting up Lurv Plus on my TV and then I'll be ready."

"No worries." I step inside, kicking off my shoes in the foyer. "I want to see your house anyway." My toe presses into a hole of some kind, and I look down to see that the floorboard has a corner missing. Marina gives me a nervous glance but scurries off with the boxes before I can ask about it.

Marina's house is…not what I expected. When I follow her into the kitchen, I see discolored rectangular outlines on the wall behind the oven, ghosts of the cabinets that must have once hung there. The cabinets on the wall by the sink are intact, but they're sagging a little, listing to the left. Marina doesn't offer any explanations as she sets the boxes on the counter and returns to entering Jen's log-in information into the Lurv Plus app on the TV, so I don't comment on it, either. The living room has several gaping holes in the drywall. In the corner, there's an opening that I think might lead to the basement, but it's covered in plastic sheeting.

"Just renovations," Marina says, following my gaze.

"Right," I say, as if I know anything about renovations. I take another look around, searching for something I can compliment. Past the kitchen is a doorway leading to a spacious dining room with a long, wooden table and mismatched vintage chairs. An ornate gold chandelier hangs above it. "Your dining room's beautiful."

I start to move toward it, but Marina blurts out, "The chandelier flickers!" like she's confessing to a crime.

I stop in my tracks. "Okay." It's only then that I notice how intently Marina is watching my every move, turning the remote over and over in her hands.

I'm reminded, then, of a time when the roles were reversed. When we were eleven, and Marina spent the night, as she'd done many Fridays in the past. We were partway into a game of Monopoly when my parents' angry voices sounded from downstairs. My dad saying, *You're being selfish*; my mom saying, *I can't do this anymore*, with unsettling finality. Marina had stopped in the middle of rolling the dice when she heard them, but I'd kept my head down, pretending to count my money, imploring her not to draw attention to what was increasingly becoming my new normal. Marina must have sensed it too, because she finished rolling the dice without a word, and we carried on with our game. We never spoke of it, but it soon became understood that sleepovers would be at her house during that rocky phase at the end of my parents' marriage.

I decide to extend Marina the same courtesy. If she's self-conscious about her house, then I won't comment on it. "Is there a bathroom I can use?" I ask instead.

Marina points toward the stairs. "Use the one upstairs. The downstairs bathroom is…scary."

"Sure," I say brightly, as though *scary* is a perfectly normal thing for a bathroom to be. I go up the stairs, which creak under my weight. I head toward the first door I see and push it open to find myself in Marina's bedroom.

She probably wouldn't want me in here if just seeing the downstairs had her on edge. But I can't help myself from stepping inside, curious to see how adult Marina's bedroom differs from the one she had as a kid, with the overflowing bookshelf and the row of stuffed animals that once lined her bed.

This Marina's bedroom is fairly spacious. Gauzy white curtains hang on either side of a large window that overlooks the dirt patch backyard and the trees lining the main road behind it. A neatly made bed sits in the center of the room, a dresser and vanity on either side. I can see touches of Marina sprinkled throughout. On the vanity, there's the Snow White jewelry box that used to sit on Marina's desk. There's a bookshelf, still packed to the brim with books. On one shelf sits a framed photo of Marina with her mom, dad, and two older sisters. A keyboard lies on the bench at the foot of the bed, haphazardly balanced on the edge like she'd just put it down and gotten distracted. It brings back memories of sitting in Marina's room years and years ago, listening to her idly tinker with melodies.

On the dresser is a mess of cards and envelopes. I have to do a double take when I catch sight of the card at the top of the stack. It's a photo of Marina and Jess. Marina wears a floral dress, Jess a pair of sharply tailored pants and a loose-fitting tweed blazer over a white shirt. They're holding hands and smiling at each other. My eyes fall on the words *Save the Date* and *December 6th* in flowy white script.

Here's something else to scribble on my sparse mental timeline of Marina's life since our friendship ended. We used to talk about being each other's maids of honor, and now I don't even make the list for a save-the-date. Marina has never once mentioned being engaged. Nothing about the way she and Jess talked to each other last week suggested they were wedding-bound. Question marks spring up to surround this new entry in my Marina timeline.

"I've got the first episode cued up," Marina calls, snapping me from my thoughts. There's a note of panic in her voice, like she's also saying, *You better not have found the swamp witch in my attic,* or whatever inconceivable issues the upstairs level has. Or maybe it's this card right here in my hand that she doesn't want me to find, this relic from a time when she and Jess were happy and in love.

"Be there in a sec!" I call back, setting the card down. I use the bathroom and remember my way back to the living room, that engagement picture still looming in my mind.

When I sink into the plush cushions of Marina's beige couch, she hands me a plate and reaches for a slice of pizza from the box on the coffee table. "You might actually like Top Slice's crust," she says. Her voice is a little too perky, too eager to fill the silence, as if she's realized that having our usual sleepover staples here doesn't mean we suddenly know how to hang out together like we used to. "They do this amazing garlic Parmesan thing."

"Sounds good." I cut a glance at her as I load up my plate. "And, um. I like crust now. So…I'm sure I will like it."

"Oh." Marina looks me over. I know she's trying to reconcile this fact with her memories of all the times I'd toss my crust back in the box, ready to move on to the next slice of pizza. Sometime in my early twenties, though, I came to appreciate the bready chew of a good pizza crust. But she'd have no way of knowing that. There's a lot we don't know about each other, I'm learning.

My eyes zero in on her left ring finger: no ring. So she and Jess were engaged, set to be married this December, and then they broke it off.

But there's something between them still. The way they looked at each other at the Chamber of Commerce meeting. Their easy banter at the mayor's office. It doesn't make sense, but I've lost the right to ask for the details. So, I take a slice of pizza and sit back while Marina presses Play.

Time passes in a glorious haze of bizarre reality-show sound effects and excessive snack consumption. Twenty-two-year-old Nancy on a dating show is a beautiful thing to behold. By the end of the first episode, two separate women have given confessionals declaring that Nancy is their archnemesis.

Wyatt, the man these women are supposed to be vying over, wears exclusively denim and plaid and speaks in horse metaphors. The real fun is in seeing the women try to look interested as Wyatt brags about his barrel-racing rank. And in watching Nancy dismiss Wyatt's brag and tell him about coming in third in her high school talent show.

Nancy is eliminated in the seventh episode, and it's honestly pretty impressive that she made it that far. Marina suggests seeing her off with a toast, so we make vodka sodas—Nancy's drink of choice throughout the show—and raise our glasses in the air during Nancy's final confessional. Nancy says rather astutely that Wyatt wouldn't love any of these women as much as he loves horses. She also says her time in LA is just getting started, which is...less astute.

The show isn't as fun without Nancy to stir up chaos, but we enjoy rooting for Alexis, the most genuine of the group, to come to her senses and stop chasing after this hopeless horse boy. We make more drinks and fall into giggles, that early awkwardness from a couple of hours ago long forgotten.

There's something beautifully familiar yet exciting and new about today. Bingeing shows and finding hilarity in whatever we're watching was one of our favorite ways to spend time together. We'd crack jokes between lines of dialogue, create elaborate backstories about unnamed extras, pitch absurd plot lines and treat them as canon. Falling back into that again makes me feel like I've stumbled into something precious, a horde of buried treasure I'd lost the map to years ago, and found every gem shiny and intact, just as I'd left it.

The newness comes from the fact that we've never drunk alcohol together before, never been drunk or so much as buzzed in each other's presence. This feels right, now: making up for lost time, hitting milestones we never got to reach together.

There are still things to discuss, still much to clear the air about. We've yet to hash out our friendship-ending argument at the last apple festival, or have a real conversation about what's going on in our lives now. I want to ask her about how she's coping with her broken engagement with Jess, about what she said back at the bar in DC about feeling like she always messes up, about why her house looks like a construction zone. I want to tell her about my FIRE plan, how I'm going to make a difference before I leave Ryser. But that could break the spell of this night, so light and full of joy. So, I push those heavy thoughts aside and take another drink.

Marina is a surprisingly loud drunk and I love her for it. As Alexis sobs about Wyatt not saying he loves her back, Marina shouts at the TV, "It's not your fault you're not a horse!" sending me into belly-aching cackles. I'm laughing at everything, probably obnoxiously so, but that doesn't feel all that different from how I used to be when I was around Marina sober. I've never laughed harder than I did when I was with Marina, when we could be silly and loud and freely ourselves.

When we start the finale, Marina suggests taking a drink every time Wyatt says the word *horse*.

Naturally, we're hammered within fifteen minutes.

We're so far gone that when her phone starts ringing, we don't even notice it. We're too busy voicing the horse Wyatt's brushing on-screen, laughing wildly as we utter equestrian innuendo between neighs. It's Marina who pauses the show and traces the sound back to a buzzing on the coffee table.

She picks it up with a giggly hello. Immediately, her eyes go wide. *It's Nancy*, she mouths. She puts the phone on speaker and places it between us on the couch.

"Hello?" Nancy's voice rings through.

"We were just watching you," I say, leaning over the phone.

"Okay," Nancy says, and I love how unfazed she sounds. Of *course* we'd be watching her. She must assume that every TV in Greenstead blares her show at all hours of the day. "Look, I need a favor, and you owe me one. I'm supposed to have a chef on the show tomorrow for a crepe-making demonstration, but he just backed out because *his mother's in the hospital,*" she says, mimicking his words with annoyance. "Can you come on? I have five minutes to fill."

"You want us to make crepes?" Marina asks, her face screwed up in confusion.

"What? No, you can talk about your festival. Or you can braid each other's hair. I really don't care, as long as you're there and you fill five minutes."

"I finally learned how to French braid!" Marina says, turning to me. "Like five years ago."

"That's amazing!" I reply. I offer her a high five, but our palms barely graze one another. We try again, letting out a cheer when our hands meet in a satisfying smack.

"Say yes, or I just might have to take Juniper Park back," Nancy says. Marina and I exchange shrugs.

"Sure," Marina says.

"Nancy, you were robbed in *Love Quest,*" I say. "I don't think you should have been enumerated. No, elemon—eliminated."

"Are you drunk?" Nancy asks.

"*No,*" I say, sounding overly aghast, and Marina and I break into a fit of laughter.

"Jesus Christ," Nancy mutters. "Be at the studio at 6:00 a.m. tomorrow. I'll text you the address."

"Six?" Marina groans. "What time is it now?"

"You—you don't know what time it is?" Nancy sputters. "Whatever, I don't care. Just be at the studio at six, okay?"

"Okay," we reply.

"You should probably drink some water and go to bed."

"You're not my mom," Marina says, and I fall into more giggles. The last thing we hear before Nancy hangs up is a tortured sigh.

Then we're left blinking at each other in the dark, lit only by the glow of the TV, paused on a still of Wyatt's horse.

"It's almost midnight," Marina marvels, checking the time on her phone.

"Wow." We sit there in wonder at the passage of time. "Can we finish the finale?" I ask in a small voice.

"Oh, obviously we have to finish the finale," Marina says. "I guess we can switch to water." She gets up to refill our water glasses, and I stretch, raising my arms above my head. "You can sleep on the couch," Marina calls from the kitchen, "and we can go to the studio together tomorrow morning."

"Okay," I agree, immediately grateful. The thought of leaving this couch in the state I'm in feels impossible right now.

We watch the finale through to its foregone conclusion. Wyatt crushes Alexis's heart by proposing to Deb, and they ride off on horseback into the sunset.

"They broke up before the show even aired," Marina says, reading from her phone.

I snort. "Checks out." I stretch again, rotating my stiff ankles. "What an amazing show."

"It's got four more seasons," she says, clicking through the menu on-screen.

"Next time?" I ask.

"Definitely."

Marina grabs me a pillow and a blanket, something heavy, soft, and plaid, that I immediately snuggle underneath. The room is spinning when I close my eyes, and the last thing I remember before I fall asleep is the creaking sound of her going up the stairs.

That night, I dream about horses, and Nancy, and engagement rings, set against the backdrop of the last apple festival Marina and I attended. Except we're not fighting this time. There's only laughter, and caramel apples, and buried treasure, and it's the only part of the dream that makes any sense.

CHAPTER FOURTEEN

S TUDIO LIGHTS HAVE NO BUSINESS being this bright.
They press on me, pushing into view, eagerly latching
onto my throbbing headache. Putting a hand over my closed
eyes helps a little, but the nausea is another problem.

"Hey," Nancy hisses. Reluctantly, I open my eyes and wince
at the light. Nancy, sitting on her stool with perfect posture and
glossy hair, smooths down the front of her yellow sheath dress.
"Don't do that," she says. "You'll smear your makeup."

"I didn't even want makeup," I groan, pulling my hand away
from my face.

"Who was your favorite contestant on the *Love Quest* set?" asks
Marina, who's sitting on my other side. She takes a sip from her
coffee, making a slurping sound that pierces my brain. "We really
liked Alexis."

"Ugh," Nancy says, which makes Marina laugh so hard she
nearly falls off her stool.

I'd ask Marina how she's not dying of a hangover right now, but I already know the answer. This morning when she was flitting around her bedroom, pulling together possible outfits for us to wear on the show, she confessed that she still felt a little drunk.

So, as I sit glued to my stool of suffering, Marina babbles away to Nancy, asking endless questions about her *Love Quest* experience. I half listen to Nancy complain about a producer who was out to get her while the rest of me concentrates on staying upright.

At thirty seconds to air, it occurs to me that Marina and I haven't planned or rehearsed a thing. I cast a questioning look at Marina, trying to telepathically ask her what the hell we're going to say about the festival.

I start to voice the question, but my stomach roils as if an open mouth is all the invitation it needs to stage a violent upheaval. I clamp my mouth shut and try not to die.

Then Nancy is talking to the camera, greeting her viewers and telling them about the special guests she's brought today. It takes everything in my power to shift my expression into something resembling pleasant neutrality.

"I hear you have some exciting news," Nancy prompts, turning to us.

I can only blink at her in misery. In the silence, Nancy's eyes widen, shifting from friendly to threatening, but my mind is a dark void.

"We're bringing Greenstead's apple festival back to town," Marina announces, grinning like a natural. "There will be vendors and apples and all sorts of other things we haven't figured out yet. It'll be the weekend of October 11 in Juniper Park, permit willing."

"Great," Nancy says through bared teeth. "All my Nancies know eleven is *my* number, so what a *special date* you chose for your festival."

"I know, right?" Marina says breezily, completely missing the barb.

"Rest assured, Nancies, the Nancy convention will *also* be taking place at the festival. When they heard about our event, they insisted on making it part of the festival."

Nancy smiles sweetly at the camera. Marina, oblivious to Nancy's lie, stares curiously at the camera, as if the Nancies are hiding somewhere inside it.

Then Nancy fixes her gaze on me, sweet smile entirely gone. I instinctively flinch. "I've heard this festival is in collaboration with Ryser, is that correct? Don't you work for Ryser?"

"Yes," I say suspiciously. "It's…" I search my empty mind for the company-approved language. "Ryser's charity division, Ryser Cares." I pause and try to swallow past my nausea. "Sponsoring the festival is part of a long line of continued support Ryser Cares has offered Greenstead over the years." I end the statement on a whisper, fearful of how my body will react if I speak a decibel louder.

"It's interesting to hear you say that," Nancy says. "I'm not sure I see a 'long line' of support when I think about the disrepair Greenstead has fallen into since the mustard flood."

I inwardly groan. Or maybe it's an outward groan. I don't

know anymore. All I know is that I'm having trouble piecing together how this self-involved mean girl has turned into a hard-hitting journalist before my bleary eyes.

"I appreciate your perspective," I manage to lie. Thankfully, years of writing press releases and communications slide decks has made me well versed in Ryser's usual self-satisfied language. "Ryser has always believed in the power of community. We don't believe in quick fixes; we believe in long-term community empowerment. That's why Ryser Cares has been—" Then another wave of queasiness hits.

I go still, entirely at the mercy of my nausea. I close my mouth and try to ride out the wave.

Nancy and Marina watch me, waiting for a response. When it's clear they're not going to get one, Marina chimes in. "I think what Lauryn is saying is that Ryser Cares has been here in Greenstead ever since the flood—"

Factory malfunction, I want to correct, but I don't trust my stomach enough to open my mouth.

"Which is true," Marina continues. "But I totally see your point. It's not enough to just *be* here. We deserve more after the devastation Ryser's caused. Not just in Greenstead, either. Did you know they have a plastic pollution footprint of over fifty thousand tons a year?"

My stomach lurches in another threat, but I'm too busy staring at Nancy and Marina in horror.

This can't be real. Nancy Fletcher can't be an investigative journalist when just last night we were watching her splash her vodka soda in Deb's face for suggesting that her brassy hair, which had clearly been brightened with highlights, wasn't her natural color. And Marina can't be capable of spouting off environmental impact statistics on the fly while drunk. Nothing about today makes sense.

I imagine adding this to my weekly email update for Amanda. Not only does the apple festival feature Nancy Fletcher idolatry, but our first and only TV spot for this festival has turned to bad-mouthing its sponsor. If Amanda knew what was happening right now, my chances of returning to the DC office would shrink exponentially. My only comfort is the knowledge that a small town's local television show would never fall on Amanda's radar. She monitors major outlets and publications for media hits. *Wake Up with Nancy*, mercifully, has yet to rise to that level.

Marina's rant continues, revealing more about Ryser's atrocities, more statistics pulled out of thin air. Nancy nods along while I sit there with a smile glued on my face, desperately hoping to mind over matter my way past the nausea. As Marina shifts to detailing the ways Ryser has depleted the waterways of entire communities to source water for their billion-dollar plastic bottled water business, the churning in my stomach crawls up to my throat and I can't hold it back anymore.

On live television, I lean forward and vomit on Nancy's shoes.

"It could have gone worse," Marina says as we leave the studio.

The sun has thankfully cut me a break today, hiding behind clouds to leave the sky gray and overcast. I still have the heat and humidity to contend with, but it's better than blinding sunlight. The road in front of us is quiet and empty—no sign of our Lyft driver yet.

I lean against the brick wall behind me, searching for steadiness. It's a relief to be out from under the studio lights, but my mouth tastes like bile, my head is pounding, and my stomach is threatening a round two.

"Why would you say all that stuff?" I moan.

"What stuff?"

"About Ryser."

Marina frowns. "Nancy asked us a question."

"Okay, but you didn't have to answer it so thoroughly. You didn't have to use statistics and cite your sources like you're writing a research paper." I huff out a sigh and scan the road—still no Lyft. I look down at the polka-dotted cotton dress Marina lent me and pinch the fabric at my chest, flapping it back and forth to fan myself.

"So this is about Ryser?" Marina asks.

I close my eyes, still fanning. "It looks bad to criticize Ryser when you're there to talk about a Ryser-sponsored event. If my boss heard that, she'd—" I stop when I realize I don't know what Amanda could do. Demote me further? Is that even possible? "It looks bad," I say again. "It makes *me* look bad."

"Okay." Her voice is quieter. "I'm sorry. It wasn't on purpose. I was trying to say Greenstead deserves more, and how this festival was gonna help with that. But then I got sidetracked, and my heart started beating too fast. I think I drank too much coffee trying to sober up, and now I'm somehow groggy and overcaffeinated at the same time."

I blink my eyes open. Her expression is sincere, and her eyes do look bloodshot. "I guess neither of us was at our best," I concede.

"Besides, no matter how important Nancy thinks she is, I don't think anyone outside of Greenstead is gonna see this."

"Yeah." I force a chuckle, letting myself find reassurance in Marina's words. Joking about Nancy is familiar, comforting territory. I'll avoid mentioning this particular media hit when I update Amanda, and maybe this awful morning can stay between us. And Nancy. And her dozen Nancies. "I hope my boss isn't a Nancy, I guess. That's my only option at this point."

I mean to say it jokingly, but my worries must seep through, because it comes out snippier than I mean for it to. Going by the way Marina glances over at me, she seems to notice.

"If she *were* a Nancy, she'd have to care at least a *little* about Greenstead, so I think you're safe." Her tone is lighthearted, but I detect a sharpness in her words.

"What are you talking about? She gave us ten thousand dollars for the festival."

"For *good PR*," she corrects. When I scoff, Marina tilts her head, studying me. "Come on. She's a Ryser exec, right? You know they only care about PR."

"No, they don't!" I raise my voice louder than I mean to.

Marina sighs, rubbing a palm into her eyes. "I wasn't trying to start anything; I was just…" Her voice trails off. "Why does it matter to you what I say about Ryser? I've never understood your obsession with them."

"I'm not *obsessed* with them," I say with a roll of my eyes. "I just—"

I don't know how to say it. That if she disapproves of Ryser, it means she disapproves of me, because Ryser and I may as well be one and the same—and always *will* be for as long as I work there. Which won't be forever, of course. I want to tell her I'll do something good before I leave, that I won't be working there forever, if she can just wait a few years for me to show her. But I'm not sure I can make the words make sense.

"You just what?" Marina asks.

Something about her exasperated tone cuts at me. Like nothing I say will ever make sense to her.

"Nothing," I mumble. "Just…I don't need your judgment. If we're judging, there's a lot I could say about your mess of a house right now, but I won't."

"Wow," she says sarcastically. "Thanks. Then the next time you invite yourself over, I'll tell you you're not welcome."

"Good," I spit.

She huffs, I cross my arms, and we spend the remainder of our time aggressively avoiding eye contact until our Lyft driver thankfully slows to a stop in front of us.

We don't talk on the ride back to Marina's. When I follow Marina into her house, the scene we step into feels like it's from another time. The pizza box, the Häagen-Dazs wrappers, the bag of Doritos, the Raisinets and Sour Skittles, the almost-empty bottle of vodka. All reminders of how close we were a matter of hours ago, and how far apart we've managed to come since.

I change out of Marina's dress and back into my skirt and top from yesterday, when everything was different. Our goodbyes are terse and brief. We make no reference to the plans we made last night to watch more *Love Quest* in the future. I close the door behind me and sit in my car with resignation.

I can't bring myself to start the car just yet. I close my eyes and lean back against the headrest, steeling myself before I have to make the fifteen-minute drive home.

When my phone chirps with a notification, my first thought is that it's Marina, apologizing or reaching out with understanding.

Instead, I see someone has tagged me in a video. The clip of me throwing up on Nancy's show has made it to the internet. Amused comments are rolling in.

For the millionth time that day, I want to die.

GEORGETOWN
UNIVERSITY

F OR THE FIRST TIME SINCE our tradition began, the Greenstead Apple Festival has been canceled.

I sit at my desk reading the news, scrolling through the article that cites the Greenstead parks department's budget cuts and a lack of volunteers as the reason for the cancelation. A pang of disappointment runs through me. It never occurred to me that the festival could be canceled, especially with just a few days' notice. I was planning to go down to Greenstead this weekend. I told myself it was because I haven't missed the festival in over a decade. But a small part of me was holding onto the hope that if I showed up, Marina might be there too, and we might just find our way back together.

I reach for my phone and pull up my texts with Marina. The last text between us was from the day of last year's festival, a simple

Leaving now! My thumb drifts over the keyboard, tempted to tap out a new message, ask how she's taking the news, ask if she's as disappointed as I am, ask if she misses having a best friend, because I do. I have friends here, but no one like Marina. No one who shares my history, trades my soggy fries for her crispy ones, can make anything, even a Slap Chop informercial, the most entertaining thing in the world to watch. She's the best person I know, a beam of goodness who makes me want to try harder, be better.

Still my thumb remains frozen. Suppose she ignores the text? What if she's still mad about our fight, and that's why she hasn't reached out to me, either? What if she was hoping she wouldn't see me at the festival, and now she's relieved that it's canceled, that last tie between us severed for good?

The cancelation does make me feel like a line has been drawn, actually. Except it's not just with Marina. Greenstead as a whole is sending a message, closing itself off to me, telling me to stop looking back, because there is nothing left for me to go back to.

I wanted to leave Greenstead, didn't I?

Why go back?

I swallow and exit our text thread. I close out of the tab with the news article. And I vow to move forward, once and for all.

CHAPTER FIFTEEN

THE GEESE ARE LESS HOSTILE with me now. In the week that's passed since the incident on Nancy's show—which resulted in a video that now has forty thousand views and climbing—I think the geese have taken pity on me.

They don't chase me anymore. They just stand in their spot behind the planter and honk angrily, which I can take. It's basically the goose version of how Marina feels about me, I'm sure. She's kept a frosty distance from me and the Ryser Cares office since last week.

Our conversations have been stilted and work-related only. After we officially secured Juniper Park as the festival location, Marina came by the office yesterday to work on a presentation we're planning to give to Solar Summit today. Last weekend, when Tessa took me to Richmond for a tour of her favorite bakeries, she mentioned that if Solar Summit sponsored the festival, we could use the funds to solicit prominent local bakers and food critics to serve as judges for an apple pie–baking contest. The promise of prestigious judges and cash prizes for contest winners could help drum up attendance.

Even if Solar Summit doesn't go for the sponsorship, just getting them to advertise it to their audience would be a win. We need all the advertising help we can get, especially because Nancy's roundabout way of promoting the festival on her show involves prattling on about the Nancy convention, advising they bring ponchos in case "Queasy Lauryn" makes an appearance, and cutting to a still of me from the moment right before I threw up. *It was hilarious*, my dad said, because he has no sense of loyalty.

The morning of our meeting with Solar Summit, we all pile into Randy's van. On the drive to Falls Point, as I listen to Marina and Arun joke about the multiple fruit bouquets listed on the rider Nancy sent us this morning, the pit in my stomach reminds me how close Marina and I came to rekindling our friendship.

When we pull up to Solar Summit's corporate office, a nondescript building just outside the amusement park gates, my eyes gravitate to the roller coaster towering in the distance. I can just barely hear the delighted screams of its passengers as the coaster plummets down.

Marina slows to watch it when she steps out of the van. I wonder if she's thinking about all the times we've ridden that coaster over the years, all those summer memories drenched in ice-cold lemonade and dusted with funnel-cake powdered sugar. But her gaze leaves the roller coaster without a trace of longing.

More than once, I catch myself watching the coaster through the window during our meeting with the Solar Summit marketing team, a broad-shouldered man named Ted and a small, blond woman named Lucy. To Tessa's delight, Ted and Lucy exclaim over the pie contest idea. Before long, they agree to not only sponsor the festival but to include ad space for it on the Solar Summit website.

I know, logically, that this is more than we even hoped for. I see the pleased looks on Randy, Jen, Arun, and Tessa's faces, and I try to mirror them. But I just can't bring myself to be excited about it when Marina and I aren't talking—again.

"Looking forward to working together," Ted says, shaking our hands firmly at the end of the meeting. "We've been looking for more opportunities to partner with Greenstead."

"These are for you." Lucy presses something colorful into each of our palms.

I examine the ticket in my hand: a one-day pass to Solar Summit. A ticket to reliving every happy memory I've had here. Beside me, Tessa breaks into a smile that I can't help but mirror. Jen raises her eyebrows in interest. Arun nudges Randy and whispers something to him. Marina turns to stare out the window at the park with a wistful expression, but she doesn't say a word.

"What are we supposed to do with these?" Marina says once we reach the parking lot.

"Uh, go to the park, obviously," Arun replies. He points a thumb toward the park behind him. "Ready?"

"Hell yes," Tessa says.

I'm about to agree when Randy interrupts to say, "Hold on. If anyone doesn't want to go, I can drive you back."

"Who wouldn't want to go?" Tessa asks. When Randy tosses a pointed glance toward Marina—who's still staring at the ticket in her hand—an understanding passes over Tessa.

"I don't think I'm up for it," Marina says. She holds her ticket out to Arun. "You should give this to your niece."

It stings that she could give it away so easily, this ticket to so many memories we shared. Like she's decided this place that once meant so much to us is nothing. I'm suddenly overcome with a desire to rip up my ticket, toss the pieces into the sky and let the breeze carry them away. If Solar Summit doesn't mean anything to her anymore, why am I holding on to it?

"Yeah, me neither." I hold out my ticket too. "You can take your niece." When Arun just stares at my outstretched ticket like it's a bomb, I offer it to Randy instead. "Or give it to Jake," I say, naming the teen he's fostering.

"No," Arun says with more finality than I've ever heard from him. "Don't pretend you're doing us a favor."

Marina frowns. "I just thought you might enjoy coming here with your niece."

"I take Hannah to Solar Summit all the time. She's not old enough to go on any of the good rides. I've ridden Pony Chase and Dizzy Kittens enough for a lifetime—but I can't remember the last time I went on the Avalanche," he says, pointing at the tallest roller coaster behind him.

"Then go," Marina says. "No one's stopping you."

Arun tilts his head to the side with a sigh. "Look, I know

things have been weird between you two lately, but I don't care. We've spent all week working on this presentation—and we crushed it! We should celebrate that. Together."

Marina hesitates, her gaze drifting from Arun to the park behind him. His earnestness has me wanting to take back my reluctance and give in—but only if Marina does, too.

"Things aren't weird between us," Marina protests, but she averts her eyes when Arun scoffs.

"Then prove it," Tessa says. "Let's go in."

Another pause. Marina's looking down at her shoes. I silently will her to care enough about this, about me, to put our past behind us and stay.

"Okay," Arun says when Marina doesn't speak. "Then I don't want to go." Beside him, Tessa's face sinks into disappointment, and she mutters something I can't hear.

Randy pulls his keys from his pocket, ready to drive us back to the Ryser Cares office—the place where I'll spend the next two and a half months having stilted, obligatory festival planning conversations with Marina. As if that evening of giggles and horse jokes last week never happened.

I breathe in the sweet smell of fried dough wafting from the funnel-cake cart just past the gates. Leaning on our old traditions brought us together last week. It has to mean something that we're back here, at the place that shaped our childhood, holding these tickets. All we have to do is use them.

"No, we should go," I say, glancing at Marina. "All of us."

The distant screams of joy sound again. Marina lifts her head to watch the roller coaster race along its tracks.

"Well…" Marina says. "I haven't had a peach cobbler funnel cake in forever."

"I wouldn't say no to a lemonade," Jen says.

Arun's grin is infectious. Together, the six of us walk through the parking lot, cross the street toward the Solar Summit entrance, and hand in our day passes.

I spin around, taking in the familiar sights and new changes. The colorful coaster tracks are the same, looping impossibly through the sky. The funnel-cake stand by the entrance has its same menu of flavors. But there's a ride I don't remember seeing before, something lime-green and steep called the Raging Cyclone. And when a man walks by carrying what looks like a burrito bowl, I gawk at the lettuce and bell peppers in disbelief. It's strange to see fresh vegetables within the walls of this park that, as far as I can remember, has only ever sold foods that are either deep-fried, full of sugar, or both at once.

I haven't been here since the tail end of my senior year of high school. Grad night, an after-hours, seniors-only trip to Solar Summit at the end of the school year, was tradition for most high schools in the surrounding area. While Marina and I had been to Solar Summit together easily over a dozen times, there was something especially magical about being here late at night, when the park was open to only us students for five precious hours, from 9:00 p.m. to 2:00 a.m. The lines for all the rides were short, and the air was electric with adrenaline and possibility.

The memory plucks a string in my heart. If nothing else, we have this: one more day here at the park before we return to our separate lives.

"What should we ride first?" Tessa asks.

Arun points to the one right in front of us. "The Speed Racer?"

"Sure," she agrees.

"Hold on," Marina says. "Shouldn't we talk strategy?"

"Strategy?" Jen repeats.

"For…roller coasters?" Arun asks.

Marina glances at me for backup. The glint in her eyes ignites a spark in me. "I'll get the map," I announce.

"Strategy meeting, picnic table, two minutes," Marina says to the others. At Arun's groan, I share a smile with Marina before darting off to the information booth. For the first time all day—all week—something feels right.

Two minutes later, we're sitting at a table with the Solar Summit map open in front of us. "We start with the Avalanche because of the short line," Marina says, circling it with her pen. "Then I say we hit up all the good coasters that usually have long lines. It's…" She checks the time on her phone. "Eleven o'clock on a Wednesday, so we can take advantage of weekday lulls."

"And when we finish the last intense coaster," I say, circling every roller coaster with high intensity ratings, "we can take a break for a light lunch, and then we'll move on to the less intense ones, like the Frozen Tundra."

"Yes," Marina says, pointing at me with her pen. She draws a square around those next, then puts a number beside each shape to note our order of operations.

We carry on like this, plotting our approach around the park based on the time of day, busy times, phases of the moon. This is exactly what we've done every time we've come here. A calculated, methodical plan of attack while our parents sigh in boredom.

"Itinerary look good?" Marina asks, holding up our annotated map, now inked with circles, squares, triangles, numbers, and asterisks.

"I don't even know what I'm looking at," Tessa says.

Arun squints at the map for several long seconds, then shrugs. "I'll go wherever you tell me to go."

"It's perfect," I decide.

With a somber nod, Marina folds the map, and we head off toward our first roller coaster of the day.

———————

The day passes in flashes of adrenaline-fueled joy.

There's the moment the Avalanche finishes its slow, clicking climb to the top, when I look over my row and take in Marina's wide-eyed anticipation and Tessa's grin—and then the coaster plunges downward to the sound of Arun's whoop, Randy's frightened scream, and Jen's laughter.

Or when we're all clustered into our kitten-shaped vehicle on Dizzy Kittens, a new ride that tempted me even though it was clearly designed for five-year-olds, and Arun is the only one who isn't turning the wheel in the center because he's too busy crossing his arms and muttering that this wasn't on the itinerary.

Our laughter when we spot our picture at the booth displaying the on-ride photos from Python's Revenge and see that, amid our wide smiles and gaping mouths, Tessa is yawning, as though two-hundred-foot drops are a bore.

The warm feeling I get a moment later when, as Randy and Marina are joking about what else Tessa would probably yawn her way through—skydiving, bungee jumping, tightrope walking—I turn to my right and see that Jen has quietly crept up to the register to purchase the photo. It makes me study the image for a little longer, seeing it in a new light—not an overpriced souvenir, but a memory to cherish. The first and only photo of the six of us together, a perfect snapshot of this day that started with a presentation and pivoted into something unexpected. And it means enough to Jen that she wants to buy it.

It's the first time it occurs to me that we might be something more than a group of people with a shared office and a collective goal. The thought—that image—stays with me for the rest of the afternoon, through cheese fries and snow cones and our last scheduled ride of the day.

As four o'clock approaches, Randy checks his watch and says we should head back. Jen, Tessa, and Arun murmur in agreement, but I'm rooted to the spot. Leave the most magical place in the world? While it's still daylight? Marina and I always stayed to see the fireworks show.

A flicker of hesitation passes over Marina, and I wonder if she's thinking the same thing.

I take a breath of hope. "I'm gonna stay for the fireworks," I announce. My words come out more certain than I am, like watching fireworks alone is something I do all the time. My eyes drift over to her, waiting for a response.

"I'm afraid I can't stay that long," Randy says. "You'd have to find your own way back."

"That's okay," I say cheerily, even though my hopes are wilting with every passing second. Marina isn't even looking at me. She's staring somewhere off in the distance.

Randy turns to the rest of the group. "Everyone ready?"

"I'll stay too," Marina blurts out.

"O-okay," Randy says, starting to sound like he's getting tired of our abrupt announcements. "Have fun." The group gives us parting waves before they turn for the exit, and then it's just Marina and me left to stare awkwardly at each other while carousel music plays in the distance.

Questions fight through the daze in my head—why she decided to stay, what it means, what we're going to do next since the fireworks don't start for another five and a half hours. All that comes out is a disbelieving, "You're staying?"

"Yeah," Marina says, a small smile perking up the edge of her mouth. "It doesn't feel right unless we stay for fireworks."

That *we* makes my hopes skyrocket. "What do you wanna do until then?"

She quirks a brow. "Second itinerary?"

"Second itinerary," I agree.

We fall right back into that sunshine-soaked magic we've been drinking in all afternoon. We take a seat at a picnic table and pore over our creased, inked-up map, charting out new courses to fill the rest of the day. Another round of rides ordered from highest to lowest intensity, a break for dinner at eight, and then we'll acquire a peach cobbler funnel cake and pick out a spot on the pavilion to watch the fireworks show.

It's a perfect plan. I don't dare bring up our fight outside

Nancy's studio, or Ryser, or anything that could break this spell. As long as we're here, retracing our old steps, there's no need. I let those words stay unsaid, and I follow her to line up for the Avalanche.

———————

There's something about spending an entire day riding roller coasters that makes a fireworks show especially enchanting.

Marina and I sit on the Solar Summit's grassy pavilion, on top of the overpriced towel we bought from the gift shop, and stare up at the colorful fireworks exploding in the night sky. I use my plastic fork to break off a piece of the peach cobbler funnel cake sitting between us and pop it into my mouth in bliss. The funnel cake is airy and crunchy, but it's the caramel peach topping that makes it, bringing a fruity freshness with a drizzle of decadence.

"Somehow we never did figure out how to make caramel right," Marina says, using her fork to scoop up some of the caramel pooled at the bottom of the plate.

I laugh, remembering our homemade caramel apple attempts from those years after Lettie retired. "Too thin the first time; glued to the pot the second time."

"Did we try a different recipe after that? I vaguely remember you sending me one."

I study the tines of my fork. I *had* sent her a recipe sometime in spring semester, something I came across on Pinterest that promised to be foolproof. But that was before the summer internship debacle, before the fight that left me standing in Juniper Park without a best friend.

Marina, clearly, hasn't made the connection. She's drinking from her novelty Solar Summit cup, tapping her foot in time to the jaunty organ music coming from the carousel. Reminding her about our fight would dredge all that history back up and ruin the carefree mood we've fallen into today.

But maybe this is the best time to bring it up. Our day of coaster-riding is behind us, that laughter and lightness cemented in amber. Here, in the dark, where we're looking at the sky instead of each other, might be the most opportune moment to talk about our friendship and hopefully open the door to becoming friends again.

With a bravery bolstered by funnel cake, lemonade, and fireworks, I venture, "I sent a recipe, but we never made it. That was the year we stopped talking." I keep my eyes on the fireworks when I say this.

Marina doesn't speak for a moment. Then, in a voice that's quiet and small, she asks, "What happened? How'd we go from best friends to…" She doesn't complete the thought.

I watch a firework burst into blue sparkles. I can't look at her as I say, "You didn't want to be my friend anymore."

"What?" I can feel Marina's eyes on me. "You didn't want to be *my* friend anymore."

I lower my gaze to face her. Her brow is wrinkled, eyes searching. She doesn't look mad. Just confused. "You said, 'I'm done,' and left me standing there by the cotton candy booth," I remind her.

"Yes, because *you* ditched me at the accounting office for an entire summer. We had all those plans, and you just…left."

The hurt in her voice is raw and pronounced, like she's recalling something that happened just yesterday.

A pang of guilt stabs at me. "I wasn't trying to ditch you; I just... Being in that office made me feel like I was suffocating. And then I got the call from Ryser offering me their internship, and it felt like the only way to escape. I was escaping the *internship*. Not you."

"Then why didn't you tell me when you were back in Greenstead at the end of the summer?"

My heart thuds harder. "What do you mean?"

I returned to Greenstead to visit my dad for the two weeks between the end of my internship and the start of the next semester, but I never texted her to let her know I was back in town. I lay low, hanging around the house, watching TV with my dad, doing puzzles, and hiding from Marina. I kept seeing her disappointed face in my head from that moment when I told her I was leaving to intern at Ryser. I didn't have the nerve to face her. Though I'm not sure how she could have known.

"I saw you," Marina says. "I was at Food Lion, and I saw you and your dad getting groceries. You came home, and you didn't even want to see me."

An ache grips me at the image of Marina standing in Food Lion, watching my dad and me check peaches for ripeness, and feeling betrayed.

"I *did*," I insist. "But I knew I'd disappointed you, and I–I couldn't face it."

"Because I'm self-righteous and no one wants to be my friend," she murmurs.

"*No.* I shouldn't have said that."

"I shouldn't have called you selfish."

A low laugh leaves me. I didn't realize until now how badly I wanted this, for her to take that word back, tell me I'm not an awful person. But now that she's finally done it, it doesn't feel like it could possibly be true.

"I am, though," I admit.

"No, you're not. Would a selfish person plan a charity festival?"

Yes, I can't stop myself from thinking. Yes, I would, if I was doing it to get my old job back.

But I don't want to think about that. I certainly don't want to admit to it. I just want to keep sitting here, on this overpriced towel, while Marina tells me the things I've always wanted to hear.

"I don't think you're selfish," she says. "I'm sorry I ever said that."

"I'm sorry about what I said. I'm sorry about not telling you when I was back in Greenstead at the end of the summer. It wasn't that I didn't want to see you. I just felt bad about letting you down."

"Yeah, well." She swallows and looks down at her shoes, playing with a shoelace. "That summer was the start of kind of a rough period for me. I thought my best friend was done with me. That internship was *so* boring. And the next semester just got shittier. We had that stupid fight. I started seeing someone who dumped me out of the blue. I came close to flunking a course and almost losing my scholarship. I was thinking about dropping out and living at home. Everything just got to be too much, and—"

"I wasn't there," I finish, wincing at the realization. Marina shrugs in silent acknowledgment. "You never told me."

"I didn't think I needed to," she replies quietly.

I think back to my sophomore year. I was preoccupied with my classes, deciding on a major, being so excited to be out of Greenstead and in a new city—a city I didn't want to leave.

"You posted less on social media," I recall. Marina's posts were so prolific our freshman year of college: anecdotes about life on campus, pictures of coffee cups with captions about late-night study sessions, group photos with her dorm mates. Just as I was eager to head to Georgetown and lose myself in a big city, Marina took comfort in the fact that her university, William & Mary, was on the smaller side, complete with a small-town tranquility that made her feel at home. One day, she'd post a photo of herself outside a blacksmith shop in Colonial Williamsburg; the next, a scenic view of a marsh-filled hiking trial on Jamestown Island. She was happy, or so I thought.

There did come a point when she was posting less, and less, and less. But at the time, I thought she'd just gotten swept up into her own life, much in the same way I had. I thought she'd finally seen the beauty of life outside Greenstead and was clinging to it as tightly as I was.

"I'm sorry," I say. "I should have reached out to you. I was just so in my own head about things, and thinking you were still mad at me, that it felt easier to ignore it all." I pull my knees up to my chest and turn to face Marina. "Do you want to talk about it now? What you were going through?"

Marina loops a shoelace around her finger, winding it and

unwinding it. "Nothing all that unique," she says with self-deprecating laugh. "It was partly feeling isolated because I lost touch with my old dorm mates. They all got places together and I had to dorm with random freshmen. And the rest of it was having an identity crisis. At nineteen," she says, rolling her eyes. "I went in thinking I was going to major in music, but I hated it. I kept trying to love it, but that just made me hate myself for not loving it. I failed a class, I got depressed, my mom made me see a therapist, and that helped me figure things out. I dropped music, took an education class on a whim, and I found my way again." She meets my gaze. "But I still missed my best friend."

"I missed you too," I murmur. How easy it would have been, to pick up the phone and give her a call. To stop thinking about my own insecurities and realize my best friend needed me. "I'm sorry I wasn't a better friend," I say. "But...I'd like to be, now."

"Thanks," Marina says quietly. "I'd like that, too."

"So we can be friends again?" I ask, hope rising in my chest. "For real?"

When Marina nods, I reach over and pull her into a hug, and she squeezes my shoulders in kind. It's freeing to not have to limit myself to polite social convention anymore. To know that I can squeeze her with all my might, enough to pull a groan out of her. That if I can't hear her, I don't have to restrict myself to the usual two *whats* to avoid awkwardness as I do for strangers and acquaintances. I can ask her to repeat herself all day long until I understand her, and she'll do it. Such are the laws of best friendship, and we're finally beholden to them again.

"I'm sorry I went off about Ryser on Nancy's show," Marina says when we pull away.

"You were drunk," I remind her.

"Yeah, but I could have stopped myself if I'd thought about it. Ryser doesn't seem that bad if they're willing to help out with the festival. And I trust your judgment."

I let out a dark laugh. "I don't know if you should."

"Too bad," Marina says, elbowing me in the side, "because I do."

That's something I need to absorb for a second, the notion that Marina trusts me. I certainly don't. But I decide to take her at her word. I want to slip her comment in my pocket like a stone and rub it smooth every time I need a reminder that someone believes in me.

"I'm sorry I got mad at you," I say. "You were just saying what you feel. I can't blame you for the way you feel about Ryser."

"I can't blame you for believing in them," Marina replies.

A quiet peace settles over us. We lie back and watch the fireworks for a while longer. We finish off the funnel cake, and the taste transports me right back to every time I've been here, nearly all of them with Marina. The laughter, the roller-coaster-induced exhilaration, the unbridled joy that feels so alien to me now.

"I can't remember the last time I had this much fun," I say, staring up at the sky.

Marina turns to me. "Really?" She asks it in the way she has where she's clearly trying to be subtle. "Isn't DC supposed to be, like, *way* more fun than Greenstead?" The light mockery in her tone makes me smile. I'm sure I was insufferable when I was rambling to her about the wonders of DC my freshman year of college.

I stick my tongue out at her. "It is."

"Then why aren't you having fun?"

"No one to have fun with," I say with a shrug.

"No friends?"

I busy myself by using my fork to scoop up a stray strand of leftover funnel cake. "I have a work friend or two." Which is a bit of a stretch. Selma's my only actual work friend. I'm not sure who else I'd count. Bill, maybe. That's a sad thought.

"And outside of work?" Marina asks.

I shrug again. "I've just been focused on working hard and retiring early. I can have fun when I'm forty."

"Did you ever adopt a dog?"

That was all I talked about as a kid. I wasn't allowed to have a dog growing up because my dad was allergic, so I fantasized endlessly about adopting one as soon as I was old enough to live on my own. I was drawn to their sweet temperaments, their playful energy, wet noses, wagging tails. Dogs don't care if you're awkward, or if you mishear their bark as a woof. Dogs are pure joy. And I do *want* that joy. Just not when I'm living in an apartment the size of a matchbox.

"Not yet," I reply. "But as soon as I move to a bigger place, I will." I keep my words light, hoping Marina will cut the line of questioning. But she's not done yet.

"Do you…date?"

Concentrating on straightening the tines of the plastic fork in my hand, I say, "I can date when I'm forty." I toyed with dating apps in my early twenties, until right in the thick of the palm oil controversy, I met someone who was interning at a legal office that was suing Ryser. We'd gotten along so well up until I learned that fact, exchanging easy banter and accidental-on-purpose nudges under the table. But as soon as he dropped that comment about doing research for a case against Ryser, I clammed up. What was I thinking, dating an environmental lawyer in training while I was practically abusing orangutans for a paycheck? How could I justify that?

After that, I spoke about my job only in vague terms, and we dated for another couple of months. But the banter didn't feel easy anymore. I spent too much time in my head, overthinking my every word, until finally I broke it off and swore off dating until I could be someone I was proud of. That hasn't happened yet.

"If that's what you want to do," Marina says after a pause. "Sounds kind of lonely to me."

She's not wrong, but I don't tell her that. "Are *you* lonely?" I ask, turning the focus on her.

She runs a finger along the plastic sun on her Solar Summit cup. "Sometimes, I guess."

"I saw a save-the-date in your room," I say carefully. "I didn't know you and Jess were engaged."

Marina swallows. "Yeah, we broke things off last year. But we're moving on."

I have to stop myself from smirking. "I don't know if either of you has moved on. From the way I saw Jess looking at you at the mayor's office, they definitely have *not* moved on."

Marina dips her head, but not before I catch her smiling into her cup. "Shut up."

So I do.

We continue to lie there, drink our lemonade, take in the dazzling magic of the fireworks above, and bask in the joy of friendship renewed.

CHAPTER SIXTEEN

I

T'S NOT LONG BEFORE ANOTHER unfortunate ripple effect emerges from my appearance on Nancy's show.

The week after the Solar Summit excursion, the *Washington Chronicle* publishes an article titled "Ryser's Throwing a Festival to Pay for Its Mistakes. Is It Enough?"

I scroll through it while I'm standing in line at Pretzel in Paradise waiting for our office's order to be ready. The article paints the festival as a calculated move on Ryser's part to distract from the backlash they're getting for their latest disaster. It points out that, just one day before Marina and I went on Nancy's show, an advocacy group filed a lawsuit against Ryser for illegally treating contaminated water and passing it off as natural mineral water.

The article ends with an ominous line: "In a way, it's chillingly apt that Ryser representative Lauryn Harper would vomit on Greensteader Nancy Fletcher's show. Ryser's biggest mark on Greenstead was, after all, a similarly uncontrolled deluge. In vomiting on television, Ms. Harper is sending a message loud and clear: Ryser isn't finished ruining this town yet."

Using my hangover humiliation as a metaphor for Ryser's transgressions seems like a bit of a stretch. Other than that, though, the article is fairly standard. It's common for journalists to put out Ryser exposés from time to time, reminding people about its shady past and present. But it always blows over. People may read it, get outraged, and decide to boycott Ryser products—until they realize just how much Ryser dominates supermarket aisles. Switching from Ryser-branded potato chips to Katz still benefits Ryser in the end. As Marina tragically discovered two years into her Ryser boycott, Ryser owns Katz. And a thousand other brands.

I can only hope Amanda sees it this way. But a slow sense of dread starts building inside me. That notion that comforted me before, about Nancy's show not being on Amanda's radar, holds less weight now it's been published in a newspaper Amanda definitely subscribes to. Any moment now, Amanda's going to read the article, watch the clip, hear Marina's rant, and ask how I could have let someone bad-mouth Ryser without putting a stop to it. (Though perhaps she'll be grateful my throwing up distracted from it. I wouldn't mind pretending that was a strategic move.)

When I don't hear from Amanda that day, the feeling lessens, and I start to think she's unbothered after all. That all changes the next day, when I see her name light up my phone. A wave of panic crashes over me. She hasn't called me once since my demotion. It's no coincidence that she's calling now, the day after the article came out.

Still, I let the phone buzz for a few seconds longer. Let her think about how hard I've been working. It might have been difficult to give off that impression last month, when the sounds of Jen watching *Love Island* and Arun and Randy playing air hockey filled the office. But that's all changed now. Right this moment, Arun's using the whiteboard to figure out where to put the apple cider dunk tank. Tessa's on the phone with the owner of a DC bakery, inviting him to serve as a judge for the festival's pie-baking contest—and from the enthusiasm in her voice, it's going well. Randy's on a call with a potential portable restroom supplier, negotiating for a lower price. And Jen is picking up lunch for us all. That moment on Nancy's show doesn't change the fact that I've been completely dedicated to Ryser and this project. That has to count for something.

I let the phone buzz one more time before I answer. "Hello," I say cautiously.

"What was that stunt you pulled on that show?" Amanda asks. "That's not what we agreed on."

Her chilly tone fires off a warning signal in my brain. A chilly Amanda is never a good sign. She doesn't yell when angry; she gets cold and terse.

"I don't think throwing up on TV is what anyone agreed on," I say, forcing a laugh. "I was only there because I owed Nancy a favor, but we used it as an opportunity to plug the festival. I talked up Ryser for sponsoring it," I venture weakly. The long pause that follows confirms that her issue isn't what I did. It's what Marina said.

"What about your friend?" Amanda says. "How do you

think it looks for a Ryser employee to stand by while someone tries to damage our reputation? I'll tell you how it looks," she carries on, "because that article in the *Washington Chronicle* lays it all out there. Have you read it?"

"Yes. It was…a bit of a stretch." I'm still thinking of that stupid vomit metaphor.

"It was damning," Amanda says firmly. "And now we're getting calls from *Newsweek*, *Business Insider*, ABC. People think we're trying to use the festival to cover up the contaminated water debacle."

"But we're not," I say, twisting a pen around in my hand. "It'll blow over." This is what we tell ourselves when we've exhausted all other options. We craft the statements, issue the press releases, plant the fluff pieces, and then we sit back and say, *It'll blow over*. And it usually does.

But when Amanda doesn't say it back, I realize she has something else in mind.

"It's time for me to take over," she says.

"Take over?"

"Remember what I told you? At the awards night?"

This goddamn mystery has been haunting me for too long. "No," I say slowly.

Amanda sighs. "I said it'd be good to have the festival in our pocket in case we need it, remember? In case Ryser makes headlines again and we need a way to spin it? You agreed that if something came up, I'd take lead on strategy."

I go still. I try to remember the gibberish I'd heard, now that I can put it into context.

Hazmat inner rocket. Lee done scatter bee.

Have that in our pocket. Lead on strategy.

Amanda was always going to use this festival as a secret weapon, something to keep on standby the next time Ryser came under fire. When that happened, she would take over.

"Now that this festival is getting national attention," she continues, "I'm going to need to have a say in how it's run. It has to have the right messaging. If people think we're doing this festival in response to the lawsuit, we need to be very careful about how we position it."

I set my pen down and sit up straighter. "So we're going to be working together again?" I try to sound nonchalant, but a thread of hope sneaks through my words.

"On this," Amanda says, "yes."

"Okay. Great!" Already my mind is racing. This is the best possible outcome. Amanda's handed me a perfect opportunity to remind her of all the reasons why I deserve to get my old job back.

Amanda tells me she'll send a meeting invitation for a standing weekly call. I never thought I'd be so excited to hear the word *meeting* again. When we hang up, I look around the office grinning like an idiot.

Arun turns to me, marker still in hand. "What is it?" he asks, his voice wary.

"That was my old boss. She wants to be involved in festival planning."

This earns skeptical looks from my colleagues. Arun caps his marker, Randy puts his call on hold, and Tessa keeps her eyes on me while she wraps up her call. They don't stop staring until Jen comes through the door, a paper bag full of sandwiches from Toasty's in her hand.

"What's going on?" Jen asks, setting the bag on the air hockey table.

"Lauryn's old boss at corporate suddenly wants to work with us on the festival," Arun says.

"Because she knows we're doing great things," I fill in.

"Because of the article," Randy guesses.

I give a shrug that they all see right through. Tessa groans. Arun sighs. And I don't let it faze me. "This is a good thing," I say. "Corporate has our back. We'll have more resources."

"Corporate's calling the shots," Arun corrects. "There's a difference."

I shake my head. "Amanda's chill. She's smart. It's gonna be great. She just wants to have a call with us once a week to check in, and that's it."

Another round of groans.

"When's the call?" Jen asks.

I check my email for the meeting invitation that's just come through. "Monday at 9:00 a.m.," I say as casually as I can.

Tessa boos me. But I just laugh and collect my sandwich. They may not see it yet, but this is the start of something good. This is the start of getting my old life back.

When Monday morning rolls around, I get to the office half an hour early.

I bring in donuts, put on a pot of coffee, and connect my laptop to the monitor in the meeting room in the back for the first time ever. I make sure the camera's working okay. I smooth a hand over my hair, pull down the hem of my dressiest flutter-sleeve top to make sure it's centered, run a finger along the neckline to check for visible bra straps. Then I watch the clock and wait for nine. It's the first Monday in August, our first meeting with Amanda. It feels like my first day of work all over again. Like the world is full of promise.

My coworkers trickle in a few minutes before nine, yawning and making a beeline for the coffeepot. They cheer up when they see the donuts on the table, but uncertainty lingers on their faces when I click the link to join the meeting.

It starts off fine. Amanda asks what we've done for the festival so far, and we go around the table giving updates. She nods approvingly as we walk through the logistics. Arun's voice is full of confidence when he answers her questions about the festival location.

"Wonderful," Amanda says, dipping her head down to make a note of something. "What about sponsors? Who have you gotten so far?"

We share a look around the table.

"Well, Ryser," I say. "And Solar Summit."

There's a pause. Amanda's expression shifts from patient to concerned. "That's it?"

My eyes drop to the notebook in front of me, as if I can magically summon a response to earn her approval. Just getting Ryser and Solar Summit to sponsor the festival felt like the biggest wins we could manage. What other company around here would have the funds to spare for this sort of thing? Even Pretzel in Paradise, the most popular shop in town, isn't immune from financial realities. Meg keeps fairly limited hours because she can't afford any more hired help beyond the one other employee she has.

"Yes," I admit.

"I think there's plenty of opportunity to go for more. You know, I'm going to that wellness innovation conference in a couple of weeks since we've been trying to branch out into the personal care space. I can see if anyone I talk to there might want to sponsor the festival. We'll be talking to some companies about potential partnerships. Deodorant, foot fungus, toothpaste, diaper cream."

"As sponsors for an apple festival?" Randy asks, alarm growing across his face.

"We want to have a healthy promotion budget so we can raise interest and draw a crowd, right? Your budget's very small compared to what we'd typically do."

"We didn't have a lot of funds to work with," Arun says pointedly.

"Speaking of the budget," I rush to say before Amanda can comment on Arun's bristled tone, "you make a good point, Amanda. But now that Ryser's getting more involved, would you be able to allocate more funds from your budget?"

Amanda gives the hum she uses when someone volunteers an idea she doesn't like. "I may have to, if it comes down to it. But let's focus on the sponsorships for now. It'll save us some money. And it wouldn't hurt for Ryser to be seen aligning with some trusted brands right about now," she adds with a chuckle.

"Right," I say, faking a laugh back.

Amanda looks down at her list. "And it has to be an apple festival? Like I said, we are trying to break into the personal care space. If this was a 5K, it would tie in a lot better with our new line of antioxidant sunscreen."

In the silence that follows, Tessa, Randy, Jen, and Arun all exchange worried glances.

The temptation to say yes and win Amanda's approval rises inside me. I start imagining the logistics of pivoting from apple festival to 5K. Ryser Cares used to hold fundraising 5Ks all the time, so this would be part of Greenstead's history too, sort of. The vendors could still exhibit their booths. A pretzel from Meg's and an ice-cold lemonade from the popcorn cart would be the perfect post-race refreshment. Though I'm not sure how many runners come away from a race wanting a jalapeño-popper burger from Prime Burger or a slice of salted peanut butter pie from Cooper Cakes—which, while delicious, always leaves me thirsty. And I can't quite picture a crowd of hot, sweaty runners crossing the finish line and stopping to sniff artisan candles, peruse handmade jewelry, or check out any of the other miscellaneous booths that don't quite match up with a 5K.

Seeing Tessa, Randy, Jen, and Arun's mounting concern brings me back down to reality. We can't make such a drastic change after we've already sold people on the concept of reinstating a beloved apple festival. I know Marina would be horrified to hear that I even entertained the thought. I remember her words at Solar Summit, so confident and sincere: *I trust your judgment.*

"It has to be an apple festival," I say. Tessa lets out a relieved sigh.

"Okay." Amanda marks something off her list. "Can you tell me about the vendors you have so far?"

That puts us back on less worrisome ground. We dive into a rundown of local businesses, and Amanda listens and takes notes. But when Jen mentions that a history buff has signed up to do a booth on the history of Greenstead, Amanda narrows her eyes.

"Will it involve the factory malfunction?" she asks.

"The flood," Jen corrects. Amanda stares at her blankly, as though her brain is incapable of processing the word *flood*. "Yes, it will include the malfunction," Jen mumbles, giving in. "It's part of Greenstead's history."

"No," Amanda says at once, "we're not doing that."

Jen presses her lips together tightly, but she doesn't argue.

"You know what we could do instead," Amanda says, perking up with an idea. "We'll put a history spin on the Ryser booth. It could have a monitor displaying the history of Ryser, our volunteer work, our contributions."

"The Ryser booth?" I repeat.

"Of course. It'll sell the usual favorites. Our mini apple pies are always a hit."

"Uh…Cooper's Cakes will be selling apple pies," Tessa points out.

Amanda nods patiently. "That's fine."

"But wouldn't it be kind of messed up for Ryser to compete with a local business?" Tessa says.

"Oh, nobody's competing," Amanda replies with a dismissive laugh. "If people see Ryser at a food festival, they're going to expect their favorite Ryser foods. The last thing we want to do is disappoint people."

"That's ironic," Tessa mutters. The others titter. I peek at the screen to see if Amanda heard, but she's busy jotting something down.

Then Amanda moves to the next item on her list. "What is a Nancy convention, and what does that have to do with the festival?"

Ignoring Arun's stifled laugh, I explain, "Oh, Nancy Fletcher's a…"—god help me—"local celebrity. Including a meet and greet for her fans at the festival is a great way to get buzz and draw more people to the event." This version sounds much more impressive than *A delusional ex-reality-show-contestant held Juniper Park hostage until we agreed to her demands.*

Amanda makes a skeptical hum. "This was the woman whose show you were on? Who was bad-mouthing Ryser? Do we really want to be associated with her? She's got a fairly unflattering picture of you on her website, by the way."

"I know," I say darkly. My dad already showed me the page with the caption contest Nancy's running. Above that same unsightly still of me looking nauseous on her show, the page reads: *What's Queasy Lauryn thinking? Funniest caption wins two free tickets to the Nancy convention!*

The worst part: My dad's spent the last week workshopping possible captions with Wendy.

Still, as much as Nancy irritates me, we did make a deal. Going back on it feels slimy. "We already made an agreement."

"Send me the agreement," Amanda says. "I'm sure we can work something out."

"It was more of a…handshake deal," Arun says.

Amanda brightens. "Then it's nonbinding. Perfect! The Nancy convention is out."

My heart drops. As awful as Nancy may be, I hate the thought of her and her Nancies being ousted, crossed off a list, just like that.

I notice, as the meeting goes on, that the others are speaking less and less. By the time the call comes to an end, Amanda and I are the only ones who have spoken in the last ten minutes. The others are statues. They glance up at the screen every once in a while, but otherwise they drink their coffee, sweep up donut crumbs with a napkin, or stare listlessly ahead at nothing.

When we sign off the call, it seems like all the air has been sucked out of the room.

"That wasn't so bad," I try. I aim for upbeat, but my voice comes out questioning.

The others don't respond.

Normally, the office has a relaxed atmosphere, loose with idle chatter. But the silence only grows louder once we're all sitting at our desks. No sounds of typing, phone calls about festival logistics, ideas being tossed out, updates from Jen about who's engaging with our festival account on social media. We just sit on our computers, occasional mouse clicks or keystrokes breaking up the overwhelming quiet.

And the first shred of doubt plants in my gut as I start to suspect that working with Amanda might not be such a good thing for us after all.

CHAPTER SEVENTEEN

As August goes on, our weekly calls with Amanda become something to dread.

I still relish the opportunity to remind her I exist, show her what a valuable asset I am, and hopefully plant the idea in her head of me returning to work on her team. But I hate seeing what it does to my coworkers—to hear their ideas shot down, see them speak less and less in meetings, watch the baffled yet defeated looks they exchange whenever Amanda raises a suggestion that clashes horrifically with the premise of the apple festival.

Most recently, it was pondering aloud if we could add the slogan for Ryser's new antioxidant sunscreen as a tagline under all festival marketing materials. But I managed to politely point out that *Greenstead Apple Festival: Shield against sun damage with the power of antioxidants* might send a misleading message about the UV protection abilities of apples.

It's always a relief when the Monday morning meeting comes

to an end and the atmosphere of our little office returns to that casual, relaxed state once again. It's all the more fun on this particular Monday: We're going on a field trip. In hopes of ensuring that our only sponsors aren't diaper rash cream and foot fungus products—which aren't confirmed yet, but every Monday we fear Amanda will announce she's secured FootHeal First as an official sponsor—we've taken it upon ourselves to seek out local sponsors to balance out the mix.

And when Bertram Mason, owner of Greenstead's apple orchard, told us he'd be delighted to not only continue the tradition of being the festival's official apple provider but also serve as a sponsor, it seemed like a perfect fit. Before long, Bertram invited us down to the farm to see his orchard, taste his apples, and talk sponsor logistics in person.

Which is how Arun, Tessa, Randy, Jen, Marina, and I find ourselves seated at a picnic table on his farm overlooking the orchard. A large umbrella above us mercifully shields us from the sun's glare, though the humidity remains stifling. Bertram doesn't seem to notice it as he gives a thorough history lesson about each of his thirteen apple varieties and passes bowls of apple slices around for us to taste.

"Doesn't this taste exactly like the last one?" Tessa whispers.

Marina, Jen, and Arun stifle their laughs while Randy tells Bertram he can absolutely pick up on the subtle grassy notes of the apple skin.

Bertram passes around a Ginger Gold after talking about its distinct sharp flavor. With its yellowish hue and faint blush, I can *see* that it looks different from the last apple, but I can't taste anything remotely sharp. From the concentration on Marina's face, neither can she. Her eyes rove around, as if she's trying to make her palate detect the sharpness through sheer force of will.

"I can't tell you how much it means to have this festival back," Bertram says. "I'd been going to that festival every year since I was a kid, until it stopped. There's nothing else like it. This is a really special thing y'all are doing, I gotta say." He lifts his blue baseball cap, ruffles the gray hair underneath, and repositions it. "You know, my favorite photo of my brother and me was taken at that apple festival back in the seventies."

From the front pocket of his faded flannel shirt, he produces a weathered photo and passes it around. I study the grainy photo of two boys, one about six and the other taller and thinner, about ten, grinning, each throwing an arm around the other's shoulders. The younger boy's face is painted like a lion, the other like a tiger.

"You're the lion?" I ask. I see traces of Bertram in the younger boy, that bulbous nose, the round shape of his eyes.

"Sure was," he says. When the photo returns to him, he takes a long look at it before tucking it back into his pocket. "My brother's not around anymore," he says, "but that apple festival always made me think of him." He smiles softly to himself, then reaches for the next bowl of apple slices. Before he picks it up, he stops and turns to us. "You're doing a face-painting booth, right?"

Those of us around the table quickly exchange looks. I don't remember face-painting at the festival I used to attend. It must have been from before my time.

"Of course," Arun says, and I make a mental note to add *Find a face-painting artist* to our list of to-dos.

It hits me then, hearing Bertram talk about how much the festival means to him, that it's not just me whose memories of the festival are intertwined with a special bond. This festival is about more than Ryser PR, more than me trying to prove myself to Amanda, more than the Ryser Cares office having a reason to feel useful again, more than Marina and me. It's even bigger than the community center we're trying to save. It's about every single person in Greenstead who loves this place and chose to call it home. It's about the people who keep making that choice, day after day, year after year, even as their world quietly crumbles around them.

How many people like Bertram have memories of this festival that they hold dear and would love the chance to revisit? How many others have been getting their hopes up for this, looking forward to it, ever since we announced that we'd be reviving it? And how would they feel if they showed up expecting cotton candy and face-painting and saw nothing but foot cream and Ryser ads?

I decide then and there that I'm going to be firmer with Amanda about what this festival should be. In our next Monday call, I'll politely insist that we uphold the festival's integrity instead of trying to cram it with Ryser promo and personal care sponsors. Greenstead deserves better.

"Now, this one's a personal favorite of mine," Bertram says, passing the next bowl of apple slices around, "but I'm biased because I invented it."

As he did with all the other apple varieties, Randy pops the whole slice into his mouth. "Oh!" he exclaims. The rest of us glance over at Randy, who's now chewing with a pained look on his face. "What a unique flavor."

Bertram laughs. "Got a real kick to it, right?"

"Definitely a kick." Randy guzzles the rest of his water down.

"What do the rest of you think?" Bertram asks.

Exchanging tentative looks, we reach into the bowl for a slice as Bertram watches in anticipation. And, even though Randy is giving us a subtle but frantic shake of his head, we slowly bring our apple slices to our mouths.

A tangy, peppery, astringent flavor explodes on my tongue. I force my wince into a smile and keep chewing, chewing, chewing through the strangeness.

"Interesting," Marina says.

Arun coughs. "Definitely unique," he chokes out.

"What…is it?" Tessa asks, sounding like she's afraid of the answer.

"I bred it to have a distinctive mustard flavor," Bertram explains proudly.

"O-oh," I say, because I have no idea what to say to that.

"What inspired that?" Jen asks.

At the same time, Tessa asks pleadingly, "Why?"

"The flood, of course," Bertram says. "My crops were useless that year, and the next. The mustard sank into the soil, gave the apples a weird taste. It went away over the years, but I wanted to create an apple inspired by that juxtaposition of flavors. The bitter, the sweet. Spent years trying to figure it out, but I finally did it. This apple is Greenstead's history in the palm of your hand." Bertram takes a slice from the bowl and crunches into it. "I'm thinking this would be the perfect apple to feature at the festival. Wouldn't you say?"

"It is…unique," Randy says, looking around at the rest of us.

"Unique, yes," Arun agrees. "But I'm not sure that—"

Bertram's face falls. "You don't like it?"

"No, we do," Randy rushes to say. "It's just…an acquired taste."

"Exactly." Bertram snaps his fingers and points at Randy. "Acquired taste. Sophisticated shit is *always* acquired. Took me years to acquire a taste for caviar. I still hate it, if I'm being honest. But I *acquired* it."

"Why not feature an apple with more mass appeal?" I ask.

"Like the Honeycrisp?" Bertram supplies in a monotone voice. Enthusiastic murmurs go around the table.

"I *love* Honeycrisps," Jen says.

"Who doesn't?" Bertram mutters under his breath. "Look, I've spent a lot of effort creating this thing. It took me over twenty years to get right, and I'd really like to show it off at the festival. I'd pay extra for the privilege."

"So you're willing to pay us more to feature your…mustard apple…in our festival programming?" Arun asks.

"Yes, sir."

"I guess that's reasonable," Arun says, looking around the table. We all nod in reluctant agreement.

"What do you call it?" Tessa asks.

Bertram beams. "The Honey Mustard."

"That's just confusing," Marina whispers, and I have to act fast to suppress my laugh.

Bertram sends us home with a basket of apple muffins and a warm sentiment that he's excited to be working with us. As we're making the long trek through the field back to the parking lot, Arun asks if the Honey-Mustard apple taste is still lingering in anyone else's mouths, and the others are quick to agree. They joke about the apple's strange flavor, but I don't join in.

My mind's too full with thoughts of a younger Bertram and his brother, the lion and the tiger, what this festival means for him, for everyone. How I'd eat a dozen Honey Mustard apples, off-putting taste and all, before I'd let Amanda walk all over our festival any further.

I add another item to my mental to-dos, this one more abstract but no less crucial: *Protect the festival.*

CHAPTER EIGHTEEN

COME AWAY FROM BERTRAM'S orchard with a renewed sense of purpose.

In our next Monday meeting, I tell Amanda firmly and clearly that we have found an official sponsor and apple supplier for the event, and that it will be Bertram Mason. I hold my gaze on the camera to sell my determination—until I can't resist lowering my eyes to the screen to gauge Amanda's response.

I'm not sure what I was expecting. Maybe slack-jawed wonder? A glimmer of pride in her eyes? A round of applause?

No, Amanda's busy dabbing a wet spot on her blouse. I watch her rub a tissue over it once, twice, three times, and start to wonder how pathetic it would be to ask if she heard me. Until she lifts her head and simply says, "No."

I hesitate. "No?"

"We should go with Clark Farms," Amanda continues. "They already supply the apples for our organic applesauce."

"But…Bertram has history with this festival. He's a local farmer. The whole point of this festival is to uplift the Greenstead community. That's Bertram."

Amanda frowns, like I need to be corrected. "*No*, the whole point of the festival is to restore Ryser's reputation."

Tessa huffs out a breath. Even Randy, normally so mild-mannered, scoffs.

"That's never been the point of the festival," I say.

"But it's the point of *this* festival. Which is funded and planned by Ryser."

I don't have a comeback for that. Seeing the disillusioned looks of my coworkers around the table, my chin drops to my chest. My resolve shrinks away. What did I expect, that telling Amanda about Bertram's misty-eyed festival nostalgia would make her forget about her job as Ryser's PR director and the ten thousand dollars she invested?

"And we can't let him draw focus to the factory malfunction with that mustard apple," Amanda continues. "Which sounds disgusting," she adds with a laugh.

I can't say why this makes me bristle. The mustard apple *was* disgusting. I had to eat a handful of mints on the drive home just to get the strange flavor out of my mouth. But Bertram was so excited to share it with us. So earnest in his recounting of what the festival meant to him. I can still see that picture in my mind of him and his brother. Something in me refuses to let her disparage Bertram like this.

"No," I say. "Bertram and his orchard are an important part of Greenstead, so they're an important part of this festival, and that includes his mustard apple. I know the funding is coming out of your budget and I'm very grateful for it, but I think my team needs to have final say over the programming decisions. We need to make sure this festival reflects Greenstead above all else. And it wouldn't be a good look for Ryser to fill the festival with Ryser promo, would it?"

I can't tell if the screen has frozen or if Amanda is just sitting still, staring in disbelief. I have to move my hands to my lap to hide the way they're shaking. Amanda and I have disagreed on occasion, but I've never unequivocally said no to her like this before. I start to worry that I've taken too much of a stand—in support of a mustard-flavored apple of all things.

I sneak a glance at my colleagues. Tessa's smiling, her eyes sparkling in a way they haven't in any other Monday meeting. Arun does an exaggerated fist pump. Randy gives me a thumbs-up, and Jen's beaming at me with pride.

My hands steady. I breathe in, then out, a sense of accomplishment flowing through me. I enjoy the thought that Marina would be proud of me for this.

Amanda doesn't look angry, just pensive. She's staring somewhere off camera, her gaze distant. "I'll talk this over with the team," she says. "I understand your point. I'll see if we can think of a way to strike the right balance."

Balance.

The word stays with me after we get off the call, after I bask in my coworkers' praise. It feels right. Amanda knows I'm just trying to do right by the Greenstead community. She knows

I'm grateful for Ryser's support and how much I enjoy working with her.

This is good. When we meet next week, we'll figure out a solution for all of us to get what we want. I doubt I've risked my chance of getting my old job back at all. If anything, I feel like I've earned more of her respect.

As the week passes, I'm actually looking forward to our next meeting. I'm excited to sit down at the table and hear Amanda's ideas for how we can keep Greenstead at the center of the festival *and* give her what she needs to repair Ryser's reputation. I type up some of my own ideas as well, just in case she asks. I make a note about reinstating everything she shut down before, from the Nancy convention to the history of Greenstead booth. Our Ryser Cares team has held off on officially canceling them out of a sort of defiant procrastination—and a reluctance to face whatever tantrum Nancy would probably inflict. But now I can get them back. In return, we'll keep the Ryser booth. It wouldn't sell food that could compete with festival vendors, but we could allow the display about Ryser's positive contributions. Balance.

When Amanda calls me on Thursday afternoon, I answer immediately, ready to talk balance strategies. I lean back in my chair and click over to the ideas I've drafted.

"I've talked this over with Dan," Amanda says, "and we've agreed that it makes sense to step back from the festival."

"Great," I say. "That's exactly what I was thinking. We could take over the planning and operations like we were doing before, but of course we'd update you as often as you want. And you can let me know what's most important to include for Ryser."

"Oh." She sounds confused, like I'm speaking another language. "No, I mean really *step back*. As in we don't need to do the festival at all."

A sinking feeling hits my stomach. "What?"

"All the backlash from that article has blown over," she explains. "No one's talking about it anymore. Our stock has bounced back, our response to the water irregularities lawsuit is going over well. At this point, the festival would just risk dredging all that stuff back up again."

I can't make sense of her words. My brain is still clinging to the word *balance*, and it can't compute how throwing away a hometown festival like a piece of trash floating in their contaminated water well is anything resembling balance.

"The point was never for Ryser to save face," I say slowly. "It was to save Greenstead."

"Okay," she says in a *That's someone else's problem* kind of way. Cool and unbothered. "Nothing's stopping Greenstead from throwing the festival. I'm just saying Ryser isn't part of it anymore."

It's too simple a declaration for a statement riddled with so much consequence. The logistical impacts zip through my brain, bouncing loudly at every angle like an air hockey puck.

"What about the ten thousand dollars?" I ask.

"We won't be contributing that any longer," she says smoothly.

The puck in my head grows more frantic, picking up speed. My eyes dart around the office, taking in Arun on the phone with a vendor, Tessa at Jen's desk chatting about social media strategy, Randy coming from the kitchen with a mug of tea in his hand. He sees me watching him and gives me a warm smile. I quickly force one out in return, but it feels strange on my face.

Suddenly wary of being overheard, I walk toward the empty reception desk by the door. Only when I'm tucked away behind the desk, my aimless gaze on the parking lot in front of me, do I speak.

"But…we were counting on that money," I say, lowering my voice. "We've already made plans."

"You can cancel them."

"No." I don't say it with any defiance, but more like it's an impossibility. It's not an option.

"You still want to go ahead with it?"

"*Yes.*"

Amanda sighs like this is all an inconvenience. "Okay. You can get the funding you need from your Greenstead sponsors. Just make sure Ryser isn't associated with it. We don't want to draw attention to Ryser's connection to Greenstead any longer. This whole thing has made me realize we need to stop fussing with Greenstead. Our image has moved on from this. We're going to be moving on, too."

A shiver snakes down my spine. "How are you moving on?"

"We're… reassessing our priorities." Her voice is smooth, the way it is when she's dancing around the truth.

"What does that mean?" I choke out.

"I'll tell you when I know more." More dancing.

"Is it about Ryser Cares?" I guess. When she doesn't answer

right away, I'm gripped with a foreboding feeling that I'm right. "What is it? Layoffs? Closures?"

Amanda pauses. "This is confidential, but we discussed the *possibility* of closing the Ryser Cares office at the end of the year. Nothing's decided yet."

I feel like my throat is closing. This office of kind people who were sent here as a punishment, who chose to stay anyway and build a life for themselves, could all be left without a job, without the small community they've formed in each other. I bite my lip and try to think.

"When will it be decided?" I ask.

"Dan's going to talk it over with Bill. I don't know when that'll be."

"What would happen to the people who work here?"

"They'd be let go," Amanda says.

"Even me?" I ask. "I wouldn't get my old job back, even though I've only been here for a couple months?"

Amanda heaves another sigh. "If we *were* going to hire back someone, it would be you. But as long as Dan works here, I'd say your chances are low. I'm not sure he'd go for the idea of you coming back to his team."

Dan goddamn Gorland.

When Amanda hangs up, I'm left to run my hands through my curls and stare hopelessly ahead. I turn at the sound of Jen and Tessa high-fiving over something. Randy walks over to join the discussion. Arun's enthusiasm on his vendor call fills the air. Behind him sits the whiteboard, once boasting a running score of Arun and Randy's air hockey games, now scribbled with our colorful hopes and plans.

How am I supposed to tell these people that the festival is off and they might lose their jobs at the end of the year?

How am I supposed to tell Marina—who came up with this idea in the first place—never mind, screw the festival our entire friendship has been built around, let's leave Greenstead and its community center to die?

Selfishly, I wonder what this means for my own goals. Everything I've worked for at Ryser, all that time slowly climbing the ladder until I got high enough to make a meaningful impact, will have been for nothing. It would mean the last decade of my life has been a lie. I'd be leaving Ryser weighted down with every sin I've contributed to, with no way to erase it. Unless I did away with my FIRE plan entirely and spent decades toiling away in a low-paying job at some dreary nonprofit. But I know myself. I couldn't even make it three hours at that accounting firm in Greenstead before I went running for Ryser. When given the choice between good and easy, I choose easy every time.

The achingly lonely thought of carrying on the way I've been for years more makes me want to cry. I swallow past the lump in my throat and start gathering my things. I sling my bag over my shoulder and make up an excuse about taking off for an appointment.

They believe me because they trust me. And I plod to my car to the sound of geese calling me a fraud.

CHAPTER NINETEEN

T HERE IS TOO MUCH CHEER here.

It's the first thing I notice when I follow Tessa, Jen, Arun, Randy, and Marina through the sprawling parking lot and up the winding path leading to Strawberry Moon Brewery. A cheer rings out from the group playing cornhole up ahead when an elderly woman gets her bag through the hole. On our left, a pair of kids toss a Frisbee back and forth. A woman sitting on a picnic blanket coos at a giggling toddler. Ahead of us, people sit at a sea of tables outside the brewery, talking, eating, laughing, drinking, being nauseatingly merry. The sun is shining, the grass is a vivid shade of green, and nothing has ever been more disgustingly perfect.

"Perfect!" Randy says, right on cue. "A table's opening up, center stage." He weaves through the tables to snag it just as its previous occupants, a young couple, take their leave. Randy waves us over, and I fake a grin when I slide in across from him.

"Art's set is an hour," Arun says, checking his watch. He cranes his neck to inspect the stage behind me. "No sign of him yet."

The name Art McKenzie probably wouldn't ring a bell for most people outside of Virginia. Music snobs would recognize him as a former guitarist for Cranefly, a Richmond-based indie band from the '90s. They never reached mainstream success, but their albums earned critical acclaim, and some musicians still cite them as an influence today. Virginians would recognize Art as the baritone-voiced singer-songwriter who frequents the local music festival circuit. When he went solo after the band broke up, Art never reached Cranefly's level of success, but he remains a beloved presence in Virginia. No music festival in the state is complete without an Art McKenzie set.

But Greenstead has a special, if one-sided, connection to Art McKenzie. One of his songs, "Green Thread," made waves throughout Greenstead when it hit the local radio in the early 2000s. Greensteaders were convinced he'd written it about our town.

Of course, there's no evidence that he ever actually lived in or even passed through Greenstead, and the lyrics make pretty clear that the song is about missing an ex who left a shirt behind. But Greensteaders decided this melancholy acoustic song was really about a longing for the way our town used to be before the flood, about a soulful desire for those bright days to return. So, naturally, the citizens of Greenstead became Art McKenzie's collective number one fan. Our local radio station cycles through his music constantly—and he hasn't put out any new albums in at least a decade. Any festivals or gigs he's playing are announced on our local news, in a special segment called "Art Alert," which has its own custom graphic featuring a cartoon image of Art playing the guitar. (Art has, coincidentally, refused any offers to come on the show.)

So when Arun told us last week that Art McKenzie was playing a gig at a brewery in Richmond, I thought he was just doing what Greensteaders do, sharing important updates about the only musician who matters—until Arun said he wanted to ask Art to play at the apple festival.

It sounded impossible, on par with calling up the king of England to invite him over for a crab boil. Art was…*Art*. He was bigger than all of us.

But Arun insisted it was worth a try, pointing out how it would help drive attendance from all over the state if our little festival could boast Art McKenzie's presence.

And so we hopped into Randy's van and made the hour-long trip to Richmond for a chance to ask Greenstead's god for a very large favor. On the drive, Arun and Tessa ran the numbers and enthusiastically debated how much of our budget we could reasonably afford to offer Art. I sat in the back seat, staring vacantly out the window, unable to reveal that those funds they're counting on don't exist anymore.

I've gone over and over the budget. I've reviewed it at the Ryser Cares office, crunching numbers while people around me joke and brainstorm and make things happen. I've reviewed it sitting at the kitchen table at home late into the night, getting puzzled looks from my dad and Wendy when they pop in to say good night on their way to bed.

No matter how I look at it, there's no way we can throw this festival without the money Ryser pledged. And after getting the buy-in from all the vendors, I can't just turn around and ask them to pay participation fees after all. Especially when it was the promise of Ryser covering those fees that made them trust us enough to agree to participate in the festival in the first place. But we need that money to cover the booth rentals, advertisements, insurance, banners, portable bathrooms, and everything else a festival requires.

We do have the funds Solar Summit provided when they agreed to sponsor the festival, but that money went toward the pie contest costs: the stage, stipends for the judges, a cash prize for the winner. We've been counting on the Ryser money to cover the necessities.

Then there's the part of me that wonders, what would Marina think? Marina only came around to thinking Ryser isn't as bad as they seem because they pledged the money to support this festival. When she discovers they're just as selfish and greedy as she'd always said they were, how would that change how she thinks of me? Only a horrible person would want to work for such a horrible company, right? I can't see her overlooking this, especially after I've gotten her hopes up about this festival and its potential to save the community center. To save our town, period.

She wouldn't look at me the same way. She couldn't, especially if she knew that even after all of this, I'm still trying to think of a way to keep my old job. That I still want to align myself with Ryser because it's the best means to an end I can conceive of.

Which is why, now, I keep my thoughts to myself. I volunteer to keep our spot at the table while the rest of them go inside the brewery to order. I glance around the picnic tables filled with people enjoying themselves and think about how unfortunate it is that I don't even get to appreciate being here at this place that feels so much livelier than anywhere in Greenstead. Tessa's been talking about wanting to show me her favorite pubs and breweries on our next weekend trip to Richmond, and now here we are, at a brewery so scenic it could be a park, and I can't enjoy anything.

I thank Marina with as much sincerity as I can muster when she presents me with a cheeseburger exactly the way I like it—cheddar cheese, grilled onions, no pickle, extra tomato, extra crispy fries on the side—without asking. She knows me so well, even now. Except for the thing I can't bring myself to tell her about.

Art takes the stage as we're finishing our food. It's easy to spot him among the backing musicians taking their places onstage with him. Though his hair is gray, close-cropped, and thinner than the shaggy style depicted in the Art Alert graphic, his tall, slender frame is the same, and he's wearing his usual jeans and Converse. He even has a distinct walk about him, a nonchalant way of shuffling onstage as if he's just wandered there by accident.

When Art greets the crowd with a quiet hello, he's met with loud cheers and applause, including an over-the-top whoop from Arun. Art's gaze flickers toward our table with a touch of wariness, and I wonder if he's pegged us for the Greensteaders that we are, if he has a security team whose sole purpose is protecting him from the frightening enthusiasm of his Greenstead fans.

His set is the same as I remember it from when he played at the DC State Fair I attended in college. It's mostly his solo work, but he always scatters in a few Cranefly songs throughout. Our table cheers loudest when "Green Thread" starts up, earning us another cautious glance. And though I'm 99 percent sure the song isn't actually about us, I can't help but feel like it is, today. Every aspect of it speaks to me. The fragile pluck of the guitar, his melancholy voice, the futile hope in the lyrics: *I'll hold onto this thread and wait for our love to be resurrected.*

I'm doing the same thing, aren't I? Holding too tightly onto a thread, hoping in vain that circumstances will change? I can't even decide what my thread is: the festival, Marina, Greenstead, Ryser Cares, my old job, that promotion I'm chasing. I just know that in this moment, no one else understands me like Art McKenzie does.

As I'm vowing to keep my TV tuned to the local news at all hours of the day so I don't miss any future Art Alerts, the song ends, the crowd breaks into applause, and I must come to the terms with the fact that I've teared up over a song about an old shirt.

Partway through the last song in the set, Arun stands and gestures for us to follow him. We weave through the crowd until we reach the side of the stage, though I'm not quite sure of the game plan. Are we going to ramble out a festival invitation in the three seconds it'll take Art to pass us on his way offstage? When the mention of Greenstead sends him into a panic, will we chase after him, shouting assurances that our town is totally normal?

When Art finishes his last song and thanks the crowd for coming, he turns to the side, sees us, and stops in his tracks, looking like a frightened deer. Before we can speak, he turns and exits from the opposite side of the stage instead.

"Maybe we shouldn't have cheered so loud," Tessa murmurs.

"It's *Art McKenzie*," Arun says, and I have to smile. The Ryser Cares folks aren't even from Greenstead and yet they've adopted the town's Art McKenzie idolatry just the same. Much like how they've adopted the entire town as their own. A worry pushes forward at what will happen when they learn the Ryser Cares office, the place keeping them employed in the town they've chosen to call home, might close. My smile drops from my face.

When Jen spots Art disappearing through the brewery's doors, we follow after. As I walk through the door, I mentally calculate the odds of this night ending with a restraining order.

We spend the first hour watching. From our table near the back, we watch Art sit at the bar with his fellow musicians as a steady stream of people walk up to him, exchanging a few words or asking for a photo. Art always obliges. When they walk away, Art turns back to continue his conversation with his group—and as we're debating whether this is the moment to make our move, someone else comes up to him and the cycle continues.

The light filtering in through the windows slowly wanes as dusk mellows into evening, and still we wait. The stream of approaching fans has lessened to nothing, but now Art seems to be arguing with one of the men he's with. He's frowning, talking animatedly, gesturing his arms out—and then he pushes back his barstool with a loud squeak and stalks off for the restroom.

"That doesn't sound good," Tessa remarks. But Arun's staring at the closed men's room door like it's an opportunity.

"I'm going in," Arun announces. His words are immediately met with groans.

"Let the poor man pee in peace," Jen says.

Already, though, Arun is standing. Moments later, he's slipped in through the restroom door, leaving Tessa to remark that we may have to allocate some of our budget to bailing Arun out of jail for stalking. The laugh that escapes my lips is forced, too bogged down by the knowledge that our budget is all but nonexistent now. I just need Art to gently let Arun down so we can leave and I can go back to holing up in my room, searching for a solution that doesn't exist.

When Arun emerges from the restroom a few minutes later, he's grinning in triumph. Even more miraculously, Art McKenzie—now back to looking friendly and personable— follows Arun to our table and pulls up a chair.

It's so counter to what I expected that my brain short-circuits. All budgetary worries fly out of my head. I become all too aware that I don't know how to act in Art McKenzie's presence. I straighten my spine, but that feels unnatural. Next to me, Marina tucks a lock of hair behind her ear, while Randy, sitting across from us, brushes his hand down the front of his shirt a few times, as if dusting away crumbs.

Arun goes around the table introducing us, and the five of us break into stilted hellos and frozen smiles. Art, ever professional, says it's nice to meet us. I mean to nod, but I think I forget to.

"Like I was saying, it would be a real honor to have you at our apple festival, if you can manage it," Arun says. "Your music means a lot to us."

"Yes, I'm…aware," Art replies, looking uncomfortable. "But I'm actually stepping back from music, some."

Marina gasps, but my hopes latch onto Art, clamoring for an easy letdown that will let me deny reality for a little bit longer.

Art chuckles, his eyes shifting to Marina. "It's true. I only did today's gig as a favor to a friend."

"But…why step back?" Randy asks. "You're a legend."

Art's smile looks forced. "Appreciate it. I've just…gone as far as I want to go with music. I'm looking to make a change. Well," he says with a tilt of his head, "some might see it as a change. For me, it's going back to my roots."

"You're reuniting with Cranefly?" Randy asks excitedly.

"No," Art says with an amused shake of his head. "Before I ever even touched a guitar, my first passion was this." He waves his hand over the straw in Arun's water glass once, twice, then lifts his hand higher and higher, his fingers rubbing together. We all watch, transfixed, as Arun's straw rises from the glass and hovers in the air.

"*Witchcraft?*" Tessa guesses.

Art laughs. He snaps his fingers and the straw drops back into the glass. "Magic."

"You're leaving music to…be a magician?" Jen says. Her voice is tinged with disbelief, but I'm still staring at the straw, trying to figure out how Art has the power to levitate. Arun sweeps his hand over the glass, but going by his puzzled expression, he can't work it out, either.

"Yep. I'm actually moving to Orlando in a couple weeks. Big magic scene down there."

Arun glances up from the glass he's still studying. "Oh. Our apple festival's in October."

My chest loosens with relief, but I try to look just as disappointed as Arun does.

Art makes a sympathetic sound. "I'll be long gone by then. Just like your wallet," he adds to Arun.

"What? My wallet's…" Arun pats his back pocket, then gazes at Art with wide eyes. "Where is it?"

"All in good time. But first, pick a card." From seemingly nowhere, Art summons a deck of cards and fans them out to Arun. What follows is a magic show I can't begin to understand. Art tells Marina to check the bottom of her shoe for Arun's card. She does, only to reveal Arun's driver's license. More and more items from Arun's wallet appear in various places—a credit card under the napkin holder, a debit card in Tessa's purse, a Luau Hut loyalty card, which explains where he gets all his colorful shirts, under my water glass—until finally, Art points up, where Arun's nine of diamonds is stuck to the ceiling above our table.

I'm sure there's a logic to how he did all this, but it truly does feel like magic. It's a pleasant feeling to lose myself in the wonder, even briefly. I join the rest of the table in applause when Art finishes his trick. Arun marvels over Art as he places his cards back in his empty wallet (which Art returned to his back pocket somehow). It's Tessa who gets us back on track.

"So there's no chance you could come out for the festival?" she asks. "It would really make a difference if you came. Greenstead's always been a big supporter of your work."

"Oh, I know," Art says. "Greensteaders are very... enthusiastic."

"We mean well," Marina pipes in. "I promise there's nothing scary about us. We're just trying to save our community center. It's the whole reason we're throwing this festival. It would mean a lot to have you."

Art seems to consider the idea, his dark eyes roving in a way that makes me think I'm not out of the woods just yet. "I do my magic act under a different name—Arthur Frost. That an issue?"

"Well..." Tessa's voice trails off.

"Art McKenzie carries a lot of weight," Arun says, an apology in his voice. "We were hoping you'd play music."

"I'm focusing on magic-only gigs to get my name out there," Art explains.

A silence falls. The uncertainty on everyone else's faces reveals their doubt that a performance by the unknown magician Arthur Frost probably wouldn't motivate any Virginians to travel to Greenstead for a festival.

"Of course your magic is impressive..." Jen begins.

"But you want Art McKenzie," Art finishes unenthusiastically. He sits back in his chair with a sigh. "It's what I was just arguing with my buddy about. He thinks I'm ridiculous for going all in on magic."

"You're not ridiculous," Arun says, subtly reaching behind him. I think he's checking to make sure his wallet is still there.

"Maybe we can compromise," Marina says. "Art McKenzie, featuring a performance by Arthur Frost."

Art lifts a brow. "I'd consider it. And you'd cover travel and lodging?"

"Yes," Tessa says slowly, exchanging a look with Arun. Art's move to Orlando wouldn't have factored into their giddy calculations this afternoon.

"Okay." Art nods slowly, interest lighting his eyes in a way that makes my stomach plummet. "We might be able to make this work. And since it's for a good cause, I'll even cut my usual fee in half."

"What does that come out to?" Tessa asks.

Art gives an elusive shrug and cocks his head in the direction of the napkin holder. "Grab a napkin."

Giving him a suspicious look, Tessa pulls the first napkin from the container. Once she smooths it out, she gapes at it in disbelief. "This is *half* your fee?" She tilts it toward Arun, whose hopeful expression falls from his face. It's terrible that this is what makes my hopes stir.

"Yep." Art checks his watch. "I've gotta head out. Just shoot me an email if you're interested."

"But I don't have your—"

"Yes, you do." With a wink, Art turns and exits the brewery, leaving the rest of us to stare in confusion—except Arun, who's grinning into his wallet.

"He put his business card in my wallet," Arun explains, lifting up a shiny black card. "He's good."

"And he knows it." Tessa waves the napkin in his direction.

"Right," Arun says with a resigned sigh.

"He's out of budget?" I guess, trying not to sound too relieved.

Tessa nods, and the table falls silent. Seeing their dejected faces, I start to worry I've caused this somehow, that my desperation for Art to let them down made this happen. Now that they've all been brought down to my level, an impulse to cheer them up tugs at me.

"Maybe his price will go down," I try. Arun lets out a dejected grunt in response.

"Maybe you can put it all on your Luau Hut credit card," Randy jokes.

A corner of Arun's lips perks upward. "It's a platinum-level *loyalty* card, thank you very much."

Tessa laughs. "And what does that get you?"

The mood lifts as Arun details Luau Hut's three loyalty tiers and starts listing the perks of platinum: one and a half points for every dollar spent, free shipping, exclusive coupons, an annual birthday gift. While the others joke about Arun's Luau Hut obsession, my mind goes somewhere else.

Suppose we took a page from Luau Hut's book? We don't have any sponsorship tiers—we were so desperate to take whatever we could get that it didn't occur to us. But if we offered additional perks, maybe we could attract more sponsors. We could create a new VIP sponsorship level. It could include some kind of special recognition, bigger ad space in the festival program and our website, swag bags with freebies of festival goodies, reserved parking spots. Maybe this could be the way we make up for the funds Ryser pulled.

For our best chance of success, we'd have to really make these potential VIP folks feel special. Sending a mass email begging for money would be impersonal and easy to ignore. But if we gathered them in a room and pitched them in person, we might get the money we need to pull this off.

I chew this over while the others finish their drinks. After we step outside into the lamplit darkness and start down the winding path to the parking lot, I raise my idea.

"We should throw a dinner party," I say, "to try to sell people on a VIP offering. It could bring in more money for the festival. People could promote what they want, and they'd get better booth placement at the festival, more advertising, freebies. Everybody wins."

No one speaks right away.

"You…want to throw a dinner party?" Marina asks. "*You?*"

She undoubtedly remembers how stressful social gatherings are for me. Large groups of people, endless small talk, people chattering into my deaf ear, the exhaustion of smiling and nodding and pretending I wouldn't rather be at home doing a puzzle and watching a movie.

Marina's not the biggest fan of parties, either. We once snuck out of her own quinceañera to sit cross-legged on the balcony and play Speed with the worn deck of cards in my purse. That half hour we spent talking, laughing, and slapping cards down—until her mom caught us and made us rejoin the party—was the highlight of my night, and I like to think it was hers, too. I can see why she'd be baffled that I'd willingly suggest throwing a party. But this feels like the only solution. I'll just have to think of it as one long presentation, slip back into Business Partner me.

"I don't know if that would be enough to cover Art's fee," Arun says. "Art was a long shot anyway. Our resources are probably better spent working on the projects we already have in motion."

The others murmur in agreement, which isn't a surprise. Since Arun's the only one of us with any events experience, we all defer to him when it comes to festival decision-making.

And Arun's response is a reasonable one. Anyone who thought we still had the ten thousand dollars Ryser pledged would think our funding was in pretty good shape. But if he knew the truth, he'd side with me.

"I think we should," I try again. "We want to make this festival a success, right?"

"Not if we're stretching ourselves too thin," Arun says.

"We won't," I promise. "I'll do all the work."

"Well…" Arun rubs the back of his neck, thinking it over. "I guess it couldn't hurt to bolster our finances a little more."

I breathe a quiet exhale. "Exactly."

"Who knows? Maybe it could bring in enough for Art."

I keep silent on that one. Right now, it doesn't matter what Arun thinks the money is for. I can tell him the truth later, after the dinner party brings in the money we're missing. *We still can't afford Art McKenzie* is a far better letdown than *The festival's canceled and nothing matters.*

"So your plan is to invite people over, cook for them, and say, 'Please give us money'?" Marina asks.

"Yep. Personal touches go a long way." I'm met with more skeptical silence, and it's hard to keep from explaining myself further to make them understand I'm not delusional.

"That *is* true," Jen says. "In the third season of *Diamond Divas*, when Kayleigh wanted Aiden to invest in her couture clothing line for cocker spaniels, she invited him over for dinner."

My heart fills with appreciation for Jen and her encyclopedic knowledge of reality TV. "See? Who are we to deny the business sense of Kayleigh from *Diamond Divas*?"

The others chuckle, and my muscles relax. I've got the go-ahead. Now I just need to secure the location.

"Hey, Marina," I say in an innocent voice.

"Yeah?"

"Now I'm thinking about where to host the dinner party."

"Okay." When I fix her with a hopeful look, she catches on and wrinkles her nose. "No. You're not using my house."

"You know my dad's dining room is tiny," I protest. "He has that little round table that only fits four people. But *your* dining room. It's enormous. It's magnificent. It has that big table, and all those chairs."

"But my house isn't…" She doesn't finish her sentence.

"Isn't what?" I prod.

"It's just not the best place for it," she says.

I keep playing innocent. "But you love your house, right? That's what you said."

Marina's jaw sets as she stares me down. There's no way she'll admit to her house's state of disrepair. I tried bringing it up once a few weeks ago, but she just changed the subject. Now, though, she can't avoid a direct question. When her eyes narrow with empty threats, I know she's falling into my trap and hating every second of it.

"I guess I see no reason why we couldn't host it at my house," she says slowly, over-enunciating every word.

"Great," I chirp at her knowing scowl. I soften the blow by saying, "I promise I'll do all the cooking and whatever it takes to get your house ready for the party."

Marina's grunt is wholly unconvinced, but I don't care. Already my sights are set on throwing my all into this dinner party to get the money we need to keep this festival going.

Another thought springs forward, gift-wrapped in hope, or possibly delusion. What if the festival is such a success that it convinces Amanda and the Ryser executives to keep the Ryser Cares office open? If the festival ends up raising enough money to save the community center and help revive Greenstead, that may be the best possible case for why Ryser Cares needs to stay open.

It's not just the festival that hinges on this dinner party, then. The future of Ryser Cares and the livelihoods of my coworkers might depend on it, too.

I just need this dinner party to be a success—no matter what it takes.

CHAPTER TWENTY

As August melts into September, I throw myself into the world of party planning. I design a fall-themed menu, from a butternut squash soup starter all the way to apple galette for dessert. For inspiration, I research events that have offered VIP packages or different sponsorship levels. And I sign up for Luau Hut's gold-tier loyalty program. They're clearly masters of marketing.

To put together a guest list, I go over our spreadsheet of vendors and pull out the biggest names. I put a question mark next to Solar Summit. They've been supportive so far, but inviting them to a dinner party could be a recipe for disaster considering how polarizing Solar Summit is for Greenstead folks. But they *do* have deeper pockets than any of the Greenstead vendors.

I delete Solar Summit, add them back in, stare at the list in uncertainty. Then I decide to put a pin in that and invite the folks I am sure about. I start with Meg, the pretzel queen herself. But when I explain why I'm calling, she's skeptical.

"Who else is coming?"

"Um." I glance down the list of people I haven't invited yet. "Other prominent business owners in the area. It's a chance to network and hear about an exclusive new opportunity for vendors."

"If I want to network, I can join a hiking group."

"Right," I say weakly. Apparently Greensteaders use hiking for dating and networking alike. I shuffle through my pages of scribbled-down dinner party notes, searching for something to entice her. I'm about to ask how she feels about butternut squash soup when she speaks again.

"You know what would really interest me? If Mayor Bradley was coming. That man has not returned any of my calls about the ridiculous meals tax bill I got this year. He needs to change his tax policy if he wants to keep my vote."

I chew on the end of my pen. "So if Mayor Bradley comes, you'll come?"

"Absolutely."

"I'll see what I can do."

When we hang up, I call a few more vendors on my list to float the idea of the dinner party, and their response is similarly lukewarm—until I mention the possibility of Mayor Bradley's attendance. Suddenly, they're all ears, talking about a pothole they need fixed outside their shop, a broken streetlight, an issue with a sign permit.

I study my invite list again, an idea taking shape. I sit with it, consider it. Then I pick up my phone and look up the number for the mayor's office.

The R on the lettering above the mayor's office is still missing when I reach the second floor of Town Hall the next morning. I wonder how long it's been gone, or if Mayor Bradley has just come to terms with his new mayonnaise-related title. Given our town's history with condiments, it is rather fitting.

Jess greets me with a wave when I enter the office. The smile I give in return feels tight and unnatural, tainted by desperation, but Jess doesn't seem to notice.

"You said you had a proposal?" Jess says as I take a seat at their desk in the back.

I take in a steeling breath. "I'm unveiling a VIP package for our most prominent vendors and collaborators. I'm inviting them to a dinner party to get them interested in being VIPs."

"And?" Jess prompts.

Out tumbles the flash of an idea I'd gotten this morning. "I'd like Mayor Bradley to attend." I can practically see Jess's eyes glaze over the second I say it. Half their job must be turning down requests on the mayor's behalf. To our right, the mayor's office door is once again closed, keeping him shut in frosted-glass isolation. Before Jess can respond, I rush to explain, leaning forward and resting my elbows on the desk between us. "People only want to come if Mayor Bradley comes," I confess. "They want to talk to him about potholes and meal taxes and other stuff they need his help with."

Jess steeples their fingers, looking doubtful. "He is the most introverted man I have ever met. He hates parties."

"I mean, don't we all?" I say, making Jess smile. I try another tactic. "Doesn't he have an election coming up? He could consider this a sort of campaign event. Meg did say he'll have to change his tax plan if he wants to keep her vote."

Jess's eyes narrow slightly. "Mayor Bradley's running unopposed."

"Right," I say slowly, trying to think. "I think Meg said she might run for mayor herself if Mayor Bradley doesn't make some changes."

Jess tilts their head. "I'm pretty sure you're bullshitting me, but Meg probably *could* get the votes if she ran against him."

"This town does run on pretzels," I reply. While they're pondering, I raise the idea I've been mulling over in my mind. "What do you think about inviting someone from Solar Summit?"

"Bold," Jess says, lifting a brow.

"They said they want to partner more with Greenstead. And, if you come, maybe you could advance your proposal."

"I don't hate it." Jess looks me over, and I try not to fidget, even though I know what they're about to ask. "Does Marina know?"

"About the dinner party?" I say. "Yes, it'll be at her house."

"Really? You got her to agree to that?"

I shrug. "All she'd have to do was admit that her house was in bad shape, and she didn't. So…"

Jess laughs, in a way that suggests it hits close to home. "Sounds kind of like why we broke up," they say, a hint of bitterness in their voice.

"Over the house?" I ask.

"Over…" Jess sighs. "Knowing when to cut your losses," they say carefully.

I nod, reading between the lines. "And she cut the wrong losses," I conclude.

Jess gives me a grim smile. "She doesn't seem to think so."

"I'm not so sure," I say. Which makes Jess perk up a little, their lips curling slightly upward. "So, are you coming to the party?" I ask. "I'm sure Marina would love to see you."

Yes, Marina would probably kill me for inviting her ex to a dinner party she doesn't want to host, but I know there's still something between them. Inviting Jess could either make everything worse, or it could be the start of something wonderful. And, frankly, I'm not sure things could get much worse anyway.

Jess's cheeks flush. "I'll think about it," they say quietly. Then, with a too-casual clear of their throat, Jess says, "What I was *going* to ask is does Marina know you want to invite people from Solar Summit to her house?" From the meaningful look Jess gives me, I can tell they already know the answer.

"No," I admit. "Not yet."

"And she doesn't know you're inviting me, either," Jess gathers.

"Nope. But I'm gonna tell her."

Jess exhales. "Make *sure* you tell her," they say. "Before I get there."

"I will," I promise.

"Okay. And I will…work on getting Mayor Bradley to come to my ex's house. Slash my old house."

"Good luck to us all," I say. The uncertainty on Jess's face mirrors exactly how I feel inside.

I know Marina wouldn't be comfortable with Solar Summit's attendance. But it's this or risk not having a festival at all. If she understood what was at stake, she'd know I'm only doing this because it's our best bet at securing this festival.

Except for the whole inviting-Jess-to-the-dinner-party-to-force-a-reunion thing. That's on me. But she'll be okay with it, probably.

When I return to the office and take my seat, I notice Randy staring at me from his desk. I offer him a friendly smile, but he just squints like he's trying to read me. Guilt immediately floods me. How could he possibly know I was just meeting with Marina's ex to discuss inviting the company that's been trying to buy her home to the dinner party she doesn't even want me to throw?

Randy stands and gestures with a tilt of his head for me to follow him. I trail after him, past Arun, past Tessa, past Jen, all obliviously working, to the kitchen in the back.

"What is it?" I ask.

After turning to peek at the others in the main office, Randy ducks back into the kitchen, then glances at the kettle on the counter. He flicks it on, and the kettle slowly starts rumbling to life. He takes a tea bag from the box in the cabinet and leans against the counter, playing with the square packet as a troubled expression clouds his face.

"I tried to buy some balloons," he says. He looks at me like *balloons* is code for something.

"Okay," I say. "How did that go?"

"Not good."

"Oh. I'm sorry." Unable to decipher the meaningful look he's giving me, I ask, "What…kind of balloons?"

His brow pinches, as if *I'm* being strange when he's the one with the sudden balloon fixation. "Latex."

"Maybe…try Mylar?"

Looking pained, he whispers, "The corporate card was declined. I'm…wondering what you know."

His meaning washes over me. "*Oh.*"

I try to get a read on him. Does he know something? Or is he just curious? If he knows, I could have a confidant, a way to feel less alone. But if he doesn't, I'd be pulling him into the same cold, unforgiving reality I've been living in for the past couple of weeks.

"What did you do when you found out it was declined?" I ask, my voice guarded.

"I called corporate."

I narrow my eyes at him. "Did they tell you something?"

Randy leans in, trying to read me right back. "Did they tell *you* something?"

"What do you think?" I ask.

"I think it's interesting that you suddenly wanted to throw a dinner party to ask for more money."

Coming out and saying it is a risk, but the words claw at me, eager for confirmation that I'm not alone in this. "They told you about pulling the funding?" I ask.

Randy nods. "And that's why you're doing the dinner party?" he fills in.

"Yes. It was the only way I could think of to get the money we need."

"I get it now," he says.

I glance from the kettle bubbling away on the counter to the tea bag. He's rubbing the wrapper like it's a worry stone. "I'm guessing you haven't told the others?" I ask.

Randy shakes his head. "And you haven't, either," he confirms.

"No. Should we?"

"I don't know," he says. "I don't want them to feel like this has all been for nothing."

"It's not," I say. "I can make this work."

"Then...maybe we don't tell them," Randy decides.

"Okay." I lean against the counter, too, and we stand there listening to the kettle throw a fit.

I want to ask Randy if he knows about the Ryser Cares office possibly closing at the end of the year—but he hasn't brought it up. And as much of a relief it is to have someone to talk to about this funding issue, I don't want to spring a new revelation on him when he's worried enough about this one. As if in agreement, the kettle finishes its cycle, slowing its rapid boiling until it falls into silence.

"Let me know how I can help with the dinner party," Randy says. He tears open the tea bag wrapper and drops the bag into his mug.

"Okay." I give him a grateful smile. "Thank you. And sorry."

"You have nothing to be sorry for," he says gently. It's a touching thing to say, even if he's wrong.

"You should buy the balloons," I say, reaching into my purse, "or whatever we need for the festival. Just put it on this." I hand him my credit card.

Randy turns it over with a frown. "Is this your personal card? You shouldn't have to pay for this."

"Just to hold us over until we get the money," I say. "I'll pay myself back after the dinner party."

"We're really putting all our eggs in this dinner-party basket," Randy says uneasily, pocketing the card.

"Because it's gonna work," I reply.

And I choose to believe it.

CHAPTER TWENTY-ONE

O NE BY ONE, THE DINNER-PARTY pieces fall into place. Jess emails me to confirm that Mayor Bradley will be attending the party, I invite our vendors, RSVPs roll in—and still I haven't told Marina that Jess and Solar Summit will be coming.

Which leaves today, the day before the dinner party. Marina's kitchen is filled with the sweet smell of butternut squash soup and spiced apple cider simmering on the stove. Occasional floorboard creaks sound from the dining room as the electrician I hired, Stan, fixes the chandelier. I'm slathering four chickens in an herby compound butter, and Marina, who I'd instructed not to lift a finger, is halving a mountain of brussels sprouts.

"How's everything going with work?" I ask.

"Good," Marina says. "It's always hard shifting back into teacher mode at the end of the summer. But I'm in a good routine now."

"Great," I say. A good mood is a plus. She'll be more receptive to the news. In theory.

"The cider smells amazing," Marina says, peering over the bubbling pot on the stove. "I don't know why I'm looking forward to tomorrow now."

"Because I bake a mean apple galette and you know it."

Marina laughs. "I know we went like a decade without talking, but I feel pretty confident that you have never baked an apple galette in your life."

"Accurate," I say with a grin.

"But I bet it'll be delicious," she replies. "As long as you don't use Honey Mustard apples."

"Well…" I wrinkle my nose. "Bertram *did* make us agree to come up with a recipe that uses them. We'll be including the recipe in the festival promo materials. He sent over a case of Honey Mustard apples for us to experiment with."

Marina grimaces. "You mean…" She points at the basket of apples on the kitchen island. "Those are his apples? And you're using them in the dessert?"

I give a helpless shrug. "I have to come up with a recipe, and I have to make dessert for tomorrow. Two birds, one stone." Seeing Marina's dubious expression—and remembering the acrid flavor of the apples—I waver. "Maybe I'll buy some Granny Smiths and save the experimenting for later."

"For the love of god, please do that," Marina says, making me laugh.

That's when Stan pops his head in to tell us he has to replace the chandelier to stop the flickering light problem. "It'll cost more," he warns.

Marina turns to me uncertainly. I did say I'd cover the costs.

"No problem," I say. I'm in too deep now. I can't serve Mayor Bradley and our potential VIPs dinner under a creepy haunted-house flickering light. Marina gives me a smile of thanks and follows Stan into the dining room to select her new chandelier.

True, my credit card has been very tired since Ryser cut us off. But it will all be worth it once the dinner-party money comes in.

By early evening, we're in a good place. Stan has finished up and left, and the dining room is now filled with a warm, steady glow of soft light. All the brussels sprouts are halved and ready to roast tomorrow. The chickens, beautifully buttered, are prepped and in the fridge. The butternut squash soup has been taken off the heat. The Honey Mustard apples are…staring at me from the counter, waiting to be useful. I look away.

Marina and I decide to take a break to watch more *Love Quest*. We've been making our way through the second season in the last few weeks. While she prepares the TV, I pour out ladles of spiced apple cider for us to sample.

As I take my seat on the couch, I glance over at Marina. She's in a good mood, her dining room is no longer haunted, she's got a drink in hand. Maybe now is the moment, before the show starts.

"There's something about the guest list I wanted to—"

Marina's so quick to frown that I start to wonder if she's psychic, until she says, "Do you hear that?"

"Well, I'm notoriously bad at hearing, so…no." I stop and try to listen anyway. I don't hear anything at first, until my ear picks up on something subtle and steady. *Drip. Drip. Drip.*

Marina walks through the kitchen into the dining room, me

trailing after her. She cranes her neck upward and lets out a deep sigh. I follow her gaze to see a wet spot forming on the ceiling.

Trepidation snakes through me. "Oh, no. Did Stan bust a pipe or something?" She doesn't answer, just keeps staring at the spot on the ceiling. "What should we do?" I ask.

"I–I don't know," she says, sounding flustered. "Jess always handled plumbing stuff."

"Then let's call Jess."

Marina nods, still staring up at the spot.

"Marina?" I prompt.

She shakes herself out of it and picks up her phone. When Jess answers, she stammers out that the ceiling is leaking, listens, and sets her phone on the table. "Jess is coming over now," Marina says, sounding like she's in a daze. "I should get a pot, I think."

"I'll grab one," I say quickly, wanting to feel like some semblance of useful. In the kitchen, I rummage through her cabinet for a pot and scramble back to the dining room. I set it on the table below the wet spot, which is slowly spreading larger on the ceiling. "Is there anything else we should do?" I ask.

Marina shakes her head listlessly. "I don't know."

I didn't expect her to fall into a stupor about this considering the state of the rest of her house, but I wonder if this is the final straw, one more unexpected inconvenience when she has so many to contend with already. I want to apologize for making this happen, for pushing her into the dinner party, for picking Stan, whose rate was cheaper than the other electricians who popped up in my search. And I want to tell her, before Jess arrives, that I've invited Jess and Solar Summit to this dinner party she didn't want to throw.

But I don't know how to say any of this when Marina is standing there blinking upward like the sky is falling. Because it sort of is.

The mood changes for the better when Jess arrives. I'm starting to suspect Jess is a superhero. They enter the house without knocking—they must still have a key—and immediately climb onto the dining table, producing a pocketknife from their key ring. They stab into the wet spot in the drywall, and a small stream of water spills into the pot beneath it. Jess cuts a hole into the drywall and pokes a finger on the pipe above it, inspecting something.

"You said an electrician was here?" they ask.

"Yeah," Marina replies. "He was fixing the chandelier, and then he said he had to replace it."

"Who was it?" Jess asks.

"Um," I say. "A guy named Stan."

"Sounds legit," Jess says with a dry laugh. "He must have disturbed a pipe." They climb down from the table and fold their knife. "It's not too bad a leak, at least." Water is steadily dripping into the pot still, but at a fairly slow pace.

Jess makes a call, squeezing Marina's arm in a comforting gesture, and I watch the way Marina leans into them. "Good news," Jess says when they get off the phone. "Plumber's on his way now. Everything should be fixed before your dinner party tomorrow."

Marina's brow wrinkles. "How do you know about the

dinner party? Oh, because of your job," she says, answering her own question. "You invited Mayor Bradley through Jess, right?" Marina turns to me.

"Yes," I say slowly, ignoring the suspicious look Jess gives me. "And because…I invited Jess." When Marina's eyebrows shoot up, I throw in, "I also invited Solar Summit."

Marina's eyes flash with anger. "You *what*?"

"Only because I really felt like I had to," I insist. "We need to tap into every resource we can. And Solar Summit wants to partner with us."

"They also want to buy my house for their stupid resort," Marina points out. "They'll come in, take one look around, and when they see all of this"—she gestures around her, then at the hole in the ceiling—"they'll find a way to use it against me."

"No, they won't," I protest. "I promise. They're just coming to support the festival."

Marina harrumphs and crosses her arms. "If they say a single word about my house—"

"We'll sic Stan on them," Jess interrupts. "Give Stan an hour and a pair of pliers, and he could accidentally turn Solar Summit into a water park."

Marina laughs despite herself. "Okay," she agrees. "If Solar Summit tries to mess with me, they have to deal with Stan."

"And me," Jess adds.

They exchange a look so loaded with emotion I feel like I shouldn't even be in the room.

"Thanks for coming," Marina murmurs.

"Of course," Jess says softly.

Marina pulls Jess into a hug, and I slowly back out of the room. I busy myself with washing dishes. As I scrub orange-colored residue off a pot, I vow not to put Marina through any more turmoil. I'll do whatever it takes to make sure tomorrow's dinner party goes perfectly—and it will.

Just...with a hole in the ceiling.

CHAPTER TWENTY-TWO

I T MAY HAVE TAKEN HALF the night, but I have transformed Marina's house into an elegant venue fit for our guests, Mayor Bradley, and Martha Stewart herself.

With velvet curtains and a tension rod, I've blocked off the entrance to the kitchen to prevent our guests from catching a glimpse of the discolored wall with the missing cabinets. I put down a colorful Persian carpet runner in the foyer to cover up the chipped floorboards. I cleared out the wall hanging aisle of a home decor shop in Falls Point, and now the living room's drywall holes are covered with framed decorative signage—including three identical LIVE, LAUGH, LOVE signs. It's a little bizarre, but it works.

When the plumber Jess found finished fixing the leaky pipe in the dining room ceiling, I asked him to take a look at the downstairs bathroom Marina deemed scary. He fixed the issue by replacing the toilet—another expense on my tired credit card, but at least now the downstairs bathroom is usable, clean, and smelling like the apple-and-clove potpourri I've placed inside.

The hole in the dining room ceiling is…larger, after the plumber had to cut into more of the drywall to fix the pipe. And none of the wall decor I bought was suitable for a ceiling. But I dug around in a box of classroom supplies in Marina's closet and found a poster to cover the hole. Now, anyone who sits at the dining room table and looks up will be greeted with the smiling face of Daveed Diggs holding a book, with the word *READ* displayed above him in large block letters. The dining room ceiling is, admittedly, an odd place to promote literacy. But it's better than a hole.

Randy volunteers to help out, which I'm grateful for. While he handles the appetizers in the kitchen with Marina, I stand in the living room and watch the door, ready to play host.

The first guest to arrive is Jaclyn, who I remember seeing at the Chamber of Commerce meeting. She'd signed up for a booth at the festival to sell items from her body boutique shop. I'm tempted to ask her how her mission to try CBD oil is going, but I'm not sure I could manage the question without laughing.

Tim Cooper greets me with a hug and hands off a pink box of cupcakes. I'm used to seeing him behind the counter of his bakery in a flour-dusted apron, but tonight he looks distinguished in a plaid blue flannel shirt and dark jeans.

Meg arrives with Elise, who serves on the Chamber of Commerce committee and owns a successful candle business. Today, Elise wears not a crop top but a long, flowy dress. I compliment the shiny purple crystal Elise is wearing around her neck, which leads her to launch into its healing properties. Meg listens with interest, but Walt, an older man who will be running the history of Greenstead booth, gives a skeptical hum. Elise pauses briefly but carries on talking, though a flash of annoyance crosses her face.

Next to show up is Sera, who runs a barbecue food truck. She's half Black like me, maybe a few years older. I recall her having a bubbly personality when I got lunch at her truck last month, but tonight her eyes are watery, her nose is red, and she disappears into the bathroom to have a sneezing fit. Which doesn't seem like a great sign.

After everything I've heard about Mayor Bradley, I expected a nervous, wild-eyed person, hair unkempt, wearing unusual clothes from centuries past, skin pale from hiding away in attics or whatever it is Mayor Bradley gets up to when he's not fulfilling his mayorly duties. (It's possible I might have been picturing Edward Scissorhands.) But the man who shows up with Jess looks mayoral enough, a dark-skinned Black man in a blazer and jeans. Though his smile is tight and forced as he thrusts a bottle of wine in my direction.

As he steps into the foyer, he glances down at his watch and fiddles with it. It gives a soft beep, and I peer over to see that it's begun counting down from two hours.

Catching my eye, Jess leans in to whisper, "He has a strict two-hour limit for social situations."

Mayor Bradley maneuvers past us, hugging the wall as he sneaks into the living room like a spy.

"What happens when the two hours are up?" I ask. Except

I don't get an answer, because Jess disappears into the kitchen to find Marina. I'm left to stare in dismay at my two-hour time bomb. He's now tucked himself into the corner of the living room, pretending to study a KEEP CALM AND DRINK WINE sign as if it's a treasured historical document.

The guests zero in on him immediately, plying him with complaints about permits and taxes, showering him with questions about how his community development project is going. He stands there looking like a hostage, nodding and grimacing his way through the conversation. It makes me wonder how this people-averse man was ever elected to office, though I suppose not many are up for the job of trying to keep a dying town going. Greenstead probably takes what it can get.

By the time Marina comes out with a tray of goat cheese crostini, Mayor Bradley has at least become verbal. With Jess standing at his side fielding questions on his behalf, Mayor Bradley takes a crostini and mutters into his watch that Pretzel in Paradise has become the cornerstone of Greenstead's community. Meg glows with pride, and I notice her comments about his tax policy are suddenly more neutral.

I take a breath when Ted and Lucy from Solar Summit arrive. They look around the living room with interest, but not in the home-inspector way Marina feared. Lucy hands Marina a box of chocolates and says her home is lovely, and Marina visibly relaxes, melting into a smile and thanking her sincerely.

The rest of the guests, however, are less civil.

"What makes you so interested in Greenstead?" asks Tim.

"We think it's a wonderful location," Ted says. "Lots of open space, great view of the Blue Ridge Mountains by the Echo Hill Overlook."

"Yeah, until you put in a roller coaster factory, and then suddenly a roller coaster flood takes over the town," shoots back Elise.

Her remark elicits titters from the other guests, loudest of all from Jaclyn. Sera is the only one who doesn't laugh, perhaps because she's from Falls Point. She just sneezes into the crook of her arm and excuses herself for a tissue.

"That doesn't even make sense," Lucy whispers into her cup.

"What was that?" Elise takes a step closer. It's hard to imagine Elise intimidating anyone. There's nothing intimidating about her soft voice or her casual paisley dress. But she's about a head taller than Lucy, and her height coupled with the intensity of her disapproval is enough to startle her.

"Nothing," Lucy says, stepping back. "I just… We have no interest in stepping on any toes. We'd like to work *with* you."

The others won't hear of it. They grumble and shoot her distrustful looks until I change the subject by asking Walt about his history booth. Walt's response quickly turns into a monologue about interesting facts he's gathered in his research. The others start to shuffle impatiently, but boredom is better than a brawl.

I have to stifle my sigh of relief when Randy interrupts Walt to announce that dinner is ready to serve. I lead the way, directing our guests to the dining room. I've arranged the seating so that the Solar Summit folks sit at one end of the table, far from the Greenstead vendors, with Jess, Marina, and me serving as buffers between them.

Despite the fall-inspired centerpiece I've placed in the middle of Marina's table—decorative mini-pumpkins and fake leaves—every guest who trickles into the dining room cranes their neck to gaze at Daveed Diggs on the ceiling.

"Reading is so important," I say to Mayor Bradley, who's still staring at the poster.

Mayor Bradley lowers his eyes to rest on me. "Right," he agrees, looking bemused. Behind him, Jess covers their laugh with a cough.

The first surprise of the night comes when the doorbell rings partway through the soup course. I lift my head at the sound of it, meeting Marina's eyes across the table.

"Are we expecting anyone else?" she asks. I shake my head, and she stands to answer the door. Moments later, a high-pitched voice tells me everything I need to know.

Nancy Fletcher has decided to crash our dinner party.

I should have known, of course. It's exactly what she did to Wyatt and Deb's one-on-one date on *Love Quest*. While the other contestants kept a respectful distance from Wyatt and Deb enjoying a candlelit meal on the back patio of the *Love Quest* house, Nancy pulled up a chair next to them and squealed that she hadn't gotten a chance to see Wyatt all day. Nancy is an expert in making everything about her, even someone else's date. And, evidently, someone else's dinner party.

"When I heard you were gathering influential figures, I figured my invitation must have gotten lost in the mail," Nancy says, draping herself in the doorway to the dining room. She must think she looks cool standing like this, her hip jutted out at one angle, one hand pressed against the doorframe. But really, it just makes her look like she's bracing for an earthquake.

"I thought you were avoiding 'Queasy Lauryn' until your hazmat suit arrives," I say through clenched teeth. "Isn't that what you've been saying on your show?"

"I believe *everyone* deserves a second chance," Nancy says sweetly, and I want to pull a page out of her *Love Quest* repertoire and throw my drink in her face.

Marina, however, doesn't let Nancy rattle her out of her polite host role. "Why don't you take a seat right over there?" she suggests, pointing to the chair she's been sitting in.

"No," Jess says, starting to stand, "I can—"

"*No*," Mayor Bradley and Marina say at the same time. Marina raises her eyebrows meaningfully at Jess, the corners of her lips fighting to hide her amusement.

"I'm mostly gonna be in the kitchen anyway," Marina explains, guiding Nancy to her seat. "Have fun."

Marina winks at me on her way to the kitchen. Mayor Bradley lets out a relieved sigh that his buffer hasn't left him. I suppress a groan and stare daggers at Nancy, who shoots me an angelic smile.

Nancy seems to have a talent for making my life worse. If she hadn't insisted we go on her show, I never would have thrown up on air while Marina ranted about Ryser's scandals. The clip never would have gone viral, and Amanda never would have seen it, gotten involved in festival planning, and decided to pull the funding and consider closing the Ryser Cares office. And Nancy wouldn't be milking the hell out of that incident on her show, turning "Queasy Lauryn" into a running joke, holding that caption contest with that godforsaken picture of me. She's having the time of her life basking in my misery.

But I clench my fists and try to be civil. Nancy's motives become clear when she gushes to Mayor Bradley that she'd love to have him on her show for an interview.

"I'll have to see," he says, sharing a look with Jess. "My schedule's pretty packed." He checks his watch, and I remember his two-hour limit. Which Nancy is wasting on herself.

"I know you'd be an exceptional guest," Nancy says. She turns to me with a pointed glare. "Unlike some people."

"You made me go on your show," I remind her, doing my best to sound friendly.

"Did I make you show up *hungover*?" Nancy replies. "Did I make you *vomit* on my Louboutins?"

All eyes around the table fly to me, sending a flush of heat to my cheeks. My mind flashes with white-hot rage, and I can't resist getting in a dig of my own. "Have I told you how much I love your highlights?" I say.

Nancy gasps, her eyes narrowing into slivers. Around the table, it's clear who's familiar with Nancy's hang-ups and who isn't. Elise, Meg, and Tim go still while Mayor Bradley and the rest of the guests continue eating and drinking.

"This. Is. My. Natural. Color," Nancy insists in a gravelly low tone I didn't even know her voice was capable of reaching.

Before I can respond, Marina calls my name. I toss Nancy a glare as I stand. When I enter the kitchen, Randy is artfully arranging roasted brussels sprouts on plates filled with roast chicken and mushroom risotto while Marina leans against the counter with crossed arms.

"What the hell are you doing?" Marina says.

I raise my palms in a gesture of innocence. "Nancy started it!"

"Nancy lives on another planet," Marina reminds me. "Fighting with her is pointless. Just let her get in her catty remarks, let her make everything about her, and move on with it. It's fine."

"Easier said than done," I grumble, lowering my eyes. I reach for a brussels sprout off the tray, but Randy swats my hand away.

Marina squints at me. "Why are you letting her get to you? Is it the Queasy Lauryn stuff?"

"I…" Behind Marina, Randy gives me a look of concern. I imagine he might have pieced together the connection between Nancy and Amanda's decision. "Nothing. Just…dinner party stress."

"This was *your* idea," Marina reminds me with an amused grin. "You did this to yourself."

I give her a rueful smile back. "I know. I shouldn't have."

She shrugs. "It seems like it's going well, actually. Just…be chill. Live, laugh, love. Keep calm and drink wine. Pick a mantra from one of those hideous signs you put in my living room and stick to it." Marina gathers a plate in each hand, fixes me with a stern look that I'm sure she saves for her most difficult fourth graders, and moves into the next room to serve the main course.

"I'm partial to the 'Grandchildren Make You Grand' one," Randy jokes, passing me with a plate in each hand. "Raises a lot of questions."

I take in a long breath through my nose and pick up two more plates. Before I leave the kitchen, I steel myself. I won't let myself get sucked into Nancy's world of pettiness. I won't take out my frustrations with Ryser on Nancy. I'll rise above, for the sake of Marina, this dinner party, and the festival. I throw on a smile as fake as Nancy's golden blond highlights and enter the dining room.

When I take my place at the table, I am a perfect hostess. I charm our guests by talking up their businesses and gushing over how excited I am to have them at the apple festival. But the conversation slips into new tangents before I have a chance to bring up the VIP package. Tim talks about taking his son camping by the lake south of Greenstead, which prompts Walt to dive into a story about a historically significant church near the lake.

Sometime around then is when Jess raises the subject of Solar Summit's hotel resort proposal. They tell Ted and Lucy that it would be a wonderful way to rejuvenate West Greenstead and bring more tourists to our town.

"Admittedly," Jess says, "on a personal level, part of my excitement is for selfish reasons. You said the resort would include a shopping center and a movie theater, right? My life would be so much easier if I didn't have to drive to Falls Point when I want to buy a pair of jeans or see a movie."

Mayor Bradley, who I suspect Jess's speech is really for, listens with interest, but Meg and Elise bristle immediately.

"Thank you," Lucy says. "We came up with the idea when we expanded to a year-round schedule this year. We needed more hotel accommodations, and we wanted to give our guests activities they could do in the winter or on bad weather days. A resort in West Greenstead felt like the perfect fit. West Greenstead would get a lot of benefit from it, too."

"West Greenstead is doing fine," Meg replies hotly. "I know you Falls Pointers think you're better than us, but you're not."

Lucy shuts up, but Sera studies Meg curiously, like she's trying to place her. "Don't you live in Falls Point?" she asks. "I think I've seen you around my condo complex."

Elise, Jaclyn, and Mayor Bradley whip their heads around to stare at Meg, who's now shifting in her seat. She gazes up at Daveed Diggs, as if he can swoop down from his perch and save her with the power of literacy.

"You moved to Falls Point?" Jaclyn asks.

"You told me you were just moving across town," Elise says, betrayal in her voice. "I helped you *pack*."

Mayor Bradley shakes his head in disappointment. "Some voters might find it insulting that you would try to run for mayor of a town you don't even live in."

Meg frowns. "What? I'm not—"

Jess gives a loud, exaggerated cough, shooting me a look across the table. I lean forward and hurriedly try to think of a distraction.

"This risotto is delicious," I say loudly. Then, realizing that complimenting my own cooking might come off a little strangely, I add, "I, um. I've never made it before."

"It *is* delicious," Jaclyn agrees, her eyes still not leaving Meg.

Sera sneezes into her napkin and mutters an apology.

"Why'd you move?" Jaclyn asks Meg, taking a swig of her wine. "What does Falls Point have that we don't?"

"I needed to, for my asthma," Meg protests. "The air's better there."

Sera sneezes again. "There *is* something to Greenstead air that always makes my allergies act up," she admits with an apologetic sniffle.

"You know, Greenstead actually has *less* ragweed, which is the common cause for fall allergies, compared to neighboring areas," Walt says. "There's an interesting story behind that."

Next to him, Elise groans, and I tense up. I saw the way Elise's patience with Walt waned back in the living room, when he was questioning her claims about healing crystals and rambling about an article he'd read on the psychology behind them.

I'd like to change the subject again, but my mind unhelpfully offers up nothing. I resign myself to biting into a roasted brussels sprout. It's the perfect balance of crispy and tender, not that any of our guests have cared to notice.

"Look, I don't know what it is," Sera says, pulling another tissue from the pack in her lap. "It could be a lot of things. Maybe it's the mus—"

Heads swivel in Sera's direction. She abruptly closes her mouth. It's an unwritten rule here that only Greensteaders are allowed to talk about the mustard flood.

"Never mind," Sera says. "I just know that if I'm parking my truck in Greenstead, I feel better when I wear a mask."

"You don't *need* a mask, because our air is plenty clean," Mayor Bradley insists. "It's in the town slogan." He sets down his fork and turns to Meg. "I take back what I said about Pretzel in Paradise. Also, some of your pretzels are too salty."

"Well…" Meg looks around the table desperately, then points at Tim. "Tim's sponge cake is made from a mix—from Ryser."

Amid the gasps, Tim startles, his eyes bulging. "With modifications!" he protests. Glancing around with unease, he adds, "I'm still working on my sponge cake recipe."

"You've been 'working on' it for thirty years!" Meg retorts.

"At least I'm not a hypocrite pretending to live in Greenstead," Tim shoots back. "You think you're better than us, with your fancy Falls Point clean air?"

"Our air is *plenty* clean," Mayor Bradley repeats, raising his voice.

"How would you even know?" Jaclyn cuts in. "You're too busy hiding in your office, locked away from all of us."

"I'm shy!" Mayor Bradley bellows, bringing his fist down on the table. It's forceful enough to make the silverware rattle like a warning bell. One of the decorative mini-pumpkins threatens to roll off the table, and I have to reach across Walt to halt it.

"Let's change the subject," I quickly say.

"Why, feeling queasy?" Nancy asks.

"Oh, shut up, Nancy," Marina says wearily, refilling Walt's wineglass. "Our appearance on your show got you more views than you've had all year, and you're obviously loving it. You're welcome."

"I don't remember thanking you for anything," Nancy snipes.

Marina laughs. "You never thank anyone. You're just as entitled as you were in high school."

"Well, you're just as short as you were in high school," Nancy retorts, looking Marina up and down. I sigh and reach for my glass of wine.

A shrill beep joins the commotion. Heads turn to Mayor Bradley, who presses a button on his watch to silence it. "Well." He breaks into his first genuine smile of the night and rises from the table. "I've got to go."

"No!" The word leaves my mouth like a reflex, making the table go silent. I set my wineglass down hard enough that the wine nearly sloshes onto the tablecloth. Everyone is staring at me, in what feels like the first time I've gotten their attention all night. "I invited you all here to have dinner, talk to Mayor Bradley, and hear about the apple festival's VIP package," I say. "We have had dinner, you have talked to Mayor Bradley, but no one has let me get a word in about our goddamn VIP package. You will stay seated, you will eat dessert, and you will listen to me talk about the benefits of being a fucking VIP."

Our guests look down at their plates, remorse on their faces.

"Sorry," Mayor Bradley mumbles, sinking back into his seat.

"I'm sorry, too," says Meg sullenly.

Sera gives a stifled sneeze into her napkin.

"I only use a mix for sponge cake," Tim clarifies in a whisper.

We sit in awkward silence while Marina and Randy clear the table and bring out plates of apple galette topped with vanilla ice cream.

"Looks good," Elise says. "What is it?"

"Honey-Mustard apple galette," I say. "It's disgusting."

Her smile withers.

After yesterday's chaos of the leaking ceiling, dealing with the plumber, running around to home decor shops, and decorating Marina's house late into the night, I never got a chance to pick up non-mustard apples, nor did I have time to figure out how to make Bertram's apple abomination taste good. Instead, this morning I dutifully sliced the Honey Mustard apples, coated them in cinnamon and sugar, folded pie crusts around them, and threw them in the oven to let the fates take it from there.

They'd *baked* like regular apples. Their juices bubbled and caramelized, and there was a smell almost like apple pie permeating the house when I'd pulled them from the oven. *Almost.* It smelled like apple pie with a little…something else.

I planned on bullshitting something about the creativity of Greenstead's farmers when I served it tonight. I was going to steal Bertram's speech from the tasting and say this galette perfectly encapsulated Greenstead's history. But I can't be bothered to do that now. Tonight, they get a mustardy apple dessert with no context.

Our guests suffer their way through the galette. Their faces are pained, but they don't complain. I try a bite, hoping I've somehow found a way to make the apples taste good, but it tastes as unpleasant as I'd feared, sweet and savory clashing together in discord.

"The crust is delicious," Meg says politely. Like everyone else, she's eating around the filling.

"It's store-bought," I mutter.

"Beautifully presented," Jaclyn chimes in.

"Nice bake on it." Tim taps the crust with his fork. "Perfectly browned. That takes skill."

My anger melts a little, watching them bend over backward to find something to compliment about this terrible dessert. "Thank you. I have zero skill, though."

"Oh, take a compliment," Tim says.

"That's Lettie's problem," Walt adds. "Try to compliment her fudge and she starts telling you every single little thing that's wrong with it."

"Lettie?" I ask. "From Lettie's Confections?" It's strange to hear her spoken about in the present tense. Since she retired, I've only thought of Lettie as existing in the past, a memory of a time when the apple festival thrived and Marina and I had an unbreakable bond.

"That's her," Walt says. "I usually drop by and see her around Christmas when I visit my sister in Tampa. Lettie always sends me home with a mountain of fudge and refuses to hear a single good word about it."

I smile at the image of Lettie loading down Walt with candy. "I loved her caramel apples." Several murmurs of agreement ring out.

"Well, don't tell her that when you see her."

I have to mentally replay his words to make sure I've heard him right. "What?"

"She's coming to the festival." Walt pauses, bite of crust halfway to his mouth, when he sees my mystified expression. "Just to visit, not to sell anything like she used to. We were talking on the phone the other week and she was excited to hear the festival was coming back. She said to thank you."

A warmth floats through me, starting at my heart and radiating outward. As the creator of the caramel apple that marks our festival tradition, Lettie has loomed larger than life in Marina's and my minds. She's a goddess, a conjurer of sugar-spun miracles, and she's coming all the way from Florida to attend our festival.

If I can summon Lettie back to Greenstead without even knowing it, I can surely sell a few folks on the VIP package. Even if tonight's dinner party isn't going according to plan, everyone's still here, wincing their way through a galette. I can still turn this around.

"Ready to hear about our VIP offering?" I ask.

I talk in-depth about the VIP package, and our guests nod, listen, and even ask questions (except for Nancy, who scrolls through her phone the entire time). When I finish my spiel and ask who would like to purchase one, nearly all of the vendors agree. Mayor Bradley even writes out a check to make a personal donation for the festival. I'm certain it's only because they're ashamed of their behavior tonight, but guilt-induced purchases are fine by me.

One by one, our guests take their departure. Mayor Bradley is first out the door, but he isn't actively sprinting away, which I choose to take as a compliment. Even Nancy is more civilized than usual, telling us dinner was delicious. More shocking, she finds some semblance of manners and apologizes for showing up unannounced.

"I was really hoping to get that interview with Mayor Bradley," she explains. "Ratings aren't what they used to be. I needed a Hail Mary."

"You haven't tried vomiting on air?" I ask.

Nancy gives a baffled chuckle, and I'm just as confused, really. I don't know why I'm joking with her when she's been such a nightmare. It has to be post-dinner-party relief.

"Maybe for sweeps," she jokes. And I laugh, and I don't know what's happening. I tell her to have a good night, and I sort of mean it.

When we close the door on our last guest, it's just Marina, Randy, and me standing in the foyer, staring at the front door in a daze.

"That was fun," Marina deadpans.

An exhausted laugh escapes me. "Thank you for letting me use your house," I say. "I'm sorry about…all of it."

Marina gives me a tired smile. "That's okay. It seems like it was worth it?"

"I think so."

I'll still have to chase people down on Monday to make good on what they promised tonight, but if everyone who agreed to buy a VIP package stays true to their word, we'll have a good chunk of money to make up for what we lost from Ryser.

Not all of it—not quite enough. But enough to eke our way forward and hope I can figure out a plan for coming up with the rest.

And soon.

CHAPTER TWENTY-THREE

MY DINNER-PARTY PLANNING STRESS FADES into pleased relief when Randy and I recap the event to the Ryser Cares office the following Monday morning.

Amid Jen's laughter, Tessa's delighted interest in learning about Meg's true place of residence, and Arun's awestruck joy at the news of how many VIP packages we sold, my memory of the dinner party grows softer around the edges, transforming from a night of stress to a sparkling evening of good food, Greenstead gossip, and hard-won accomplishment.

Arun sends out the VIP agreements, and it's another relief when all six come back signed, promised payments made in full. I tell Arun I'm sorry it's not enough to afford Art McKenzie, he smiles and shrugs it off, and I feel deliciously at peace with what feels like the most satisfying lie I've ever told.

My next challenge is getting the rest of the money, but I give myself a break from worrying. I deserve a little more time holding on to that peaceful feeling.

I only get two days, though. On Wednesday morning, as I'm drinking an iced pumpkin chai latte and working my way through the daily crossword on my phone, Arun disappears into the meeting room in the back for a call, which isn't out of the ordinary. He'll use the room sometimes for lengthy calls with suppliers—or with Walt, who tends to talk his ear off. But when he returns from this one, he's a different person, strutting to his desk with his laptop tucked under one arm and a proud grin on his face.

"Guess who I was just talking to," he says.

"Walt?" Tessa guesses from the kitchen. After hearing about my failed attempt to bake with Bertram's Honey Mustard apple, she's been doing some experimenting with them.

"Nope." Arun sets his laptop down and hops onto his desk. "That was Art McKenzie."

Jen and Randy look up. Tessa peeks her head out from the kitchen down the hall. My stomach tenses.

"Why were you talking to Art McKenzie?" I ask, growing fearful of the answer.

"Because he's performing at the apple festival," he reveals.

Tessa gasps, Jen squeals, and my brain doesn't know how to process this.

"But...how?" I ask.

"I negotiated. He was willing to take less if his set was more magic than music. Not ideal, but...we got him. You put in all that effort trying to get the money, and we were so close. I didn't want it to go to waste." His eyes are shining, and his words are so sincere, and I'm a horrible person for wanting to strangle him.

I agonized over that dinner party for nothing, and now I'm back to square one. I once again need to conjure thousands of dollars, except this time the festival is only three and a half weeks away. All the air in my lungs leaves me in a shuddering breath.

Seeing Arun's expectant look, I plaster on a thin smile. "Wow," I say weakly.

I ignore Randy's sympathetic glance as Arun launches into next steps in words that sound faraway. He says we'll pay Art half the money once he signs the agreement and the other half after the festival, and that we'll need to book Art's flight and hotel reservation. He recaps their careful negotiation, how Art was doing sleight-of-hand tricks all throughout the video call, expertly making a coin disappear. A fitting trick, considering.

The office is abuzz with energy after that. Jen begins creating graphics to advertise Art's presence, and Tessa ponders how quickly the local news station will update its "Art Alert" segment. Randy comments that this all hinges on whether Art sends back the signed agreement. And as I'm finding reassurance in Randy's words and hoping Art proves himself a flaky disappointment, Arun's computer unhelpfully chimes with an email. Within seconds, Arun cheers that Art is an official part of our apple festival.

As the others celebrate, Randy edges over to my desk, where I'm doggedly staring at the crossword puzzle on my phone, trying to think of a seven-letter city in Silicon Valley.

"What do you want to do about this?" Randy asks quietly. "How can I help?"

I look up with a listless shrug. "It's fine," I say. "I'll figure it out." When Randy hesitates, I add, "I'll think of something. Don't worry about it."

Randy's not convinced, but I don't have the mental capacity to reassure him any more than that. I go back to my phone, and I enter in *San Jose*, and Randy gives up and returns to his desk.

I do intend to think of something, when I'm more capable. Yet I start slipping into procrastination instead, deciding I'll figure it out the next day, then the next. Somewhere along the way, that procrastination turns into blissful, numb denial.

The apple festival has been largely hypothetical in my mind, anyway. For so long, it's been an idea, a concept. Something we discuss and plan for that hasn't actually come into fruition—which makes it all too easy for me to downplay the realities of what I'm up against.

Yes, I need to come up with the money we lost—again—but no one's stopping me from continuing on with the festival preparations. We're still sending our vendors email updates, hanging up flyers, approving brochures. No one bats an eye when I suggest removing the Ryser name and logo from the festival signage and make up a lie about getting Amanda's approval to keep the festival Greenstead-centric. There's nothing to doubt. This is normal. Business as usual. I carry on acting like everything's fine and the world keeps on turning.

Until Jen gets a call one drizzly Friday morning in early October while I'm settling into my desk with a mug of tea.

"It's Waterfront Party Rentals," she says, walking up to my desk with her phone in hand. "They said the card was declined."

My head shoots up. Behind Jen, Randy glances over with worry. I rifle through my mind for a response.

"Right," I say, like I'm just remembering something. "Amanda said they're sending us a new corporate card. There was some kind of security issue with the old one."

Jen nods, seeming to accept this. "They need the deposit for the chair and table rentals by Monday. Would you mind letting them know how we're handling the payment?" She holds up her phone.

"Sure." I bring her phone to my ear, even though I want to toss it across the room and hide in my delusion for a while longer. Jen stands by as I recite my excuse and promise to have the deposit by Monday.

"So you're getting the new card by Monday?" Jen asks when I hand the phone back to her.

"Yeah," I say, "it's on its way." The lie is easier the more I repeat it.

When Jen returns to her desk, I catch Randy's eye again and look away. I'm not interested in being pulled into the panic I've spent the last few weeks trying to numb myself to. I want to pretend for as long as I can. I'm good at it.

Later that morning, I volunteer to pick up pretzels for everyone. I could use some time to clear my head. But being alone with my thoughts makes it worse somehow. The worries I've been avoiding pile up and multiply, and as I lean against the wall at Pretzel in Paradise and wait for my order to be called, I feel more acutely than ever that time is running out. I have to come up with a thousand dollars for a deposit on the chair and table rentals by Monday. I can't put it on my credit card because it's dangerously close to being maxed out with all the festival-related purchases I've put on it already. And when I called the rental company on my way to the pretzel shop to ask for an extension, they cited their policy and said it wouldn't be possible.

I could transfer the money from my savings, but touching that would set my FIRE plan back even further. And what would be the point of all the years I've spent working for Ryser and hating myself for it, if I was just going to end up setting my plans back anyway? The last decade of my life can't really have been for nothing, can it?

I take the warm paper bag Meg hands me when my name is called. I thank her when she tells me she threw in a few samples of her new cheddar jalapeño pretzel bites. As I pass through the exit and into the brisk autumn air, I turn around and stare at the cute Pretzel in Paradise storefront with its cartoon images of flavored pretzels adorning the window on this otherwise deserted block. And I wonder, will Meg and her pretzel shop that Mayor Bradley called the cornerstone of the community be able to thrive and stay in business in the years to come? Or will this place, too, fall into disrepair, just like the ghosts of the shops that used to be next to it? Like the community center is surely destined for, and all the other places that used to be beloved in Greenstead?

I'm so in my head when I return to the Ryser Cares office that it takes me a few seconds to notice the office is empty. A smell hangs in the air, something fruity yet savory, and there are voices coming from somewhere. I walk past our empty desks and peek into the meeting room—empty—then the kitchen. It's there that

I find Tessa standing at the stove, stirring a pot of brown goop as the others look on. Arun's sitting on the counter, Jen stands at the stove beside Tessa, and Randy's washing a cutting board in the sink.

"She's here," Arun sings when he spots me.

"What's this?" I ask.

Tessa turns to me with a proud smile. "Okay. This might be my most promising mustard apple attempt yet."

The memory of her last attempt—a sour-tasting cinnamon apple cake—makes my taste buds cower. I take a closer look at the goop. "What…is it?"

"Honey-Mustard apple butter," she replies. "Remember that sandwich place we went to in Richmond last weekend? They had that grilled cheese with mustard and apricot jam? It made me wonder if a Honey-Mustard apple butter would be good on grilled cheese. We don't have grilled cheese, but…" She gestures to the bag of pretzels in my hand.

"Let's do it." Arun reaches into the bag and pulls out a pretzel. He offers it around, and we each take a piece like this is part of some sacred ceremony. We dip our pieces into the pot and hope for the best.

When the flavor hits me, I stop chewing. I share a perplexed look with Jen, whose eyes have widened.

I resume chewing, trying to pin down the flavor. It's sweet, like jam, but there's a savory edge that complements the sweetness, prevents it from being cloying. And the sweetness in turn tames that savory flavor, adds a complexity that makes me want to go back for more.

"How is this so good?" Arun says, reaching for another.

"The universe took pity on me," Tessa jokes.

Arun shakes his head. "This is not the universe. It's you being awesome."

Her smile is shy and reluctant. "Fine," she relents. She dips another pretzel piece into the apple butter and chews it thoughtfully. "I need to try it on grilled cheese. I think the flavors will really come through then."

"I *do* want a grilled cheese sandwich, now that you've mentioned it," Jen says.

Randy, reaching into the pretzel bag, stops his movements. "I could go pick up some bread and cheese right now." There's a question in his voice. In seconds, we all silently agree on the answer.

And so the workday devolves into an exploration of the grilled cheese sandwich. We stand in the kitchen while butter sizzles on the stove, talking about what we love about grilled cheese, the memories we associate with it: cold rainy days, tomato soup, comfort and indulgence. We decide there's no better day for a warm, melty grilled cheese than today, the first day that actually *feels* like fall, with that crispness in the air outside that demands sweaters and scarves.

This doesn't feel like work. These people don't feel like my coworkers. We've slipped into something else, something that feels solid and real. It's connecting me to a feeling I haven't known since childhood. It's something that crawls inside my heart and radiates a warm glow. I feel like I belong.

How strange and sad that I've gone my entire adulthood

without it. How wonderful that I get to experience it now, here, surrounded by these people and grilled cheese sandwiches sizzling on the stove beside a pot of something sweet and delicious.

The Honey-Mustard apple butter makes the grilled cheese sing. It elevates it into something tantalizingly complex and mouthwatering. The creamy tang of the sharp cheddar is the perfect contrast to the bright, refreshing sweetness of the apple butter.

"You could bottle this," Randy says, gesturing to the apple butter with the half-finished sandwich in his hand. "You'd make millions."

"Or sell the recipe to one of those fancy judges you're bringing in for the festival," says Jen, who's leaning against the counter across from him.

Tessa wears her usual reluctance whenever she's met with sincerity, but a glimmer of excitement peeks from her eyes. "Actually, um, one of them did say there was some kind of opportunity she wanted to talk to me about. I was telling June Davis from Bread and Butter about how I love baking but haven't ever tried doing it professionally, and she said she was gonna send me something she thought I should apply for."

"You gonna go for it?" Arun asks. From his spot at the stove where he's making a second grilled cheese sandwich for himself, he turns to gauge Tessa's response.

"I don't even know what it is yet."

"Yeah, but if it's, like, a job at her bakery or something?"

The Tessa from a few months ago would have rolled her eyes and reminded us for the thousandth time about her salad-dressing botulism incident that landed her in the Flop House. But this Tessa scrunches up her face with the agony of believing in herself and says, "I might." Against our cheers, she's quick to add, "Not that she's actually offering me a job. We're daydreaming here."

Arun flips his sandwich. The butter hisses when he presses it into the pan. "While we're daydreaming? Can I say something delusional?" When we nod, he says, "I was thinking, if the festival goes well, I might...start my own event management company. Is that stupid?"

"Of course not," Randy says with a surprised laugh. "You'd be great at it."

"Thanks." Arun inspects his spatula. "This festival's been a reminder that maybe I don't suck ass at events."

"Beautifully put," Jen jokes. She tilts her head, considering. "There *has* been a sort of hair of the dog to all this. After the *Bachelorette* incident with Ryser, I thought I'd never want to run social media for anyone ever again. But...it's been fun, running the festival account."

"You're good at it," Tessa says, and I join her in agreeing. Jen's tongue-in-cheek replies to Nancy's "Queasy Lauryn" posts have been garnering more and more likes.

Jen shrugs, looking pleased. "Maybe, after the festival, I'll ask corporate about dusting off their old Ryser Cares account."

Randy takes a sip from his mug of tea. "We should take on another project when the festival's over. I think...maybe I'm good for something besides having a van and throwing Christmas parties."

A timid satisfaction takes over Randy. In his face, I see the quiet confidence he's taken on over the last few months, how he's gone from making himself invisible to navigating vendor calls and negotiating contracts with an expertise I didn't know he had.

This festival has given us all a sense of purpose beyond what I ever expected. It's helped us tap back into the versions of ourselves we thought we lost. Even me, I think. I never felt like I was a screwup like my colleagues have, but I did feel more alone than I realized. Until Marina walked into this office and gave me a reason to step out of my bubble and find connection with the people around me.

I remain lost in thought after our impromptu pre-lunch lunch comes to an end. Tessa heads off to write up the recipe and work with Jen to design it into a recipe card for the festival. Randy starts on the dishes. I wander to my desk, where I watch Arun cross *Honey Mustard apple recipe???* off the whiteboard.

I sit there, sweeping the last few grilled cheese crumbs into my mouth, staring at the whiteboard that has only a few outstanding items remaining, the calendar in the corner showing the festival is just eight days away, and this beautiful group of people working away to make it happen. And I know what I have to do.

When I get home that afternoon, I log into my bank account and initiate a transfer from my savings—not just the deposit for the chair and table rentals, but everything I need to cover the festival costs. Seeing the money I worked so hard for leave my account in a few taps of a button pains me—as does opening my FIRE spreadsheet, adding the deduction, and seeing that shiny early retirement goal move even further away.

But it feels worth it for this, to hold on to our little community for a while longer. To help my coworkers see this project through so they can use this success to propel them into whatever next chapter they envision for themselves—whether that's starting something new like Arun and Tessa, or staying here at Ryser Cares and finding more ways to uplift Greenstead like Jen and Randy. To keep Greenstead's community center going and ensure Greensteaders will always have a place to gather and connect. To give me an excuse to hold on to that blissful feeling of belonging for as long as I possibly can.

Even if it has an expiration date.

CHAPTER TWENTY-FOUR

IT'S STRANGE TO THINK THE festival is just hours away.

The evening before we open, my colleagues and I survey Juniper Park, admiring our work. The sign hangs over the arch we set up at the entrance beside the customary stack of hay bales. The booths we assembled line the park in neat rows, forming aisles for crowds to walk down. Even the trees have seen fit to dress up for the occasion, with orange-bronze leaves that adorn their branches and scatter across the grass like confetti. Save for the roped-off Nancy convention section at the other end of the park—and the stage, chairs, and enclosed tent for the greenroom she requested, arranged exactly as her rider dictated—the scene before us comes strikingly close to the festival Marina and I attended every year.

All that's missing are the people—who should, we hope, fill the park tomorrow. Soon these empty tables will be full of vendors selling their goods. This park will be swarming with attendees, hopefully not just Greensteaders but Virginians from all over, here to support this town and celebrate what makes Greenstead unique.

When we part ways that evening, my work still isn't done. Marina volunteered to assemble the gift bags for our VIP sponsors, but she texted me that afternoon to confess that helping out with set design for a school play kept her so busy that she hadn't touched them. I told her I'd come over to help when we were finished at Juniper Park. There was a pause, and then Marina texted Can we do it at your place? My AC's acting up.

I wanted to press her on it. It's so rare that Marina acknowledges the state of her house that this felt like an opportunity to get more out of her while she was willing to talk about it. But, knowing what it took for her to admit this much, I just replied that she was welcome to come over.

She arrives not long after I get home. My dad treats Marina's arrival with such fanfare that I feel like a teenager again, mouthing apologies about my uncool dad while he peppers her with questions and marvels over how long it's been since she was last here.

Once I manage to extract Marina from the parental chitchat, we head to my room and soon fall into a rhythm. We form a two-person assembly line, loading each bag with our designated items, from tote bags stamped with the festival logo to mini bottles of apple mead we sourced from a vendor. With the bags filled, Marina moves on to filling out the handwritten thank-you cards for each of our VIPs. As I'm trying to separate two layers of the colorful tissue paper we bought, I look over to watch her write Meg's name in the elegant handwriting I recognize well.

All throughout school, whenever we were paired together on a project, Marina has always been the one to do the writing, be it notebook paper or poster boards. Her handwriting has always been neater than mine.

I don't think I ever would have expected, some fifteen years ago—or whenever we last did an assignment together—that we would be here at thirty-two, in my same childhood bedroom in Greenstead, working on what's essentially one big shared assignment. I would have expected the being-with-Marina part, but not so much the Greenstead part. Or the fact that Marina and I went a decade without talking. There's a lot about my life I don't think my teenage self would have predicted. Which is strange to think, because on the surface level, I'd always thought I was following my dreams—getting the hell out of Greenstead, moving to DC.

But I have to admit that those dreams involved more than a city. They involved being close to friends and family, having a dog with a wagging tail to greet me at the end of each day. Not wrestling with my conscience while I draft press releases for the company that devastated my hometown. Not putting in long hours at work, coming home to my empty apartment, and constantly checking the balance of my savings account like a bored student watching the clock, waiting for class to be over.

But I'll still fulfill those dreams eventually, I remind myself. I'm just postponing them. You can put a pin in dreams, I'm pretty sure. They're not balloons; they won't burst. But they *can* change. Or maybe I've changed. The vision feels close in some ways, and so far away in others.

"I'm almost nervous about tomorrow," Marina says, pulling me from my thoughts. She closes the last envelope in her stack and begins sliding each one into the gift bags I've decorated with yellow-and-orange tissue paper. With the last card nestled into its bag, she leans back against my bed railing. We're sitting on the floor of my bedroom, bags, tissue paper, stickers, and festival goods all around us. "I just hope it's as good as everyone remembers."

"It will be," I tell her. It *has* to be, after everything we've poured into it.

"I hope it becomes an annual thing again, if it goes well," Marina says. "It could be the thing that people keep coming back to Greenstead for every year, like it was before. We could use the proceeds to reinvest in the town, make improvements. I know one festival might not be enough to save the community center forever, but over time, maybe?"

Her eyes are sparkling with hope, and I'm tempted to suggest she temper her expectations. This festival probably won't happen in future years. Not without the money Ryser pulled from us. And while I'm still clinging to the chance that Amanda won't close the Ryser Cares office once she hears about the festival's success, there's no way she'd contribute to the festival budget next year after she made such a big deal about revoking the funds.

But I remember my decision to wait until after the festival to come clean about all this, and I remind myself that I'll tell Marina on Monday.

For this weekend, though, I need to let her enjoy it. I need to let *myself* enjoy it. I've spent so much time these last few weeks worrying and panicking and letting the pit in my stomach weigh down my every feeling. Why shouldn't I set that aside for once and enjoy this weekend too? Life after the apple festival may be murky—job prospects uncertain, no clue whether Marina and the folks at Ryser Cares will understand why I've kept this news from them—but before I face all of that, I get to enjoy this festival. I'll see the results of our hard work, taste the mustard-flavored fruits of our labor. All the harsh realities that follow will still be there, and I can face them then—and not one moment sooner.

It's almost ten o'clock by the time we place the final VIP bag on my desk. Marina stretches her arms over her head like she's going to get up—but she doesn't.

She sighs and turns to me, leaning her head against the side of my bed. "Do you still have that air mattress?" she asks. Her tone is almost apologetic.

"Yeah," I reply, trying to get a read on her face. "I think my dad still has it somewhere. You…want to spend the night?"

Marina purses her lips, eyes roving. Wrestling with whatever it is she wants to say. "I don't like sleeping in my house," she says quietly.

There's reluctance in her voice. She's dreading that I'll ask follow-up questions, try to dig deeper to the root of it. But now's not the time.

I don't point out how she used to grumble about that air mattress back when she used to sleep over. She used to say it deflated too easily, that we'd fill it up before we went to bed and then she'd wake up in the middle of the night and feel like she was slowly sinking into a sagging heap. I simply ask my dad for it, which of course makes him sentimental all over again—and then he pops his head back into the room to ask if we want him to make us chocolate chip pancakes in the morning, as if we're still little kids (and yes, we do).

After Marina and I set up the mattress, I rummage through my dresser and lend her an old T-shirt from a volunteer event we did together in high school—which of course gets us talking about school. Marina shares updates on what our old teachers and classmates are up to. Before long, we're catching each other up on our own lives. Even after we set our alarms for early tomorrow morning and turn off the lights, we still lie in the dark talking, just like we used to do at sleepovers past.

"I like mushrooms now," Marina announces, as if she's revealing a scandalous piece of gossip, and she sort of is. My mental Marina file has a whole chapter dedicated to her hatred of mushrooms, with subsections for her complaints about them: too squishy, too earthy, they ruin pizza.

I turn on my side, propping up my elbow, and ask for every detail. She complies, talking about how a bowl of ramen she had in college expanded her horizons, how those enoki mushrooms were a gateway into the world of mushrooms she didn't hate. (But she still hates portabellos, she tells me gravely, and I nod with the deepest of understandings and update my file accordingly.)

I tell her that I stopped getting my hair relaxed a couple of years after college, when I decided I wanted to learn how to do my natural hair. I detail all the hair care tutorials I watched, the hair routines and product reviews, and how all that knowledge has been wasted in these last few years, when I've been so preoccupied with work that it was easier to fall into a routine of throwing my hair in a ponytail or slapping on a headband.

She tells me her new favorite pen has changed from the Pilot G2 to the Pentel EnerGel because it writes more smoothly and the ink doesn't smear on her hands as often. I tell her my favorite peanut butter brand has switched from Jif to Teddie. She tells me about getting stung by a bee for the first time five years ago and discovering she's allergic to beestings.

On and on we go, trading anecdotes and factoids, updating our mental files, bringing our knowledge of one another into the present. I don't ask her about her house or Jess. She doesn't ask me about Ryser or DC. We just talk about the details that feel the most compelling as we lie in the dark and stare at the ceiling where my glow-in-the-dark stars used to be.

It's Marina who falls asleep first. Her breaths slow as I'm explaining how I came to start preferring vanilla cake over chocolate. And when I ask if her favorite cake flavor is still strawberry, she doesn't respond. I roll over and close my eyes, pulling my blankets closer.

As I fall asleep, I think about everything I still want to tell Marina, everything I don't, and all that awaits us tomorrow.

CHAPTER TWENTY-FIVE

S ATURDAY BRINGS PERFECT FALL WEATHER. The sky is bright, and the sun's providing enough warmth to make an outdoor festival comfortable. But there's still a bite to the air that invites cardigans, pullovers, and an abundance of plaid.

When Marina and I arrive at Juniper Park on Saturday morning, I'm wearing an oversized plaid shirt unbuttoned over my bright-orange festival volunteer top. It's the perfect ensemble for the weather, but not so much for my nerves. I can feel myself starting to sweat through my festival shirt as my worries shape-shift and multiply. No one could show up. A fight could break out among the vendors when Solar Summit arrives. Everyone could get apple poisoning from Bertram's Honey Mustard apple.

I glance around at Marina and the Ryser Cares folks as they arrive, but no one else seems to share my worry. Today, everyone is all smiles and excitement.

"Everything good?" Randy asks me quietly, taking a seat next to me at the festival volunteer table.

His concern pierces through me. It's harder to lie to him when he knows the truth—or part of it, anyway. "Yeah." I manage a grin. "All good."

Randy's forehead creases. "How did you manage...?" He gestures toward the park around us, filled with the tables, chairs, tents, stages, and everything else Ryser didn't pay for.

"I just..."

I'm not sure how he'd react if I told him I paid for everything. Would he whip out his wallet, try to write me a check on the spot? Tell the others so they can pitch in, and then they'll ask questions until I cave and tell them about the office possibly closing? I'm not doing anything to put a damper on this day. We've worked too hard for this.

"I just made it happen," I say. "I talked to Amanda. Everything's fine."

Randy gives me a puzzled smile that tells me more questions are coming. Luckily, that's when a vendor approaches to ask about power sources, and I duck away to help them.

As the next hour passes, more vendors arrive and set up their booths, and I spot some early attendees driving up. Marina, the Ryser Cares folks, and I move around the park switching between different roles: checking on vendors, answering questions, manning the ticketing and information booth. As the last of the vendors take their places and finish setting up, I blink around the park in disbelief.

This...looks like a festival. Booths and tents stretch

throughout the park in the exact formation we planned out on the whiteboard back at the office. The sweet smell of kettle corn wafts through the air, and as I stroll along the perimeter of the park, the other festival attractions take over my senses. The woven lattice on the apple pies Tim is selling. The gentle snuffles and snorts coming from the pigs at the petting zoo stall. The tantalizing aroma of apple cider donuts from the donut booth. The produce stall, Pretzel in Paradise, Sera's barbecue truck, Elise's candle stand, Walt's history of Greenstead booth, on and on and on the attractions go.

I pass by Bertram, apple crates on full display in the tent behind him, and give him a nod. He grins back. I hope he likes that we placed the face-painting booth across from him. I imagine he'll enjoy seeing all the smiling, painted faces coming away from it. I hope he sees a tiger who reminds him of his brother.

By the time I return to the information booth, a long line has formed. More people than I expected are entering the raffle and making donations. A small, hopeful part of me wonders if we might get enough money to save the community center after all.

Every time I think we've cleared the line, a new wave of people approaches. When we hit a lull at last, I take a look around. The festival is swarming with people wandering around the booths, lining up for kettle corn, tearing chunks off pastel clouds of cotton candy, clambering to the petting zoo fence. A toddler runs around, and her harried father chases after her. Even the Nancy convention on the other side of the park seems to be going well. Nancy's sitting on the stage, chattering away to her audience of twenty or so Nancies. This is more crowded than the dying festival of our teens, maybe even bigger than that first festival that cemented our friendship.

"What are you thinking?" Marina asks.

I'm not sure I can think in words. The only thing running through my head is emotions, colors. Shades of coppery orange and golden yellow, pride and joy, all wrapped in a sparkle of magic. It's a passionate protectiveness that pulls at me, telling me that even though I spent my entire childhood wanting to leave Greenstead, that doesn't mean this isn't a beautiful place that deserves to be cherished.

This makes me feel like I can do good things. It's not the large-scale good I've hoped for. But, for now, this good is good enough.

I turn to Marina with a dazed smile. "I think this is a perfect festival."

She nods, her eyes shining. "Me too." She stands and surveys the park. "I'm getting a donut. Do you want anything?"

I shake my head and stay where I am. There are no new incoming attendees approaching our booth, so I pull out my phone to keep me occupied while I hold down the fort. I'm surprised when I see that it's just past noon. The flurry of last-minute preparations and checking in the long line of attendees has made time pass in a blur.

A notification tells me Selma texted me hours ago. I tap on it.

I forgot to tell you! I got drinks with Colby yesterday and he said he heard Dan's leaving! Nothing's announced yet, but apparently Dan got a new job at Atlas.

My first reaction is spiteful relief. I don't love that Dan's being rewarded with another job after he cost me mine, but there's still a satisfaction in knowing he won't be around at Ryser anymore to call the shots.

That's when it dawns on me: Dan leaving means I might actually get my job back. Amanda said my chances were low as long as Dan was in charge. But with Dan out of the picture…I could be back at Ryser by next month.

I lift my head, staring aimlessly ahead at the crowds enjoying the festival. This feels like the last missing piece slotting into place. I've done some good here, and now I have something to go back to after I leave Greenstead. I can take my rightful place on that corporate ladder and keep on climbing until I reach the rung that lets me make a bigger difference.

My brain latches onto the security of having a job ready and waiting for me. It flits to my FIRE spreadsheet and replaces the blank cells and question marks with numbers, making my calculations make sense again. Confetti rains over the spreadsheet in my mind.

Except, through the confetti, I see the faces of Marina, Tessa, Jen, Randy, Arun. Taking my old job and returning to DC means leaving them behind. It means washing my hands of whatever Amanda decides to do with the Ryser Cares office, whatever happens to Greenstead, and floating back to my old life without a second thought.

Strangely, the more I sit with this news, the more detached I feel from it. I don't quite know how to picture going from here, this open field full of activity, and returning to that towering, stuffy DC office. But I know this is just the bizarre sensation of getting what you've always wanted. You spend so much time hoping and wishing, and when you finally do get it, you don't know what to do with yourself.

The same thing happened when I got promoted to senior communications specialist a couple of years ago. I spent a year obsessively working toward it, taking on leadership roles for projects beyond my level, trying my very best to prove myself. When I got the promotion, I felt an initial burst of excitement at changing the title in my email signature and updating my spreadsheet with my new salary. After that faded, though, I felt a similar sort of dumbfounded for a few hours. A sense of...*Now what?* But it passed, my happiness returned, and Selma and I celebrated with cupcakes that Friday.

When Randy comes to the information booth to relieve me, I walk around the park, stopping at booths to chat up vendors, going up to the stage to help Tessa finish setting up the judges' table for the pie-baking contest. But all throughout, my mind is teeming with the realities of next steps. I'll need to call Amanda to ask about my old job. Will she grant it back to me as soon as Dan leaves? If that's the case, I'd be leaving the Ryser Cares office while its fate is still up in the air. Maybe once I'm back to working on Amanda's team, I could convince her why Ryser Cares's work is so important. Maybe we could even partner with them for a new project.

I'm still thinking about this as I peruse the display in Walt's History of Greenstead tent. I tune out the sound of Walt monologuing to an attendee and focus on the images.

Black-and-white photos of farmland appear above descriptions of Greenstead's origins as a rural farming town. A photo of the Ryser mustard factory accompanies a paragraph about how the factory's opening brought jobs and economic prosperity to Greenstead. The next few sections focus on Greenstead's growth: the opening of the community center, the uptick in population, the start of traditions like the apple festival.

I have to wait my turn for the next panel, where a cluster of people are gathered to read about the devastation of the mustard flood. That's always been the most interesting thing people associate with Greenstead. I can't blame outsiders for thinking that way, but there's more to Greenstead than the catastrophe that happened here nearly thirty years ago. Even though there were a lot of times when I couldn't see past it myself.

Now, I mentally paint those panels with the important details that wouldn't make the history books. The friendship two girls formed around this festival, memories wrapped in laughter and ribbons of caramel. The community-center-organized hikes up Echo Hill Overlook where Dad met Wendy, where Randy met Marge, where Meg apparently does her networking. The tight-knit sense of kinship that threads people together and makes them feel like this place is worth sticking around for.

"You're Lauryn Harper?"

I turn to find a stocky Asian man around my age watching me expectantly.

"Yes," I say slowly.

He extends a hand. "Peter Guo."

The name rings a bell. I stare from his outstretched hand to the polite expression on his face. "You wrote that article in the *Washington Chronicle.*"

He breaks into a proud smile. "I did."

A rush of annoyance overcomes me. "You compared me vomiting to the mustard factory exploding."

"My editor added that," he says, rubbing the back of his neck. "I thought it was a little heavy-handed."

"So did I."

He seems to register the steel in my voice, but he doesn't back down. "I was hoping I could ask you a few questions."

I narrow my eyes at him. "You're writing another article?"

"Of course. People want to know how the festival turned out."

I give a skeptical hum. As tempted as I am to turn him away, he's going to write the article regardless. Without my participation, he'll write another one-sided attack piece on Ryser. If I talk to him, I can at least nudge his perspective in the right direction, make sure his article focuses on Greenstead and the success of this festival. Greenstead deserves to be the main focus, not a launching pad for more Ryser discourse.

"Okay," I say begrudgingly.

Peter and I walk around the park, sticking to the outskirts where it's quieter. When he presses Record on his phone, I'm mindful of my every word. I imagine my words going straight from my lips to the article, picture Amanda reading everything I say in undeniable black ink. I stick to talking up the festival, its history, Greenstead's spirit of community and resilience.

The edge of Peter's mouth pulls downward slightly as he

ends the recording, but I feel a glow of satisfaction at avoiding whatever trap he was hoping I might fall into.

The rest of the afternoon passes without a hitch. I return to the information booth and tally up the familiar faces of people who stop by. My dad and Wendy tell me they're proud of me, which makes my chest inflate. Jess greets Marina warmly when they come by to make a donation, and Marina stands to hug them in an embrace that goes on a beat too long for exes.

I know better than to look for my mom. I invited her weeks ago, and she said she'd try to come. But she texted this morning that she wouldn't be able to make it after all. I don't know if it's truly because of a last-minute flight schedule change as she claimed, or if she just couldn't bring herself to come back to the town that made her feel trapped. But instead of commiserating with that instinct as I always do, I decide it's her loss if she's choosing to miss out on what makes this town special. I may still share her desire to never get stuck here, but the thought of coming back to Greenstead to visit my dad and Wendy for Christmas, or even just because, doesn't seem so bad anymore.

Marina's mom comes by and exclaims that she hasn't seen me in years, and I bask in the hug she pulls me into, this woman who I sometimes liked to think of as a stand-in mother after my mom left. I see a few people I remember from high school, who stop by and say hello. Even Nancy deigns to cross the velvet rope separating her convention from our festival.

"I had an extra minute to fill on Friday, and I mentioned that you *probably* wouldn't get sick on anyone at the festival," she tells me. "So, you're welcome. And congratulations. I brought these for you." She hands us each a small jar.

I stare down at the handwritten label: *Wrinkle cream.*

"One of my Nancies makes beauty products," Nancy explains. "I don't need them, but I thought you might."

Marina and I share a look, disbelief mixed with amusement.

"Thank…you," I finally say.

Nancy beams. "You're welcome." Then she flits off, leaving Marina and me to marvel in her wake.

"Was that her trying to be nice to us?" Marina asks. "Or was this a fuck you?"

"I…" I shrug, lost for words. "I think it was just Nancy being Nancy. There's no other way to decipher it."

My heart soars when a woman with wiry white hair and a familiar gap-toothed smile approaches us. Lettie thanks us for bringing back the festival and says it's just like she remembered it. "Almost," she adds, tossing a glance over her shoulder at the Nancy convention.

"Th-thank you for coming," I say, surprised to find myself feeling so starstruck in her presence. For all those years Marina and I came to this festival, she was always just *there.* It never occurred to me how much we'd come to rely on her presence until she was gone.

"This is for y'all." Lettie slides a square white box toward us. I see the stick first—the thin white stick poking out from the top could only belong to a caramel apple. I think back to the dinner party, telling Walt how much I'd loved Lettie's caramel apples. He must have passed the message along to her. But then my eyes fall on the cellophane window at the front of the box. It's not her standard plain caramel apple. It's the same exact one Marina and I always ordered, down to the crushed peanut coating and milk chocolate drizzle.

I share an incredulous look with Marina. "How did you know...?"

Lettie lets out a satisfied cackle. "You think I don't know my regulars?"

It takes a moment for that to sink in. That just as Lettie was a constant for us, maybe we were for her. That maybe we were figures in her story just as she was in ours. That maybe that's the beauty of this festival, of Greenstead, the ways our threads weave and connect like strands of yarn in a sweater, coming together into something bigger than its parts.

A sense of excitement floats through the attendees as Art McKenzie's set draws closer. When he takes the stage at last, the crowd gravitates toward him immediately. Instead of his usual T-shirt and jeans, he's dressed in all black, which I'm assuming is his Arthur Frost uniform. His show begins like a normal set, starting off with a song from one of his solo albums. Some confused murmurs go through the crowd when the song finishes and he sets his guitar down to pull out a deck of cards. But the audience gets into it after a few minutes, applauding when he pulls an attendee's card from his shirt pocket. Then he picks up his guitar for another song, and so the set continues, alternating between songs and magic tricks. By the end, he has people straining to raise their hands, clamoring to be volunteers for his next trick. Arthur Frost just might have a long career ahead of him after all.

Art saves "Green Thread" for last. The second he strums the familiar melody, Greensteaders burst into cheers and applause. With a silent look of understanding, Marina and I decide this is the perfect moment to break out the caramel apple. We take turns passing it back and forth, savoring every morsel of this sweet, nutty dessert we thought was lost to us forever.

Just like at the brewery, I fall under the song's spell, lulled by Art's baritone voice. I lean back in my chair, chin propped in hand, and let the words wash over me. When he sings about holding onto the thread and waiting for love to be resurrected, I look around at the crowd gathered around the stage, at the booths stretching out throughout the park, the half-eaten caramel apple sitting between Marina and me, and think *We did it*. We *did* hold on to the thread of Greenstead. We *did* resurrect this dying town. Not permanently, I know. We might not save the community center, and this might be the last apple festival Greenstead ever sees. But for this weekend, today, *this moment*, Greenstead is more alive than it's been in decades, and that's something to be proud of.

CHAPTER TWENTY-SIX

W E'RE ALL A LITTLE LOOPY when we show up to the Ryser
Cares office on Monday.

We're still riding the high of the festival's success.
Sunday didn't bring as large a crowd as Saturday, but the park was
still bursting with attendees and activity all day. The close of the
festival brought a long evening of folding up the tables and tents
to be returned to the rental company, packing up our decor, and
cleaning up the park grounds. We didn't stumble home until the
sky was a dark shade of night—and still we dragged ourselves into
the Ryser Cares office the next day.

We did take the morning off, at least. I'd have preferred to
skip work entirely that day, but Marina said she'd come by when
she got off work to go over the festival donations, and Jen wanted
to send a post-event thank-you email to our vendors. So, come
Monday at one o'clock, we're sitting at our desks in the Ryser
Cares office, bleary-eyed but present, at least physically. None of

us has done anything remotely productive so far. Tessa's playing sudoku on her phone, Randy's reading, Arun's napping at his desk, I'm taking my time doing the crossword while sipping my tea. Even Jen hasn't made a move to send the vendor email yet. She's watching an episode of *Love Island*. I think we're waiting for Marina to arrive before we turn to business.

At four o'clock, Marina walks through the doors, lockbox in hand. "Afternoon!"

Our mumbled greetings are more subdued. Marina looks around at us, clearly not impressed.

"You could try to look alive," she says.

"Too much effort," Arun says, his head resting on his folded arms.

"Come on." Marina strides into the meeting room in the back. "Don't you want to know how the festival did?"

Slowly, we follow after her and take our seats around the table.

"That's more like it." Marina taps the lockbox in front of her. "I counted this out last night, and—well, it's not enough to keep the community center going indefinitely. But it's enough that I think…we're onto something. It's enough to keep the community center open for the next six months, I think. I was talking to some of the vendors yesterday, and they all said this should be a regular thing. As long as Ryser continues to fund it, we can afford to bring the festival back every year and keep putting the profits toward Greenstead. I really believe we could turn this town around in a few years. What do you think?"

Amid Jen, Arun, and Tessa's cheerful exclamations and

excited questions, a sense of anxiety curdles in my stomach. I share a look with Randy, who eyes me with that same worried scrutiny he gave me when I dodged his questions a couple of days ago.

I take a breath to confess the truth, but then Arun's sharing his estimate for how many attendees came to the festival, and Jen runs off to grab her laptop to note down the specifics for an infographic she's planning, and reality is slipping away from me.

When Jen returns to her seat, she's frowning at her laptop. "That's weird."

"What?" Tessa asks.

"It's not letting me log in."

"Do you have Caps Lock on again?" Arun asks.

"No." Jen types a few keys and hits Enter. Her frown deepens. "I don't understand. My log-in worked fine a couple of hours ago."

"Maybe you didn't reset your password in time?" Tessa guesses.

A weight presses on my chest. Amanda said they hadn't yet decided whether to close the Ryser Cares office. But they wouldn't have made that decision without telling us, would they?

Unless we gave them reason to.

The only reason that pops into my head is the very thing that I thought might save our office: the apple festival. Amanda had been clear about distancing Ryser from the festival, and from Greenstead in general. But she hadn't forbidden us from throwing it. If our festival was more successful than Amanda counted on, how could she possibly hold that against us?

That's when it hits me. Peter Guo. The article he was working on.

His last article kicked off a storm of bad press that sent Amanda into a frenzy. If he's published another one today…

With a shaky hand, I pick up my phone and search Peter's name. And there it is, published just this morning: *The Small Town Making a Comeback Despite Ryser's Best Efforts to Destroy It.*

I scroll through it quickly, piecing together phrases and tuning out the sounds of the office trying to troubleshoot Jen's log-in issue. It seems that Peter grew suspicious of the way I danced around his Ryser-related questions and minimized Ryser's role in the festival. He points out that this didn't align with the statement Ryser put out in late July, which talked up its efforts to support the apple festival. He correctly guesses that Ryser pounced on the opportunity to support the festival as a knee-jerk reaction to his first article, then abandoned the strategy when it no longer suited them. The article includes quotes from Greenstead locals he interviewed at the festival, who happily tell him how little Ryser Cares actually cares. There's a particularly condemning quote from Walt—riddled with ellipses, though it still somehow takes up two paragraphs even in its heavily abridged state—that details how Ryser's support of Greenstead gradually diminished to nothing.

In short, the article celebrates Greenstead and exposes Ryser as a fraud. It would be enough to make Amanda furious. Enough to incite her to take action.

"Lauryn?"

I look up. Randy's watching me with worry.

"You okay?" he asks.

"Yes." Slowly, I rise. "I just have to…check something."

I try to keep my steps even on the walk to my desk. Save for Randy, the others are still in conversation. Marina's advising Jen to restart her computer. Jen says she doesn't think that's going to solve it, and I have a terrible feeling she's right.

I sit down at my computer and slowly press the power button. When it boots up, I enter my password.

It's denied.

I take in a shuddering breath and glance back at the meeting room. Randy's leaning against the doorframe, watching me. I can see the pieces starting to come together in his mind.

I turn away. I can't face any of them until I hear it from Amanda herself. I mutter an excuse about calling IT and dash into the parking lot. The geese are chillingly silent.

I call Amanda and lean against my car, my back to the office to avoid making eye contact with anyone through the window. It rings once, twice—and then she picks up.

"Hi, Lauryn." There's a knowing tone in her voice. Like she's been expecting this.

I open my mouth to speak, but my throat is too dry to get out a single syllable. I clear my throat and try again. "I'm having some trouble logging on to my computer."

"I know."

Well, that's not a great sign. Ignoring the way my muscles tense, I ask, "Can you tell me what's going on?"

"I think you know the festival isn't what we agreed on."

"How? First you wanted to be more involved in planning,

so we involved you. Then you wanted us to distance Ryser from the festival, so we did." It's a struggle to keep my voice even. "We did what you told us. How is that not what we agreed on?"

"It wasn't supposed to draw this much attention," Amanda says coldly. "It wasn't supposed to get that reporter digging again, making up theories about Ryser."

I let out a huffy breath and kick a pebble near my shoe. "I can't control who shows up. I can't control him deciding to write an article."

"But you spoke to him."

"Just about Greenstead," I insist. "When he asked about Ryser, I gave our usual talking points and redirected the conversation."

"Which he found suspicious," she points out.

I sigh. If it's suspicious, it's because Ryser's behavior *is* suspicious, and it's not my fault he caught on to that. "What does this have to do with our log-in trouble?"

"I met with leadership this morning, and we decided it would be best to shut down Ryser Cares immediately."

My breath leaves me. "Without any notice?"

"We felt it was safer this way. Dan was concerned that if we gave you a notice period, you might retaliate somehow. He thought it would be safer for the company if we removed access first and informed you after."

I break into a bitter laugh. Just when I thought it wasn't possible to hate Dan Gorland more. "Thanks for informing us," I spit out. "I thought Dan was leaving."

"He is." She sounds surprised that I know this. "But he still works here until next week."

"So *he* gets a notice period." When she doesn't respond, I breathe out a controlled exhale through my nose. I don't want to ask, but the question claws at me, desperate and unashamed. "You said before..."

"Yes?"

I swallow and try again. "You said before that I wouldn't get my old job back while Dan was still around. Does, um...does him leaving change anything? About the possibility of getting my old job?"

It's humiliating to get the words out. Then I'm left stewing in the silence stretching out before me. Amanda must be shocked I asked. She must be trying to understand how I could bring this up when the answer is written all around us. But apparently this is what I'm willing to do for my FIRE spreadsheet, for a stable life. I'm willing to make myself look like an idiot in front of my ex-boss who, I'm realizing, doesn't understand me at all.

"No," Amanda replies. She says it gently, at least. "With the festival, and the article...we're past that now. You won't be getting your job back."

"So that's it? We're all just fired?"

She tells me to expect a letter from HR, and then the call is over. I'm left to stare at my phone and try to come to terms with the fact that I'm unemployed for the first time in a decade.

"What do you mean, we're all fired?"

I turn at the sound of Tessa's voice. Marina and the Ryser Cares folks are standing just outside the office, watching me. I bite my lip and come closer, crossing the parking lot to stand in front of them. Like I'm facing a firing squad.

I fiddle with my phone, running my thumbnail around the edge of the case. How are the geese not running out to interrupt this scene? It's like they know the worst torture lies in me staying put.

"Amanda says they're closing the Ryser Cares office. Today." My voice comes out hoarse, just above a whisper. "Because of the festival buzz, that reporter wrote another article attacking Ryser and…Ryser took it personally. They want to distance themselves from Greenstead to improve their image."

Arun glances at his colleagues in disbelief. "So we've lost our jobs? Just like that?"

I nod reluctantly. "HR's gonna send us letters in the mail, apparently."

"I don't understand," Marina says. "Why would Ryser punish you all if they're the ones who invested in the festival in the first place?"

I wince. I look to Randy, hoping for an ounce of sympathy. But he's staring at me with just as much confusion as everyone else.

"They—they didn't," I confess. "After the first article came out, Amanda wanted to get more involved in the festival planning. But when she started trying to turn the festival into something it isn't, I told her no." They're nodding. They know this much. I swallow and have to force out the rest. "And she…pulled the funding. She said Ryser was stepping back from Greenstead."

Tessa's blinking in disbelief. "Why didn't you tell us?"

It's a reasonable question. But when I search for an explanation, nothing I come up with makes sense. I *should* have told them. But that would have been admitting that Ryser is every bit as soulless as Marina has long insisted. It would have been admitting that *I'm* soulless for continuing to work for them. It was easier to hide the truth, keep my head down, and let myself believe the lie that we were all working toward a common good, hand in hand with Ryser.

"I–I guess I didn't want to admit it," I stumble out. "That Ryser's as bad as Marina says."

"We *all* know Ryser's terrible," Tessa says with an eye roll. "What does that have to do with anything?"

"How have we been paying for the festival?" Jen asks. "If Ryser hasn't been providing the money?"

"I did," I say quietly. "From my savings."

Surprise passes over their faces, but this admission isn't enough to clear the hurt and anger reflected in their eyes.

"Did you know they were gonna close the office?" Randy asks.

I meet his eyes for only a second before I have to look away. "Not for sure. I didn't know they were gonna close it today."

"But you knew something," Randy guesses.

"Yes," I admit. "When Amanda said she was pulling the funding, she also said they were considering closing the office. She said she felt like Ryser has moved on."

Marina lets out a skeptical laugh. "Wow, okay. I'm so glad *they've* moved on, even though Greenstead can't."

"You should have told us." Randy's voice is serious, tinged

with hurt. I remember that moment we shared in the kitchen, our hushed conversation over the boiling kettle, how I made the split-second decision to keep quiet about the possibility of the office closing. I think of him by my side at the festival, asking how I pulled it off, and how I lied to his face about working something out with Amanda. It felt like the right decision at the time, a kindness to keep up morale and let us stay in our festival bubble for as long as we could. But now, I see it as he does: a betrayal.

"I was going to, after the festival," I try to explain. "I didn't want to bring everyone down."

Tessa scoffs. "Thank you for being so considerate of our feelings."

"You don't think we could have helped you figure something out?" Arun asks. "We're a team."

"No, *we're* a team," Tessa corrects him, gesturing to the five of them. "Lauryn always said she was sent here by mistake. She's the messiah from corporate and we're just the Flop House. How could we *possibly* help?"

"That's not it," I whisper. But I can't blame her for thinking that way. I cringe to imagine what they thought when that version of me showed up here a few months ago, with her blazers and her belief that she was better than this place. She didn't know anything.

I glance at Jen, who normally has a kind word to say. She may even have the urge to, going by the conflicted look on her face. But she remains silent.

"Okay," Arun says, throwing his hands up in the air. "I guess I'll pack my shit and…wait for my letter at home." He disappears into the office. Randy, Tessa, and Jen follow suit, giving me disappointed looks on their way in.

Then it's just Marina and me, standing across from each other. Marina's eyes are round, her brow knit. "Was all of this really just because...you wanted me to think Ryser wasn't evil?"

I hang my head. It sounds so stupid spoken aloud. "I wanted you to think *I* was..." I stop, not sure how to finish the sentence. Not as evil as Ryser? Good? Noble, even? Was I delusional enough to believe there was a world where Marina would consider me a good person just because I helped her throw a festival and stretched the truth enough to trick her into respecting the company that destroyed our town?

Marina casts her gaze skyward. "I don't know where you're going with that, but I have *never* thought you're evil, or anything close to it. I think you're confused. And I think you spend way too much time worrying about how the company you work for reflects on you. Which makes it pretty clear what working for Ryser is doing to you."

I can't quite make sense of her words. They pass over me without sinking in. "What's that?" I ask listlessly.

She tilts her head, like she can't believe she has to spell it out for me. "From everything you've told me, you sound miserable. You hate your apartment, your job is clearly messing with your head, you don't seem to have friends or do anything fun. You keep saying you're gonna start living your life once you're forty and retired, but...is that worth being this miserable over?"

"I'm not *miserable*," I protest, heat rushing to my cheeks. "I'm...planning. I'm a planner."

"Okay." The word is hard with sarcasm.

"Besides, you're one to talk. You live in a house you hate, but you won't admit you're in over your head. You keep complaining that Greenstead is dying, but you're too stubborn to sell your house and let Solar Summit build something new here. And I'm pretty sure your weird, stubborn attachment to your run-down house is getting in the way of you actually being happy with Jess—who you're obviously still in love with."

Marina's shaking her head when I bring up her house—but at the mention of Jess, something in her softens for an instant before her indignance takes over again. "You don't know what you're talking about."

"Maybe I don't. But you don't get to lecture me about how miserable I am if you can't listen to the truth about yourself."

"Fine." She pointedly keeps her glare somewhere behind me.

"Fine," I shoot back. I glance toward the windows behind her, where the others are packing up their things. I can't go back in and face their disappointment. But I have no interest in staying out here with Marina's judgment. Finally, I turn on my heel and start toward my car.

"You're leaving?" Marina says.

"Yep," I say without turning around.

"You're good at that," she calls after me.

The remark stings, but I don't bother responding. I get in my car and slam the door shut. As Marina stands there watching, I pull out of the parking lot and head for anywhere that isn't filled with people I've let down.

CHAPTER TWENTY-SEVEN

THERE ARE TWO ROUTES I'VE taken more than any other when leaving Ryser Cares: the way home and the way to Pretzel in Paradise. All those runs to pick up pretzels when I'm on snack duty have made the route something akin to muscle memory.

I don't much feel like going home. The thought of sitting alone in my room reminds me of all the days I've spent by myself in my apartment over the years. Just the idea of it makes me feel lonelier than ever.

Which is why I find myself pulling into the Pretzel in Paradise parking lot. When I get out of my car, I notice that the store is busier than I've ever seen it. Normally a few people are milling inside, but now it's bustling with activity, so cramped the line almost extends out the door. At the apple festival, Meg sold out of stock by early afternoon on both days. This surge in business must have something to do with that.

I know this is a good thing, but seeing the busy shop fills me with reluctance. I don't want to be surrounded by people. I have no interest in hearing Meg rave about what a success the festival was when I've never felt like more of a failure.

A fiftysomething woman stands outside the shop, eating a pepperoni pizza pretzel and staring at the empty storefront beside Meg's. I eye her curiously, wondering how I recognize her, when I realize she's one of the attendees I checked in at the festival. She made a twenty-dollar donation.

"You were running the festival booth," she says when she spots me.

I force a smile. "Yeah."

"I knew these pretzels had to be something special when I saw that line. I couldn't get them out of my head." She takes a bite and closes her eyes as she chews. "Even better than I expected." The woman turns back to the empty storefront. "Do you know if this is for sale?"

I glance from her to the vacant shop window. "Probably. Why?"

"I own a restaurant in Falls Point and I've been thinking about opening up another."

I don't know how to not sound judgy when I ask, "*Here?*"

My question doesn't faze her. She dunks a piece of pretzel into her dipping cup of marinara sauce. "It's next to a successful business, the rent would be cheaper, and I hear Greenstead's making a comeback. Could be smart to get in now." She says goodbye, pops the pretzel piece into her mouth, and walks off.

I stand there, wondering why the term *making a comeback*

sounds oddly familiar, until I realize it's from the headline of Peter Guo's article. If my brain were rational, I'd be grateful to Peter for publishing a piece that helps uplift Greenstead.

But it's not, so: I mentally curse him and get in my car.

I do drive home this time, but I feel aimless once I sit down at my desk. There's no work to do, no one to impress. I don't know how to cope with being unemployed. Robotically, I open up a job search site and click on listings, and I can't stop myself from comparing every job to Ryser.

Significantly lower salary. Less vacation time. No free snacks. Far from my apartment.

Right, my apartment that I hate, according to Marina. The thought of it pings something in my brain. I got an email about it last week, sometime during the blur of festival preparations. I click over to my inbox and search for it.

Lease Renewal Offer

I scroll through the document, see the space at the bottom for a signature. I should want to sign this. Even with the minor rent increase, it's still the cheapest apartment I've seen in the area. Cheap apartment means more money for savings, which means I'm one step closer to early retirement.

Marina's words come back to me, and I tamp them down, tell myself she doesn't know what she's talking about, that I should sign it just to spite her.

But I don't. I close out of the file and decide to postpone it until later. Which I'm sure Marina would say is typical of me.

I postpone so much of my life already, the Marina in my head says. I shoo her away.

I end up passing the afternoon watching a dating show on Lurv Plus. I can still log in to Jen's account, and the profile Marina set up for us, under the name Marina & Lauryn, is still there. Seeing our names linked in this account Jen shared with us feels like a vestige from an era past. I don't touch *Love Quest*—even after our argument, it feels wrong to watch a show we were watching together—but I do pick out a different show: *Loving on the Edge*, in which a group of singles is mixed and matched into pairs to go on dates centered around adventurous activities like skydiving and white water rafting. As I watch a woman comfort a fellow contestant who's tearfully confessing her fear of heights, I wonder what Nancy would do if she were on this show. I wonder what inside jokes Marina and I would concoct if we were watching this together.

It's not nearly as fun, bingeing this by myself. But turning it off would force me to think about what happened at Ryser Cares today, about all the things Marina said, about the job applications I haven't filled out, about the lease renewal offer I can't think about.

So, I dig my hand deep into a bag of Cool Ranch Doritos and watch a bunch of adrenaline-filled singles zip-line through treetops in the name of love and television.

"What's this?" my dad asks when he comes home. At this point, several episodes deep, I'm lying on the couch, bag of Doritos on the floor for easy access.

"*Loving on the Edge.*" I point at the woman on the TV. "Aaron thinks Caroline is going to give him her golden power bar after they make it through the cave expedition—but he doesn't realize Caroline is saving it for Benny, even though Benny's on a skydiving date with Ingrid."

"Right," my dad says slowly, shoving his hands in the pockets of his chinos as he watches Aaron and Caroline move through a narrow passage. He turns to stare at me, even though Aaron and Caroline are far more interesting. I don't have to look at him to know he's got his scrutinizing face on, eyes serious and shrewd behind his glasses.

"What?" I ask.

"I thought you'd be...happier."

"Why?" I dig a hand into the bag of Doritos and shove one in my mouth.

"The festival was a success! You should be celebrating."

"Yeah, and I lost my job over it," I grumble. When my dad gapes, I pause the TV with my hand that isn't covered in Doritos dust. "It's no big deal."

"It seems like it's a big deal to you," he says carefully. He approaches the other end of the couch, and I reluctantly sit upright to make room. "What happened?"

I sigh and relay the terrible details of the day: the news I'd kept secret, the firing, coming clean to the Ryser Cares team, the argument with Marina. I have to blink several times to keep tears from welling up in my eyes.

My dad is sympathetic but direct. "I have to say, I'm with Marina on this one. I've never understood why you'd stay on with Ryser all these years."

"Of course *you* don't," I say before I can think better of it. "You're stuck."

He pulls back. "What do you mean?"

"Mom always talked about feeling stuck here," I explain, reaching into the bag for a handful of Doritos. "She said she felt like she was suffocating in Greenstead. So, she got out. But you stayed here."

"Because my life is here! That doesn't make me stuck."

The Doritos in my hand drop back into the bag. "You *like* living here?"

"Of course. Why wouldn't I?"

"Because, it's…sad. And empty."

"Not to me," he says with a shrug. "To me, it's home."

Home. Said with such ease, such pride. I look around at the framed photos on the walls showing Dad and Wendy with various friends, the calendar with scribbles denoting *Taco Tuesday* and *Hiking with the Forresters*, the Pretzel in Paradise coupon affixed to the fridge with a WAKE UP WITH NANCY magnet. There's so much joy here.

His gaze lingers on me. "I have to admit, there are times I've wondered if *you* feel stuck."

I frown. "Why?"

"Well…your apartment is…the saddest thing I've ever seen," he says with an apologetic chuckle. "When I call, you never talk about doing anything fun. You always used to pester me about getting a dog when you were little, and now that you're grown, you've never gotten one. I just…I worry about you, all alone in that apartment. You don't seem happy." He eyes me like he's afraid I might take this the wrong way.

My first instinct when Marina brought up my apartment was to lash out and deny it, and that same impulse comes to me now, too. It's easier to deny it than to dig deeper and consider the possibility that it might be true. To think about the time I've spent watching the potted plants in my living room—which I bought for the sole purpose of brightening up my apartment—wilt and wither away from lack of sunlight.

How much unhappiness are you supposed to put up with to set yourself up for a happy future? And how happy would my future be if all the years before it were spent alone, isolating myself out of shame? Even if I got that promotion and did something good at Ryser, it wouldn't cancel out everything I did, and everything I put myself through, to get here. Doing good at Ryser wouldn't improve my life overnight or turn me into a different person.

My dad's right: I've spent so much time trying to avoid being stuck that all I ended up doing was getting myself stuck. But not in Greenstead, where people have made lives for themselves, where they wake up every day and choose this place because they believe in it. I've been stuck in a deep, dark hole of my own making. If I keep burrowing deeper into myself and pushing people away, there won't be anyone left standing at the top to pull me out.

But I *do* have people, ready and willing. There's my dad, who I don't visit as often as I should. There are the people I've only gotten to know in the last few months but whose presence has been a greater comfort than I've realized: Randy, Jen, Arun, Tessa. And there's Marina, whose renewed friendship has felt like righting a terrible wrong—until we went wrong again today. But it might not be too late to right us back again.

"I haven't been happy," I confess. "But I think I'm learning how to be."

His mouth perks into a smile. "I've noticed. See, we just needed to get you out of that sad apartment."

I laugh when he elbows me in the side. "It wasn't just the apartment. I had everything wrong. I was letting the way I felt about my job take over my life."

"Well, you don't have to worry about that job anymore," he says. "You know, it's funny that they'd decide to fire you all now, when they were so afraid to do it before. Guess they can't make up their minds."

While my dad picks the Doritos bag off the carpet and grumbles about my inability to use a bowl, his comment stays with me. The Ryser Cares team told me about how they'd messed up at work, how Ryser chose to demote them and ship them off to Greenstead instead of firing them—because they knew too much. Even when Ryser did fire us, they did it in secret, removing our access from the company systems because they were afraid of retaliation.

Our small Ryser Cares team is capable of so much more than any of us thought. We got an entire festival off the ground, didn't we? We planned it to such success that it drew more attention than we—or Ryser—could ever bargain for.

We've managed to do a lot of good in our time here. We showed people how much Greenstead has to offer. We helped Bertram tap back into one of his most cherished childhood memories. We convinced Art McKenzie to come to Greenstead. We brought Mayor Bradley out of hiding. We got a respected journalist to declare that Greenstead is making a comeback. We made a goddamn mustard apple taste good.

I can't take back all the questionable things I've contributed to in my years at Ryser. The blatant denials of completely true allegations, the way we've spun narratives to discredit innocent people, the picture-perfect image I've painted of an organization that's done irreparable damage on a monumental scale. All while telling myself I'm not really causing any harm, because one day I'll do something good to absolve it. That fantasy wasn't enough to lessen my shame.

But I *can* try to do more good. I don't have to wait for a promotion to make an impact. I can do something now, something that makes me feel better about myself before I close out this chapter of my life. I can try to undo the harm I've caused—by any means necessary.

Now that we've lost our jobs, we have nothing left to lose. I have absolutely no desire to return to work at Ryser ever again.

So, why not show Ryser what we're really capable of?

I turn off the TV and rise to my feet with purpose. I've got a team to assemble.

CHAPTER TWENTY-EIGHT

THE NEXT MORNING, I SIT at my desk in the Ryser Cares office, my eyes trained on the window.

I texted the team asking them to meet me at the office, but for all I know, they could have blown off the message and decided I wasn't worth their time anymore. Thinking about the way they looked at me yesterday still sends a ripple of guilt through me. I push the thought out of my mind and focus instead on what I'll say when I see them. *If* I see them.

I check my phone—no messages—then glance back at the window when I see a flicker of movement, but it's just the geese. I sigh and check my phone again. Still no messages.

Randy arrives first. When he steps through the door, he gives me a quick, perfunctory nod in greeting. I'll take an acknowledgment of my existence as a positive sign.

"Hey," I say as he takes his seat at his desk. I open my mouth to ask how he's doing, but the apology I've been rehearsing in my head spills out instead. "I'm sorry I didn't tell you the office might be closing. It wasn't decided yet, and I hoped the festival might convince them not to if it went well, and…we'd *just* decided not to tell everyone about the funding until after the festival, so I just sort of…applied that same logic about telling you."

He gives a humorless chuckle. "Yesterday made it clear how everyone felt about that logic," he says. A note of remorse passes over his face. "I'm sorry I gave you bad advice."

"Not your fault. It was the advice I wanted to hear."

Something like understanding passes between us. We sit in the office quietly—me obsessively checking my phone, Randy reading his book. One by one, the others filter through the door. First Jen, then Arun, and finally Tessa, her eyes curious but wary. They take their seats at their desks, as if it were any other workday. But instead of the warm, casual atmosphere that usually permeates the office, this one is uncertain and heavy.

"I'm sorry for keeping so much from you," I begin. "I really loved working with you all, and I was afraid telling you what was really going on would ruin it. And, selfishly, I wanted to keep pretending Ryser was interested in helping Greenstead, because…I didn't want Marina knowing Ryser was as bad as they are. Because then it would mean *I'm* a bad person."

"You're not a bad person," Tessa says. The words leave her with some reluctance, but still, she says them.

"I know," I say, though it still sounds strange to say. "Or, I'm trying to get better about knowing that. But…these last few months, working with you has made me feel like…I can do something good."

"That goes both ways," Arun says quietly. He's looking down, picking at a thread on his narwhal shirt. "Before you came here, I'd gotten so used to thinking I couldn't do anything." The others murmur in agreement.

"Of course you can," I reply. "That was just Ryser trying to tell us we're failures, and we're not. We're also not powerless. They were so afraid to fire us before, remember? We knew too much?"

"I don't know if that's true," Jen says. "It was just a theory."

"But we do know a lot, don't we?" I ask. "We've all seen sides of Ryser they wouldn't want the public to know. Peter Guo's articles have shown there's a lot of interest in exposing Ryser for who they really are. So…why don't we?"

"Why don't we…?" Randy echoes.

"Use the information we have to expose Ryser?" I suggest. "It's not like they can fire us again. We could show everyone how little they've done to actually support Greenstead. Maybe that would force them to really help rebuild our town."

Tessa's eyes flicker with interest. But Randy, Arun, and Jen exchange doubtful looks.

"What could we do, though?" Randy asks. "We don't have access to the company systems anymore."

"I have emails," Tessa says. "Things I forwarded to myself when I had to submit stuff for our finances. Our budget's pretty small, and it's only gotten smaller over the years."

"I've printed some things," Jen remembers. She opens her desk drawer and rifles through some papers before passing a page to Tessa, who reaches over her desk to pass it to me. "Corporate sent us reimbursement guidelines for the claims we processed. I only printed them for reference, but…take a look. There were so many stupid rules that meant we had to deny most of the claims that came in."

I scan the paper, reading the narrow limits of claims they would consider, the excessive burden they placed on claimants to prove that the issue they raised was directly related to the mustard flood, the absurd levels of proof they required: photo or video evidence, multiple witness statements, a professional assessment by a certified home inspector. The guidelines were clearly designed to be so narrow that almost no one would qualify for a claim. Ryser designed these rules to make sure they paid as little as possible, all while outwardly pretending their claims program was helping to rebuild Greenstead.

"I have some texts and emails from my dad," Arun says. "There's a lot he's told me over the years that could be useful."

"This is all great," I say. Already my mind is piecing together how to fit all of this into an impactful proclamation against Ryser.

"Could they sue us for this?" Randy asks.

I shrug. "If they want more bad press, sure." I can't be sure of anything, but a retaliatory lawsuit against the individuals living in the small town they wrecked would be at odds with Ryser's usual deflect-and-deny approach. I'm willing to take the gamble.

"But is it enough?" Jen asks. "To really make a difference?"

"I have something too," I say. "The communications department has a database where they keep all their cheat sheets for the terms we're supposed to use to downplay everything Ryser does.

A lot of it revolves around how to make Ryser look as innocent as possible…but it also includes tons of stuff about everything Ryser's guilty of."

It came to me last night when I was trying to think of what we could use against Ryser. Good old Bill, the Brand Learning Library that played a part in getting me banished to Greenstead in the first place, is an external platform. Amanda gushed about how this enabled us to benefit from a world of features Ryser didn't have, from its (un)intuitive interface to its (laggy) animation abilities.

Last night, I visited Bill's website and checked to see if the communications department's log-in still worked.

It did.

I've never loved Bill more.

I log on to Bill now and show the Ryser Cares folks around his wonderful, clunky platform. I point out the documents I think might be most useful, and we gather all the other information we have: Tessa's emails, Jen's printed documents, Arun's emails and texts.

Next, we reach out to our Greenstead contacts. We sift through the long list of denied claims and call people asking for their side of the story. I call Marina, and though our conversation is heavy with unsaid apologies, she agrees to come down to the office after work and contribute whatever she can to our growing pile of Ryser evidence.

When she arrives, she details the extensive damage her house took due to the flood, and how the records the previous owners shared with her showed that Ryser had covered only bare minimum repairs but refused to compensate the owners for the more extensive damage, again citing their excessive criteria for what qualified as a claim. The effects of the damage had only multiplied as the years wore on, and by the time Marina purchased the house a few years ago, for what felt like a steal, it was on the verge of falling apart. Marina shows us the inspection report detailing the many repairs her house needs. She outlines how she'd submitted claims to Ryser Cares out of desperation, hoping their policy might have changed, only to discover the criteria were even more strict.

I'm the one who sends the email to Peter Guo. I include a link to the repository of evidence we've gathered, all the proof of how little Ryser actually cares about anything besides profits and maintaining a pristine image. We even include a statement from Randy, alluding ominously to his knowing a secret that could spell trouble for the company: *I heard two executives in particular having a discussion that would raise some serious concerns. I wouldn't even feel comfortable repeating it, unless I had to.* It's pure bluffing, of course, but if it can scare Ryser into action, it's worth a try.

When I hit Send, the finality of what I've done makes my heart hammer. I've waged a direct attack on the company I've spent the last decade of my life defending. Any chance of mending that bridge with Amanda has gone up in flames.

It's terrifying. But it's liberating at the same time. I feel like I've done something truly important. It's not a feeling I often get. But I like feeling this way—powerful. Good.

I assume Marina and the Ryser Cares team must be getting

a similar rush, but when I announce that the email's sent, they just tell me to let them know what I hear back. Marina says she has to go and leaves without another word. The rest of them start putting away the documents they've gathered, like there's nothing more to say.

I reluctantly close my laptop, watching them tidy up with their impersonal, businesslike focus. I was hoping for a little more camaraderie. Not that we'd go out for drinks like the night we did after the awards event, or cavort around riding roller coasters like we did after our Solar Summit meeting, but…something to commemorate the moment we took a stand against Ryser.

But that's what friends do, I realize with a twinge. That's what we were, and now, after yesterday, we're not in that place anymore. The Ryser Cares team has accepted my apology, but that doesn't mean we're automatically whisked back into that same carefree ease we had before.

I also still need to apologize to Marina. I need to be really, truly honest with her. I don't want to lose the friendship we've just rebuilt. I don't want to go another decade without talking to her and then catch each other up on all we'd missed out on. Now that I'm back in her life, I want it to stay that way.

And I believe it can. I believe we did something today that's going to make a difference. The others may not have much faith in it—or in me—but I'm choosing to believe goodness will prevail. I'm choosing to believe I fall on the side of goodness, even if that hasn't always come naturally to me.

All I can do now is wait.

CHAPTER TWENTY-NINE

QUICKLY DEVELOP A NEW morning routine.

It starts with checking my phone for any news of Ryser. I've set several alerts for Ryser, for Peter Guo, for my own name. Six days have passed since I sent the email—and five days since Peter called me for another interview, in which I answered his questions in full, holding nothing back—but nothing's been published yet.

Next, I eat my breakfast while searching for apartments. But not in the DC area this time. Now, I take my search to Richmond. After the weekends Tessa spent showing me around Richmond, I've fallen in love with it. It turns out that when you actually explore the city instead of dismissing it as the place where you failed a lot of hearing tests, Richmond is kind of amazing. It has that city excitement Greenstead is missing, the energetic atmosphere, the walkability, blocks and blocks of unique restaurants, cafés, markets, and more. It's affordable enough that I could live in something bigger than a basement matchbox. It's closer to

Greenstead, to my family and the people who—I hope—I can consider my friends.

I click through pictures of sunlit rooms and imagine myself living in a new neighborhood. My FIRE spreadsheet is full on sobbing at the sight of these rent prices, but I can't go back to my old apartment. I want windows. I want sunshine. I want everything I've denied myself before.

That's why my apartment website perusals include looking up their pet policies. I immediately click away from the ones that don't allow dogs. Which feels presumptuous. But it also feels right.

Next, I scour job listings. Which is a little tough considering I'm not really sure what I'm looking for. Setting aside the fact that publicly exposing Ryser will essentially blacklist me in the world of corporate PR and communications, I'm not sure that's a world I'd even want to reenter. After these last few months at Ryser Cares doing work that actually feels valuable, polishing a company's image doesn't interest me. I start gravitating toward jobs in the nonprofit sector, even though the roles are less special- ized and the salaries would make my FIRE spreadsheet wail. Seeing listings that use terms like *mission-driven* or *community- centered* puts a flutter in my belly, and I think that's something worth listening to.

I inevitably watch an episode of *Loving on the Edge* after that. I tell myself it's my reward for doing all of the above.

Also inevitable: fighting the impulse to text Marina about something I know we'd have joked about. The impulse wants me to ask if she's watched *Love Quest* at all since we last did together, because I haven't. It wants me to ask if she misses hanging out together, because I do. But I resist. I carry on watching *Loving on the Edge*, and I check Jen's social media to see if she's ever posted about it (she hasn't).

On day seven post-email, I don't get through my entire routine. I wake up to a notification about a new Peter Guo article, and my heart leaps.

Ryser Employees Tell All: Inside the Web of Cover-Ups and Lies

Peter Guo has taken everything we've handed him and used it to craft a detailed exposé on Ryser's misdeeds. He cites our evidence, interviews with the Ryser Cares team—Randy's bluff included—as well as quotes from Marina about her house, and from people in Greenstead sharing their accounts of how life in town has changed since the flood. Mayor Bradley is also cited, giving a quote that denounces Ryser and asserts Greenstead's strength and spirit. A Ryser exec is quoted saying a few lines that I'm sure were meticulously crafted by Amanda and her team: "We are saddened to hear that our efforts to support Greenstead through its challenges have not been found sufficient. We vow to take action to provide further assistance in hopes of a brighter tomorrow."

It's the vow that intrigues me. Ryser rarely alludes to taking concrete action to address an issue. Our go-to approach was always to dance around the subject, share some meaningless words that sound good on paper. But the vow changes things. They have to be planning something.

I send the article link to Marina and the Ryser Cares team. They respond with celebratory remarks and emojis, but nothing that invites conversation. I can feel their distance through the screen.

I think Ryser's going to announce something, I reply. I'll keep you posted.

No one responds.

I skip the job hunt and apartment search today. I'm too busy searching for more on Ryser, refreshing the press releases page of their website. In my desperation, I even try to log on to Bill to see if they're working on something behind the scenes, but that's when I discover they've changed the password. Understandably.

And then, at 2:00 p.m., a new post appears: *Ryser Pledges Funds to Support Local Community.*

In a glowing statement effused with self-congratulatory positivity, the press release announces that Ryser has pledged to invest five million dollars to uplift the town of Greenstead, Virginia. In typical PR fashion, it doesn't mention the mustard flood, but it also doesn't use the term *factory malfunction* either, now that Peter Guo has revealed the transparency of their preferred language. It simply states that Ryser has a long history with Greenstead after building a factory there in the early twentieth century and reiterates Ryser's belief in supporting small communities.

It's fake, and it's trite, but that doesn't matter. Unlike their other press releases, this one comes with money attached. Five million dollars, all for Greenstead. Perhaps to avoid allegations that this may be another repeat of the Ryser Cares debacle Peter

Guo shed such light on, the press release specifies that the money will be donated directly to Greenstead's town council, which can decide how to manage the funds.

I think of the community center, the vacant storefronts, the dilapidated houses in West Greenstead. This money has the power to make a difference.

I paste the link to the statement in the group chat. Immediately, bouncing dots appear. I brace myself for another tepid response—but before a message comes through, my phone rings.

"Five million dollars?" Marina exclaims. Her squeal instantly brings a smile to my face.

"I know!" My phone vibrates against my ear, singing with messages from the Ryser Cares folks.

"Thank you for doing this," Marina says.

"We *all* did it. And this was your idea in the first place. None of this would have happened if you didn't get the idea to throw the festival."

"A festival that lost you all your jobs," she points out, her voice going quieter.

"A lot of that was my fault."

"It wasn't *all* your fault." She's almost whispering now. The words are heavy with emotion.

I can hardly hear her over the continued buzzing of incoming texts. I'm curious to know what they're saying, but I don't want to pull my phone away for a single second while I'm talking to Marina. I wish we could all be together, in the office, like we used to.

The thought gives way to a question that flies out of my mouth before I can stop myself.

"Do you want to get together tonight?" I ask. "All of us? To celebrate?"

Marina's response comes quickly. It's glittering with joy, relief, and maybe even forgiveness. "Definitely."

We may not work at Ryser Cares anymore, but it feels right to meet here, gathering again at the place where we've spent so many hours planning the festival, getting to know one another, talking over pretzels and grilled cheese sandwiches, forming the bonds that tie us together still.

Plus Randy still has the key to the office.

Randy and Tessa are already there when I arrive, standing around the air hockey table talking. On the table between them sits a stack of pizzas from Top Slice, soda bottles, and paper plates and cups. Randy and Tessa pull me into hugs, and as the others stream in, we pull up chairs and share theories about what the money Ryser pledged will be used for.

"Jess says Mayor Bradley's talking about putting together a task force to decide what to do with the money," Marina announces, leaning over the table to grab a slice of pizza.

While the others continue chatting, I place a couple of slices on my plate and turn to Marina beside me. "You talked to Jess, did you?"

Marina's eye roll doesn't hide the soft smile growing across her face. "Yes."

"Do you two talk often?" I tease.

"Mind your business," she says, making me laugh.

"Do you think you might get some of the money for your house?"

Marina takes a sip of her drink, her expression thoughtful. "I think...I think I'd rather sell it."

Part of me wants to celebrate her decision to let go of a house that's done nothing but cause her problems. But the rest of me is thinking about the argument we had outside Ryser Cares.

"Are you sure that's what you want to do?" I ask carefully. "Because I said some things I shouldn't have, and—"

"So did I," Marina says, looking at me with serious eyes. "I had no right to judge you like that."

"Neither did I. And...you were right." My eyes fall to my hands in my lap, studying my nails as I summon the courage to admit the truth. "I was miserable. I was just so busy planning for a future when I maybe wouldn't be unhappy that I didn't realize what it's been doing to me now."

Marina scoots closer and puts an arm around me, giving my shoulder a sympathetic squeeze before dropping her arm back to her side. "I just want you to be happy."

"I will be," I say, giving her a small smile. "I'm working on it."

"Me too. Which is why I'm gonna sell my house. You were right, too. I was just being stubborn. That house was so much more work than I thought it was gonna be. I thought I could handle it. I felt like giving up on the house would be, like, quitting. Or giving up on Greenstead. So many people leave town every year, and I didn't want to be like them. I wanted to prove it's possible to stay."

"It *is* possible," I say. I know now, from talking to my dad, from seeing the lives people here made for themselves, that they're not just staying because they don't have any better options. They're staying because they want to.

"But maybe not in that house," she adds.

"Definitely not in that death house," I confirm, and she laughs. I take a bite of pizza, thinking through my conversation with my dad, Marina's words, the tension-filled Solar Summit discussions at the dinner party and the Chamber of Commerce meeting. "I'm glad you're selling it. I think there's this belief that the only way to be loyal to Greenstead is to recreate the past. But I think building something new can be better sometimes."

"I'm starting to see that," Marina says.

I glance into my drink, trying to hide my surprise. "And if there's a successful theme park one town over that wants to build a resort in your town and shuttle in a ton of tourists, maybe that's a good thing."

She chuckles reluctantly. "I'm selling the house, aren't I? They can have West Greenstead."

"Really? So you're okay with it now?"

Marina nods. "I've accepted the fact that I can't single-handedly save West Greenstead. Why not let Solar Summit clean it up and give it a try? I don't think it can get any worse."

"You say that now, until they install a funnel-cake factory and there's a batter flood," I joke.

She makes a face, but then she says, "So be it. I love funnel cake and I'm done fighting change."

When we tune back in to the larger conversation, Randy's listing the office manager jobs he's applied for in Falls Point, which leads Jen to talk about a remote social media position she's applied to at an association in DC. Tessa tells us that the baking contest judge she's been in talks with offered her an apprenticeship at her bakery in Richmond, where she can learn the ropes of baking at a professional level and see if it's right for her. We raise a toast when she says she's already accepted the offer. We toast again when Arun shares that he's bought a domain for the event management business he's starting.

"Anything you're working on?" Marina asks me.

I don't know why I'm suddenly nervous to share that I've been looking at job posts and apartment listings in Richmond. It's not like this would be a surprise considering how hell-bent I've been on finding a way to leave Greenstead ever since I got here. But it still feels like a betrayal, to want to leave my hometown behind again.

"I'm thinking about moving to Richmond," I say tentatively, looking around to check for their reactions. But no one expresses an ounce of surprise or judgment. Marina just smiles, and Tessa starts talking about her favorite neighborhoods, and that's that.

A calming relief runs through my veins. I just might be starting to have my life figured out. I don't have a job, and my lease is going to be up soon. I still don't know where I'm going to live, or what I'm going to do. But for the first time in years, I know who I am, and I *like* who I am. I have people in my life who I can trust and lean on, because I've actually let them in this time.

I'm going to Richmond because it excites me, but that doesn't mean I've abandoned the town I'm from—not this time, anyway. I know I'll be back. I'll visit my dad and Wendy more. I'll come to see Marina, and Randy, and Jen, and Arun. I'll be back for the next apple festival, if Greenstead uses some of the funding to continue the tradition. Maybe I can even explore Solar Summit's resort hotel, if they get it up and running.

I know my life in Richmond will be different. I'll see Tessa at her bakery. I'll fulfill my childhood dream at long last and adopt a dog. I'll reach out to Selma, break that work-friendship barrier we've always maintained, and see if she wants to hang out the next time I visit DC. I'll go places, do things, make friends, make a profile on a dating app, and start living my life now instead of planning for a future when I might be too numb to enjoy anything.

Everything seems possible. The thought fills me with such lightness that I may as well be floating.

After we eat, Randy and Arun clear the table so they can get in a few last rounds of air hockey. Marina talks to Jen about a Lurv Plus show, *Mingle and Match*, which makes me realize with a spark of joy that she's also been avoiding watching *Love Quest* without me. Tessa rolls her chair over and shows me a listing on her phone of an apartment in the Fan that she's submitted an application for.

Our conversation fills this office that once seemed so barren and depressing just a few short months ago. We talk, we reminisce. Randy, Jen, Arun, and Tessa tell us stories about the office from before my time here, explaining why the clock on the wall is a little off-center, peeling the tape from the flyer hung strategically on the far wall to show us the drywall hole from when Randy and Arun first moved the air hockey table into the office years ago. We tour the office like it's a sacred site. It is, for us.

We engage in some light theft, because morals and Ryser don't mix anyway. Arun rolls his desk chair near the exit, saying he wants to use it at home. Randy packs up the party planning supplies he bought on Ryser's dime, from a weathered HAPPY BIRTHDAY banner to a half-empty box of birthday candles. Jen packs her keyboard in her purse, saying it's more comfortable than the one she has at home. Tessa claims her monitor without explanation.

I can't think of anything I want to take. I look around the office, but nothing calls to me. I haven't bonded with this place in the same way they have. I don't have the years of history they do.

But these people, though: this group of self-professed screwups walking out the door with me, Tessa lugging her monitor under one arm, Arun rolling his chair, Jen and Marina talking behind us, Randy locking the doors of the office for the last time. These people, I will take with me. I will stay in their lives and keep them in mine. And that is the very best souvenir I can possibly imagine.

CHAPTER THIRTY

His name is Leo.

That's not the name he has when I meet him. The volunteer at the Richmond animal shelter tells Marina and me they've named him Steven. But when I look into his large, sad brown eyes, see how his floppy brown ears sway when he tilts his head, see the disciplined way he sits when I approach his cage, I know he is not a Steven.

And when the volunteer opens his cage and lets me walk him around their fenced-in outdoor area out back, I fall in love with the careful, meticulous way he sniffs the bush next to us, like it's a specimen to be studied. He's patient with me; at one point I accidentally drop his leash, and he waits for me to grab hold of it before he resumes walking. While he conducts a thorough examination of a tall blade of grass he deems suspicious, I admire his multicolored fur: white chest, legs, and snout; brown face and ears; large black patches on his back; brown markings at the top of this thighs. He's a beagle mix, he's no taller than my knee, and something about him just makes sense. As the walk comes to an end and we approach the shelter's back door, he turns around and fixes his serious eyes on me, and something about his expression seems to say *Are we doing this?*

We are.

"Why Leo?" Marina asks on the slow, cautious drive to my apartment. She's sitting in the back seat of my car, one arm braced around Leo. He stands on the seat next to her, refusing to lie down.

"He's just a Leo." From the driver's seat, I sneak another glance at him. He's still there. Still perfect. "I can't explain it."

At my apartment, Leo sniffs every piece of furniture, taking what I imagine to be an exhaustive list of mental notes. Marina and I watch him from the couch, entranced by his studiousness.

Eventually, he makes his way to the floor-to-ceiling living room window, and I feel a sense of pride when he stares through the glass. I want to tell him, *Look at how much light we have.* I want to take him on a tour of all the windows in the apartment, not just this one but the one in the kitchen, the one in the bedroom, the one in the bathroom. I want to tell him how big a deal all of this is: the windows, the sidewalks outside, this apartment, Marina next to me, him, here, existing. But I decide he's already gathered all of this through his research. I won't insult his intelligence by telling him what he already knows.

Marina's phone chimes with a text. I tear my gaze away from Leo to watch the smile that lights her face when she reads it. "Jess?" I guess.

"Yeah." She holds up her phone to show me a picture of a wide, light-brown dresser. "They found a dresser that'll work in our bedroom."

Just hearing Marina say *our* makes me smile. She got back together with Jess immediately after putting the house up for sale, and she moved into Jess's apartment soon after that. Now they live near downtown Greenstead, where the atmosphere is much livelier than the abandoned neighborhood Marina used to live in—which is saying something, considering Greenstead isn't known for its energy. But in her new place, Marina has neighbors again, and a coffee shop within walking distance. She'll have a good view of the swimming pool and basketball courts outside the community center. Funding the community center was one of the first projects the city council approved when Ryser's money came in.

Over texts, lunches, and visits, Marina has kept me updated on all the other Greenstead goings-on. Mayor Bradley came around on Solar Summit's resort hotel proposal, and Marina told me Jess suspects our dinner party had something to do with it. After the dinner, the mayor exchanged contact information with the Solar Summit team, and they met a few times to discuss the proposal more extensively. Apparently, Mayor Bradley developed a begrudging respect for Solar Summit after seeing their support for the apple festival.

With Solar Summit committing to cleaning up West Greenstead for their resort hotel venture, the city council has set its sights on other endeavors, like the community development ventures Mayor Bradley hoped to invest in, back when he was focusing all his energies on getting the federal grant Greenstead ultimately failed to receive. With this money, Mayor Bradley can finally start to fulfill his campaign promises of making infrastructure improvements and creating financial incentives for small businesses. Marina also told me there's talk of setting aside money to fund the apple festival in future years. It's gratifying to hear the ways our festival has gone on to impact the town. And all of us too, I suppose.

Randy got the office manager job in Falls Point. He texted our group chat with the news and added that while he hasn't been a manager of anything in years, he feels up to the challenge again. Jen, who's been settling into her role as a remote social media manager for an association in DC, is enjoying having the flexibility to work from anywhere. Last week, she sent us a picture of her and Randy out to lunch at a restaurant in Falls Point. Seeing their smiling faces filled me with fondness and a wistful nostalgia for the dawdling days we spent together in the Ryser Cares office, but I know I'll see them soon enough. We already have plans for the group to get dinner together in a couple of weeks, when Arun wraps up an event for his first client under his new business: Nancy Fletcher enlisted him to throw an elaborate birthday party for her Scottish terrier. None of us are invited, but I will be pressing Arun for details.

Tessa's the Ryser Cares person I've seen most often. She ended up getting a place in the Fan, and we've hung out several times. On days when she's not apprenticing at the bakery—which she seems to love, going by the way her eyes light up whenever she mentions it—she's been showing me more of her favorite eateries in Richmond, from Up All Night Bakery and its flaky croissants to Mama J's tantalizing fried chicken. It's been fun to explore the city through her eyes and get to know my new home a little better.

I've been making an effort to explore the city on my own, too. I'm slowly finding my favorite spots in my neighborhood and near the office at my new job, where I now work as a marketing manager at a healthcare nonprofit in Richmond. The money isn't much, but I get to feel good about myself, and that's all I can really ask for. When I met up with Selma for lunch in DC last weekend, she told me I seemed different—happier. Which may be partly because I'm not complaining to her about Bill anymore, but I'm sure there's more to it. I *feel* different. More self-assured. More me. And life feels so much easier this way, when I'm content with my choices and I like who I am.

Leo finishes his inspection of the living room and cautiously approaches the couch. I reach a hand out, just as timidly, and he gives it a sniff before taking a step forward and ducking his head under my hand. I pet him, stroking the soft fur at the top of his head. Leo closes his eyes and comes a step closer, coming to rest his chin on my knee. I decide this means he likes who I am, too.

"Jess is calling," Marina says, standing up. "I think it's about the dresser. Can you listen out for tacos?"

"No promises," I reply as she disappears into my bedroom. She ordered us tacos when we got back to my apartment, and I'd been counting on her to listen out for the door. Listening for a knock always feels stressful, like I'm taking another hearing test I'll inevitably fail.

Left alone with Leo, I take the moment to lean forward and cup his face in my hands. I tell him I think we're going to have a very good life together. I tell him I've been waiting my whole life to have a dog like him. I say I'm sorry it took me so long to become the person I needed to be first, but that I'm so glad I got there in the end.

Suddenly Leo freezes, then whips his head around to face the door, his ears perked. I watch him curiously—and then, as if he's psychic, a knock sounds a few seconds later.

As I follow Leo to the door, I can only marvel at how perfectly he fits into my life. We've got three working ears between us—two more than I've ever had. Hearing is about to get a whole lot easier.

READ ON FOR A LOOK AT SHAUNA ROBINSON'S *THE TOWNSEND FAMILY RECIPE FOR DISASTER*

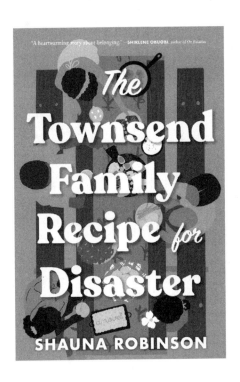

CHAPTER ONE

MAE DIDN'T REALIZE SHE WAS drunk until she nuzzled the peony.

Her future mother-in-law, Susan, paused mid-sentence to watch Mae across the table. Tracing a petal down her cheek, luxuriating in how velvety it was, Mae wondered if Susan had lost her train of thought, and Mae was going to say *You were talking about*—except she couldn't remember. It was something to do with the centerpieces, a debate about roses versus peonies, and then Mae had plucked a petal from the peony in front of her and wondered how that surprising softness might feel on her face. Were peonies good for the skin? If jade rollers were a thing, there had to be a market for face-flowers. What would she call it? Flower facial? Petal peel? Floratherapy? The name needed workshopping, but she was onto something.

But now, staring into Susan's baffled blue eyes, it occurred to Mae that perhaps that look had nothing to do with centerpieces and everything to do with Mae. Mae glanced at Connor, her fiancé. He was watching her, too, except the corner of his lips twitched in the hint of a smile.

In an instant, Mae noticed the warmth in her face, the floating in her head, the flower on her cheek, and realized she might have hit the Cabernets too hard. They'd all tasted about a dozen wines that afternoon and yet Mae was the only one fondling flowers. Then again, Connor's parents owned a winery, and she guessed wine-tasting expertise ran in their blood. Even Connor had probably swirled and sniffed from a baby bottle before he'd taken his first steps. Mae, on the other hand, had made it to thirty-one without grasping the basics of wine appreciation. While they went on about hidden flavors and aromas she never picked up on—apricot, mushroom, tobacco, wet gravel, as if anyone in their right mind would want to drink something with notes of *wet gravel*—she'd guzzled every glass, just trying to get the acidic taste over with.

If only today had been a pizza tasting. She was great at appreciating pizza.

Mae lowered her hand to her lap and studied the petal, now patchy with grease. Susan resumed speaking, gushing about the timelessness of peonies, and Mae let the petal flutter to her feet. Her mind was still drifting past the cloud of conversation, but that was how all wedding planning discussions felt. For the last year, talk of table settings and color schemes had swirled around her in words she couldn't quite grasp. Who cared about irrelevant details when her wedding might be the catalyst that finally brought her estranged family together?

"But you don't need to worry about the cost," Susan was saying, her voice faraway.

"I know," Connor said. "But if Mae and I don't care about the flowers, then what's the point of splurging?"

John, Connor's father, laughed like it was the silliest question he'd ever heard. "Because we can."

"You prefer the peonies, don't you, Mae?" Susan said.

Mae snapped to attention. Three expectant faces watched her, waiting for signs of life. Even the fountain behind them, which normally brought a soothing sound to John and Susan's patio, seemed to silence its steady trickle. Mae should say something smart, something relevant at the very least, but her last competent brain cell was busy designing colorful T-shirts stamped with *TOWNSEND FAMILY REUNION*.

Her gaze darted around the table for a distraction: empty wine glasses, assorted flowers, one of Susan's three-ring binders. It was open to a glossy page showing leaves running down a white backdrop. "What's that?" she asked.

Susan perked up. "It's a vine wall, like the one we're doing for the wedding. If we're agreed on peonies for the centerpieces, I was thinking we could put some on the wall too. I have a picture of that somewhere." She licked a finger and flipped through a never-ending fun house of themed walls: sunflowers, balloons, glowing light bulbs.

Of course Susan had a wall binder. This wedding was serious business for John and Susan Rutherford. It was decreed long ago that their only child's wedding would be held at their picturesque winery. With a coveted venue at their disposal, and their many contacts in the wedding industry, the Rutherfords were determined to make this wedding the event of the century. And Mae and Connor would be there, too.

"Wait," Mae said when she caught a glimpse of food. "What was that one?"

"This?" Susan turned back to a page where colorful donuts hung on wooden pegs. "Oh. This is a donut wall we did for a wedding a few years back."

"The Harrington-Chambers wedding," John said. "May 2019."

Mae always thought it was impressive that John could remember every wedding. Though he could just be spouting off random names and dates for all she knew. He could have said, *The Crumpet-Trolleybottom wedding, January 1593,* and they would have all nodded knowingly. The thought made her laugh, and John gave her a puzzled look, and she cleared her throat and went back to staring at the donut wall.

"I love donuts." Mae rested her elbows on the table with a dreamy sigh. "I love when the glaze hardens and gets a little bit country." She frowned. "Crunchy." Yes, that was it. Her head swimming with glazes and sprinkles, she gasped and turned to Susan. "Hey, what if we did a donut wall? Instead of the vines?"

Susan did a double take, looking from Mae to the binder. "You…want to do a donut wall?"

Mae couldn't tell what Susan found more surprising: that Mae was finally expressing a wedding-related opinion after a year of nods and shrugs, or that a wall—and not flowers, or music, or anything else Susan had a dedicated binder for—was the one detail Mae chose to speak on.

But donuts were delicious. Mae could go for a donut right now. And maybe her dad's side of the family liked donuts too. In fact, maybe this whole, elaborate wedding wasn't so absurd if the spectacle of it drew them in.

"Yeah," Mae said. "Is that possible?"

"It *is*. It's just…" Susan's brow pinched. "This was for a morning wedding. Donuts went with the breakfast theme. But your wedding's in the evening." She spoke like there was something unspoken in her words.

"I'd eat donuts day or night," Mae said. She glanced around the table. John was squinting thoughtfully into the distance, the temple tip of his glasses between his lips, like he was trying his hardest to imagine a world with night donuts.

But Connor, smirking at Mae, was already in that world with her. "Let's do it," he said. "Donut wall."

"Donut wall!" Mae echoed, lifting her water glass. Connor clinked his glass against hers, his eyes dancing with mirth.

"Okay." There was a touch of pain in Susan's voice. She tucked a blond flyaway into place, surveying the two of them uncertainly. "Let's have a donut wall…at night."

"Night donuts!" Mae raised her hand for a high-five.

A range of emotions passed over Susan's face: confusion, surprise, maybe joy? Susan gave a delighted laugh and slapped her hand neatly against Mae's in the demurest high-five Mae had ever received.

"I didn't know you liked donuts so much," John said. "We could have picked some up for you today."

Alarm bells sounded in the small part of Mae's brain that

hadn't succumbed to the wine fog, flashing a bright-yellow caution sign, slow down, yield to oncoming intimacy.

For years, she'd curated the perfect balance of geniality and distance around Connor's family. Semi-regular lunches and dinners with Connor and his parents? Sure. Pedicures with Susan? No, thank you—she was busy that day. Coming over to admire the Rutherfords' kitchen remodel? Certainly, and she'd even gift them some fancy olive oil to mark the occasion. Being left alone with them when Connor had to step out to take a call? Oh, actually, she had to use the bathroom for the exact duration of Connor's call, please excuse her a moment.

There was a logic behind her avoidance. Mae knew that if she let her guard down around his parents, they would do the same around her—and that was when the danger set in.

Yet, John's donut offer and Susan's high-five excitement had Mae's resolve crumbling a little, as it always did when their kindnesses caught her off-guard. She studied John and Susan, searching for traces of Connor. With that gray hair lining the sides of John's bald head, he didn't much resemble him—but those warm brown eyes were the same. Susan's hair was lighter and thinner than Connor's honey blond, but her crooked smile mirrored his. Mae could choose to believe in them, accept that John and Susan might be every bit as good as their son.

"That would be great," Mae said. "We'll have to get donuts sometime."

A strangely fuzzy feeling came over her as she took in John and Susan's pleased expressions. Was this growth? Had she really overcome her fears about Connor's parents *and* invented floratherapy (patent pending) in a single afternoon? She should get drunk more often.

While John and Susan debated potential donut vendors for the wedding, the talk of flavors and toppings had Mae's mouth watering—except someone must have taken the snack platter inside. The old Mae might have politely toughed it out around the Rutherfords, but she was evolved now. She was Cabernet Mae. CaberMae, if you will.

"I'm gonna grab a snack," she announced, standing abruptly. "Can I get anyone anything?" A wave of dizziness washed over her. She gripped her chair to avoid swaying.

"You good?" Connor asked, watching her closely.

"I'm great," Mae assured him. She even believed it.

READING GROUP GUIDE

1. Compare and contrast Lauryn and Marina. Who do you relate to more? Why? What do you think makes their friendship last over so many years, even through their disagreements?

2. What is your relationship with your hometown like? Did you find yourself wanting to leave, like Lauryn? Did something make you want to stay?

3. Discuss the difference between the relationship Lauryn has with her mom and the relationship she has with her dad. In what ways is she like each of her parents? Did you prefer one of her parents over the other?

4. When Lauryn learns what Amanda plans to do to Ryser Cares, she decides it's best not to tell her team. What did you think about that decision? What would you do?

5. Lauryn often worries that others see her as selfish for working at

Ryser—the company that left her hometown devastated—in order to further her own goals. If you were from Greenstead, what would you think of Lauryn? Would you do the same as she did?

6. Discuss the significance of Marina's house. Why do you think it was so important to her?

7. Marina and Lauryn had many traditions together that meant a lot to them. Do you and your friends have any traditions that remain special to you?

8. Both Ryser and Solar Summit are large companies with a stake in Greenstead. Compare and contrast them. How are they alike and how are they different? Do you think those in Greenstead prefer one to the other? Why?

9. When Lauryn meets the Ryser Cares team, they are all hesitant to help with the fall festival due to their past mishaps. Are there moments when you have made a mistake you didn't think you could come back from? What helped you push through?

10. For much of the novel, Lauryn finds herself balancing long-term goals (promotions, early retirement, etc.) with day-to-day happiness (friendships, getting a dog, dating, etc.). Have you ever found yourself balancing those things? What feels more important to you? What ends up being more important to Lauryn?

A CONVERSATION
WITH THE AUTHOR

What inspired this story?

This story came from a mix of sources and inspirations. Like Lauryn, I'm completely deaf in one ear. I thought it would be funny to write about someone who gets into a mishearing mishap with unfortunate consequences. And I'm always thinking about the ways the working world warps us. I once aspired to have a job where I'd "make a difference"—only to realize that if making that difference involves lots of meetings and stress and things I'd rather not do, I'm fully willing to abandon those aspirations. It's so much easier to not be noble. Which naturally led me to wonder what it would look like if someone took that philosophy to an extreme.

The final source is my publisher. I think of a story idea as a Jenga tower. When I sent them my tower, they pulled out some blocks that set the tower tumbling down. They tossed a few of their own blocks onto the pile, and I had to figure out how to build something new. I took parts of what I wanted and parts of what they wanted, and somehow, from some corner of my mind dedicated to odd bits of trivia like food floods, a mustard flood became key to tying it all together—and so a new tower was built.

Lauryn has a complicated relationship with Greenstead. What is your relationship like with your hometown?

I can relate to Lauryn's desire to leave her hometown but to a much smaller extent. San Diego is a beautiful city with incredible food, people, and sights. I love going back there to see my family and indulge in all my favorites (Burritos! Fish tacos! Copious amounts of tamarind candy!). But I always knew San Diego wasn't for me. I daydreamed about rainy days, snowy winters, getting to experience all four seasons. I'm happy living in Virginia (though I wouldn't mind a little more snow…), but I'll always have love for California.

If you had any advice for someone considering if they should stay in their hometown or leave, what would it be?

I suppose it's less advice and more a question: Why not? There are many valid reasons to stay where you are. But if those aren't enough and you still feel an itch to leave, why not give it a try? Even if it doesn't work out and you decide to move back, at least you'll know—it's better than always wondering.

While temporarily solved, the futures of the community center and the fall festival aren't set by the end of the novel. Do you think the fall festival will happen again next year?

I think the fall festival will come back next year, the year after that, and beyond. I also think the community center is safe for the foreseeable future. Greenstead just needed a little help reminding everyone what's great about it—and to understand that help is a good thing!

Everyone in the Ryser Cares team, on the surface, seems so different. What do you think drew them all together?

The Ryser Cares team formed a friendship founded on failure. They were convinced they had nothing to contribute, so they gave up on trying and took solace in one another. They know all too well how it feels to be rejected and cast out, which is why they're so quick to lead with kindness and embrace Lauryn as one of their own—even if she's a little horrified at the thought of being considered a failure.

Is there anything you hope readers take away from this novel?

I hope readers come away from this book with a smile. One of my favorite things about reading is the escapism it provides. If readers enjoyed even a little time reading about friendship, pretzels, roller coasters, apple festivals, and the lingering smell of mustard, I'll be happy.

ACKNOWLEDGMENTS

Katelyn Detweiler, thank you for being a wonderfully encouraging source of support during the idea development (and reworking) process for this book. MJ Johnston and Jenna Jankowski, thank you for your keen editorial insight and funny comments that always make the editorial process a little more enjoyable.

Many thanks to Sam Farkas, Denise Page, and the rest of the team at Jill Grinberg Literary for all that they do. And thank you to BrocheAroe Fabian, Cristina Arreola, Aubrey Clemans, Beth Sochacki, Valerie Pierce, Anna Venckus, Jessica Thelander, Mary Wheelehan, and everyone else at Sourcebooks for all they've done to support this book and my previous books. And thank you Diane Dannenfeldt for copyediting!

I'm thankful for the writing community, especially Camille Baker, Bethany Baptiste, Gabi Burton, Sami Ellis, Elnora Gunter, Jas Hammonds, Avionne Lee, Britney Lewis, Deb Makuma, Allegra Martschenko, Melody Simpson, KJ Micciche, and Eden

Robins. Sierra Godfrey, Sara Goodman Confino, and Anna Johnston, thank you for being kind enough to read my book and say nice things about it!

Kate Reed's friendship has seen me through the last two-plus decades. Lauryn and Marina are fictional, but I did sprinkle a few details from our real-life friendship into theirs, namely our amusement park itineraries, our mental files of minutiae, our sacred traditions built around food, and Kate's dedication to always finding my hearing side. Kate, you and your friendship make my life so much better.

The friends I've had growing up inspired some additional tidbits I sprinkled in. Yasmin Hernandez, thank you for being my confidante and partner in crime (and by "crime" I mean escaping social gatherings to play Monopoly in secret). Diana Chávez, I loved being your scribe on all the group projects we shared. Val Yazon, spending grad night at Disneyland with you and Diana remains one of my favorite high school memories.

I'm grateful to my family for their love and support. Matt Hocker is the first person I tell new book ideas to. He listens patiently while I think aloud the specifics, he offers ideas when I'm stuck, and he suggests random names when I need to quickly name a character while I'm drafting (like Art McKenzie). Thank you for being my partner in all things and in all ways.

To booksellers, librarians, and readers everywhere, thank you for uplifting my books. It fills me with joy to see you reading, sharing, and embracing my books. Thank you for making space for me on your shelves.

ABOUT THE AUTHOR

Photo © Rachel E.H. Photography

Shauna Robinson writes contemporary fiction with humor and heart. Originally from San Diego, she now lives in Virginia with her husband and their sleepy greyhound. Shauna is an introvert at heart—she spends most of her time reading, baking, and figuring out the politest way to avoid social interaction.